CW00433783

CONTENTS

Note To Reader

This book contains content that may be troubling to some readers.

Please read the content warning list at the end of the book should you be concerned before reading.

Thank you.

DEDICATION

THIS IS FOR THE GIRLIES WHO JUST NEED A SECOND CHANCE.

GET IT, GIRL.
WE ALL MAKE MISTAKES.

TRUST ME.
MY LIST OF EX-BOYFRIENDS IS PROOF OF THIS.

PROLOGUE

"YOU CAN'T DO THIS! You can't just cut me off!"

My father looms over me, his wrinkled face set into a cold, indifferent mask I've seen him use on a hundred different people: restaurant servers, business partners, so-called friends, and even my mother.

But never with me.

I was the one softness he allowed himself.

Until now.

Anger churning in his eyes, he lifts his finger and shakes it at me, like I'm a disobedient dog that chewed his favorite slippers. Except what I've done is worse; I've made him look bad to his business colleagues. And that's something I should never, ever hope he'll forgive.

"I told you. I told you that if you were intent on blackmailing the Baxter family, then you had better make sure you succeed. You had better make sure it was going to work. But it didn't, did it? Damien Baxter left you. Again!" The spittle on his lips flies as he hisses the words. Eyes glistening like glaciers as he shakes his head. Drenched with disappointment. "You failed, dear daughter of mine. And I do not tolerate failure."

And I had.

I had failed.

When I tried to use my father to blackmail Damien into marrying me, it had worked. For a while. But I had misjudged how much he had changed since the last time we were engaged. And when he called off our engagement for the second time, I knew this day would come.

Father takes a deep breath, looking away from me for a moment before he squares his shoulders and says, "I want you out of this house by tomorrow morning. The jet will take you to New York, and you can stay in one of our apartments there. For three months. Then you'll have to find your own place. With your own money. I think that's more than fair."

It sounds anything but fair. "But, Father—"

"Hush. I don't want to hear another word out of your mouth. I told you before you insisted on this ridiculous plan that if it didn't work, there would be consequences. So go, start a new life in the United States. Or Paris. Or the planet Jupiter. I don't care. I just don't want to see your face..."

"You can't do this to me!"

He walks over to his desk and pulls out a thick yellow envelope with my name on it. "Here," he says, dropping it on the table. "Your cards and accounts have been frozen. This should be enough for a few months. After that... well, maybe it's time to find out what it's like to earn your own living for once."

No, he wouldn't...he couldn't do this to me...

"What about Damien? You're just going to let him do this to me? To us? I thought you said you'd never let anyone besmirch the Masters name?"

Somehow his eyes get even colder. "My relationship with the Baxters, and as the chairman of the board of their company, is my business. You should start worrying about your own life."

"But... Damien..."

He slams his hand down on the table, his voice terrifying as he shouts, "Enough!! You never loved him, and he sure as hell never loved you. He found his way out of your ridiculous arrangement, and you need to as well. Best you can do, Clarissa, is try to forget you ever heard the name 'Baxter.'"

One

MATTHIAS

FROM ENTERTAINME.COM

"Playboy billionaire Matthias Baxter is once again in deep water after two women have come forward claiming that he is the father of their unborn children after he forced them to have unprotected sex. The women have contacted the media after they say that all efforts to contact Baxter have been in vain.

This news comes after a string of scandals involving the bachelor billionaire, including a dalliance with an ambassador's daughter and taking her on a joyride on the Hudson on a jet ski last month. As usual, there has been no comment from Baxter Enterprises. No doubt, though, that behind the scenes, there must be some discussion as to whether this will affect the public listing of their subsidiary child care company, Kids & Care, in three months' time.

Anyone want to take bets to see if Matthias Baxter can keep it in his pants until then?"

"Harder. Do it harder!"

A grunt. "I'm doing it as hard as I can!"

"Come on, Katie," I say, my voice muffled against the hole in the massage table, as my masseuse drills her elbow into the small of my back. "I have a lot of tension to work out."

"I would think that you have had more than enough help to relieve your tension," Katie snickers.

She hasn't really stopped laughing since I came down to her massage room twenty minutes ago. After the news broke this morning, I hightailed it downstairs to the spa I'd set up in my company's headquarters for moments just like this.

"It's not fucking funny, Katie. I'm no one's baby daddy. And that unprotected sex bullshit is just that.," I grumble. "Hey, I'd double bag if I had to to make sure that no woman can go around saying that she has Matthias Baxter, Jr. in her belly."

Katie moves around the table and jabs her elbow into my shoulder blade, making me yelp. "Um, I don't think that's where the baby is—"

"You know what I mean!"

This time it's not just a snicker, she outright guffaws and slaps her hand across my bare ass.

Considering we slept together a few times about four years ago, there doesn't really seem to be any need to be modest around her. I scowl into the hole, glad she can't see me, or else she'd be laughing even harder. These bogus news stories are the bane of my existence. After living here in Manhattan for seven years now, I would've thought that the entertainment channels would be more than sick of plastering my fucking face on their big screens.

It's not the allegations themselves that annoy me—they're always quickly quietened with a fat check—it's how they affect business. I'm spending more time putting out fires than actually getting any work done.

We don't say anything for a few minutes as she grunts, trying to dig the pointy parts of her body into the sore parts of mine, finally working out some of the tension. That is until the door flings open and my assistant's voice comes crashing down over my trying-to-relax state.

"Matthias! Where have you been?"

Judging by the tone of her voice, my massage is over.

I sit up, ignoring the fact that I'm buck naked. There isn't much she hasn't seen of me either, but not in any kind of sexual state. She's just walked in on me showering or changing enough times not to be fazed in the slightest about the sight of my back and front bits. If anything, I feel like she silently scoffs, as if she's disappointed in me for even having genitalia.

That's what you get when you hire an assistant who's ten years older than you.

"You know, Hannah," I say, "all of my brothers' assistants call them *'Mr. Baxter.'*"

Her eyes roll up so high in her head she can probably see what's hung on the wall behind her. "Well, then, you wouldn't want to be mistaken for them, would you? Aren't you always complaining about how you hate being in your older brother's shadow and overtaken by your younger brothers' intelligence?" she says, her voice deadpan as she throws a robe at me.

It lands over my head and drapes over my face, the scent of fabric softener permeating my breath. "Touché. What are you doing here, anyway? You said I had a half hour break before my next meeting."

"Mr. Baxter is on the phone," she says.

"*Which* Mr. Baxter?"

A smug smile settles on her lips as she realizes I have just made her point. "Your uncle."

A string of curses spills from my lips. Gerry, my uncle, the interim CEO of Baxter Enterprises, is more of a pain in my ass than my masseuse and assistant put together. Times a thousand. As far as I know, they're not trying to throw my three brothers and me out of the company.

"What does he want?" I growl, pulling on the robe. Any day that has Gerry in it is a bad day.

She purses her lips. "I think you know what he wants."

I do. It's about the news that he's allegedly about to be a great-uncle to two baby Baxters. I slide off the massage table and shrug. "He'll get over it. It's not the first time."

"I don't know. He sounded angry. He sent Paula from PR to come talk to you."

"What makes this time important enough for him to stick his nose into it?" I ask, but it's a rhetorical question.

We know exactly why.

Because in eight months, the company's board is due for a vote, and as agreed between the board and my late grandfather, when my eldest brother Kingsley turns forty-two years old, he is to be voted in as CEO. So, Gerry, as interim CEO, has eight months left to get us thrown out and get the board to vote him permanently into the position. Since my grandfather's passing, he's been trying to pick all of us off, one by one. He hasn't succeeded with any of my brothers yet, and I'll be fucking damned if I'm going to be the weak link.

Hannah hands me my clothes and turns away while I quickly get changed in my private elevator as it whizzes up to my office floor. "You don't have to turn away, you know. You're welcome to enjoy the show."

"No, thank you. I'm not much for horror movies, Matthias."

"Ouch!" I mock wince, as the elevator comes to a stop, and I catch a smirk on her face as she steps out onto the floor ahead of me. "Paula," I say as soon as I step into my office to see my PR rep standing there, looking about as pissed with my uncle as I am. "Tell me what I have to do to make this all go away, and fast, so I can actually get some work done around here."

"Yes, Mr. Baxter. But frankly, sir, you're going to fucking hate it."

Two

CLARISSA

THE EAR-PIERCING SHRIEK FROM the sound system feels like someone is slashing at a spot behind my eyes with a nail file. If the sound check goes on for a minute longer, my brain might actually explode.

"Ms. Masters?"

I shake my head at the sound of my name and scowl at my head bartender, half-annoyed, half embarrassed that I'd been caught not paying attention to what he was saying.

"What?" I snap.

A look of confusion flashes over his face at my tone, but he doesn't say anything about it, just holds out the clipboard to me. "Erm, I was just saying, I think we're going to need to up our ice shipment. I think another five twenty-pound bags should do it. We can store them in the cool room and then bring them out when we need them. But we were out almost an hour before we closed last night. Had to hit the kitchen freezer up for some. And that's hardly ideal."

In the background, the speakers let out another screech, and I use every ounce of presence to plaster a neutral look on my face. "Sure, whatever you think is right, James. Update me in a week."

"Sure thing, Ms. Masters." He pauses, then asks the question on his lips. "Are you okay?"

No.

No, I'm not.

And nothing makes it worse than being asked that question for the tenth fucking time of the day.

I wave my hand. "I'm fine. Just go back to work, I have things to do," I hastily say, in a voice almost as shrill as the sound coming out of the speakers.

Before he can ask any follow-up questions, or the façade fades, I walk to my office, slamming the door closed behind me, and lean against it. My eyes flicker erratically back and forth, and fall on my reflection on the mirror across from the door. I almost find myself without breath again when I see what I look like - messy bun, face still bare, eyes circled by dark, purple rings.

I haven't slept properly in a week.

More like six months, a niggling voice in my head insists. I push it back as far as I can because it doesn't matter how long it's been. Last night was the opening night of my whisky club, Malt, so it's no wonder that I've barely slept a wink wanting to make sure everything was ready.

Opening night had gone about as well as expected, with a few inevitable and unavoidable hiccups that come with any opening night.

The few friends who are still talking to me after I moved to New York City showed up. I'd been touched to see them. It's easy to take friends for granted, even casual acquaintances. Maybe after the last few months of nothing but unanswered phone calls and indefinitely postponed lunches has taught me to not rely on promises from the people who I used to call friends.

Last night's entertainment, Georgana Best, a local blues singer, had turned out to be quite the draw card. And as high priced as she is, I've made sure to book her for the coming three Saturdays. The half-price drinks for opening night had also proven to be incredibly popular, and we still managed to break even despite the Mt. Everest-high stacks of empty bottles of high-end liqueur currently clogging up the alley behind the club.

And while it was only the first night, the early success gives me a little hope that I can make this work.

Which is exactly the lift I need.

Since moving out of my family's apartment three months ago, I've been living in the upstairs storage space of the club. Dusty. Roach infested. And only a stained, lumpy, abandoned couch as my bed. But it's free and my commute is the forty-five seconds it takes me to go downstairs. Which is convenient considering I will regularly be finishing work after two a.m.

Not that anyone knows. Not that anyone can *ever* know.

Closing my eyes, I do some quick additions in my head of the upcoming costs that are going to have to come out of my quickly depleting savings. Building rent, wages, promotions, finishing the renovations... This place is going to have to start bringing in regular money and fast.

The thought makes my lung suddenly unable to inflate, and my blood starts to pound in my ears. A sweat breaks out all over my body.

Fuck.

Not again.

I stagger over to my desk, grabbing the little pill bottle from the drawer and tip four little white pills into my hand and swallow them, wishing the drugs could be delivered to me in the form of an IV instead.

Why, just why?

The desk chair creaks under me as I sink into it, my head falling into my hands, the sweat from my forehead dripping down my forearms as I drag air into my chest.

And I can't help wondering...if it's going to be like this forever. Is this panic is ever going to stop fucking up every single day of my life?

I shake the thought from my head, focusing on my breathing.

And I calm down.

A glance down at the sleeve of my dress shows me a small thread unraveling from the sleeve. They must've done it at the dry cleaners. I can't afford to get a new shirt right now. A rummage around in my drawer for a small pair of scissors comes up empty, and the prospect of stepping out of my office into the club edges me back on another anxiety attack.

Fuck!

I sweep my hand across my desk, scattering a pile of papers into the air.

Watching the sheets flutter to the ground brings me a small sense of peace, however, and when there's a small knock on my door a few seconds later, I feel like I can brave the day again.

"Yes?" I call out, hoping my voice doesn't give me away.

A soft voice pipes up behind the door. They must've played rock paper scissors to see who would have to talk to me. "Ms. Masters, you told me to tell you when it was time for your appointment with Leanne."

My decorator. She's here to discuss how the club looked last night in the dark and full of customers. I stand up, wiping my hands down over my shirt and pants, and then pat any errant hair into place.

My reflection shows a woman who has it much more together than I feel inside.

And that is just going to have to do.

I'm doing the best I fucking can.

Three

CLARISSA

A WEEK LATER, MY cab stops outside of a brownstone in the West Village, a few buildings down from where a group of girls are squealing and taking pictures in front of the house used for the exterior shots of Carrie Bradshaw's apartment in Sex and the City.

My lip curls in distaste.

I can't imagine any of my friends causing such a scene in London in front of Sherlock Holmes's building.

You don't have any friends to cause a scene with, a bitchy voice in my head reminds me. Wow. My inner voice is even more of a bitch than I am.

I climb up the stairs just as they come skipping down the sidewalk, hands-in-hands, faces flushed with the excitement of squealing.

"Hi!" one of them says to me. "I love your shoes!" Her eyes are locked on my pink Ferragamo pumps. "Guys, look! This lady is so pretty!"

They all stop in a pile of matching outfits, smiles, and coos.

It takes me completely by surprise, and all I can do is respond with a curt nod.

The other girls start walking forward, while the girl who's been speaking stays and says to me, "We've got a reservation at *Via Carota* for tonight! We've never been to such a fancy restaurant before."

I bite back a little snicker. *Via Carota*, while definitely delicious, is hardly a fancy restaurant in the scheme of "fancy" restaurants in Manhattan. But the sheer unadulterated joy on her face touches me and I surprise myself by saying, "That's nice. Have a lovely dinner."

"You have an English accent!" she squeals.

Sometimes I forget that I sound different than most of the people I talk to. "Oh, yes, I grew up there. But I live here now."

She clasps her hands together and visibly swoons. "You're so lucky! Where else have you lived?"

This young girl is very chatty, but it's the first conversation I've had in a long time that wasn't about the club. Something makes me want to answer her. "Well, I lived in Sydney, Australia, for a few years before I moved here." The memory still hurts.

"Sydney!! That's next on my bucket list. Did you see anyone famous?"

That makes me laugh despite my initial bad mood. "I saw Nicole Kidman at a party once..."

The girl practically faints right there on the sidewalk. "She's so pretty. You kinda look like her. Tall, with long beautiful hair. And pretty shoes."

That elicits a laugh from me. Almost unheard of these days. "Why thank you. How long are you here for?"

"I'm just visiting for now, but I'm coming back to study at NYU in the fall. What do you do?"

The answer tickles on the end of my tongue, I'm not used to telling people yet. "I actually own a whisky and cigar club a few blocks from here. Malt."

This time she squeals so loudly I'm sure only the dogs in the neighboring houses can hear her. "A club! I am so jealous!"

"Mandy, come on!" her friends yell from the end of the street.

She jumps and runs before stopping. "I better go! We're going to go over to the Friends' house before dinner."

"Well, I hope you enjoy your time in the city, Mandy. And definitely try the charred leeks at *Via Carota*." I press my friend's buzzer on the panel.

"I will! Thank you! Bye!" She gives me a smile that looks like it stretches all the way around her head, and then runs to her friends, almost tripping on a raised crack in the sidewalk.

They welcome her back with open arms and then skip around the corner, out of sight.

I guess being excited isn't such a bad thing after all.

The door buzzes, I push it open and make my way up to Leanne's apartment. We'd talked the day after my club's opening night and had decided to make some fabric changes and repaint some of the light fixtures to make them better catch the light in the dark. This morning, she'd asked me to come over to have a look at some color and fabric swatches she narrowed down.

Her apartment takes up the whole third floor, but I can hear music and chatter filtering down the stairwell even as I approach the second floor.

Did I misunderstand her? Am I actually about to crash a private soiree?

I don't even have a chance to turn around and hightail it down the stairs before she appears, walking someone down to meet me on the landing.

"Clarissa! There you are! I was just coming down to make sure the door had buzzed open for you."

She lifts her hand in a wave and her friend gives me a nod as they brush past me and continue down the steps.

"Hey, Leanne. Am I interrupting? I can come back at another time! Or I can wait here if you want to grab the swatches." This is the exact reason I prefer my contractors and suppliers to meet me at the club. Home advantage is priceless. But she had sounded so busy and I had been in such a rush to finish the final work on the club that I'd offered to come pick them up.

"Absolute nonsense! Some friends just stopped by and we're just having a few drinks. Come." She links her arm in mine and leads me up the stairs. I go with her because she was one of the first people to befriend me and offer her services to the club. She's become a trusted friend in the last few months even though she's incredibly chatty. And while I'm not actively looking for any friends, I really don't think I can afford to alienate the ones I do have.

It's not the first time I've been to her apartment; in fact, the first time I saw her home, I knew that I'd picked the right person to help with my club's décor.

As we get to her floor, I see that what Leanne described as "a few friends" looks more like happy hour at a Wall Street bar on a Friday afternoon. There must be thirty or forty people crammed into her living room, each with a glass in his or her hand, and some with some sort of food stuck on a toothpick.

"*Some* friends just dropped by?" I ask, teasing her. I'm not actually that surprised, I imagine she has a lot of friends.

Leanne laughs as she shrugs. "Well, just a few to start off with, then we may have called some more. Grab a drink, I've just got to say hi to someone and then I'll grab the swatch binder, okay?"

I swallow the apprehension as she pats me on the shoulder, leaving me standing alone in the kitchen among the discarded lipstick-stained wine glasses and emptied crackers packets.

This is fucking stupid.

When have I ever been afraid before to walk into a room of people I don't know? This used to be my playground. I could walk into any room and have everyone's eyes on me, puppets to my pulled strings.

Well, you're not exactly the same person you used to be, are you? that little bitch snickers. I'm going to have to do something about her. I start by numbing her voice by picking up the bottle of vodka and pouring myself a glass, downing half of it. My cheeks instantly burn from the alcohol.

But it helps.

I top up the glass, take a deep breath and step into the crowd.

A quick glance around returns no familiar faces but somehow that calms me rather than scares me.

No familiar faces means no one here to bring up my baggage, of which there is so much that sometimes, maybe too many times recently, I feel like I'm suffocating under a never-ending cascade of LV suitcases crushing my chest.

I walk around the main crowd, most swarming around the table of appetizers, to make my way over to the window where there's an empty spot to stand.

"Hello," a man appears to my right, when I get there, his face a picture of friendliness. "I'm Halifax."

I take a sip, keeping my eyes locked on his as I tip the glass against my lips before I say, "As in Nova Scotia, Halifax?"

He grins. "Let's just say my parents went there on my honeymoon, and nine months later, I was gifted a life of knowing way too much about my parent's love life."

I can't help but smile at him as he shrugs awkwardly, and runs his hand through his floppy brown fringe, his self-deprecating manner instantly relaxing me.

He eyes me when I don't respond and asks, "What's your name?"

"As far as I know, there are no honeymoon destinations that carry my name," I say, mysteriously. Men always love a little mystery. Makes them feel smart when they figure things out.

He narrows his eyes at me for a second, then breaks into a grin. "Okay, so not Paris, Florence... or god forbid, Bora Bora."

"Damn. You guessed it." I sigh prettily, shaking my head so that the curls flutter and frame my face as I fix a doe-eyed look at him. It's a move I've perfected over the years, so much that I don't even notice when I'm using it. I'm not even sure why I'm using it now. I have no interest in twirling Halifax around my little finger. Or maybe I do. Just... to remember what it used to feel like.

"Which one is it? Not Bora Bora? Say it isn't so!" he exclaims, grabbing a little triangle of avocado and salmon toast off a plate that's making the rounds.

I politely decline the food and he passes it over to the couple standing next to us.

"Look, we can't all be named after George Montagu-Dunk," I tease him and take satisfaction from the look of utter confusion on his face.

Finally, he gives up, throwing his hands up into the air. "Okay, Bora Bora, or can I just call you Bora, who is George Montagu-Dunk?"

I grin. "George Montagu-Dunk is the earl of Halifax. Or, if you like, the earl of you."

His mouth drops open. "How on earth do you know that?"

"What can I say, useless information, isn't as useless as you might think."

"You're a fascinating woman, Bora Bora."

This time I don't even stop the laugh. It's been a long time since I've had such an easy conversation. It probably helps that he doesn't know that I tried to blackmail my ex-fiancé into getting back together with me. Not tried. *Did.* I actually blackmailed Damien Baxter, only for him to dump me, for the second time, and go running back to the woman I made him leave for me.

I continue to chat to this funny, friendly man for a few more minutes. It turns out he's a buyer for a coffee company. It makes perfect sense. He looks and talks like a coffee hipster nerd. At twenty-nine, I feel like an old hag to his twenty-two years.

"Anyway, I'm going to Australia in a few weeks. They have an amazing coffee culture compared to us," he says, excitedly. I don't offer the information that I lived in Australia for three years. No use digging that up. "You look like you drink a lot of coffee," he says once he finishes telling me about his upcoming trip.

I frown. "I'm not really sure how to take that. Do I look hyper? Or strung out?"

He blinks and then trips over himself saying, "No, no! Not at all. I think coffee drinkers are the best people. That's all that I meant by that."

I enjoy the way I can unbalance him with a single sentence. Well, I would, if I wasn't entertaining the idea of actually becoming friends with this guy. I like him. He's sweet and unaffected. "You know, I don't even know your last name."

"It's Holland."

"Well, Halifax Holland, it's been lovely to meet you." The wide smile I give him is as genuine a smile as I have.

He returns it, his puppy dog eyes soft and kind. "It was lovely to meet you too. You know. I feel like I should know your actual name now. I feel like we're past the Bora stage."

"My name?"

"Yes, what's your name?"

I hesitate, thinking about all the reasons why I want to remain anonymous for just a few more moments when a voice speaks up behind it.

"Clarissa. Her name is Clarissa Masters."

Four

MATTHIAS

DEALING WITH THE AFTERMATH of the women who'd accused me of knocking them up has been utter hell. Meeting after freaking meeting trying to figure out how to rehabilitate my so-called manwhore reputation. So, when I receive Leanne's text asking if I want to come have a drink at her place, I'm only too happy to accept the invitation instead of going back to the office.

Kevin, my driver, lets me out and I walk the five blocks to her apartment, not sure what to expect when I get there. Leanne is known for rarely having a quiet night in her own apartment. In fact, I'm sure I've been there multiple times when she wasn't even there.

I can't help wondering what her neighbors must think. Not that it matters. I own the building, which is how I met her in the first place.

As usual, when I enter her open apartment using my own security key, she is nowhere to be seen. I recognize a few people and chat for a few minutes, before someone points to the drinks trolley near the window and offers to get me a drink. I excuse myself from the conversation to get the drink myself.

And run into someone I never expected... and had hoped...never to see again.

My brother's ex-fiancée.

She's talking to a guy, who looks like he's ready to crawl onto his hands and knees and do whatever she asks. I've seen the look before. On the face of pretty much every man who comes into contact with her. Except Damien.

What is she even doing here?

I'd heard she'd moved to the USA, but I'm surprised I haven't heard anything about her living in New York City. Because wherever Clarissa is, she makes sure that everyone knows she's there.

She's dressed in a pair of white silk pants that make her legs look like they go on for days, and a sleeveless cream colored satin shirt with a ruffle running down the front. Her hair is perfectly curled, falling around her face like she'd moved each strand into place. As usual, she looks perfectly put together. The only thing that stands out as different about her is that she's not blinding me with diamonds on every surface of her skin.

At least she's toned down that part of her outfit.

I take a step closer out of pure curiosity, working out how long it's been since I last saw her.

Seven months, give or take. Since the day I went with Damien to her apartment to tell her that he was calling off the engagement.

It had turned out just as we expected, with an array of vases, shoes and chinaware thrown at each of our heads.

I'd stayed with Damien there that night, as he'd sat outside her bedroom, making sure she was going to be okay before we left. As far as we'd heard, a week later, she got on a plane and hasn't been heard from since.

Good.

Good fucking riddance.

The sound of her giggling drifts over to where I'm standing by the drinks trolley, my back turned.

Ugh. Poor guy. He has no idea what the fuck he's getting himself into.

Surely, it's my role to help him out.

I take a step closer and hear him ask for her name.

Another step takes me into their circle, and I give the guy a big smile, just as he asks her name again.

"Clarissa. Her name is Clarissa Masters," I say, giving him the answer she seems reluctant to give him.

She turns to me, her pupils a whirlwind of recognition and anger. I forgot how beautiful she looks when she's brimming with fury. If nothing else, Clarissa is a true beauty. Outward class and elegance. Turning heads wherever she goes. It's too bad it just masks the desperation and deception inside.

I bestow on her a smile even bigger than I gave the guy. "Hi, Clarissa. It's *so* nice to see you."

A soft hiss draws itself from between her gritted teeth, and then she turns back to the guy without a word to me.

"Halifax, I'm so sorry to cut our conversation short," she says, her voice genuinely sorry. "Suddenly, I don't feel very well. A bad smell or something is giving me a headache."

Halifax's face instantly shapes itself into concern. "Oh, I'm sorry. Can I take you home?"

"No!" she shouts, a little too loudly, and she flicks her eyes to me as if hoping I didn't notice.

The innocent look I give her in return does nothing to ease her misplaced concern. But she doesn't have to worry. I have absolutely no intention of following her back to whatever hellhole she crawled out of.

"I'm sorry, Halifax, I didn't mean to snap." She gives him a small smile. "I just meant I don't live that far from here. I'm just going to walk to get some fresh air," she responds, her voice transformed into a coquettish tone. Whatever she was worried about when she practically screamed at him, it hasn't taken her long to recover from it. Or maybe she's just so good at the façade she puts on that it just comes naturally to her now.

But I'm not done with her. The raw memory of what she put my brother through makes me want to see her squirm again, want to twist the knife. I address the young guy, sticking my hand out. "Halifax, is it? It's nice to meet you. Clarissa and I go way back."

He takes my outstretched hand and gives it a shake, a small dent in his forehead as he looks at Clarissa and back at me, seemingly smart enough to pick up that there's something going on between us. "Oh. Yes, I'm Halifax...and you are?"

I keep Halifax's hand gripped in mine. It had long ago become apparent to me that every first impression starts with the handshake, and you won't ever see me pulling away first. It sets the tone for my relationships, personal and business, and has never let me down yet. The light sheen of sweat along Halifax's hairline that wasn't there before tells me it's working on him too. Drawing out my answer to his question doesn't hurt either.

Next to me, I feel Clarissa shift and huff before she says, "His name's Matthias."

"Matthias Baxter," I finish and give his hand one more pump before letting him pull his hand away.

A question flashes across his forehead. I don't have to be a mind reader to know what he's asking. And he confirms it when he shoves his hand into his pocket and asks, "Matthias Baxter? As in Baxter Enterprises?"

"One and the same. Well, one of four Baxters, that is." There's no need to mention the skid mark that is my uncle. Before he can finish the thought on his lips, I cut him off. "Well, Halifax, it was lovely to meet you. And Clarissa... well, it's been the same experience as always."

I turn to leave, catching her narrowed eyes as I go, but a hand on my arm pulls me back.

"Matthias! I didn't see you come!" Leanne greets me, brushing a kiss on my cheek. "Have you got a drink?"

"Just about to grab one, gorgeous," I say, giving her ass a playful squeeze, which makes her squeal and swat at my arm. "I was just saying hello to some of your friends."

Leanne beams and takes a step over to the drinks trolley and pours me a cognac, neat. "Oh yes, Clarissa owns the new whisky bar around the corner from Sushi Nakazawa. It just opened last weekend and is amazing. You should stop over there sometime."

That...was not what I'd been expecting to hear. I was sure they'd met at some private club or another. Somewhere where the greeting of choice was air kisses and comparing Louboutin's new season's shoes. Owner of a whisky club? That was unexpected. Curiosity gets the better of me and I hear myself ask, "What kind of club is it, Rissie?"

"*Rissie*?!" Leanne catches and roars with laughter, grabbing my arm as she bends over. I grab the glass from her before she spills it. "Where did that come from?"

"Oh, don't you know?" I say to her, "Rissie and I go way back. Actually, she's engaged to my brother."

Leanne stops laughing, her mouth falling open, and both she and Halifax turn toward Clarissa, who looks like she wants to grab the ice bucket and swing it at my head. And keep swinging it. Until they'd need dental records to identify my head. "What?! Clarissa, you didn't tell me you're engaged. I thought you were dati—"

Clarissa cuts her off with a hand slash right down the middle of our group. "Was! I *was* engaged to Damie—, er, to his brother. That's long over. *Long* over." The restraint in her voice is admirable. Considering how she looks, if the ice bucket thing doesn't work, she might try grabbing the bottles of wine on the trolley and knock my head with them both, one on each side, until my brains come spilling out of my ears. It's exactly the look I want her to have.

Leanne turns back to me, her eyes unreadable. "Well, I guess my plan is both brilliant and stupid then."

That sounds ominous. "What plan? What mischief have you cooked up in your head?"

She chuckles, somewhat nervously, something I've never heard before. "Well, I actually texted you because I thought... you know ..." She points at Clarissa and then back at me, her finger swinging back and forth between us.

"What? No!" Clarissa yells, her face mirroring the horror I'm sure is plastered on mine.

"Leanne, sweetheart, that is without a doubt the worst idea you've ever had. Ever. And don't forget you wanted to put one of those rotating beds in my apartment."

Leanne screws up her face and swats me away. "That was a *joke*. You and your revolving door and all. Why not have a revolving bed?"

"I... think I'm just going to get another drink," Halifax finally speaks up, and the three of us turn toward him, apparently forgetting he was there.

"No, I'm going," Clarissa says, her lips set in a thin line.

"Hey, don't let me stop you," I say, holding my hands up. "I'm sure there's a shoe sale somewhere out there that you haven't hit yet."

Fury and loathing is the look of choice that she shoots me before she pushes through the circle and disappears into the crowd, leaving a faint waft of Dior's Balade Sauvage. A fitting scent. Savage, indeed.

"So, how've you been?" I ask Leanne, ready to forget the unpleasantness of an unexpected run-in with my brother's ex.

She just shakes her head at me, as if disappointed in something I've said.

Frankly, I'm kind of getting used to that.

Five

CLARISSA

I walk, no, *run*, toward the stairs, practically flinging myself down them.

Fucking Baxters.

Does nothing good ever come out of them? Fucking fuckhead, fucktard, fucking dickface fuckers! Every single fucking one of them.

Not just Damien and Matthias, but fucking Gerry too, who'd promised me that our plan was going to work. Gerry, who I'd believed even when I knew he was the last person who should ever be believed.

And now, they're all flying high while I'm stuck in a fucking run-down building, sleeping on a dusty couch and showering at the gym a block away from my "home".

And to think that Leanne was trying to set me up with one of them. The worst of them, in fact. At least Damien was serious with his work and wasn't a manwhore. Wasn't it just a few weeks ago that Matthias was reported to have knocked up two women?

I hope he catches something that turns his dick green and oozing and it falls off, then it's dipped in rancid hot sauce and fed to him. Hope he chokes on his pustulating, gangrenous pickledick!

Fuck!

And he'd outed my business to everyone.

The front door sticks so I slam my body against it and fall out into the warm late spring afternoon. I inhale deeply, then exhale with a loud "pahhhh" trying to expel the anger from my mind and body.

Fuck!

Blinded by rage, I step out onto the street, trying to flag a cab. But it's five p.m. and they're all full. I don't really have the presence of mind to book a Lyft on my phone so I just keep my arm in the air, taking in deep, deep breaths.

A few seconds go by before I realize my cheeks are dripping with tears. I can't remember the last time I cried, or at least the last time I let myself cry. But these are tears of anger, of frustration, spurred on by a man from the same family who's responsible for where I am in my life right now.

A car horn startles me out of self-pity as a cab rushes by me, leaving a hot cloud of fuel fumes in its wake.

Shit.

I'm going to get myself run over if I don't start paying attention.

Another cab turns onto the road and it looks empty. I raise my hand, just as someone wraps their arms around my bicep and yanks me back.

It's Matthias, with a smug fucking grin on his face.

"Hey," he snickers, his voice saturated with self-satisfaction. Can one word make you want to slap someone? Because he's just proven it can.

"What do you want? Shouldn't you go inside to perform for your adoring audience?"

The left side of his mouth lifts into an ironic curl. "Oh, Rissie, have you forgotten? Everywhere I go, there's an adoring audience." I can't help but let out a snort. "Oh, so you agree? Why I'm flattered." He bends at the waist in a deep bow. It makes me want to shove him down and knee him in the fucking balls.

"I agree about as much as I agree that you should step out onto the road in front of that truck!"

"Can't. Expensive suit." He pats the front of his jacket vainly. "Just got it back from the tailor."

"It'll definitely be worth more with your blood splattered all over it."

Annoyingly, he just laughs, which only makes me scowl even harder.

"I'm going to ask you again," I hiss, "what do you want?"

"Leanne sent me to give you this. You forgot to take it with you." He holds up a thick binder with Leanne's logo on the front cover. I'm sure it is filled with the swatches and paint samples that she painstakingly picked out for me.

My fingers itch to grab for it. I'm been waiting all day to see her ideas. I just didn't expect that I'd have to deal with Matthias Baxter to get to it. "I didn't forget it. I had to get out of these because... as I said, there was a bad smell."

He lifts his arm and gives his armpit a sniff. If my memory serves me right, he's getting a nose full of *Aventus by Creed*. Too bad he didn't swallow the bottle and poison himself. "Actually, I smell divine. Want a sniff? Or did your last nose job affect your olfactory nerves."

My foot itches on the ground to swing at his shin. But that would mean touching him. "Big word for such a small brain."

"Oh, darling, it's the only small thing about me."

Okay, that's fucking enough. I reach over to grab the folder but just as my fingers touch its edge, he takes a step back. And a step for Matthias, who towers over me at six foot six inches, is a big fucking step.

I refuse to let go of my swatches, however, and for my trouble I fall on him, my face flat against his chest.

And I was right.

He still smells just like ambergris and Moroccan jasmine, and it is fucking divine.

"Well, well, well, Clarissa. If you wanted me to hug you, all you had to do was ask."

With a hand against his firm chest, I push myself away from him, taking the folder with me as I stand up. "Matthias Baxter, I wouldn't want you to touch me, if you were the only man alive, and your touch saved me from a flesh-eating bacterium that killed off everyone else on this earth by gnawing their skin off an inch at a time."

He grins, sticks his fingers into his mouth, and blows, letting out a loud dog whistle. A car pulls out from the curb and drives up to us. Grabbing my arms, he pulls me toward the car, and opens the back seat door. "Rissie, you're not going to get a cab at this time." He leans into the car. "Kevin, please take Ms. Masters wherever she wants to go. But don't take any money she gives you. It could be laced with arsenic."

"I don't need a ride," I shout, even though I do.

"Then why were you trying to get a taxi?" He's got me there. "Take the ride. Consider it an apology for telling everyone we were almost siblings-in-law."

The reminder stings. I'd had a relatively quiet existence here with no one really knowing who I was. And now he's announced it to one of the friendliest but most chatty people in town.

"Am I supposed to thank you for the ride?" I hiss, the rudeness surprising even myself. "Because, as far as I remember, Matthias, you've never done anything for anyone out of the goodness of your heart."

He locks his eyes on me, pinning me against the car, his hand on my chin, stopping me from looking away. "You don't know anything about me. Not a fucking thing. But if you're going to know one thing, it's this. I don't take kindly to someone attacking my company or my family. And you did both. That doesn't bode well for you, darling." He pulls away from me. "And no, I don't expect anything from you, Clarissa Masters, except to be everything you've always been."

He walks away, smirking. "You can close the car door yourself. Unlike poor Halifax in there, I'm not a fucking simp," he calls out as he throws his suit jacket over his shoulder and disappears down the street.

And as I climb into his car, slamming the door, I can only hope it's the last I will see of Matthias Baxter.

Six

MATTHIAS

FOUR YEARS AGO, OUR grandfather passed away leaving express instructions with the company's board of directors that he wanted my brothers and I to retain our positions as the regional directors of Baxter Enterprises, me in North America; Kylian, the youngest Baxter brother, in Asia; Damien heading up the Australia and Oceanic region; and Kingsley, the eldest, in Europe. And for Uncle Douchebag Gerry, to be the interim CEO until Kingsley turns forty-two.

Gerry is a fucktard with no business acumen or talent. He rides on everyone else's coattails and never takes responsibility for his bad calls. We are all convinced that he was adopted at birth, considering he neither looks like any of us nor has any integrity to speak of. But Grandpa felt that the board of directors wouldn't be on board with Kingsley taking the realm at such a young age, and that appointing Gerry would appease them.

And now we're stuck with dealing with him.

Luckily, other than regular meetings and the occasional check-in when he's trying to stir up some shit, he mostly leaves us to our own devices. So, when I return to my desk after a meeting and see a message that Gerry called, it conjures up all sorts of annoyance.

Before I can decide whether to return the call or not, Paula, my PR rep, comes running up to me, her face contorting like someone is shoving something up somewhere something shouldn't be shoved. "We need to talk," she pants.

"Yeah, Paula, I... don't think I want to talk to you," I say, backing away. "I'm guessing it has something to do with this message from my uncle." I wave the post-it in front of her.

"Mr. Baxter." She sounds like she's about to reprimand me for something, and frankly, I'm still smarting from some of the lines that Clarissa landed on me the other day.

I point to my assistant, who's pretending that she's not eavesdropping on the conversation. "Can you tell Hannah instead, and then she can tell me?"

Paula huffs impatiently, so I give in and gesture for her to go into my office. I seriously consider locking the door behind her and hightailing it out of there.

"Get inside," Hannah commands, coming up behind me, clearly trying to block my escape.

"Hey, Hannah, I'd just like to remind you that you work for me."

She shrugs. "Technically, I work for Baxter Enterprises. You want to pay me out of your own pocket?"

My head shakes so hard, my brain almost comes loose. "Hell no, I don't know who negotiated your contract, but I think you're way overpaid."

"*You* negotiated it for me."

"Hmm. Maybe I'm not such a good businessman after all."

She shoves me as hard as she can, which isn't very hard at all, but I still pretend to go flying. "Just go inside!"

"Don't make me send you to one of my brothers!"

"I'd gladly go!"

I pretend to stomp into my office with a sulky scowl, but when I see Paula's voice, it dies on my lips. She does not look happy.

"Okay, what did I do now?" I say, sinking into the leather couch.

She drops a stack of photos on top of the coffee table in front of me. "See for yourself, sir."

With a frown, I pick up the photos. Instantly, I recognize the location as the street in front of Leanne's apartment building. The rest of the subject matter, I've actually been trying to forget. But can't. Me, leaning in so close to a woman, it almost looks like we're kissing.

Clarissa.

One hand is tucked under her chin, the other braced on the car over her head. It looks much more intimate than it was. Too bad they can't see her face because if my memory serves me correctly, they'd see her looking at me with pure and unadulterated loathing. Hatred aside, the photograph does paint the picture of two people caught in an embrace.

"Oops?" I say.

Paula's face tells me that her reaction to these pictures is not "oops.". "Mr. Baxter, what did I tell you just a week ago?"

I sigh. "You said that I was not allowed to be publicly flirting... with women."

"I'm pretty sure I said *'manwhoring.'*"

"That sounded a little too crass for me. I'm a classy gentleman." I lean back onto the couch and lift my feet up onto my coffee table.

"Mr. Baxter!" she yells, her face turning red, looking like she's on the verge of stomping her foot like a toddler.

I stop talking for a minute because I understand that she has a genuine worry that her job is on the line. Not everyone is as privileged to work at a job where their name is on the plastered in neon lighting on the side of the building. I take a breath and straighten my face. "Paula, would you relax? It's nothing. This was... definitely not me *manwhoring.* Trust me. It was just a conversation. A very *unwhorey* conversation." I jab my finger on Clarissa's head. "If you knew who that was, you'd know this wasn't a problem. Where did you get these photos, anyway? I didn't see any paps there."

"I know who it is." She points to the watermark. "And my friend over at EntertainMe.com sent it to me. They're recording the video right now but the text is already on their website, which means it's going to be picked up by the wider media at any time."

A thought occurs to me. "You're not the one leaking information, are you?" I get a glare for my joke. "What's the accompanying text?"

She shakes her head and rests her hand on her forehead. "You do *not* want to know."

"It can't be that bad."

She glares at me, and struggles to her feet before handing me her phone, open to an email.

"Serial womanizer and alleged soon-to-be father of at least two children, Matthias Baxter, was recently seen embracing his brother's former fiancée in West Village on Thursday. Do we now know the real reason that Damien Baxter and Clarissa Masters called it quits? Could Matthias Baxter be the reason Masters fled Sydney after the breakup and moved to New York? Matthias Baxter is fast winning the race for the most immoral man in Manhattan. Should investors be supporting a child care company under his watch?"

"Shit." I exhale and sit up . Okay, this actually isn't good, and it couldn't have come at a worse time.

"Yeah, *shit*."

I've heard Paula swear more in the last week than in the entire time she's been with Baxter Enterprises. I guess I just bring that out in women.

With the IPO for Kids & Care happening in two months, this is monumentally bad timing. This has been in the works for the last year and a half and is expected to be big news in the business space. Which is probably exactly why this is the angle the tabloids are targeting.

Now I'm worried. "So, Paula, what am I supposed to do? Or should I say, what do you want me to do?"

The recent surveys have made it clear, investors did not want to buy into a child care company whose director has a reputation for whoring it up. The projected asking price for our IPO is going to drop because of this. And I'm not okay with that.

Paula sits down on the couch next to me. "You know how I said that you better not be photographed with another woman?"

I hesitate to answer. This sounds like a path that's not going to end in anything fun for me. "I guess..."

She sits up until she's eye level with me. "What did I say? Repeat it to me."

"You said that... if I did get photographed with a woman in the next three months...then it better be with the *same* woman."

Paula nods. "Right. I think you see where I'm going with this."

"I don't see." A shake of my head. I refuse to see.

"I think you do, Mr. Baxter. "

"Yeah, I think I might, but I'm hoping that that's not really where you're going."

"You've now chosen the woman you're going to be taking photos with until the IPO." She holds up two fingers. "For two months."

I recoil just at her words. "No. You don't get it. She and I can't be in the same place for more than thirty seconds without wanting to rip each other's throats out. And it's always been this way. She's just a spoiled rich bitch. And I can promise you now, she's not going to want to have any part of this either."

"You can ask."

I get up, and just for one second try to imagine what Paula is suggesting. Me. And Clarissa. In some kind of... public... thing to stabilize my reputation? Fuck. No. "I'm serious. You don't know what you're suggesting. It's not going to be my manwhoring that's going to screw the IPO up, it's going to be the explosion that takes out half of Manhattan if we sit in the same room for more than ten minutes."

My PR rep stands up, looking a lot happier than when she came in here. "Well, whatever it is you do, just make sure that the press is there to see you two doing it together."

I'd rather suck my balls off with a Dyson, deep-fry them in human lard and have Hannah shoot them into my mouth with a T-shirt canon before I voluntarily spend time with Clarissa. And I have zero doubt that the feeling is mutual; the run-in at Leanne's place more than proved that.

After Paula leaves, I do a Google search to see what everyone really is saying about me, as well as to read the latest reports of the predictions for Kids & Care going public. And none of it looks good. In fact, it looks progressively worse the longer that I look.

Shit.

Is there really no other way?

I pour a drink, sit and contemplate my life for a few minutes, then I sigh, grab my phone and dial Leanne's number.

"Hey, it's your lucky day," I say when she answers. "What are you doing tonight?"

Seven

CLARISSA

I WENT TO MY first blues and whiskey club when I was six years old.

My father used to have a standing appointment at the local club a few blocks away from his office. One day, I was shipped off to spend the day with him at the office while my mother spent hers at the spa. After work, my father packed up his things, took my hand in his and said, *"Let's go to my favorite place in the city."*

The cigar smoke choked me the second I walked through the door, but everything else mesmerized me.

My father sat me in the corner with a soda and a coloring book while he made his way around the room, shaking hands with almost everyone. He looked like a different person there... comfortable? At home? More at home than he'd ever looked at our actual home, anyway.

After an hour or so, he came back, a humidor in his hands, and handed me one cigar after the other, teaching me how to distinguish them. When we finally emerged from the club out into the darkening day I had with a cigar tucked into my pocket and I hobby that would stay with me until now. Sometimes, when I wanted to remember that day, I'd take out that cigar and run it along my top lip. It's dry and smells of nostalgia now. I don't like smoking cigars, I just like everything about the process of making them and enjoying them. A lost art. A dying pleasure. And whether I want to admit it or not, it's how I knew, if I had to start a business, a whiskey and cigar bar would be what I would choose. Something about it is second nature to me, something that bleeds in my veins. I can't help wondering if my father would be proud of this place or if he just wouldn't care.

I guess I'll never know.

The club is already almost full when I replace my hostess, Penny, at the front of house so she can take a bathroom break. A quick glance into the clubroom had shown that only one or two of the twenty tables still sat empty. Leanne's suggestions for the changes are almost completely implemented, and the room looks infinitely more cozy, but still lush with the beautiful décor. When I look out into the main room of the club I know I'm proud of myself, even if my father isn't.

Luscious turquoise velvet curtains drape in dramatic flourishes from the ceiling, revealing oak wooded slats adorning the walls. In the beginning, I considered a theme of mismatched reclaimed antique chairs to save on cost, but Leanne was able to negotiate a deal with one of her furniture stores for a custom bulk order of distressed leather wingback chairs that completely transformed the whole space. Everything was of the highest quality, and it felt that way.

James, my bartender, gives me a wink as I walk past just as he's reaching for a bottle off the top shelf. The bar we had installed is a thing of beauty. From the moment I saw this empty space, I'd envisioned a mahogany bar that stretched the length of the room with inbuilt soft light panels along the front. A bar that could accommodate almost twenty bar stools. It's a stunning statement piece against the backdrop of the stage and classic furniture.

The cigar girls, charming and knowledgeable, weave in and out between the tables and guests. I'd put them through rigorous training and tested them relentlessly before we opened. Everything I know, they now know too. As a result, in the two weeks since we've been open, we've sold almost double the number of cigars I had conservatively projected.

And what a two weeks it has been.

I can't remember the last time I was this tired. Or had such a sense of achievement.

The write up of Malt on the EatDrinkNYC app was basically a rave. And with other positive reviews trickling in, our tables have been all taken every night. I can only hope the momentum continues, because I think I could be happy doing this for a long time.

The door opens and a couple steps into the club. I look up to greet them, a scowl quickly settling on my face when I see who they are.

It's Leanne and *him*. And every thought of happiness flees from my mind.

"What the fuck are you doing here?" I say, only realizing at the last minute that I'd said it out loud.

Matthias grins, brushing his unnecessarily blond hair out of his face. "Is that how you greet all your guests?"

Leanne throws her head back and laughs, laying her slender, perfectly manicured hand on Matthias's arm. "You two are hilarious. I could watch you argue all day."

"Us? Argue? No, I told you, we're old friends, aren't we, Rissie?" He winks at me, and if I weren't standing at the hostess's stand at my own club, I might have reached out and poked him in the eye. Both eyes.

"Friends, foes, same difference." I swallow down the annoyance of seeing him here in my space. "What can I do for you, Leanne? Did you come to see how the changes are looking?"

Her pretty mouth spreads into an excited grin. "Yes! I can't wait. Did the new paint on the light fixtures work out?"

Her enthusiasm temporarily sweeps me along in excitement. "It looks absolutely stunning. We tried out some colored light themes this afternoon, and it makes everything look so beautiful."

Beaming, she elbows Matthias in the chest and twitters, "You're going to absolutely love it inside. Clarissa has done a phenomenal job with this place. Would you believe, three months ago, this was basically just a hollowed out old Subway."

"I believe you," he says, his eyes warm when he speaks to her. Then he turns to me and they harden, grow cold. "Clarissa has always been very accomplished. *Ambitious.*"

Cold eyes meet even colder eyes. "Some of us have to be. Not everyone is handed everything on a silver platter," I spit, and instantly regret it. I don't know how much the Baxters know about the way my father had basically disowned me, and I'd rather not give them that satisfaction.

"Not everyone, true. But none of those people are here, are they?" he says. It tells me that he has no idea about my current financial predicament. Good. I'm going to keep it that way. The last thing I need or want is Matthias's pity.

Before I can throw another insult his way, someone comes running up behind me.

"Ms. Masters!" Clementine, one of the cigar girls, loudly whispers, her face blazing red.

I touch her shoulder. "Clementine. No running, okay? Not in front of the guests."

She turns even more red but nods, acknowledging my instruction. "Ms. Masters, there's a guest who is asking if we can get the Brick House Churchills. But we don't have any! I don't think we've ever had any!" Her voice rises in volume and pitch with each word, panicked.

Out of the corner of my eye, Leanne and Matthias step aside, giving us some room. "Clementine, that's okay. Customers can ask.

In fact, it's good that they ask. It'll give us a chance to make sure we have it in stock." I give her a nod of reassurance and grab a gift voucher and scribble the name of the cigar he'd requested on it, tuck it into an envelope, and hand it back to Clementine. "Tell the customer that we're getting a shipment next Wednesday. Give him this envelope, and ask him to bring it in with him next time he comes and his first one will be on the house, okay?" She looks down at the envelope and back up at me with a nod. "Thank you. And while you're there, can you please lead Ms. Marshall and Mr. Baxter to my table? And send someone to take their order, please."

"Of course, Ms. Masters," she answers, calmed down.

I look up just in time to see Matthias giving me a strange look. Indecipherable. And then it's gone before I can figure out what it means.

"Have a good night," I say as they follow Clementine into the salon.

"Thank you, Clarissa," he says, voice soft.

The rare moment of respite from his insults emboldens me. "Actually, I was talking to Leanne. I hope *you* choke on your cognac," I say with the widest smile I can muster.

The response I get from him is a laugh that, inexplicably, warms right through me.

I ignore it and make a note to check the thermostat.

An hour later, the lights dim while the stage lights come to life. There's a smattering of applause as the band makes it onto the stage and performs a quick sound check. I wait until they give me a quick nod, signaling me to walk onto the stage.

"Good evening, everyone, and welcome to Malt!" I greet my customers, trying not to squint under the stage light. "Tonight, once again, we have the absolute pleasure of welcoming one of Manhattan's best talents, Georgana Best! We hope you enjoy the show." This time the applause is thumping, deliberate, anticipatory. I can't help feeling a thrill. I had taken a chance with Georgana, spending almost twice as much as I had intended for the opening night. But tonight is the third night she'll perform since then, and each time she's had to do two encores before the customers let her leave the stage.

Georgana steps onto the stage, bowing low to the audience before the band launches into their six song set.

I listen until the first chorus, just to make sure everything is running smoothly before turning toward my table. I should take a minute to make sure that Leanne and her *plus one* have everything they need. I refuse to think of him as anything but that.

As my eyes land on my table in the far left corner, I notice him watching me.

And even though the room is dark, lit only by a soft orange glow from the stage, I know the eyes watching me are an unnerving hue of blue. *Baxter Blue*, I used to call it. The Baxter brothers might have gotten their business and tenacity from their grandfather, but their piercing, crystal blue eyes and almost bleached blond hair are their mother through and through. Even with Matthias, who might be the one who looks least like her, there is no doubt where his looks came from. Damien used to say that was the very reason Matthias was even more neglected by their mother than the others. Whereas Damien, who most resembled her, was the "favorite" and the focus of his mother's attention, both good and very, very bad, Matthias was the forgotten child when it came to her. And thus, probably the reason he's more immune to her games than the others.

I meet his eyes, just for a second, then I look away. Or maybe he does first. I don't know. I just know that someone has turned the heat up again, and I'm flushed.

It's a rare moment shared between the two of us, where one of us isn't insulting the other.

But it doesn't last.

The next time I look over, he's leaning into Leanne, his hand on her back, whispering something that makes her eyes twinkle, and she leans back, pressing her hand against his cheek.

Ugh.

Come on, Leanne, you're better than that.

I bite back the acid burning the inside of my mouth and make my way over to them.

"Clarissa! Babe, I am stunned!" Leanne squeals when she sees me, and gets to her feet, pulling my hand to the empty seat next to hers. "The gold flecks in the paint shimmer even more than I thought they would. And you did such a good job with the light show." She twirls her finger in the air toward the ceiling.

But I'm not looking at her.

He's looking at me again, with that unreadable look on his face. Neutral, but with something flickering in his eyes.

"Matthias! Isn't Clarissa's club amazing?" Leanne continues squealing.

His lip lifts, not into a smirk as I'd expected, but just in a look of amusement. I can't tell if it's about me, or about Leanne's excitement. It *is* infectious.

"Tell her!" Leanne yells at him, slapping a hand against his thigh in a way that's too intimate for just friends.

"It's okay," I say, not wanting to admit that I'm actually wondering what he really thinks about my club. He's one of the top twenty richest men in New York City and the director of a Fortune 100 company. He's been in the most luxurious, most exclusive, hardest to get into places in the world, and if I know a thing about Matthias, there isn't a vice he hasn't partaken in. My stomach suddenly sinks and I hope he's not comparing Malt to the best places he's been.

Stop it, who the fuck cares with this twat waffle thinks? I didn't build this place for him! He's just lucky to be here.

"Rissie," he finally says. "You've done an amazing job with this place."

The words pierce through the background noise of the band and chatter around us.

Did he actually sound sincere?

No.

I haven't eaten all day, and on top of sharing a few drinks with some of the patrons, maybe my head just isn't working right.

Or maybe it's because Matthias has never, not once, not even in my dreams, *ever* complimented me.

And now is hardly the time to start.

I crook my finger at Clementine and point her to Matthias. She shuffles over, cigar box at the ready.

I reach in and pull one out, handing it to him. "You won't find this anywhere else. Can you guess what it is?"

He looks at the cigar I put in his hands and then his face completely brightens. "*La Tormenta by Fermin*? Where and *how* did you get this? He only makes a thousand of these a year!"

"For himself and as gifts, I know." A little flicker of pride tickles in the center of my chest. It's only fun showing off when your audience knows what you're bragging about. "I may have convinced him to sell me a very small amount. Just as a gift for my VIP guests."

He opens his mouth and then closes it. "I'm speechless."

The heat in my stomach comes flaring back. "Well, that's my cue to go. Matthias's speechlessness is a sign of only dark things to come." I rise to my feet, feeling a need to flee. "Let Clementine know if you need anything, okay, Leanne? Don't forget, I grew up with him"—I point to Matthias—"and I know what he's capable of. Hold on to your purse." Leanne guffaws at my joke, lightly slapping her hand on the table.

Before I leave, Matthias twirls the cigar in his hands, and gives me an appreciative nod, before turning his attention back to Leanne. It's unnerving. And I don't have time to be unnerved.

I walk a little too fast back to the front, trying not to replay the look in Matthias's eyes. Luckily, I'm soon saved by the sound of the club door opening. I recognize the guest and make my way over to the door, a smile plastered on my face.

"Patrick? You're here," I say, with all the warmth I can muster.

"Ah, Clarissa, hello." He returns my smile and reaches for me. I let him give me a soft kiss on the cheek before I subtly extract myself.

"I have a full house," I tell him. Both as a reason for not wanting to be seen canoodling while trying to be professional, as well as something to distract him. He's prone to fixating on why I say and/or do anything that he doesn't like.

But this time, he doesn't seem to be miffed. Maybe my explanation is enough to placate him.

"Full house, what's that... every night now?" He beams, proudly.

"We've been lucky."

"Nonsense, you have worked very hard on your little club."

The smile freezes on my face and I bite down so hard on my tongue, a metallic tang fills my mouth. Once my blood temperature lowers to a notch below boiling, I swallow and nod. "I *have* worked. *Very* hard."

"Yes, I know, Clarissa. And it looks like it's paid off. Now, shall we go in? I'd like to catch the last part of the show." He steps forward, but I grab his sleeve to hold him back.

"Erm, actually, we're so full, even my table is full."

He blinks, as if he hasn't processed what I've said.

"I can't turn away paying customers," I continue, spelling it out.

"But you *did* know I was coming."

I let go of his sleeve, rubbing my hand on the back of my skirt. "Yes."

"As your boyfriend and your biggest supporter, surely I get to have some special privileges."

My annoyance intensifies. The word "boyfriend" sounds so ridiculous coming out of his 45-year-old mouth, especially considering what we really are to each other. I grit my teeth as I say lightly, "Um, well, why don't you have a seat at the bar, and as soon as my table is free, I'll come get you."

He's about to reply, no doubt, to disagree, when Leanne joins us on her way to the restroom.

"Patrick! You handsome devil!". She beelines for Patrick and presses her cheek to his, making the smacking noise of an exaggerated air kiss. To his side, she gives me a wink. She abhors Patrick, having only met him a few times when she'd come to help outfit the club. *"A sniveling Wall Street finance bro who doesn't realize that he's too old to be any kind of bro,"* she'd called him the second he'd left.

I'd had to agree, albeit secretly.

But beggars can't be choosers.

And like it or not, I am one rent payment away from holding a Styrofoam cup outside of Grey's Papaya.

Patrick has deep pockets and likes to throw his money around to show just how deep they are. It helps that he doesn't know that I'd come from pockets that make his pockets look like a pothole compared to my family's moon crater.

"Leanne," Patrick says, about as impressed with her as she is with him. *Crass and a terrible gossip,* had been his impression of her. "How lovely to see you."

She grins at his obvious effort to be polite. "It is, isn't it? Are you coming over to Clarissa's table?"

"Er, actually..." he looks at me, uncertainly. As much as a dick as he was, he's taking care now not to upset me. That's what happens when you tell a man that you're not going to sleep with him until you're married.

"Come, Pat. You like cognac, don't you?" She winks at me. "Matthias is waiting there, and he just ordered a bottle of Remy Martin XO Louis XIII."

"Matthias?" Patrick's eyes sharpen.

"Matthias Baxter, you know him, don't you?"

Patrick practically drools on the spot. Having inherited a healthy $15 million from his father, Patrick feels like a king amongst the peasants. But he is always aiming for more.

Matthias Baxter-level more. *Unachievable* more.

"I-I've actually tried to get a meeting with him," he stammers. "But he's always busy... probably getting some stripper pregnant. Hehe." His nervous laughter at his dumb joke makes me glad his focus is on Leanne and not me.

I don't know how Leanne keeps her face from scrunching up, but she does. Instead, she grabs him by the arm and tugs him toward the table. "Well, now seems like as good a time as any. And he's all liquored up, great time to ask him for his business."

"Oh. My. Oh... okay," he stutters, and follows dutifully behind her.

Poor Patrick. He's nice enough, I guess. But he's lived his whole life in the shadow of those far more successful than him. Unfortunately, for him, he's about to talk to a man whose light has only ever been shadowed by his own brothers. Liquored up or not, Matthias is going to eat Patrick alive and spit out the leftovers for the sewer rats to feast on.

I follow, a little concerned that my meal ticket is about to become mincemeat.

Leanne stops at the table, and a stiff Patrick stands there mute until Matthias stands and offers him his hand. "Matthias Baxter."

Patrick takes the outstretched hand and holds it like a dead fish, mute. Like I said, mincemeat. And Matthias hasn't even really said anything yet.

Leanna rolls her eyes. "Matthias, this is Pat Linzer. He's Clarissa's—"

"I'm Clarissa's boyfriend," Patrick finally speaks up, and I inwardly groan.

Matthias, on the other hand, turns to stare at me, and then cuts his eyes back to Patrick who's standing there, staring at Matthias as if he's a seafood buffet, and he's been fasting for a week.

"Nice to meet you, Pat," Matthias finally says.

"Um, it's Patrick. I don't like 'Pat.'"

Matthias gives his hand another hard pump. "Patrick, it is. Do you like cognac, Patrick?"

Patrick pulls his hand away. "Love it."

Matthias passes him a glass of amber liquid. "Well, then please, take this glass, Patrick. I'll get another one."

"No, I'll get it," I say, torn between wanting to watch the scene unfold and wanting to be anywhere but here.

"Nonsense. Sit," Matthias commands, pointing to the empty chair next to Patrick.

My legs bend of their own accord and I feel my ass sink into the seat. Matthias gives me another one of those indecipherable looks and gets up out of his chair. "I can get my own glass. You've been running around all night and god knows for how long before that."

My stomach swoops at his concern, but before I can argue, he's gone. His blond head towers above the crowd all the way over to the bar. He says something to James that makes him laugh, and he comes back with another brandy balloon and a glass of orange juice.

The glass gets placed in front of me.

"Drink that," he whispers into my ear.

And for a moment, I forget that I hate him. "Um, what?"

"I said, 'drink that'. When's the last time you ate or drank something?"

I can't even remember when. Might have been this morning. Might have even been yesterday.

For no reason other than to take a moment to process what is happening, I lift the glass to my lips. I've downed the whole glass when realize I must've been thirsty. My stomach rumbles from the addition of acidity into it. Luckily, the music drowns it out.

"Another one?" Matthias asks, his voice low against my ear, sending shivers down my spine.

What is he doing?

I shake my head, glancing past him to see Leanne watching us both intently.

Is she jealous?

She doesn't have anything to be jealous of.

I'm putting Matthias's interest in me down to him having already downed half of the bottle of Louis XIII all on his own. Most men turn into disgusting sleazebags. Who would have guessed that Matthias turns into a gentleman?

He's about to say something else when Patrick turns his attention back to us.

"So, Matthias, how do you know Clarissa?" he asks, reaching for the bottle sitting in the middle of the table. He fills up his own glass almost all the way to the rim, licking at the drop that spills over the sides.

I catch a look of disgust ripple across Matthias's face. He steadies his face and opens his mouth about to answer. Just before he speaks, he glances at me, cocking his eyebrow at the pleading look in my eyes.

Instead, he just says, "Oh, we're old family friends. You?"

I mouth a thank you to him, but he's not looking at me. He's sizing Patrick up, from his thinning hair to the way he slurps down his drink.

Patrick coughs, wiping his hand across his mouth. "Oh, well, it was a meeting destined in the stars, wasn't it, dear?"

I focus on a stain on the tablecloth, so I don't have to meet Matthias's eyes. Why am I so scared of him finding out about what's going on here? Why do I suddenly care? "Um, yes. We met at... a restaurant."

Patrick continues filling in the holes I'd purposely left out. "She was there, looking for a friend who didn't show up. So I asked her to join me instead. And the rest is history!"

Matthias cocks his eyebrow. "The rest?"

"Oh yes, she didn't tell you?" Patrick puts his hand on my thigh. "I guess she wants to make the announcement together."

Leanne can't help joining the conversation. "Announcement?" she asks.

Please, please stop, I silently beg,

Patrick beams. "Oh yes, Clarissa has finally agreed to make an honest man out of me."

"I'm sorry?" Leanna splutters.

"Clarissa and I are getting married."

Eight

MATTHIAS

"I'm sorry, I must have misheard you over the music. Did you say that you're getting married?"

I address Patrick, but my eyes are locked on Clarissa, who's squirming under my gaze. Why in the fuck is she marrying this loser? I know exactly who Patrick Linzer is. He's a barnacle in an ocean of sharks. Living off his inheritance while trying to make a name for himself in the stock brokering business, most of his clients are people who owed his father a favor. He's been trying to get a meeting with me for months. Maybe years. He can keep waiting. What is she doing? Surely, she can do better than him.

While I continue to glare at Clarissa while she avoids my eyes, Patrick drones on. "Yes, we're planning for a fall wedding. I mean, we'd like to have more time to plan, but, well, you know. It's time sensitive."

Instantly, my eyes flick down to her stomach as her hands come up to cover her torso. Hiding something? God, no. This is even worse than I thought.

"No!" she yells at me, then tries to cover it with a cough. "I'm sorry, I mean... no, I'm not pregnant."

"Oh. No." Patrick laughs. "It's nothing as sordid as that. No, Clarissa needs her green card to stay in the country. So, since we're getting married one day anyway, I suggested that we do it as soon as possible so she can stay. And make me the happiest man in the world." He reaches for her hand.

Relief floods through me. I tell myself it's because my plan to rope my brother's ex-fiancée into helping me clean up my image for the next three months isn't completely hopeless yet.

Unless she's really in love with Patrick.

If she is, then she's doing a really good job at pretending she isn't. Every time he moves closer to her, she shifts away. Subtly, politely, always under the guise that she's reaching across the table to grab something, or straightening her clothes, but each and every time, she ends up a few inches further away from him than she was before. She's practically sitting in Leanne's lap.

Not a chance in hell she's interested in this man.

Using him for a green card sounds imminently more believable. The strange part is that somehow, she's managed to convince him that it's his idea.

Still the consummate con artist.

For some reason, there's a swelling of pride in my chest.

Probably because I wouldn't mind seeing her taking this loser for every dime he has.

Next to me, Leanne twitters, congratulating the couple, but there's a dangerous edge to her voice. She doesn't mean a word of it, and if I know anything about my friend, she's coming up with a way to save her friend from Patrick.

"Matthias? Isn't it wonderful news?" Her words sound like she's congratulating them. But I hear, *"Really? This loser?"*

"Sure. Yes, it's wonderful, the best bloody news I've ever heard in my whole damn life." I reach for my glass, lifting it in a toast before downing the entire contents. I bite back a hiss as it slides down the back of my throat, almost choking me.

In the corner of my eye, I see it's Clarissa's turn to stare. But she needs to look away if she doesn't want to see how I really feel about this news.

Despite everything that our families have been through together, I can't imagine her father being okay with this shit. What happened to the man who wanted his daughter to marry my brother, and stop at nothing less? He must be throwing a fit. She's either doing this to piss him off, or he doesn't know about it yet. Either way, I can't see her getting out of this without being the target of his considerable ire. Terry Masters didn't get to where he is by being *nice*.

"Well, since your wedding is so soon, I won't have time to get you something really special, Rissie. So, I might as well just ask you, what gift can I give the happy couple?" The words sound sardonic even to me. There's no way everyone else at the table hasn't picked up on it. "Anything, anything at all, just name it," I say, trying to lighten my tone.

Patrick slides to the end of his seat, visibly drooling at my offer. Disgusting. He glances at Clarissa, who gives him a smile that barely reaches the corner of her mouth, let alone her eyes. "Well, that is awfully generous of you, Matthias. Um, if you really mean it, h-how about you gift me just thirty minutes of your time? There's some business I'd love to talk to you about."

Clarissa lets out a little choked sound, revealing how she's utterly embarrassed about her fiancé's behavior. If I had had just a bit more to drink, I would find it hard not to stand up and shout, *"Can't you see what everyone, including your fiancée, thinks about you?"* I don't want to embarrass Clarissa. Although why I even care is a surprise to me.

So, all I say when I finally open my mouth is, "Sure. Call my office and set up a meeting. Sometime early next week. I'm busy later in the week."

He nods like I've offered him the secret to regrowing hair and reaches out to shake my hand. I just pick up the bottle of cognac and hold it out, as if to pour him some more. His excitement wavers for a split nanosecond when I don't take his hand, but then he holds out his glass. I fill it up all the way to the rim even though it hurts me to do so. Cognac should have room to breathe in the glass. The particles lifting in the glass, mixing with the air and delighting the olfactory nerves as you take a sip. Not sucking it down like you're upside down over a keg at a frat party.

Idiot.

He should've pulled his hand away, knowing that drinking out of a full glass is as good as drinking champagne through a dissolving paper straw.

Leanne shifts next to me, and I turn to her, the bottle still in my hand. "Can I top you up, Lea?"

"Are you just trying to get me drunk, Mattie?" she says, calling me by the nickname she knows I hate.

"And why would I do that?" I tip the bottle into her glass and she pulls her glass back once it's just a little over an inch full as she should.

"You tell me. Why do you ever get women drunk?" Her eyelids flutter and then we both laughs.

Out of the corner of my eye, Clarissa watches us out of... interest? Morbid curiosity? Whatever it is, it can't be jealousy.

"I better get back to work," Clarissa mumbles, jumping to her feet.

Leanne does the same. "Oh, great, walk me to the ladies' room?"

"Of course." Clarissa smiles, more warmly than she ever did at Pat. Then, arm in arm, they disappear into the crowd,

Patrick doesn't even notice. His eyes are trained on one of the cigar girls' asses so hard, I'm surprised there isn't a burn hole in the back of her shorts.

"Nice, eh?" he says when he finally turns and sees me watching him.

I fix him with a steely stare. "I assure you; I haven't got a clue what you're talking about."

An eye roll. "Please, man. You're no monk and everyone knows it."

"They do? What do they know, exactly?" I haven't looked away yet, and it has the desired effect of making him squirm.

"Never mind," he mutters into his already empty glass.

Two hours later, Leanna and I make our way out of the club, her having a little more to drink than usual. She leans against me as I wait for my car to show up.

"Did you have a good night?" she asks, putting one hand on my shoulder as she adjusts her shoes strap.

"I did. How could I not with such wonderful company?" I answer, holding her steady.

"You flatter me."

"I meant Patrick."

She laughs so loud it echoes all the way down the emptying road. "What a dickweed. What's she doing with him?"

"Well, apparently that's what it takes to move to the United States these days," I respond with a nonchalant shrug.

"Ugh, she should marry you instead."

"Yes, that sounds like exactly what everyone wants." Well, me at least. But not for the reason she thinks.

She rifles through her handbag for her ChapStick. "She warned me off you, you know?"

"What? When?" And why?

"When we went to the restroom, she asked me if I was involved with you. By the time I stopped laughing three minutes later, she finally got the message. But that didn't stop her from telling me that you're a horndog caring about nothing but what's between a woman's legs."

I drop my mouth in mock shock. "Rude. I'm a tit man and everyone knows it. So, what did you say?"

Her lips stretch over his teeth for a minute as she lines her lips with the ChapStick. "I told her that kissing you felt like kissing my brother, but even worse."

"My ego's taking a beating today." I frown and fidget with my belt buckle as I think about what Leanne's just told me. "I wonder why she cares."

She grins and punches me on the arm, a little harder than I actually thought she could punch. "Yeah, right! You don't know?"

"Should I?"

A sigh, and a patronizing pat on the shoulder she just punched. "You're really fucking dumb for a billionaire."

I have the distinct feeling that I'm being insulted. "You'd actually be surprised how dumb billionaires are. But no, I have no idea why she cares."

"You will. Until then, it's a good thing you're good looking."

My car shows up and I gesture at Kevin to not to worry about getting out. I open the door and help Leanne into the car. She sighs and leans against the seat. "You're going to make someone such a wonderful husband someday."

I wait until the taillights are just dots in the distance before I tuck my hands in my pockets and turn to start my walk home. My nightly walks are the most important part of my day, a jog first thing in the morning and a long, quiet walk to go over the thoughts at the end of the day before I go to sleep. Some day I barely have a moment to myself, that I need the time to really examine some of my decisions. I've been known to be a hot head and it's taken a long time for me to learn ways to not make rash decisions that affect more than just me but thousands of employees.

There's a cough in the alleyway as I walk away from the club. I look up to see Clarissa, in her heels, carrying two large trash bags toward the curb. Toward me. I have to rub my eyes to make sure I haven't inadvertently fallen asleep from a little too much cognac. But I haven't. She gets to the end of the alley and steps into the light, stopping in her tracks when she sees me.

Some primitive masculine instinct inside me compels me to walk over and take the bags from her. But she holds on tight, trying to turn her body to block me.

"Let go of the trash bag, Clarissa," I growl.

She just tugs on the bag, trying to free it from my hold. "*You* let go, Matthias."

"I'm just trying to help you!" I knew she was a bitch, but was she always this stubborn?

She kicks her leg out with a grunt, and I can't tell if it's out of frustration or if she's actually trying to kick me. "Oh, I'm sorry, but I don't remember *asking* you to help me."

"You *will* be sorry when the bags rips and those cans spill all over your precious Ferragamo's!"

"So then I'll be sorry! I'd rather that than ask for your help!"

I huff and turn my body so that my back is against her chest, and block her as I yank one of the bags, pulling it out of her hand. She catches on quickly; she turns away from me, and swings the other bag away.

In an almost Stooges-worthy sequence, both bags rip at the same time, just as I'd predicted and what looks like a million cans spill out all over the street.

"Shit!" she yells and throws what's left of her bag on the ground and drops to her knees. I watch, openmouthed, as she starts gathering the cans closest to her into a pile that keeps toppling over and falling all over the ground again.

"Clarissa, stop. Let me do it. It's my fault."

She doesn't say anything, just spins around on her ruined shoes, reaching for the can behind her.

Guilt creeps in, settling on my skin, to see her this way. I kneel down next to her, grabbing the cans she can't reach.

"Go home, Matthias," she mumbles under her breath. "Just go home."

My voice drops, soft. "I'm trying to help you."

"I don't want you to! Stop! I don't fucking want anything from you!" This time she yells and looks up at me for a second before lowering her face again.

But it's long enough for me to see the tears streaming down her face.

Fuck.

A pressure builds in my chest.

Is she actually crying?

I was just trying to help. Something tells me that whatever is happening right now probably has less to do with me than something else going on with her.

"Clarissa," I say, the guilt now moved to my voice. "Are you okay?"

She doesn't answer, just crawls a little further away, her arms full with crumpling cans of Duvel beer and imported grape soda. A little sniffle escapes, but she swallows it down.

"Clarissa. Look at me. Please."

She doesn't.

I have no choice. I grab her arm and drag her to her feet, pushing her up against the front entrance of her club.

"What are you doing, Matthias? Are you fucking mad?" she yells, the confusion in her voice raising the volume and it momentarily sends a bolt of relief to me. The angry, fighting Clarissa is the one I know. But when I catch a glance at her face again, my stomach sinks.

Her cheeks are completely drenched with tears, her eyes still filling with more, and every time she blinks, she sends another torrent of saltwater down her face.

The pressure in my chest builds to an almost unbearable level. This girl I've known all my life, broken. "Oh, Clarissa. Tell me what's wrong."

My out of character gentleness does nothing to soften her anger. "You mean you causing my recycling bags to burst? Do you know how long it took to crush them and put them in the bag? And now I'm going to have to go back inside and grab another bag!" she yells, each word getting louder and angrier.

I wait for her to finish and say, "No. Not that."

Red tendrils creep up the skin of her chest and neck. "Well, then what? For insulting my fiancé and making him feel like an idiot and making him mad at me!"

Fucking Patrick. "Wait. What did he say?" I should've known it would have something to do with that asswipe. He'd spent all night taking turns leering at Clarissa, me and every woman who walked past. By the end of the night, I could barely look at him, let alone be friendly.

Her face freezes, as if she's only just realized what she said from my short response. "I-It's nothing. I... didn't mean to say that."

I ask the question everyone wants to ask. "What are you doing with him, Clarissa?" Her mouth falls open, the tears seemingly freezing in their tracks. But it doesn't stop me from saying what I've been wanting to say all night. "You're too good for him, Rissie."

This time she snickers and drags the back of her hand across her face. "It's really fucking rich of you to say that."

"What did I say?" I throw my hands into the air. This woman is unbelievable. It was a compliment.

She jabs her fingers into my chest. "You. Of all people, saying that is utter bullshit. When everyone knows you never thought I was good enough for Damien."

She isn't good enough for him. She never was. I never disputed saying or thinking that.

"We're not talking about my brother, Rissie. I'm talking about that piece of useless skin that seems to think he can hold a green card over your head to make you marry him. You *are* too good for him. Why are you doing this?"

She pulls away from the wall and stares me down, her jaw twitching. "I'm in this position because of you. All of you fucking Baxters. So, I'd really appreciate it if you didn't fuck this engagement up for me, too." Her hands push against my chest with a force I wasn't expecting and propels me a few steps back. "So, tell me, Matthias, if I'm too good for Patrick, but not good enough for Damien, then who the fuck am I good enough for?"

I open my mouth and then clamp it shut, surprised by the answer that sprang to my lips.

Why am I even having this conversation with her? If this is the life she's chosen for herself, then what the fuck do I care? But something tugs at my brain... or somewhere in my chest. And it won't go away. And even though it might be the biggest mistake I've ever made, I rest my hand on my chest and say, "If you're really going to sell your soul just to stay in the U.S., I think I might have a better offer for you..."

Nine

MATTHIAS

AFTER LEAVING THE CLUB, I walked around the city until almost five a.m. Somehow, I'd managed to leave my phone at the club after I'd pulled it out to let Patrick type in his number. When he was done, I'd gestured for him to just put it on the table, not wanting to touch it when I saw it was streaked with his sweat.

I walked until the sun had slowly started to glow in a thin blue-orange line along the horizon. By that time, it was too late to go home as I had an early meeting for which I had no intention of being late.

Instead, I jogged to the office, and took a quick shower in the ensuite. But it didn't matter what I did. Walk, run, shower...I could not shake the thoughts sprinting through my mind. Not thoughts of what had happened, so much as thoughts of... the person.

I couldn't forget the way she'd looked at me in horror after I'd said, *"I could make you a better offer,"* and then fled down the alley to get away from me.

I don't know how to describe the look on her face - it was half hatred, half hope. Those two expressions together did things to her face I'd never have thought possible. She'd looked vulnerable, human. Compounded with the tears down her face, I'd almost reached out to cup her cheek and tell her everything was okay, she was going to be okay.

It all had to be because I was still reeling from the news that she was going to marry Patrick. I'd gone to the club to scope out the likelihood that she would agree to some sort of arranged relationship. Something, *anything,* that would help get the tabloids off my back after I'd already been photographed with her. I'd gone to see what I could offer her in return. After her experience with Damien, maybe she had been burned for life and would never consider another relationship of convenience again.

Hearing that she was in a similar agreement with Patrick was shocking. But it also offered me a glimmer of hope. Surely, I was better than that hagfish.

But after her reaction outside the club, it's a mystery whether she would even stay in a room with me long enough to hear me out.

I guess there's really nothing to do but try.

"Cancel my last meeting," I call out to Hannah as I run out of my office and to the elevator.

The ride over to the club provides no inspiration for the perfect speech to get Clarissa to dump Patrick and help me instead.

I'll just have to wing it.

Telling Kevin to wait, I jump out of the car. I could be back out with my tail between my legs in minutes. The club's front entrance is locked and after I knock a few times, there's still no answer. I remember Clarissa walking toward me last night with the trash bag in her hands, and figure there might be a back entrance.

The back door is closed but unlocked when I get there, and I push on it to see it open into a cramped but spotless kitchen.

"Clarissa?" I call out into the quiet and listen for her response. There's a sound from somewhere, not close, and it doesn't appear to be a reply to me. Maybe it's one of her employees doing some early preps for the night.

The salon door of the kitchen opens into the side of the bar and into the main area of the club. Considering what this place looked like last night, I'm surprised by how tidy it is now. All the chairs are stacked on one side of the room, and about twenty tables of varying shapes and sizes are pushed against the other wall. The floor is spotless. On the end of the bar, there are two half full glasses that look out of place. One of them lipstick stained.

There's a soft glow from the lamps on the wall, but the main overhead lights are off.

"Clarissa?" I call out again.

Silence.

I'm about to take a step toward the front of the club when I hear a loud crash and a scream.

It's not from the front of the club or from the kitchen. It's further than that, maybe upstairs.

The hairs on my back stand on end.

"Clarissa?" I shout, this time. "It's Matthias. Where are you?"

In the distance, someone yells out a desperate, "No!"

Fuck.

My entire body ices over and I run to the side of the clubroom where I remember seeing a small locked gate that led up a set of stairs.

Another scream, and then a low rumble of a male voice as I approach the stairs.

Shit.

The gate is open when I get there and I launch myself up the stairs two, and sometimes three, at a time, almost falling all the way back down when my shin knocks up against the highest step.

"No!" the voice screams. It's definitely her.

God.

At the top of the stairs, I run down the short hallway and into the room at the end.

"Clarissa!" I shout, my heart beating about ten times its normal speed.

They don't hear me; Patrick just keeps his body crushing Clarissa's against the broken couch. One of his hands grips her wrist to the side of her body, and the other is raised.

And then, as if in slow motion, his hand slaps across her face. Her whole head snaps to the side. Sickening.

He raises his hand again, and this time, I move in time.

I run over and reach for Patrick's shoulders and yank him back. "Get the fuck off her!"

He falls backward, stumbling, crushing Clarissa's legs into the couch, and grunts trying to fight me off. Gripping his shoulders again, I drag him off the bed, off Clarissa, and onto the floor.

Out of the corner of my eye, I see her sit up, touching the side of her face, gasping.

Grabbing his shirt collar, I pull him to his feet and shove him against the wall. "What the fuck do you think were you doing, you fucking bastard?" I shout, the blood screeching through my whole body.

Gritting my teeth, I rush at Patrick, ramming my shoulder into his solar plexus. His lungs empty of air as he grunts and chokes at the same time, and he falls on the floor again, clutching at his chest.

A red haze clouds my vision and I see nothing in my mind's eye but blood.

Fiery, furious.

I know I should pull back.

I know myself better than to give into this.

Nothing good can come out of it.

But I can't.

I can't pull back.

This shit of a human just raised his hand to a woman. He doesn't deserve me to hold back. He deserves everything that's coming to him... *and more.*

Pulling my elbow back, I hold it for a moment and then release my balled-up fist like a slingshot and launch it at him. My knuckles catch him right on the philtrum, and I push up, feeling the crack of his nose under my fist.

It fuels the beast inside me.

As I drag my fist back, readying it for another punch, his entire face crumples into a bloody pulp, blood spraying from his nose. I grab him by the shoulders and pull him against me, ramming my knee into his stomach.

"You filthy piece of shit. You're about to find out what it's like when someone puts a hand on you. Every single part of your body is about to break," I hiss, my voice cold, dangerous.

I never make promises I don't keep.

I let go of his shoulders only to reach for his throat, digging my fingers into the sides of his trachea. I'm going to strangle the son of a bitch until he's nothing but a gasping puddle on the floor.

"Matthias."

Somehow, the soft sound of my name penetrates the red cloud. My hand still gripping his throat, I turn to look at Clarissa.

She's slid to the end of the couch, her hand holding her torn shirt closed, her hair tangled into a messy nest. A bruise is already forming on her right cheek.

What kind of man would do this to a woman?

I face the fucker, ready to finish him off, but as I lift my hand, she speaks again. "Let him go, Matthias."

"Clarissa. No!"

"Just let him go." She barely has the energy to speak, and she's wasting it asking for mercy for him?

Patrick takes advantage of my hesitation to straighten up, spitting a mouthful of blood onto the floor. He takes a step to the side, pushing my hand off him. "You asshole, you heard what my fiancée said. This is between her and me." His breath is thick with alcohol.

Is he still drunk from last night? He takes another step, this time forward toward her, and I shove him back against the wall.

"Stay away from her," I hiss.

"Can't do that. I need to give her a little taste of what to expect when she doesn't listen to me when we're together."

I grit my teeth, and before Clarissa can stop me, I spin him around, grab by the hair and slam his face against the wall. The sound of breaking teeth makes me smile.

I yank his head back. "No. Listen to me, and listen carefully, you're done here. I don't ever want to see you around here again. She's not your fiancée anymore."

"Then whose is she?" he snickers, as if he doesn't expect me to actually have an answer.

But today is not his day.

I grip the back of his neck and slam him against the wall again. "She's mine."

Ten

MATTHIAS

I LEAVE CLARISSA ALONE only long enough to drag Patrick's barely alive body out of the club and dump him in the back alley. I text Kevin to come and pick him up and drop him off somewhere, anywhere; I don't fucking care.

Just away from the club.

Away from Clarissa.

As I run back up the stairs to her, I'm scared of what I might find when I get there.

She's still sitting on the edge of the couch when I get to the room, her hand touching the side of her cheeks, her eyes almost as colorless as her face. Staring off into the distance, I can only guess what's going through her head.

The silence is eerie.

I wish she were crying or screaming or something... *anything...*

The thumping in my chest has evolved into an urgent tugging on my rib cage, pulling me to her, an inexplicable need to comfort her, snap her out of this trance. I run over and kneel by her side, my hand reaching out to touch her before realizing she might not want that. "Hey... he's gone." My voice comes out shakier than I expected. "Are you okay?"

She doesn't say anything, doesn't even move, not a breath, not a blink.

"Hey... Clarissa." I reach out and this time I make contact, touching her shoulder as gently as I can.

She flinches and her pupils visibly focus and she looks at me, as if she's only just noticing me there.

"Hey." I clear my throat. "Are you okay?" I ask again, because, what else do you ask at a time like this? "Can I get you something?" Every inch of the skin on her arms is covered in goosebumps. "You're cold. Have you got a jacket somewhere?" I get up to grab a sweater I see hanging on the back of a nearby chair.

"No!" she yells, color finally flooding into her eyes. Her scared, glistening eyes. "Don't... don't go... please."

I'm immediately kneeling next to her again, locking my eyes on hers, watching the transformation of her coming back to life.

Her chin trembles as she blinks, sending tears down her face.

The effect is heartbreaking.

Or... *something.*

Something inexplicable that's making my heart race and my breath quicken.

Something that's making my skin prickle and my fingertips itch, twitch. An urge to reach out and touch her pale cheek and brush the single tear that's falling down her face.

"Matthias," she finally says, her voice weak, her chin shaking.

Shit.

God fucking help me.

The tremor in her voice sends a lightning bolt streaking through my body. The white-hot heat settling in the last place it should be right now.

Seriously, Matthias?

What kind of sick fuck am I?

Apparently an uncontrollably manwhorish one, just like the tabloids are saying. I tuck my hand into my pockets, not trusting what they might do given free rein.

Maybe it's just nervousness, I try to tell myself. I hope it's not some misplaced, badly timed arousal at seeing Clarissa in a rare, vulnerable moment.

I shake my head and push the urgings of my traitorous body down and focus on her.

"Can I get you some water?" I ask, hoping she will snap back into the bitchy woman I know and am used to hating.

But she just blinks and another fat tear falls down her translucent cheek.

Shit.

This time there's no restraining myself. I reach out and cup the side of her cheek as a flash of confusion flashes across her face. My eyes aren't even focused on hers as I watch the tear drip halfway down her face and pool on my thumb.

Then I lean in, my mouth trained on her trembling bottom lip.

And suddenly, I can think of nothing but what her mouth tastes like.

Our mouths are barely a breath apart when she lets out a little gasp.

And it shatters the illusion.

The illusion that there could be a single scenario where I would want to kiss Clarissa and her to let me.

Her face locks into a shocked mask as my head snaps back. I jump to my feet and try to put as much distance between us as possible. My balled-up fist slams against the wall I'd just knocked Patrick's head against, for trying to take advantage of her.

And now I was doing the same fucking thing.

"What in the fuck am I doing?" I yell. "What the fuck is wrong with me?"

I rest my head against the wall, not ready to face her, taking in three deep, slow breaths.

One.

Two.

Three.

Sense slowly returns and I know I'm going to have to face her soon. I can't stare at this damn wall forever.

But when I pivot away from the wall and back to her, all I see is a streak of white as she rushes past me, out the door, and down the stairs. The sound of her sobs follows close behind.

Well, if this isn't a good start to a betrothal, I don't know what is.

Eleven

CLARISSA

OH, MY GOD. OH, my god. *Oh, my god.*

What the fuck just happened? What *the fuck* is happening?

I run into my office and slam the door behind me, leaning against it, head shaking.

Did Matthias Baxter almost kiss me? Did I want him to? Did that actually happen, or am I still so affected by what happened with Patrick that I've literally lost my mind?

The memory of Patrick's face as I'd turned him down when he tried to reach around to lift my skirt, burns scars into my blood. Disgust filled me as his face slipped into an ugly mask. What humanity there had been in his eyes fled and left something inhuman behind.

When he lifted his hand the first time, even then I didn't expect him to strike me, hadn't wanted to believe that he would. That he could.

But he did.

Once.

Twice.

Three skull-aching times.

Each time, a hiss leaving his lips as he said unrepeatable things about what he expected from me as his fiancée, as his future wife. Things I'd never been exposed to in my sheltered life.

And who knows what else he would've done if Matthias hadn't shown up?

God, *Matthias.*

What was he even doing there? Why did he say that thing about being his fiancée to Patrick? And why the hell did he almost kiss me?

Did I... *want* him to kiss me? No. *No!* I refuse to believe that, but the fact is that I didn't pull away. I couldn't.

There's a soft knock on the door and fear floods me, my breath stilling in my lungs. It can't be Patrick. Even in my haze, I saw what he looked like when Matthias dragged him out of the room. He wasn't in any condition to be knocking on my door.

Another knock.

"Clarissa, it's me. It's Matthias."

The realization doesn't bring me any more comfort.

I'm not sure I'm any more ready to face him.

"Clarissa. Open the door." This time, the knock is harder. More insistent. "I just want to check that you're okay."

I take a step away from the door, a mistake when I hear the wooden floor creak under my feet.

"Clarissa. Open the fucking door." There's a pause. "Please."

My chest lurches. The way he said *"please"* sounds like nothing I've ever heard come out of his mouth in the twenty something years I've known him. That's been happening a lot lately. Being surprised by Matthias. and not in a negative way. Has he changed? Or have I? That's a scab I definitely don't want to be picking at.

"Clarissa." His voice is gentle, kind, as he says my name. More surprises. "I don't want to ram this door down after what you've just been through. But I'm worried about you, and you might not know this, but I'm not good at controlling my actions when my emotions take over. So, if you don't open this door within fifteen seconds, I'm going to break this door in. Don't say I didn't warn you. Please. Open. The. Fucking. Door. I'm not going to hurt you."

Part of me wants to see how he's going to react. Surely, he's not actually going to ram the door down. As he said, he only would do that if his emotions take over, and there's no reason for him to be feeling any sort of emotions about me. He's probably feeling nothing.

But I know that's not true.

It's *not* nothing.

"Five more seconds, Clarissa."

I reach for the door handle and slowly turn it, wondering what I'm going to find on the other side. Hands shaking, I pull the door back a few inches.

A hand shoots through and Matthias pushes it open, pushing me back with it.

"Oh!" I gasp, tripping over my feet as the door almost rips my arm out of my socket.

For some reason, it doesn't occur to me to let go. I'm halfway to the ground when I feel myself pulled upright and up against a firm chest.

A warm, strong, heaving chest.

"Let go of the door, Clarissa," I hear, and a rumble spreads over the chest.

Unclasping my hand, I glance up to see him looking down at me, something burning in his eyes.

Not nothing.

But I don't know what it is.

He takes a deep breath and says, "You alright?"

"Um, yes," I mumble, my brain completely blank. "Thank you for catching me."

There's an almost imperceptible shake of his head that makes his fringe fall over his eyes. "No, I meant from before. Are you okay?" His hands contract around my biceps as he asks the question.

"Oh. Um... sure... I'm just fine..." I can't think with him touching me. The two of us have never voluntarily touched each other before. And now, in the space of twenty-four hours, he's touched me on my hands, my arms...my cheeks.

"You're lying," he accuses.

I wouldn't know if I was. My blank brain was not yet working.

He opens his mouth and then closes it, rethinking what he was going to ask. I do the same, opening my mouth, wanting to know what he was going to say, then clamping it shut, suddenly remembering who he is.

A fucking Baxter.

I step back, shaking him off me. "I said I'm okay," my voice instantly cold.

His hands, still hovering in the air where I stood, clench. Then, as if he notices, he drops them and shoves them into his pockets. A scowl plants itself firmly over his face.

"Fine," he mumbles, but the confusion in his voice is clear. I can't blame him. I'm fucking confused about what's going on as well. And not just about him, here. The entire last fifteen minutes have been one giant headfuck.

"What are you doing here?" I ask, taking another step back, brushing the hair off my face.

His eyes follow my hand for a split second and then back to my face. "I... er, I left my phone here last night. I came to get it."

That's not a surprise; in the last week, I've already collected a healthy pile of belongings left behind, such that one whole desk drawer has been dedicated to the lost and found.

Just last night, after I'd come back from taking the trash out, Clementine had handed three phones to me.

My spine freezes over, remembering the conversation Matthias and I had had in front of the club last night. And how, after I sent James out to clean up the mess of scattered cans, he had come back telling me that all the cans had been gathered, piled into the ripped bag, and placed on the curb. It could only have been Matthias. It had been only minutes after I'd run away from him.

"Have you got it?" Matthias asks, interrupting my thoughts.

"Have I got what?" I snap, embarrassed that he'd caught me in a daydream about him.

A little smirk pulls at his lips. "Have you got my phone? I left it here last night. It must've been on our table."

"*My* table," I snap again. I don't know why I do, maybe it's something in the way he said *"our table"* when it's *my* table, in *my* club. It's completely irrational, and it just makes me even more annoyed.

He sucks in his cheeks, trying not to let the corner of his lips turn into a full-fledged smirk. Asshole. "Well, do you?"

"I don't know. I don't know what your phone looks like!" I shout.

"Clarissa?" He cocks an eyebrow, amused instead of annoyed at my behavior as he should be.

"What?"

"There's no need to yell at me."

I scoff and turn away from him, partly because I need to grab the lost and found box from my drawer, partly because the way his Baxter blue eyes are staring at me is making me forget my own name. "I wasn't yelling. I just have a terrible headache."

As I sit down at my desk, I look up to see the smirk instantly dissolve from his face and in its place, his teeth gritted in anger, eyes narrowed. Was it something I said?

He walks over to the table, leaning over, eyes scanning over my face. "I'm taking you to the hospital, and I'm calling the police."

Fear pushed every other emotion out of my body. "No."

"Clarissa, he was going to—That little fuck was going to hurt you. He"—he glances at the side of my face—"already had."

I shake my head, jumping to my feet. Necessity dictates that I try to fight the urge to steady myself by grabbing the edge of the desk. The last thing I need right now is to show Matthias even more weakness. Suddenly, it's like the table isn't between us, and he leans right across it, his eyes peering right through mine and into a soft spot in my brain.

"He hurt you. Don't pretend that didn't happen."

"I have to!" I yell; the force makes me dizzy, and I fall back into the chair.

"Clarissa, be careful," he warns.

"I said I'm fine."

I bend at the waist to open the bottom drawer to reach for the box of forgotten phones, wallets, and keys. When I sit back up, he's right there beside me, his hand reaching out, touching my shoulder.

"Ahhhh!!" I yell. "What the fuck? Why did you scare me!"

He scowls. "I thought you were *falling*."

"I was grabbing your phone. Isn't that what you came here for?" I slam the box of phones onto the table, and the top three phones fall onto the desk. Even without looking, I know his is there.

How?

I can smell it.

It smells like the person standing right next to me.

Strong, masculine, powerful. *Sexy*.

Fuck.

Patrick's slap must've really dislodged something in my brain.

Matthias's body emanates a warmth that's unnerving. And I should push him away. Instead, I set one phone aside and then busy myself with locking the rest of the phones away in my desk.

When I look back up, he's still there, chest heaving.

"What?" I snap. The way he unnerves me makes me rude.

He cocks an eyebrow. "I thought you said you didn't know what my phone looked like?"

Seriously? "I didn't. I just figured it was the top one in the pile." I tilt my head. "I mean, I don't think I remember anyone being so scatterbrained as to leave their phone here last night." I pin my eyes on his as I lie. "Right?"

I expect a comeback.

A scathing, sarcastic, infuriatingly witty, comeback.

That I'm prepared for.

What I wasn't prepared for was for him to kneel down next to me, his hand brushing my thigh as he brings it down onto his own knee. "I guess someone scattered my brain last night."

The air thickens between us and he dares me to look away.

He wasn't suggesting it was me, was he?

He just said it to unnerve me. And it fucking worked.

And I almost fell for him. *It*. Almost fell for it.

The memory of him says *"She's mine"* in response to Patrick has changed everything I have ever felt about him. He still hasn't mentioned it. And I hope he never does, because if he does, I'm not sure what I'm going to say. Between the declaration that we were engaged and the almost kiss, the faster there's distance between me and Matthias, the better. I push to my feet and the desk chair clatters against the wall behind me.

"You got your phone. You can leave now."

He stands up and takes a step back. It makes me long for the moments when he was pushed up against me. At least then I didn't have to deal with the full force of his face.

I'll give him this, the bastard was handsome. Cheekbones that would make Adonis weep, a jaw that you could use as a square ruler. Eyes that make you feel like nothing other than you is worth gazing upon.

"Let's go to the hospital to get you checked out," he says.

I shake my head. "I can't, I have to get the club ready to open."

"Get someone else to do it."

I scoff. Typical. "Contrary to your misguided belief, I'm the one who has to be here. It's *my* club."

"But we need to get that checked out." He points at my head. It's only then that I notice the side of my temple burning. A cut. "What time do you finish work?" he insists.

"Four a.m.," I lie.

"You got off work at two a.m. last night," he says matter-of-factly. Ugh. Then why did he ask? "Fine. Two."

"I'll be here before then. You'll be okay until then?"

I throw him my biggest and brightest smile. "I'm perfect."

He holds my gaze for a second longer and then turns toward the door. His hand presses down on the door handle before I open my mouth to say one last thing before he goes that surprises even me.

of business adversaries, charm the men, and befriend the women. And Clarissa would be taken care of for the rest of her life.

Damien, never having the tiniest interest in romance, had more or less found this a palatable enough deal. But Clarissa, being Clarissa, had pushed his patience and Damien had called off the wedding.

Through it all, all the summers spent together, all the family dinners, all the late nights with my brothers when she'd loiter in the background, hoping we'd let her play with us, she was only there because Damien made sure to include her.

Even now, I remember her cheating at games; I remember her fiercely arguing her position on everything; I remember her storming off if we teased her and coming back with insults she'd practiced until they became second nature to her.

But never with tears in her eyes.

Never.

Until now; and it's a memory I wish I could burn from my brain.

I knock on the front door of Malt until she appears, a look of annoyance on her perfect features.

"What are you doing here?" She says, glaring at me through the closed door over the closed sign.

"I heard there's a good performance here tonight?"

She scowls and points to the painted opening hours on the glass. "Club opens at nine. Come back then."

I glance at my watch although I know perfectly well what time it is. "It's 8:39 now."

She blinks and just points again to a sign on the door. "You can spend the next twenty minutes learning how to follow simple instructions."

I can't help but grin. This is a little more like the Clarissa I know. "Save me a table?"

"Can't. All reserved. So sorry and all that."

I adopt a pleading look, clasping my hands together. "Please? We're old friends. You were engaged to my brother, remember?"

She definitely doesn't like that. Even through the door, I see her eyes flash red before she walks away.

I laugh out loud as I tap on the glass door. "Rissie. Rissie. Rissie. Open the door. Rissie. Rissie."

I'm too busy knocking and singing her name to notice someone approaching the door and pull it open. I lurch forward as I reach forward to knock again, and end up rapping my fist on the forehead of a short woman wearing the cigar girl uniform.

"Oh. Shit. Sorry. I didn't see you." A weak excuse but it's true.

She blinks, stunned that I'd basically just used my knuckles against her forehead like a door knocker.

"Um. Is Clarissa here?" I ask.

She blinks again, and then just points inside the club. "She said you could sit at the bar. All the tables are booked up."

"I'm really sorry again. I was just trying to get Clarissa to come out. Is your forehead okay?"

She frowns and rubs it.

"Matthias. Leave her alone. She has a boyfriend." Clarissa stands in the entrance into the main room, matching the woman's glare. She's dressed in the same white silk shirt and skirt I'd seen her wear last night. That was a first, seeing her wearing the same clothes.

"I'm not doing anything. I was just making sure she's okay!" I reply defensively.

"Why? What did you do?" She looks at the cigar girl. "Amelia?"

Amelia has no problem choosing her loyalties. "He knocked on my forehead."

Clarissa looks at me and then back to her employee.

I try to find a way to explain myself, but there is nothing.

"Why?" she asks, exasperated.

I shrug and wink at Amelia. "Why not?" I'm not easily embarrassed, but I have to say, I've never knocked on someone's forehead before.

"What are you doing here?" Clarissa demands, joining me at the bar.

"I'm taking you to the hospital, remember? Wow, you're forgetting already, better tell the ER doc about that."

"Matthias!"

I'm getting too much of a thrill out of the way she says my name. "What? I told you I was coming back for you."

"At two!"

"No, *you* said that. Like I said, I came to enjoy the music and"—I give the bartender a little wave and say to him—"I'm in the mood for something different, what can you recommend me?"

He comes over, flinging a tea towel over his shoulder. "Do we have a budget?"

I grin. "No. Let's break a record tonight."

He grins back. "I have a 21-year-old Suntory Hibiki."

"Sold." I like him already. "And don't stop them coming." I turn back to Clarissa. "Don't you have a club to run?"

She narrows her eyes and storms off.

I grin at the bartender, who's trying his hardest to keep a straight face. Call me crazy, but I bet her employees probably don't dare speak to her like I do.

Five and a half hours later, the lights come back on in the club.

It sheds a light on the uncollected glasses on the tables, strewn napkins under the seat, and scattered coasters along the bar. James, the bartender, collects the glasses the servers bring back to the bar and places them into a tub to take back to the kitchen.

He's been great company all night, serving me some of his favorite drinks as well as even taking some of my suggestions. One of those things is how to make a drink that costs $35 feel like you're getting your money's worth.

Sliding my business card across the bar, I say, "Call Jaxon, he'll be able to hook you up with some of his suppliers."

He takes it with a nod. "Will do. Thanks, Matthias."

"And you'll have to come and see my ice ball press collection."

"James. Are you done?" Clarissa asks from across the room, carrying four wine glasses in each hand like she's done it a thousand times before.

"Impressive," I say, lifting my eyebrow in the direction of her filled hands.

James takes them from her, placing them into his dirty drinkware tub. "Don't you know? Ms. Masters is an old hand."

"No. I can honestly say the only time I've seen her with a glass in her hand, she was lifting it to her mouth." The words were meant to be a joke but they come out a little more acerbic than I had intended. She scowls. Something about her reaction digs at me, like a stone in my shoe. I thought it was funny. She obviously didn't feel that the same.

"You ready?" I ask, to break the tension.

"I have to make sure everything is wrapped up here."

James comes back from another trip to the kitchen. "You can go, Ms. Masters. We've got it. You look tired."

I almost have to hold her back.

Calling a woman tired is a surefire way to get yourself killed. Or, at least, fired.

"Er, James, I have a feeling you're going to need that number for more than equipment. Call me if you need a job." I reach my hand out to shake his, and slip five one-hundred notes into his palm. He pulls his hand back and gives me a discreet nod. "I'll share it with the rest of the bar staff."

I shake my head. "It's yours. I've got the others covered. You do a phenomenal job." I mean it. If this place ever goes under, I might just buy it right out from under Clarissa. I feel guilty for the thought. It's obvious that this place is Clarissa's creation, through and through. She might be one of Lucifer's demons, but she has good taste.

"Clarissa, let's go," I prompt her.

She scowls and starts walking away. "One more minute! I'll be right back."

I don't trust her; I wouldn't put it past her to leave me here, even though I'd been here for the last five hours just waiting for her. So, I follow.

"What are you doing?" she asks when she sees me beside her.

"What does it look like?"

"It looks like you're following me," she grumbles.

"Clever Rissie."

She scoffs and continues making her way to her office, walking faster with every step, as if trying to get away from me. But my longer legs make it easier to match her step for step, making it clear she isn't going to shake me.

"Matthias! I'm just going to my office."

"Go ahead, don't let me stop you."

"You're so annoying!" She brakes to a stop, and shoves my shoulder with her hand, her face a clear picture of frustration. I take a step back, giving her some space as she takes a deep breath. "Why are you here?" she shouts. She sways a little from the effort and it makes my heart stop.

"Clarissa, will you please just go to your office so we can get out of here?"

"That's where I was going, dickhead!"

"Then why did you stop?"

Her whole face scrunches up and, for a moment, I expect steam to come out of her ears. "Because you're one of the most infuriating men, I've ever met in my fucking life, Matthias Baxter."

I can't help but grin. "Why, little Rissie Masters, that might just be the nicest thing you've ever said to me."

She huffs, but the tension from the earlier moment seems gone and she stomps to her office with me right on her tail.

Once inside, I close the door behind us and she stands behind her desk, as if she's trying to put a barrier between us. That's fine by me, I've talked to leaders of G7 nations, the richest men in the world, fuck that, I *am* one of the richest men in the fucking world, but something about this woman completely unnerves me.

Probably because you know that she'd stab you in the back while smiling right to your face.

"Clarissa. Get your stuff. I'm taking you to the hospital."

"I. Don't. Need. To. Go. To. The. Hospital." Tired, purple ringed eyes stare at me in defiance.

But I'm not here to play around. "I. Don't. Care. What. You. Think. You. Need." I brace my hands on the edge of the table. "Let's go."

I don't know what I expect her to do, but it's not this.

She leans forward in her seat and stares right back, challenging me.

"Why are you doing this, Matthias? What do you want from me? Because I know for fucking sure that you don't give a shit about me or the bump on my head."

My stomach drops to the floor, as well as my voice. "You have a bump on your head?" An ice cube feels like it's making its way up my esophagus and I swallow it down with an audible gulp.

She notices something in my face, but I'm not sure what it is.

But her face opens, just a little, like a crack in the door.

I take advantage of the moment. "One, I *do* give a shit if you have a bump on your head, that's why I'm here to get you checked out, and two, I want to talk about... the thing I said... before... upstairs when... the thing... happened. Before."

It's barely coherent. It's like I was the one who'd been attacked.

"The thing about me being your fiancée?" she says.

I nod. "Yes, that."

Her hand waves in the air dismissively. "I'm ignoring that. I don't care what kind of fucked up prank you're trying to play on me, but I am not biting. Look, I've been good. I've left all of you alone, so why can't you just forget that I exist? *Please.*"

I'm winded. The hurt in her voice is palpable. Hating me because I've always been a dick to her is one thing. Thinking that I would play a cruel prank like this hurts. She must really hate me. She always has in some way. But this seems different.

"Clarissa."

She shakes her head and covers her face. "Please, just go. Just leave me alone."

I ignore her. "What's going on? Why are you here?"

She moves her hand away, looking confused. "What are you talking about?"

"I mean, what are you doing at this club? Is this some side project that you're doing for your family's business?"

She spits. She literally purses her lips and spits, right there on the floor by her feet. Like she'd been chewing cud except that it's resentment. Anger courses through the irises of her almost violet eyes.

Unnerving.

Beautiful.

Other worldly.

Right now, even as she bites her glistening lip, she looks like an ethereal demon from hell.

Hungry. Angry.

"My family?" she snickers. "You've got to be fucking kidding."

I'm confused. "What's going on with your family?"

"You don't know?" she looks genuinely surprised.

I throw my hands up. "Apparently I don't know anything!"

Her face settles into a contemptuous mask. "You don't know that after the debacle with Damien, my father disowned me? And practically sent me off like a convict in the 1600's to rot away in New York out of his sight?"

No.

I can't believe what she's just told me. Yes, we'd all heard that she moved to the USA, but Terry had made it sound as though that was her choice. That she didn't want to live in Sydney anymore, not where Damien had publicly gotten back together with his now fiancée. And Clarissa had always famously hated England anyway. *"Too cold,"* she complained her entire childhood. I had always joked that she should probably get used to the cold. She wouldn't run the risk of her icy heart melting in an English summer.

But this, the idea that Terry Masters had cut her off and sent her here, is news I wish I hadn't heard. That heartless fuck. He was getting worse with age. He's always been a ruthless bastard, but under my grandfather's eagle eye, he had kept that ruthlessness under wraps. But now he's apparently let it run free. Maybe Terry Masters has let being the chairman of the board for Baxter Enterprises go to his head.

Or to whatever he had for a heart.

"Oh, Clarissa. No..."

Her eyes harden under my words.

And her throat constricts as though she's trying to force down a swallow. "No, what? No, he didn't give me twenty-four hours to pack up my things before he put me on the company plane? No, he didn't freeze all my accounts and give me nothing but an envelope of money, a key for an apartment he was going to kick me out of after three months, and the explicit instructions to never try to contact the family ever again? No, I think it's very much what happens. Or do you need evidence?"

She reaches into her desk and pulls something out of a drawer and drops it onto the desk. It's a yellow envelope, crumpled, wrinkled, as if it's been folded and unfolded a hundred times. Pushing it across the desk, she looks at me, as if watching for my expression as she flips it over.

A Baxter Enterprises logo in the top right corner and then, across the middle, a scribble in Terry's writing. *Clarissa.* That's all. Just her name.

I pick it up, giving it a little shake, weighing. There is still something in it. Pointing at the flap of the envelope, I lift an eyebrow, silently asking if I can look inside. She just shrugs. I take that as permission, and peer inside.

There's one single hundred-dollar bill left.

Flat, smooth, like it's been ironed.

"What's this?" I don't pull it out. It feels sacrilegious to for some reason.

"That's the last of the money I have left of my father's money," she says, matter-of-factly.

My mouth dries. "It's a hundred dollars. What do you mean, that's the last of the money?"

"You heard me. Of the money my dad gave me, that's it. That's all that's left."

"Use it." A shake of her head. I don't understand. "Why not?"

She slams her hands on the desk, the anger that's been simmering during this whole exchange boiling over. "Because I want a reminder that I didn't spend everything he gave me. I didn't. I almost did. But not everything. I figured it out. I figured out a way to make it on my own. And I don't need him anymore." Each word drips with sulfuric acid.

Did he really cast her out? His darling daughter? All because she'd made a few bad decisions? Who the fuck hasn't?

"Clarissa. Why didn't you tell us? Why didn't you tell *me*? You knew I lived in New York."

She exhales derisively and just the sound of it tells me how much she hates me, my whole family.

Oh my god, she thinks of us as the same as she thinks of him. Worse. She thinks it's our fault.

"We didn't know about any of this, Clarissa. I swear. Do you think we had anything to do with it? That Damien did?"

Her snicker prickles at my skin. "You're telling me you didn't?"

"I swear to you, none of us did!" I yell, her misunderstanding about something so important making me desperate.

"Maybe Damien did, and he just didn't tell you."

"He *wouldn't*."

"Because he's such a man of his word? You remember what he did to me, don't you?"

It's my turn to be angry. I'm sorry for her predicament, but she can't hide from all of the responsibility. "You can't blame him for leaving you."

She looks at me blankly. "Twice."

"You blackmailed him the second time!"

"Girl's gotta do what she's got to do."

I know she's trying to get a rise out of me, and it works. I lose control of my tongue and say, "And what's that? Marrying Patrick Linzer?" It's a low blow, especially now, but I'm too angry to apologize.

I expect a retaliation. But the tables turned at some point in the conversation, and while I'm seething with fury, she's calm, cold.

"What do you want me to do? I can't go back to England; I can't go to Australia. And I like it here and I want to stay. This is the only way."

"Marry me."

Her expression mirrors the surprise I feel. I had not intended to broach the subject this way.

"What?!"

I swallow. "You heard me. You heard me earlier today too. Marry me. We'll get you your green card. Isn't that what you need?"

"Are you insane? I'm not dating you!" she splutters.

I'd be offended if I didn't feel the same about her. "Who the fuck said anything about dating? I said *marry*." I guess this is how we were going to talk about this. "You for your green card, and me, me because apparently my lifestyle is affecting my business. It's a little too—" I clamor for the right word.

"Manwhorish?" she suggests.

She gets it. She knows what my world is about. "I prefer the phrase *'friendly to all.'*"

Her face screws up. "*Naked* to all, you mean."

I can't help but grin. "See how well we fit, Clarissa? Couldn't you do this every day for a few years?"

She makes a cross with her fingers. "Look at your face? No thanks. I'll take my chances with Patrick."

That's not funny. And I make that clear when I slam my hands down on the table, my own anger bubbling over again. "The fuck you will. Come on, Clarissa, be smart about this. You know it's in your best interest. I promise I won't touch you. I promise you won't have to touch me. All I need is for you to smile adoringly at me for a few pictures, come to a few dinners with me, get some free meals out of it, and charm a shitload of people who have nothing better to do than worry about my sex life." I stand back up. "Nothing you haven't done before. Except now, you'll finally be married to a Baxter. I mean, isn't that what you always wanted?"

The air sizzles with hate.

"You are a fucking asshole." But in her eyes, the resolve is crumbling. She's going to go through with it. I know she is.

Why am I celebrating? Is this really something I want to be doing?

She knows, she can see that I need this too. And that puts us both at each other's mercy.

"But I hate you," she proclaims.

"Well, darling, that's okay. Because I fucking hate you, too."

Thirteen

CLARISSA

"YOU HATE ME?" I don't know why I'm asking since it's a given considering our history. But something about him actually saying it out loud... *hurts*.

Annoyingly, he looks amused. "That's a surprise? You know you're not innocent, right? You made Damien breakup with his girlfriend to take you back. And even though you saw how miserable he was, you still tried to make him go through with it."

"But he *didn't* go through with it." The mention of Damien still stings. My ego, not my heart. My heart was never in play.

"No. He didn't want to marry you, Rissie. You can't blame him for wanting to be happy."

The use of my childhood nickname catches me off guard. "But now *you* want to marry me?"

"What can I say? I'm a glutton for punishment. And I probably have more experience handling someone who hates my guts."

It takes more restraint than I have not to throw something at him. I grab the stapler off my desk and launch at his head. He just side steps it, and it clatters on the floor. "Matthias Baxter, you're easily the biggest jerk I've ever met in my life."

"Please. Stop with the sweet talk. We're trying to have a serious conversation."

The only thing left on my desk to throw is my phone and I'm not going to wreck that just to see it hit him on the head. "Do you really think that I'm so desperate that I'm going to take you up on this? If I can't marry Patrick—"

"You can't, Clarissa," he interrupts.

Every time I mention Patrick, his fists ball up and I'm worried that he's going to punch a hole in the glass window of my office door. And frankly, I can't really afford more renovations, so I should probably cool it with the Patrick talk.

In fact, I'd like to end all of this talk. My head is pounding, and I'd really like to just kick everyone out of the club, go upstairs, lay down in the dark, and try to get some sleep.

I bite back the dread. I haven't even been back up there since it happened. Luckily, I keep a change of clothes in my office in case I spill something and need to do a quick change.

"By the way, this whole conversation isn't going to get you out of going to the hospital," he says, looking at me pointedly.

Fucker. How did he know I was thinking about that? "I wasn't thinking that. I was thinking about—" Is there really any use lying when someone knows you are?

He waves his hand impatiently. "We can finish this later. Clock's ticking. My friend gets off his shift at the clinic in half an hour. I figured that you wouldn't really want to go to Urgent Care." How does he understand these things about me that I've never told anyone? "And just think, after we get married, you can go to the doctor as often as you like. For Botox, a boob job..."

I know he's joking, but rage still streaks through me, probably a byproduct of everything that's happened today. I step out from behind the desk and before I realize what I'm doing, I've walked up to him and my hand makes contact with his face.

I didn't think I could slap that hard, but if I'm honest, I've probably wanted to slap him for years.

He hisses and cricks his neck before he's facing me again. I'm expecting a look of anger, but he's just smirking.

It makes me want to slap him again.

"Feel better?"

I actually do. "Yes."

"Want to do it again?"

Called it. "Yes."

He laughs. "Fine, once we get you checked out, you can slap me again."

My eyes narrow. I probably shouldn't get into a negotiation with someone who negotiates billion-dollar deals for a living. "I want to do it now."

"No deal. What do I get out of you slapping me now?

"What do you get out of taking me to the hospital?" I ask, before realizing that I'm too scared to know the answer.

"You mean making sure my fiancée is okay?" He cocks his eyebrow.

If I could, I'd reach out and slap him again, but the pounding in my head suddenly becomes a loud shriek that pierces, and then... everything turns black.

My head hurts.

Like someone slashed at my head with an ax.

Or maybe... slapped me so hard, I almost fainted?

The memory of Patrick hitting me breaks through the fog and I feel my body jolt awake and upright. My eyes flip open and I'm suddenly staring at Matthias.

"Hey." A single word. That's not like him. Nor is the look of worry on his face that seems to be directed at me.

"Mrs. Masters, I think it's better if you lie back down," a gentle voice says to the side of me. He's got my wrist in his hand, and a stethoscope around his neck.

But I'm definitely not at a hospital.

Unless it's a hospital that has 600 square foot rooms, king-size beds with opulent bedding, mahogany cabinets that I'm sure are hiding an 80-inch state-of-the-art TV, and views right over Central Park.

"Where am I?" I ask, afraid to hear the answer.

Matthias presses his finger to his lips, quieting me. "Just listen to the doctor and lie back. I'll answer all your questions when he's done."

"But—"

He rubs his forehead, looking tired. "Lie the fuck down, Clarissa. Before I make you."

Something about the way he says it makes me obey, just as the doctor says, "Yes, please, Mrs. Masters—"

I rip my hand out of his hold, swing my legs off the side of the bed, and stand up. Instantly, I'm on my back again on the bed, the room swirling around me, making me glad that I haven't eaten anything since... well, I don't remember since when.

"Mrs. Masters!" the doctor exclaims, grabbing my hand.

Matthias bites back a laugh that makes me wonder when I'm going to get to slap him again. "Yeah, you should probably stop calling her that. She's a 'Ms'. Doc, give me a hand."

The bed dips as he kneels onto it. Two hands cradle the back of my head and shoulders as two other hands swing my legs back onto the bed.

"Leave me alone, Titwaffle," I grumble, the pounding in my head making me even more irritable than I normally am.

"Well, at least we know her mouth works," the Titwaffle chuckles.

I would continue to argue, but I feel as though I used every ounce of my energy to stand up. And now, I couldn't walk out of this room if there were a suitcase with fifty million dollars and a residential suite plane ticket to Bora Bora waiting for me on the other side.

Matthias climbs off the bed, but I can still feel him standing there.

The doctor asks me some questions. Some I answer in the way I think will get me out of here faster, and some of them, I answer honestly because I can't think of a different response.

After about five minutes, and a thorough exam of my face and head, I hear the sound of a pen click. I peek out of my eye to see the doctor scribbling on the pad and Matthias moving closer. I clamp my eyes closed as soon as he comes into view.

"How is she doing, Jordan?"

"Mrs—er, *Ms.* Masters has some bruising on her cheek. It's lucky that the strikes didn't land directly on her temple, that could've had dire consequences. But with some rest"—he addresses me directly—"you should heal okay. But... Ms. Masters—"

"*Clarissa*, please."

He nods. "*Clarissa.* You are severely dehydrated, and I'm guessing it's been a while since you've had something to eat. Have you eaten today?"

"Sure I have."

"She's lying," Matthias says. "I've seen her at work, twice. She never drinks or eats anything."

I try not to think about the fact that he's been watching me at work. "I...Hey, you don't... know..." I argue, although every person in the room, including the one I just met five minutes ago, knows I'm lying.

"Well, Clarissa, you need to at least drink something, right away." He turns to Matthias. "Can you get something for her to drink?"

"Already done, Doc."

The doctor stands up and gives me a little smile. "Get some rest. I've written a prescription for some painkillers but you should get a more thorough workup, some blood work. You look a little pale." He glances at Matthias. "I'll come check in on her in a few days if that's okay."

"Wait, doctor." I clear my dry throat, embarrassed about what I have to say. "You don't have my insurance info." Probably because I don't currently have health insurance. A hot, humiliated flush creeps up my chest. It was just a luxury I didn't have the budget for.

He just smiles and shakes his head. "I'll see you in a few days," he says with a little wave and walks toward the door.

Matthias follows him. "Give the prescription to Kevin, he'll take care of it," he says to the docter in a lowered voice. "Thanks again, man. I owe you," he finishes and pats him on the back before closing the door.

I feel my teeth grit as Matthias takes the seat that the doctor just vacated, eyes on me.

"How are you feeling?" he asks.

"Fine."

"Fine people don't faint."

"You don't know." I'm being stubborn and I know it. "I was tired. It must've been almost three in the morning."

His exasperation hangs in the air for a moment. "You're up at three a.m. every day, Rissie. You're telling me you faint every day after work?"

This isn't going well for me. "What's your point?"

"You should've let me take you to get checked out before." Guilt cracks his voice. "I should've made you go."

I don't have the energy to argue with him. I just want to close my eyes and fall asleep for a hundred years. The doctor was right;

I haven't really been eating and drinking enough water. It's a little embarrassing to admit that I've been scrimping and saving. Pouring every dime into the club, for months, so that I feel like even money for the cheapest meal food could pay for nicer napkins or better straws.

You fainted in front of Matthias and now you're lying in his bed. I think being worried about being embarrassed is far gone. That bitch in my head never takes a day off, does she?

"I'll just lay here for a few minutes, and then I'll be on my way," I say, closing my eyes, laying back against the pillow.

"You're going to stay here until you feel better and I don't want to fucking talk about it." He looks agitated. Like he has the audacity to be pissed at *me* for not wanting to be a burden to him.

Owing Matthias for anything doesn't sit well with me.

We don't talk for a few minutes. Me because the pounding in my head feels like it is playing a Strauss waltz on my optic nerve; Matthias probably because he's trying to figure out what we can argue about next.

A soft knock on the door interrupts our silence and he gets up to answer it. There's a rattling and a few murmurs and then the door closes.

Something weighs on the bed and out of pure curiosity, I open my eyes. Matthias has put down a silver tray next to me on the bed and is pouring something out of the teapot into a cup. Seeing it dislodges a painful memory from the past. The fine bone china tea set with this distinct robin's egg wheat pattern was designed just for the Baxter family by *Annette by Baxter*, the china and porcelain manufacturing business started by Matthias's great grandmother. Only a direct descendant of the Baxter line can own the tea set. Damien had a set too. And when I left, I smashed every last item he owned. Not that it mattered. He could just get another set out of the family vault. But it was strangely satisfying.

The fragrance wafting from the cup is warming, a soft but permeating spice, with a touch of lavender. I don't recognize it. And that's hard for an Englishwoman to admit. Tea is my only luxury. And when I packed up my things, I took as many clothes as I could shove into my suitcases and three canisters of the special brew of Harney & Sons Assam tea from my father's kitchen.

Matthias walks around the bed, the cup and saucer in his hands. Concern clouds his eyes. "Um." He looks down at his hands, over at me and then back at his hands. "Can you hold the saucer, or should I get you a mug?"

His thoughtfulness is touching. "I can hold it, thank you."

"Are you sure?" I look up to see if he's mocking me, but his eyes are open, genuine.

I just hold out my hand and take the saucer from him, concentrating to make sure my hand doesn't shake. "This smells amazing. What is it?"

"It's—" he starts and then closes his mouth. "It's a tea I found in an Asian tea shop. It's chrysanthemum, lavender and nutmeg. It should help your headache while we wait for the meds. And maybe help you sleep a little."

It surprises me that he has this concoction, but I think he might be right, even the scent wafting up my nose is already working its magic in my lungs. I take a little sip, the hot tea burning, momentarily helping to distract me from the other pains in my body.

"It's good?" Matthias asks after a minute. And I look down to see my cup is already empty.

He takes the cup from me, and I try to ignore the way he doesn't react when our fingers touch. He pours me another cup and holds it out to me, but I gesture to the nightstand next to me.

We sit in silence again. I don't know what he's thinking, but if it's anything like the thoughts running through my head, any minute now, he's going to get up out of his chair and make a run for it.

"Where's your apartment?" he asks when I open my eyes. "I'll have someone go grab some things for you."

The warmth that had spread through my body instantly cools.

He continues, "I know you don't want to stay here and I don't want to stress you out by talking about that right now. But you might feel more comfortable if you had your own clothes. I've put some t-shirts and tracks pants on that chair for you. But... I have a feeling they might not fit on you."

"Um." No matter what... he can never, ever know where I'm living right now. *Never.* So, I do the only thing I can think of... I redirect him. Leaning back on the pillows, I drape my hand over my head. "I really need to get some sleep. Do you mind if I just close my eyes for a few minutes?"

"Of course," he stands. I'm not exactly lying, but somehow it still feels deceitful. "I'm in the bedroom right next door. Just get me if you need anything, okay? Anything at all."

I don't know what to say to that, so I just nod.

He lingers.

And even after I close my eyes, minutes later, I can still feel him there.

Finally, he speaks up. "I know that there's shit going on between us, our families. But Clarissa, you're wrong if you think that I don't care what happens to you." He looks at me for a moment and then turns away, wishing me a soft "Good night."

Even before he's closed the door behind him, tears have already sprung from my eyes.

I can't remember the last time someone *cared* about me, really cared.

And I never expected it to come from a person I would've been happy to see fall off the face of the earth, probably after I pushed him.

I take another sip of tea, and wonder, would he still feel the same way if he knew the whole truth about me.

Fourteen

MATTHIAS

IT'S TOO HOT TO be out jogging.

It's too hot to be out doing anything but walking directly from the car into the building.

But I'm a highly impulsive creature, and if I don't make an effort to add some routine into my life, chaos would reign.

I also need to get out of the house and clear my head.

Get away from Clarissa, you mean.

I thought our brains worked for us. Mine's been somewhat of a traitor recently.

I increase the pace of my stride, silently counting the breaths. Like my nightly walks, my morning jogs are meant for me to mentally prepare for the day, go over the meetings I have, and hit the ground running the moment I arrive at the office. It's a habit all of us have. Damien, like me, jogs, or in his case, runs for his life, his sanity; Kylian has his martial arts and meditations; and Kingsley, well, who knows what the fuck he does since he never leaves the office. Reading finance reports is his cardio, and he never has to prepare to go into the office since he's always there.

I worry about him. As high stress as my, Kylian's, and Damien's jobs are, Kingsley's is more pressure than ours put together, not to mention worrying about the CEO vote coming up in eight months. As much as it's on my mind, it must have been keeping him up since the day Grandfather died. He's absolutely the right person for the job. Like all of us, he lives and breathes Baxter Enterprises, but while the rest of us have outside hobbies, Kingsley's hobby is... *more Baxter*. But that's not always enough. Not in the world of office politics.

I make a mental note to give him a call.

On the advice of a counselor, my brothers and I have a standing Wednesday appointment where we're supposed to talk about anything but work. We stick to it about 50% of the time which is better than I thought we would do. It's good to catch up with them as a group, our dynamic set since childhood. But it's also nice to also have one-on-one conversations now and then. Kylian is both my and Damien's brother of choice to confide in, probably because he's so cheery, he makes you feel better after talking to him, but I don't know who Kingsley would call if he needed to talk.

We all need someone to understand us.

"Matthias?" A female voice pulls me out of my thoughts and I see a woman falling into stride next to me.

Ugh.

I hate anyone interrupting my morning jog; I try to get out here at five thirty a.m. for that reason. Everyone's trying to avoid other people at that time. But she looks familiar so I spend a few seconds trying to place her.

"Oh, hi, how are you doing?" I ask, running my wrist band over my face, stalling as I try to burrow in my brain for her name.

It's not fooling anyone.

She rolls her eyes but with a smile. "You don't know who I am, do you?"

"I'm sorry, I'm just focused on my work." Lame, but true. Kinda.

"I'm Carrie. We met at the Ash Foundation fundraiser a few weeks ago. I left a pair of sunglasses at your place. I've been calling trying to see if I can come pick them up?"

Oh. Well. I would say that this is awkward, but it's a pretty common occurrence. Women come home with me even after I make it clear that I'm not looking for anything serious. And then they try to manufacture ways for us to see each other again. What they don't understand is, if I'd wanted to see them again, I would have. I'm not shy, and I've never been afraid of going after what I want. And I certainly don't need to hear another conversation about how I *just haven't found the right woman.* If I gave two shits about finding "the right woman" I would've already found her. I live in New York City, the epicenter of beautiful, talented, accomplished women who are great to spend a night with. But I'm just not looking for someone I have to text if I want to go out for a drink after a hard day at work.

"I'll have it sent to you," I say sharply. "What's your address?"

She runs beside me in silence for a few beats, probably trying to figure out another way after I didn't take the bait. "Well, tonight's my last night in New York, I was only here for a month, remember?"

"Of course," I lie. I vaguely remember she works for a finance firm and that she likes sushi, but that's probably it.

"Could we maybe catch up for a drink?" she finally asks outright.

I give her points for directness. But that's all. I stop and pull my sunglasses up over my head. I owe her directness in return for hers. "You know what, Carrie? I'm sorry, I'm just not interested. It was nice to meet you, though. Enjoy the rest of your time in New York."

And I run.

I'll find a way to replace her sunglasses. I'm sure Marika, my housekeeper, has it somewhere in a lost and found box, just like the one in Clarissa's bottom draw.

Clarissa.

The thought of her fuels something in my feet and I run faster than I have in a long time.

Last night was... *confusing.*

After she fainted at the office, I sprang into action, carrying her out to the car, then calling Jordan on the way to the apartment. He was just finishing up his shift at the clinic and offered to meet me at home.

The whole time he was examining her, I barely took a breath, just hoping for him to say that she'd be okay.

She'd looked like a rag doll, limp, weak, lifeless.

Unlike any version of Clarissa I've ever known.

Fucking Patrick. He is going to fucking pay.

Afterwards, the way she'd lain there, pale and wincing as I poured her the tea, I'd wanted to take her into my arms and tell her that she'd be okay.

Something is wrong with me.

Not only have I never, ever had that urge for any woman, but why is it about Clarissa of all people?

What is it about her vulnerability that excites and calms me both at once?

Getting into this arrangement with her, it's suddenly seeming like a bad idea. Speaking of the arrangement, I stop at a bench and collapse onto it, tapping on my ear bud. "Call Paula."

She picks up on the second ring, probably after groaning at seeing my name. "Yes?"

"Paula. Come see me at ten a.m."

A pause. "I have—"

I cut her off. "I think you're going to want to be there. I'm bringing my fiancée to meet you."

I don't give her the chance to respond before I hang up, because she's going to ask questions. A lot of them. And I don't have any answers for her.

My phone rings just as I get to my feet.

It's Kevin. "She left, sir. I'm following her."

Shit. I thought she might do this. I'd had Kevin keep an eye on her to see if she'd sneak out. Not ideal considering I was going to bring her some breakfast to make sure she was okay. But at least I'm going to find out where she lives.

"Where is she now?"

Kevin grunts, he's probably turning into a street. It's funny what you learn about people when you spend so much time together. "I think she's going straight to her club, sir."

She couldn't say away from work for one morning? "Let me know if she leaves there. I'll be there in twenty minutes."

"Yes, sir."

"And, Kevin"—I hate that I even have to tell him this—"make sure no one is waiting outside the club when she gets there, okay?"

Something about the thought that that fucking low life is just lingering around there makes me want to murder him.

My legs forget that they've already run ten miles; I leg it all the way to Malt.

"She hasn't left," Kevin tells me when I get there.

"How did she look?"

He grimaces. "Not great, sir. She was carrying her clothes in her arms, though, and wearing a pair of sweatpants and a big T-shirt."

My clothes. She doesn't hate me enough not to wear my clothes. I itch to see how she looks in them.

The club's back door is locked, and while it stops me going inside, I'm glad that she's at least trying to be cautious.

So, I knock.

I knock for ten minutes, trying not to scare her after her ordeal yesterday.

"Clarissa, it's Matthias. Let me in," I shout until my throat is hoarse. I knock until my knuckles are sore and red, but I still keep trying, banging on the door.

Suddenly, the door flings open.

She's still dressed in my T-shirt and track pants but her hair is wet, face clean, clear of makeup.

"Matthias, what are you doing here?" she says, wary.

Seriously? "*What am I doing here?* You just snuck out of the apartment."

"I didn't sneak!" She frowns. "I just left to go home." Something unreadable flashes across her face and it's gone before I can catch it.

"You're not feeling well." It's a statement rather than a question. It's impossible trying to argue with her.

"I'm feeling fine. I got some sleep and now I'm ready just to be alone." She tries to close the door on me but I step in past her into the club. "What are you doing?" she yells.

My hand tangles in my hair, which is still dripping with sweat from my run. "What am *I* doing? I'm about to make some things very clear."

Worry fills her face. "Okay..."

I take a moment, walking away for a few seconds and then swing back to her. "We're doing this, right? I mean, that's what it seemed like. You didn't say it outright but, before you fainted it looked like... well, it looked like you were in."

She sighs. "I'm not sure, Matthias. It's going to be miserable for both of us."

"It doesn't have to be." Do I really think that? We can't go two minutes without wanting to rip the other's head off with our bare hands.

She's thinking the same thing because she says, "How can it not? We can't look at each other without fighting!"

I can't help but grin. "Well, maybe if you stopped being such a bitch."

Her eyes narrow and she points to the door. "Get the fuck out, ballbreath."

I laugh. Why does her annoyance feel so good? And where did she learn all these new insulting names? "I was joking, Rissie. Sheesh. I know you can't stop being a bitch!"

"Matthias!" she yells but then winces and her hand come up to cradle her head.

All the jokes instantly flee from my brain. "Hey, easy. Come with me." I take her hand, and despite her very loud protests I lead her into the main room of the club, pulling a chair from the stack and gently lowering her into it.

"I said, I'm fine!" she argues, even while she grabs her head.

I don't want to antagonize her more while she's hurting. "Yeah, I didn't say anything, Rissie."

"You were thinking it," she sulks.

I get up to grab a bottle of water behind the bar, and hand it to her, opened. "I'm thinking that you need to just calm down for a moment and let me talk."

"Fine."

I might as well bring up the engagement again, while she's sitting there quietly. "Look, is it ideal? Fuck, no. Will it be some great love story? Even more no. You hate me even more than I dislike you. But I know you need this. And come on, I'm better than other options."

She takes a sip of the water, mulling over my words. "And what about you? What makes this worth it for you? I can't do this halfway, again, Matthias. I just can't."

I'm so used to seeing it from the other side, sometimes I forget she had just acted out of desperation. Was she right? But was it fair to expect anything from her than to be human?

"Well, obviously I'm madly in love with you, so this all fits into my master plan."

She just shakes her head and pinches the bridge of her nose.

"Sheesh, you're a tough crowd. Look. I need help, okay? I don't want to be the sole reason the Kids & Care IPO goes south. Just because, as my PR rep says, I can't keep my pants zipped. Are the tabloids totally out of order for this? Fuck, yes. But that's just the world we live in." We share a look. "I need help, Clarissa. And I'd rather annoy you than another woman. You know me. So, please?"

The way she looks at me mirrors what's going through my own brain. *Me giving a heartfelt, genuine plea? Where is the Matthias we both know?*

She sighs and lowers her head. "Okay."

"Okay?" I shout.

"Yes. But! We have to have some guidelines."

I pump my fist and give her a big grin. "Perfect, I love a good rousing talk about guidelines. I actually have already set up a meeting for us at ten a.m. with my PR rep and she can help us figure out how to proceed."

"Matthias! Listen to me!"

I sit down, and I listen. And learn.

"One, don't interfere with my life. I've worked very hard to get where I am now. I'm not giving it up because you have delusions of grandeur about what we're really about. I don't want this arrangement to interfere or affect my business."

"Darling, this arrangement is going to help your business. And you know it."

She bites her lips and her nose scrunches up. It's unbearably cute.

"Fine. My turn. You have to attend events with me and be seen... you know, liking me."

"That's going to be hard but okay. And that's not really a guide-line, that just sounds like a given." She takes a big breath. "The moment I get my permanent residency... we're done."

"How long will that take?"

I was afraid you were going to ask that - about a year. But... I think, maybe with some encouragement from you to an immigra-tion agent, it could be faster."

She's thought about this. I wonder if she suggested Patrick "en-courage" the immigration agent. "Fine by me, IPO should be well done by then. Anything else? We should talk about everything while we're here. Money, where we'll live..." Something finally reg-isters while I talk. "Wait, you didn't go home. You came straight here."

She blanches. "So, what?"

She's hiding something. She's hiding something and she's really afraid that I'm about to figure out what it is. "When I first got here, you said you wanted to go home, but you came straight here."

She waves her hand. "Anyway, so money—"

I don't let her finish. "Where do you live, Clarissa?"

She blinks. And doesn't reply.

Fine. If she doesn't want to tell me, I'll confirm it myself.

I run up the stairs, ignoring her protests, and into the room where I found her yesterday. Looking around, I see things I didn't yesterday, or didn't care to.

Worn suitcases in the corner, a stack of business books in a pile on the floor next to the stained, broken down couch. A rolled up yoga mat against the wall. And an array of clothes, draped over the chairs, and hanging on the back of the door. A make up bag and some pill bottles in a little white storage tub next to a small lamp. Three roach traps in a far corner complete the picture. Dust on every surface.

"You live here?" I shout, unable to keep the anger out of my voice. How could Terry be okay with this? How could he let his daughter live this way after everything he had raised her to be accustomed to?

"Matthias. It's fine," she says.

It just makes me angrier, that she's lived like this for so long, she's used to it. "No, it's not fucking fine! Get your things. You're coming back to my place."

Somehow, she remains calm. "I think this is why we have the guidelines in place."

I fume. I'm surprised the air that comes out of me isn't steaming. She might be okay living here, but I'm not okay with it. She deserves better. She deserves to live somewhere safe, not roach ridden, and dusty. "Clarissa. I'm not negotiating this."

The air between weighs with disagreement.

She hunkers down. "Me either. If you say one more word about the living arrangements, I'm going to pull out of this agreement."

I clamp my mouth shut. Now that she's agreed to this, I don't know how I'll feel if she backs out. "Fine."

She nods, pleased with her win. "Now will you kindly go outside so I can get dressed so I can get ready for our meeting?"

I laugh, making my way out the door. "You worried I'm going to watch? Don't worry, you're not my type."

"Intelligent?"

"A little hellion."

Fifteen

CLARISSA

EVERYONE WATCHES US AS we walk through the lobby of Baxter Tower. I don't know if it's just because they know something is happening, or if this is just what it's like to be with Matthias. Damien is a Baxter brother, but Sydney is a different beast to Manhattan. It's like a den of vipers, and no one pretends it's anything but that.

A striking older woman is waiting outside Matthias's private elevator when the door opens on his office floor.

"Hello, *Mr. Baxter*. Ms. Masters," she greets us with a nod.

He rolls his eyes and his hand gently presses against my back as he leads me out of the elevator and into his office. I'm still not used to him touching me, and my skin tingles where he touched.

"Hannah doesn't usually call me *'Mr. Baxter'* so she's probably just trying to impress you. That, or trying to make me look good to you. Hannah knows everything around here. Right?"

She huffs, dropping a stack of files onto Matthias's desk. "I don't know what you mean. But if you don't like 'Mr. Baxter,' would you like me to call you 'master' like you normally make me do in private?"

I can't help but look at them both with my mouth open. I have had my own assistants and also worked with my family's and never have we ever spoken to each other like that. Melissa, Damien's assistant, was initially much too familiar with me, and I made it known that I preferred that she didn't. She pretty much ignored me after that, and I'm sure she didn't pass my messages on to Damien. But he wouldn't hear a word against her.

I'm getting the eerie feeling that Matthias and Hannah have the same kind of relationship and I'm not sure how I feel about it.

"Ms. Masters, can I get you anything? We make a mean latte, or would you like some tea? There isn't a kind we don't have. Ms. Tran always makes sure we have enough."

Ms. Tran? I glance at Matthias who is making a signal to his assistant to stop talking, and then it occurs to me: Ms. Tran is My-Linh, Damien's fiancée. The tea, it's hers. Of course, it is. Even half way around the world I can't escape her.

Hannah leans in, touching me gently on the shoulder. "Or I can get you absolutely anything you would like." Her friendliness toward me is more unnerving than comforting. For the first time, I can't help wondering if that's just me, and that at some point in my life I chose to doubt people's kindness rather than trust it. I can't tell if that instinct has helped me or hurt me more.

"I'm okay, thank you," I respond.

"Get her a bottle of water," Matthias says, "a chamomile tea and a croissant, please, Hannah. And close the door behind you."

"I don't need anything," I argue, almost out of habit. Truth is, I'm both parched and hungry. I'd drunken all of the tea Matthias had brought me last night in the few hours I'd been there. When I woke up, there was a bottle of orange juice left on the nightstand and I'd downed all, as well. It's like, once I'd actually started to drink, my brain remembered what it was like to be hydrated and demanded more.

"Sit down." He points to the leather couch as he strides over to his desk, grabbing one of the folders.

I sit, only because I have a feeling that I'm going to have to pick my battles with him. And this isn't one I really care about winning.

The office door opens, and a head pokes through. Matthias waves for him to come in and gestures to me.

The man smiles and places a tray with a bottle of cold water, a teapot, and a plate with three pastries on them in front of me. "Can I get anything else for you, Ms. Masters?"

I shake my head. Which is a mistake. It instantly feels like my brain has crashed against the side of my skull. I grab my temples and grimace.

"I hate when you do that," Matthias says as he walks over and joins me on the couch.

"Do what?"

"This." He adopts a wince. Then he reaches over and pours a cup of tea for me. "Drink this."

I scowl. "You're really fucking bossy. I can pour my own tea."

"Literally no one has ever called me bossy before," he says, looking offended.

The expression combined with his words makes me let out a laugh that surprises us both. "Sorry. I just have never heard anyone ever say anything so ridiculous before."

"It's okay. It's been a while since I last heard you laugh. Anyway, I wasn't being bossy." I give him a look. "I wasn't *just* being bossy. You need the tea for these." He pulls a little orange bottle out of his suit pocket and holds it out to me.

My meds from the doctor.

I take one, with a silent prayer that they're going to kick in fast. I tuck the bottle into my pocket just as there's a knock on the door.

"Come in," Matthias calls out. "That's Paula. Don't be scared. She's a PR rep. She's supposed to be mean."

I find out over the next half an hour that Paula is anything but mean; if anything, she deserves a medal for having to put out all of Matthias's fires.

When Matthias tells her about our plan, it takes him a few minutes to convince her that he isn't playing a prank on her. Frankly, I didn't blame her. He can't be serious if his life depends on it. Considering how serious Paula is about her job, his life might. If I received a dollar for every time she says, *"Mr. Baxter, I don't have to remind you how serious this is,"* I wouldn't have to worry about working ever again.

But finally, after rigorous intervention and confirmation from me, she believes that he and I have voluntarily entered into the agreement. We spend the next twenty minutes talking about how we're going to make this all work. It starts with a schedule for announcing our engagement. There are going to be a lot of questions. The least of which is going to be about why Matthias, notorious playboy, is now engaged to his brother's ex-*ex*-fiancée.

The answer we agree on is that we started seeing each other a little after I moved here. As old friends, it didn't taken us long to realize we had feelings for each other. My problem is what will we do if Patrick decides to talk to the media about his relationship with me.

But when I bring it up, Matthias just fixes his eyes dead ahead and says, "I'll take care of him."

He doesn't invite any questions.

Based on the plan we agree on, in the next two weeks, Matthias and I will make some public outings, soft launching our relationship. And in two weeks, we will leak the news of our engagement.

It all sounds very clinical.

Just the way I want it.

It helps me remember that this is just about business, about doing each other a favor.

At one point, though, while we talk about when we should actually get married, I go a little quiet. Matthias must notice because he reaches over and squeezes my hand and gives me a little smile.

"Okay?" he asks.

Not really. But I will be. At least the thought of marrying him doesn't fill me with the dread that I've been pushing down since I met Patrick.

"So, I think that's it for today. I'll look into a few things and get back to you," Paula says as she gets up. "It was very nice to meet you, Clarissa. I look forward to getting to know you more." She's warm and genuine, and I see why she must be good at her job. Baxter Enterprises doesn't hire anyone but the best, after all.

When it's just us alone, Matthias lets out a big sigh and sinks back into the couch.

I follow suit.

My head feels a little better since taking the medication, but I'm suddenly feeling bone tired.

"Paula seems nice," I say to break the silence.

"It's all an act. It's her job," he jokes. It's clear how much he likes and trusts her.

But it still makes me chuckle, and having a plan makes me feel a little more at ease with what we're doing. "It's a hard job. I hope she gets handsomely rewarded for it," I say, already knowing that she is. Baxter Enterprises is one of the companies with the highest employee satisfaction.

"We pay well. We make sure of it," Matthias mumbles, eyes closed. "You'll see. I'll make sure you're paid well after this."

The comfort we've settled into in the last few minutes fizzes into instant tension.

"What?" I ask, my voice tight.

He opens his eyes and looks at me, uncertain. "It's why you're doing all this, right? You know I'm going to pay you an obscene amount of money? I'll take care of you, don't worry."

My stomach fills with hot lead. "Fuck all the way to fucking hell, Matthias." I jump to my feet and storm out of the office, ignoring the looks from everyone on the floor, and run toward the row of elevators.

"Clarissa!" Matthias shouts as he follows me. Something in his voice almost stills my feet, but then I remember what he said and my feet move even faster under me.

"I said, go to fucking hell, you asshole!" I shout without turning around. I don't want him to see the tears streaming down my face.

I don't even know what I'm angry about. Isn't what he said the truth? Aren't I marrying him to get what I want? Isn't that what I've always done? Isn't that why I'm in the situation? It didn't bother me with Damien, and it didn't bother me with Patrick.

But something has changed.

Hearing Matthias break our arrangement down like a transaction felt like a spear to my heart.

Not what was said, but *who* said it.

I'm going crazy.

Why am I so upset for getting what I always wanted?

"Clarissa!" He catches up with me. Grabbing my wrist, he spins me around so that I'm facing him.

Electricity instantly sparks between our eyes.

"Let me go!" I shout.

He grits his teeth as he anchors me. "No. Don't run again. God, just stop fucking running." His face is shrouded in confusion. "Tell me, what happened?"

Out of the corner of my eye, I see his employees surreptitiously trying to back away.

But he doesn't care.

I try to rip my wrist out of his hand, but he just grips even tighter. "You hurt me!" I fling the words at him.

But he could only hurt me if I let him. If I cared what he thought about me. How did I let this happen?

"How? What the fuck did I do?"

My top front teeth bite down so hard on my lip, I draw blood. "You said... it like you can just buy me."

His shoulders drop in regret. "Oh, Clarissa. I didn't mean that."

But they're just empty words. "Matthias, if I had a choice, I wouldn't do this. But sometimes, to get what we want, we have to do the hard things."

His hand cups my face, and he looks anything but pitying. "Shhh, I know, I know. Do you not know how incredible I think you are for everything you've done since your family did this to you? Do you have any idea?"

I don't believe it. I can't. No good can come of it.

"Clarissa. Look at me. God, look at me." His hand grips my chin and forces me to look at him. "Do you think I would say that to you if I didn't mean it? Me? The person who used to drench you with water balloons? The person who drove my brother to your house to dump you? Do you honestly think this is something I would say if I didn't mean it from the bottom of my heart?"

I hold a hand up. I need him to stop.

"Matthias... stop. Please. You don't have to say these things." I don't really feel like being on the end of Matthias's sweet nothings. I've had too much of nothings. I just want to feel something real.

He ignores me. "I think you're fucking amazing for everything you've done. I'm proud of you, Clarissa."

His words cut through all the fog in my brain and flashes like a neon sign. *I'm proud of you.*

"Matthias..."

Our eyes lock.

The desperation turns into something dark, liquid.

And he leans in and kisses me.

I don't stop him.

I kiss him back.

Hard, desperately, inexplicably.

I kiss him back, his lips hard, crushing mine.

Until there's no air left in my lungs and I snap out of it. I shove my hands against his chest and he flies backward, the look on his face showing he is as shocked as I am. I gather all the sense I still have in my body and hiss, "Don't you ever fucking do that again."

Sixteen

CLARISSA

"MR. BAXTER IS HERE, Clarissa," Clementine says to me sometime around nine-thirty p.m. while I'm standing by the bar.

"Ugh." The groan slips out of its own accord. "What the hell does he want?"

She shifts uncomfortably. I immediately feel bad for putting her in the middle of a dispute with my... *fiancé.* That's weird to say.

"Um, I thought you told him to come. He went straight over to your table."

I flick my eyes over to my table and sure enough, he's settling into a seat and gives me a big wave when he sees me looking. What the hell is he holding? It looks likes a present.

"It's fine. Please, go back to the front, Clementine."

She flees, happy to get away from me. Guilt floods me, and I make a mental note to speak more kindly to my employees. Fortunately, I don't feel like I need to make the same concessions with my newly betrothed.

"Hi honey," Matthias says when I reach him, flashing me a grin that could probably melt 90% of the women's hearts in Manhattan. Unfortunately for him, my heart has an armor around it and can't be touched by any toothy smile.

"What do you want?" I snap, fully aware that I'm overcompensating for the kiss earlier today with abject rudeness. The elevator had appeared just after I'd pushed him away, and I'd jumped onto it and escaped. I haven't had to see him since.

I've spent the entire day stuck in a loop, replaying the kiss and the moments leading up to it.

I think you're fucking amazing for everything you've done. I'm proud of you, Clarissa.

I don't know what to make of that information, but in the moment, it had had such an extreme effect on me that I had kissed him.

And when the kiss was over, all I'd wanted was more.

I'd gotten almost nothing accomplished all day, constantly checking my phone for a text from him, and the door for his shadow. But it had been radio silence all day. But now that I'm finally distracted by work, he appears, acting like nothing happened.

"I'm just here to see my sweet. And look, I brought sweets for my sweet," he says with a cheesy grin, then stands up and holds out the box. I take it, surprised at the gesture. I hardly even notice when he leans over and presses a kiss to my cheek.

I give the box a shake. It's heavy, about the size of a shoe box. "What is this?"

"Open it and see," he answers infuriatingly vaguely.

I consider the box and then hold it out to him. "I don't want it." It's been a weird enough day, I'm not sure if I can handle an unsolicited, surprise gift.

His eyes flash hurt. "I wasn't asking if you wanted it or not. Open the damn box, Clarissa," he whispers through gritted teeth." Everyone is looking." Matthias turns to the neighboring table and says, "It's just a belated birthday gift. Her birthday was last month. I'm a terrible boyfriend." His self-deprecating explanation makes them break out into smiles, and I want to throw the box at them for falling for his charm.

Not entirely convinced that it's not a prank, I tear away a strip of the wrapping paper. It reveals the corner of the box. And I instantly know what it is. There's a hint of yellow, green, red, and, of course, Cadbury's trademarked purple.

It's a box of Caramello Koalas. I can tell by just a corner of the box.

Grumpiness gives way to awkward speechlessness as I stare at the box in my hands, mouth dropped open.

"This is a box of Caramello Koalas," I state.

He nods with a proud smile.

"H-How did you get this?" I'm stunned. For a bunch of different reasons.

"Um." He laughs. "You don't want to know. Don't you like them?"

I don't *like* them. I *fucking love* them. In Sydney, I'd pretty much lived on them. A supermarket chocolate treat common in Australia, it is basically a chocolate shaped koala with caramel inside. It is hardly haute cuisine, but I couldn't get enough of them. Everywhere I went, I carried a stash of Caramello Koalas. But how would he know that?

"I cannot even imagine how you would know that."

He shakes his head and looks disappointed. "You're kidding, right? You don't remember when I came over to Sydney one time? There was a big bowl of chocolates on the table in the employee kitchen, I accidentally *touched* a Caramello Koala and you snatched it out of the bowl."

I have no recollection of the incident, but to be honest, there's really no reason not to believe him. I will stab a bitch who touches my Caramello Koalas. Especially now that I haven't had one in six long months.

"I... don't know what to say, Matthias." The gift is extremely thoughtful. Monetarily insignificant, but something only someone who knew me would know to get me. Why is that someone continuing to be Matthias?

"Well, you could say, 'thanks for this giant box of Caramello Koalas. Aorry I almost amputated your arm that one time you accidentally touched one trying to dig through the box for a Flake?'"

I pretend to consider what he said. "That's kind of long-winded. How about just a thank you?"

He smiles, his eyes twinkling in the dark. "Happy belated birthday, Clarissa. I hope you have a wonderful year."

I hug the box to my chest and wander off, in a daze, to my office. Inside, I sit staring at the opened box for a minute. There must be a hundred in here. If I ate two a day, that would last me almost two months.

I grab one and rip it open.

The little line etchings, filling in the details of a koala in the chocolate, make me laugh. And I break off the head of my chocolate koala and pop it into my mouth.

It's just like I remember.

I never knew a supermarket treat could bring me so much joy. I practically hoover down the other half and sit back, feeling the sugar rush around my body. The chocolate hasn't even fully melted before I rip open another one and cram it into my mouth.

Divine.

Other than the tea and croissant that I had earlier in the day in Matthias's office, I haven't had much else to eat today.

I need to do better with that.

A shout comes from the club room and I reluctantly hide the box of Caramello Koalas in one of my locked drawers. I almost laugh at the security overkill, but I'd rather not have to fire anyone for stealing my treats.

Matthias is standing there with his hand up, like he's about to knock on the door when I emerge.

"Wow. That... happens a lot," he mutters to himself. "I just came to see if you are okay. You'd been gone for a while. I wanted to check that you hadn't fainted in a sugar coma.

"Close!" I laugh. "I only ate one."

He cocks his eyebrow.

"Fine, *two*. But don't tell anyone." I let out a sigh, remembering the first bite, and only stop sighing when he laughs.

"Shut up. I like them, okay?" I poke my tongue out at him, the chocolate making me playful.

"Hey, trust me, it was my arm and I remember." He rubs the back of his hand, wincing dramatically.

Curiosity fuels my next question. "Where did you even get them? I can never find them anywhere."

He grins guiltily. "There's an Aussie snacks website based in D.C. I... may have sent someone on the company plane to get them. You looked like you needed a treat. So, I looked, and you're right"—he lets out a chuckle—"you cannot get them anywhere in the tri-state area."

"But... why?" Caramello Koalas make me monosyllabic, apparently.

His lips stretch into a wide smile. "Because I wanted to. If I could find one thing that I knew you'd eat every day, then it was worth the trip. Hey, I had a bowl of phở at my favorite Vietnamese restaurant while I was there—" His face freezes and then he runs his tongue over his bottom lip.

Realization dawns. "Wait. You had... *You* went to get these for me?"

Sheepishness edges his face and he tucks his hands into his pockets, like a teenager trying to ask his crush to the prom. When he looks up at me again, though, he's Matthias Baxter, 36-year-old, ninth-richest man in New York City, director of a Fortune 100 company. Someone who knows exactly what he wants. And for some inexplicable reason, right now he looks like what he wants is me.

"I like seeing you smile, Rissie," he murmurs. He leans forward, pressing the tip of his tongue against the corner of my mouth.

My heart stills.

It's only there for a second, but my mind swirls in a tornado of Baxter blue.

When he pulls back, his eyes are dark, smoky. "There was a little bit of chocolate there."

"We can't do this!" I squeak out. "The kiss, this, whatever you just did, it can't happen again."

"Why not?" he replies with no hesitation. With no doubt. Is this what it's like to be wooed by Matthias? To be swept away by his attention, thoughtfulness, and overpowering... *himness*. No wonder there's a trail of broken hearts wherever he goes and headlines about his escapades splashed on every paper.

"You have no idea what you're saying."

Heat colors his cheeks. "Sure I do. I said, *'why not?'* Why can't we kiss? Didn't you want me to?" He's closer now. He smells like cognac and ambergris, and I want to drown in it.

I can't want this, can't want *him*. It doesn't make sense. But my body, cleaving to him, doesn't give a fuck about sense. Every cell in my body is vibrating to his frequency.

"Because we agreed." It's the lamest, weakest argument for anything anyone has ever made.

He cocks his eyebrow. "Did we?"

He's not even touching me. It's just his closeness is making my breath shallow, useless.

I give him a shaky nod. "We did, Matthias. Just this morning, it was one of our guidelines that we wouldn't let this confuse anything, remember? Purely business."

He shrugs, and lowers his forehead until our hair touches, but not our skin. "That sounds boring. I abhor boring, Clarissa."

I agree. But I can't tell him that. "Well, I could use a little boring. You're drunk. Go back to our table and I'll talk to you later."

The corner of his lip lifts and my insides do a backflip. When did his arrogant, smug grin become something that would endear him to me? "I've only had one sip, darling. To get the courage to come here and talk to you."

This time I audibly guffaw.

If there was ever a man who had never experienced a second of insecurity when it comes to women, it's the man standing in front of me. All sleek blond hair, chiseled cheekbones, eyes like blue gemstones. And a smirk that makes you want to kiss him and slap him both at once.

"Shut up. Don't tease me about the kiss, it's not funny," I hiss, embarrassed by his effect on me. "I have to go back to work."

"In a minute." He takes a step forward and pins me against the door frame and his chest. "I don't know what the fuck is going on between us. I'm more confused than anyone, trust me. But I'm not a coward. Kissing you, it did something to me. It broke something, or fixed something, I don't know. But I think it did something to you as well." His hand ghosts my chin and brands me with its ectoplasm. "And you don't know me very well if you think I'm not going to expend every moment trying to find out what that is. I *meant* that kiss, Clarissa, don't you dare think for a single second that I didn't." His words incinerate any semblance of pretension between us. "Tell me you didn't want me to kiss you again, tell me that it meant nothing to you, but don't tell me that it didn't fuck with *my* head. I would never use your feelings against you, I'm a better man than that. Don't you fucking forget it."

He takes a step back and I can finally breathe again.

We stare at each other, me in disbelief, him in nervous apprehension.

"Um, Clarissa?" A meek voice cuts through the tension between us.

Without looking away from Matthias, I say, "What can I do for you, Clementine?"

Poor girl has been my messenger all night. She's probably going to ask to be relieved of hostess duties. "Um, there's a man here to see you. He says he's the landlord."

I blink, cutting the connection between me and Matthias, and glance over at my employee. She looks worried, and it sends a streak of worry through my body. I flick my eyes back to Matthias, who frowns.

"Why is he here?" he asks.

"Damned if I know. I've only met him twice. When I signed the papers and then when he had to do some maintenance." A visit from my landlord at 10 p.m. is hardly going to be good news.

"Um, what should I tell him?" Clementine asks.

"I'll be right out, Clementine. Thank you."

"Clarissa," Matthias says, his hand catching my wrist as I push past him. "We're not done here."

I wave my hands at him, pushing him back. "You. Stay here. We'll talk later."

I follow Clementine out, and the landlord is standing there in the front entrance. "Ms. Masters," he says when he sees me, eyes serious.

"Yes, good evening, Mr. Walker. How can I help you?"

He wrings his fingers, obviously uncomfortable. Well, that makes two of us. "I'm sorry to have to ask this but, I was wondering, is anyone living here?"

My mind empties. "I'm sorry?"

He grimaces. "It's not just you, Ms. Masters. There have been some anonymous reports that there are people living in some of the units on this strip. And I just wanted to make sure that yours wasn't one of them. That's against the lease agreement. We're not in a residential zone, and this building is not up to residential code. So, if someone is living here, I'm sorry, I'd have to evict you and I really don't want to do that. It's against the law. It's not my choice, unfortunately." He looks genuinely sorry. I wonder how many of these conversations he's had to have. And if anyone else was actually living in their building, like I was.

But I still shake my head. "Er, no. Of course not. Um, this is purely a place of business."

I'm not sure if he's not convinced or if he's just naturally predisposed to distrust. Can't say I blame him. "Okay. As long as you're sure. I really don't want either of us to get in any trouble." It sounds like a warning.

I don't even have a chance to lie again though, because Matthias steps in behind me. "Sir, I suggest you leave now. I don't appreciate you questioning my fiancée like this. *She* lives with me. Why would anyone be living here?" Matthias's presence strangely calms me. His chest is warm against my back.

"Yes, of course. Again, I was asking everyone. Have a good evening, Ms. Masters. And Mr—"

"Matthias Baxter," he says coolly.

Mr. Walker pales and then apologizes as he backs out of the club.

When we're alone, Matthias leans in. "You'll come back to my apartment. I don't want to say another word about it," he says, his voice tight, and then leaves me to return to my table.

And this time, I have no desire to argue.

Seventeen

MATTHIAS

I NEED MY HEAD split open and examined.

Scientific research could discover new and horrifying things. And hopefully give me an explanation as to what the hell I was doing when I cornered Clarissa outside her office and gave her a speech right out of a cringey romcom.

And what about canceling all my meetings to fly to D.C. to buy her a box of chocolates?

The only explanation I have for everything that's happened in the last few days, is that Clarissa is a hellion and she has put some sort of demonic curse over me.

I have no control over anything I'm thinking, saying, doing, since she fainted last night.

When she's close to me, I can't think about anything except how her skin would taste, and how she'd feel, naked against me.

Matthias, stop.

Get a fucking grip, man.

It's just because you haven't seen her in a while, and she is an incredibly attractive, intelligent, argumentative woman and you miss having a sparring partner. Sure, she's obviously working so hard to turn her life around, but no. *It's Clarissa.*

"Hey, where are you?" Kingsley's face appears on the screen, staring straight into the camera. Somehow it feels like he can see right through my skull and into my thoughts.

"I'm in the car. I, er, just came out of a meeting," I explain.

My weekly meeting with my brothers falls at two a.m. on Wednesday mornings for me. My choice. I never know what, *or who*, I'm doing, and that's the best way to ensure that I won't be busy with other commitments. Unfortunately, it also means that I'm still at the club when it comes time to meet them. I snuck out to my car, hoping that Clarissa will be busy for awhile tidying up the club and packing the things she wants to with her back to my apartment.

"Sure, 'a meeting,'" Kingsley says, rolling his eyes. It's seven a.m. for him in London. But he looks like he's been up for hours.

Music floods the video conference room and I know Kylian has logged on.

"Kiara! I'm in my Baxter bros meeting!" he yells.

"So what?" his fiancée yells back

"So, I need you to turn the music down!"

"Just talk louder!" she suggests helpfully.

Kylian's face fills the screen, rubbing his hand over his face. He and I look the most similar, with Damien and Kingsley favoring each other. Kind of like our personalities. We're the chatterboxes to their grumpy asses.

"Sorry, guys. I'm working from home today and Kiara thinks she's"—Kylian raises his voice—"the next David Guetta."

"Yeah, I have no idea who that is," Kingsley says, deadpan. But it's the truth, pop culture is not something Kingsley spends too much time partaking in.

"Hi!" A bright, cheery voice pipes up and that tells us all that Damien has entered the chat. Or specifically, Damien and My-Linh. My-Linh is the closest thing to a human ray of sunshine that exists. Sometimes if she's in the Baxter Tower in Sydney when it's time for the meetings, she pops in to say hello, and makes us all smile.

Even Kingsley likes her.

"Is that My-Linh?" Kiara appears on the screen, pushing Kylian away from the camera. "Hi, future sis!" Kiara says, waving at the camera.

"Hi, future sis!" My-Linh replies, breaking out into a wider grin than any she's ever given any of us. "Oh, you look so cute in that dress, Kiara!"

Kiara beams, "Thanks! I got it at Verde Rosa, they have a pop up shop at the casino!" Kiara employs poker prop players for Baxter's casino in Macau. She's the right person for it too. Beautiful and mysterious, she smiles as she takes you for every dollar you have on the poker table.

Kylian smooshes his face up next to his fiancée's and covers her face with his hand. "Hi, My-Linh, how's my favorite future sister-in-law?" Kylian quickly appointed himself My-Linh's favorite Baxter brother from the moment he first met her. Luckily for him, Kiara fell just as in love with her as the rest of us have.

It's also a good thing that Kylian lives on a completely different continent to My-Linh or else Damien might have disemboweled him by now. Damien does not like anyone looking at or talking to My-Linh too long. Which is too bad for him, because everyone loves her. We've all warmed to Kiara as well, who is as sharp as a tack but also incredibly kind in her own way. It's hard not to be happy that my brothers have found women who love them the way they need to be loved.

We listen to the women and Kylian chatter for a little while. In his little box on the screen, I see Kingsley completely tuned out, flipping papers on his desk, Damien sits behind My-Linh, eyes trained on her and only her.

I wonder what he's going to say, when he finds out about Clarissa. Jealous, no. Angry that I've brought her back into the family fold, yes . And he won't bother hiding it either.

"So, are you guys all ready for your wedding in a few weeks?" Kylian's question somehow makes My-Linh's face brighten even more. The question doesn't have the same effect on Damien though. He throws his head back in a groan while still keeping his arms wrapped around his fiancée's waist.

"Guys, it's become a thousand-headed tulle monster," he groans. "What happened to our little ceremony in the park with appetizers in the apartment before I kick everyone out before I ravage you?" Damien asks his fiancée. I'll never get over how playful he is with her. How he isn't afraid to show that side of him now.

My-Linh rolls her eyes, lovingly, and leans over and kisses him on the cheek. "How about I let you ravage me right now?"

"Ewwwww!" Kylian shouts and covers his eyes.

Ironic, considering I've managed to walk in on him and Kiara having sex every single time I've visited Hong Kong in the last three months.

"Anyway, I better go, let you guys do whatever you guys do in these meetings," My-Linh jokes. "Kiara, are you free for a Facetime?"

"Absolutely, sis, this was getting boring anyway."

The two women disappear off screen and I almost wish they hadn't. With them here, I don't have to deal with the questions coming my way. I'm not quite ready to tell them about my arrangement with Clarissa. I know it's wrong to withhold it, but until she and I start showing up in public and Paula announces our engagement, I'm hoping I can start warming them up to the idea.

A knock on my car window startles me while Kylian talks about the construction on the new apartment building he bought in Macau for Kiara's business.

I cover the webcam and wind the window down to see who it is. Clarissa peeks in saying, "Um, I've got my stuff. Are you ready?"

I hold my finger up and turn back to the screen. "Er, guys, I'm going to have to go. Last minute meeting, you get it. Catch up next week."

It's only a second before I close my laptop, but it's enough to hear Kylian heckle me, and to see a glimmer of a shadow cross Damien's face.

"I'm sorry, I... had a meeting." I say, getting out to help her with her things.

"At two thirty in the morning?"

"Brother meeting."

She nods, "Oh, yes, the infamous Wednesday meetings. I always wondered if those were an actual thing. Damien always kicked me out when it came time for one."

Her sadness makes me angry at my brother. There's such a difference between how he treats My-Linh now and how he treated Clarissa in the past. I don't blame her for her bitterness even if I know she brought some of it on herself.

I open the passenger door for her with a flourish. "Ready?"

She gives me an unsure smile and nods.

And then I drive us home.

"So, you can choose the main bedroom or this one here." I flick the light on and she follows me into one of the guest bedrooms. There's one further from my bedroom but I show her to this one first. *Just in case she needs anything in the middle of the night, she can call out to me,* I try to tell myself.

She looks around appreciatively, taking in the décor. The bedroom is large, especially by New York City standards. When I had my penthouse floor renovated, I wanted half of the apartment to be an open plan, and the other half with cozy areas, so that if I needed to, I could close the door on the world.

"This one is fine," she says, so I drop her bags on the floor by the bed. "I wouldn't want to put you out."

"You're not, Clarissa. You never could."

"Besides, I don't have to think about what ungodly things have happened on this bed," she jokes, her voice light.

"Um, sure. If that makes you feel better," I respond matching her tone.

She makes a fake gagging motion, but it does seem to relax her.

"Come on, I'll show you the rest of the apartment. I don't think you ever really saw more than the foyer and the lounge room when you came here before."

Before. With Damien. Her ex. My brother.

"Actually... do you mind if I just take a shower and go to sleep? It's been a few really long days."

It's the first time she's every really acknowledged her fatigue, and it makes me wonder if it's gotten worse.

"Do you need—"

She holds up her hand. "Just a shower and some sleep, please."

"Okay. Come with me."

She follows me into the full size ensuite, although calling it 'full size' is like calling Mt. Everest a zit. The bathroom is almost as big as the bedroom, with a two-person jacuzzi, a shower four people could fit in, a six-foot long dressing table with a lighted vanity mirror, and ample space for getting dressed.

"The button to turn the jacuzzi on is here," I say, pointing to a button on the side of the tub. "You can also hook your phone to the Wi-Fi speakers or screen share to that screen." I lead her over to the dressing table. "You can find products in those drawers, but if you need anything else, just write me a note and I'll get it Kevin to go pick some up tomorrow."

When I turn around, though, she's sitting on the chair in front of the dressing table, eyes closed.

I consider leaving, but then decide to draw a bath for her instead. She doesn't stir at the sound of the tub filling, so I tiptoe around, gathering bath salts, toiletries she might need, and grab a bottle of water from the drinks fridge in the bedroom to leave by the tub.

"Hey," I gently wake her once the tub is full.

Her eyes flutter open. "Hmm? I wasn't sleeping."

The stubbornness makes me chuckle. "I think you were. I drew you a bath. Have a soak and get some sleep, okay?"

She nods, looking up at me. "Why are you doing this?"

The direct question surprises me. "You know why."

Her head shakes. "Not the whole marriage thing. The taking care of me part. Why are you doing it, Matthias? Is this just a game to you?"

I walk to her, bracing one hand on either side of her on the dressing table. Her breath washes against my face, sweet and chocolatey.

"I want you to listen really, really well. Because I am not going to say this again. I don't play games. Not with people. You understand me?" She just swallows. "Remember that. Because if one of us hurts the other? I'm telling you now, it's not going to be me."

And as I walk away, leaving her alone in the bathroom watching me, I wonder if I'm going to make it out of this alive.

Eighteen

CLARISSA

THE NEXT FEW DAYS go by relatively without incident. We have a meeting with Paula and with Matthias's personal lawyer about our plan, and they tell us everything is ready to move forward. They're the only two people who know both what we're about to do, as well as the truth of the situation.

That this is *not real*.

And it's something that I have to remind myself every day.

Usually, by the time I wake up, Matthias is gone. It works for me. The thing about living in the upstairs of the club is that it was my space, utterly and completely. I didn't have to worry about doing something someone didn't want, touching something I shouldn't be touching. It's the only time a space has ever been mine and mine alone.

Even in Australia, I lived in my family's apartment, or stayed at Damien's, which, honestly, resembled a mausoleum more than a home.

So even though it was cramped and dusty, without an actual bed, with clothes that I'd washed myself and hung on anything that could be used as a hook, the club felt more like home that anything had in a long time.

But Matthias has done his best to make me feel welcome; he sent me a questionnaire asking me about what food I want, toiletries I need, told me I should decorate my room however I see fit.

Without actually saying it, he knows I can't afford the luxuries I'm used to. I'm just not comfortable asking him for anything yet.

There is one thing about having money that I miss more than all the other things put together. But no matter how much I scrimp and save, there is no way I can afford a new dress, a designer dress. I miss everything about the process, the parade, the choosing, the fitting, the putting it on when everything is done, and feeling like that dress was made just for me.

One day, I promise myself. One day, I'll be back in a designer's studio getting fitted.

Matthias texts me at lunchtime on the third day I've stayed with him.

Matthias: You didn't answer my questionnaire.

Me: I didn't have anything I want to answer.

Matthias: Then don't blame me when I get something you don't like.

Matthias: Hello?

Matthias: So now you're not even going to answer my texts?

Matthias: Rissieeeeeee, I need to know what soda you like!

Me: I was working. One of us has to.

Matthias: Ouch. I'll have you know, I just spent half an hour designing my new business card. Now the font is 12 points instead of 13 points. Just call me Mr. Business Mastermind.

Me: BM? As in... in Bowel... M...?

Matthias: Hmm. Never mind. Just call me Genus.

Me: What kind of genus? Fungi? I should call you Candida?

Matthias: That was a typo and you know it. Why are you so mean to me?

Me: Because you like it.

Matthias: Well, I like you...

I put my phone into a locked drawer so I don't respond to him again, and lock my office for good measure. But that proves to be even more detrimental than just answering the message.

Around lunchtime, Matthias comes bounding into the club, large paper bags in both of his arms.

"What are you doing here?" I ask, suspicious. Even after just spending a few days with him, I know that where Matthias goes, chaos ensues. He riles my staff up, and while it makes them excited for work, it's annoying that they have quickly taken to him more than me.

"You ask me that question a lot," he says, exasperated.

I laugh, realizing that I do, indeed, ask him that a lot. "Well, you're around where you shouldn't be a lot!"

"Darling, I am *everywhere*. You should just get used to it." He winks and disappears into the kitchen. After a minute of chatter from him and my staff, he reappears with only one bag

"What's that?"

He dangles it in the air. "This? It's food."

"Why?"

He frowns. "Why is food? That's an existential question if I've ever heard one."

I'm going to strangle him one day. "Why do you *have* food?"

He grins. "It's just some subs, I didn't know what you like because *you didn't answer my questionnaire*, so I got a Mediterranean roast vegetable one, a Greek gyro sub and a crispy skin pork belly roll. Someone told me the best place to get them in the city so I wanted to try out."

He lays the food out on the bar and then pours us each a glass of apple cider from the bar fridge.

"Come on," he calls me over. "Try to eat at least a little bit of each one. You can wrap up the rest and save it for later. Maybe try to eat some before you start work tonight."

I pick up the plate he's made for me, and bring it to my nose. It's an explosion of flavor. And even though they're all inspired from different countries in the world, somehow the smells mix together in a delicious cacophony of spices.

He takes a bite out of the roast vegetable sub and groans. "Damn, that's delicious. Hurry up and eat yours or else I'm going to steal it." I hurriedly take a bite as he says, "So, what have you been doing today?"

Almost choking because I forget to swallow before answering, I take a sip of the cider before taking a breath. "Um, I'm trying to work out the entertainment schedule for the next week. One band had to pull out because"—I slap my palm against my face—"their bass player is grounded. Something about bad grades."

"*Grounded?*" he repeats, laughing so hard he almost chokes as well.

I roll my eyes. "Yeah, they start them young these days."

"No kidding. Well, what kind of entertainment are you looking to fill the space? I might know a few people. There's a pianist I know who would kill to play in a place like this. And he is good." He suggests a few people, including a guy he saw in the park who plays a piano that he pulls behind his bike, but also does blues performances.

"Thank you. I'll call some of these people today."

He beams, reaching over to touch me. It's always him first. I've never initiated contact. Maybe I'm just afraid he'll reject me...

He comes again for lunch for the next two days.

Each time surprising me with something new and delicious, and never forgetting to bring some for the rest of my staff as well. One day, he brings a picnic basket that has a bottle of Dom poking out of it and takes me up to the roof. Up there, we share a salad and enjoy the cool breeze, respite from the day and the heat.

We talk about the club, mostly, but he shares stories about work, and slowly I feel us getting closer by the minute. We still bicker, but somehow, it's different, maybe because I feel like we're in this together.

And when I'm not with him, I'm waiting until I can be again.

Nineteen

MATTHIAS

GOD.

Her lips are around my cock, sucking softly as her hands wrap around the base, squeezing me.

My hands tangle in her hair, molding around her head, ready to hold her still so I can fuck her mouth when I'm ready.

"Yes, darling, just like that. Take my cock."

She moans, sending shock waves all through my body, and I thrust up into her throat, needing more.

"Don't stop, I'm so close, it feels so fucking good."

Her head bobs up and down, each time taking a little more of me, her tongue pressed flat against the underside of my cock. Each time her lips graze over the seam of my cockhead, I edge a little closer to climax.

"Look at me, darling...let me see you sucking me off..."

Her eyelids widen and I almost come. Sweet and sexy both at once, she's the perfect combination.

I'm close. I'm so fucking close.

I grab her head and drive into her throat. The sound of her gagging spurs me on, her eyes still locked on mine.

"Just a little more, god, I'm so close, darling."

Her eyes glisten with tears as she relaxes her throat, taking me so deep.

*My balls start to—*knock, knock!

Fuck!

My hand stills, wrapped around the head of my cock, as I'm pulled out of my fantasy, seconds from coming.

"Matthias?" Clarissa calls through the door. The sound of her voice makes my cock jerk in my hand.

Another knock.

"Matthias? Are you there?" she calls through the door.

"You've got to be fucking kidding me," I groan. I don't know what's worse, having my orgasm interrupted after working on it for almost an hour, or being caught jacking off by the person the fantasy is about.

Grumbling, I throw on a robe, and crack the door.

"What?" I snap. An unsatisfying jack off session will make anyone grumpy.

She takes a step back, a little surprised. "Um, I watched the video of your piano friend and I'm going to try to see him some time in the next few days."

"Great. Anything else?"

I don't even really give her a chance to reply. As soon as she starts to shake her head, I say, "Okay, fine. Good night."

I close the door just as her face falls.

Matthias.

Stop it.

Stop thinking about throwing the door open and fucking her right now against the wall.

Just stop.

My cock refuses to behave, though, still achingly hard, precum dripping from the tip. But when I return to the shower, the water is cold, and touching my own cock pales in comparison to what I actually want to do.

I'm a coward.

Like actually a spineless, sniveling coward.

After a few hours of restlessness, I leave the apartment at five-thirty a.m. and make my way to Teterboro where the company jet is waiting.

I send her a coward's text. *I'll be gone until Wednesday. Kevin will pick you up every night at the club.*

And then mute her so I don't have to see what she replies.

I need some space.

I need to be in a place where she's not just in the next bedroom, where I can actually smell her and feel her moving.

Because if this continues, the next step I'll take is one that can never be undone.

My cock twitches with need at the memory of how close I'd come to coming with her name on my lips last night. I hadn't been able to stop visualizing what might've happened if she'd just come in without knocking and seen me there, leaning back on the shower bench, fisting my cock as I called out her name.

Either way, the consequences would've been earth shattering.

So, I'm running.

Or even better, flying.

I get the okay over the radio that I'm free for take-off and minutes later, I'm in the air.

But she's still all around me.

Twenty

CLARISSA

THE HOUSE, THE CLUB, the whole damn city feels empty without him here. But the anger I feel at him rages and swells so violently, sometime I feel like it might just flood the earth.

What is his deal?

One moment he's telling me that he's feeling something for me and wants to find out what this *thing* is between us, and the next he acts like he can't stand the sight of me.

Like he can't wait to get rid of me.

Like... he was hiding something.

Oh, my god.

Clarissa, you stupid, fucking fool.

He had someone in there with him in his room. Why else would it have taken him so long to answer the door? And then when he did, he was panting, in a robe, barely opening the door and trying to get rid of me as quickly as possible/

My stomach ties itself into a knot a sailor would be proud of, and I let out strings of curses that would cause those same sailors to blush and call their mommy.

"Ms. Masters?" Henry, James's bar assistant, appears in the door way, interrupting my thoughts.

"Guys! Would you call me '*Clarissa*', please? How many times do I have to ask you?"

Henry turns to eye James, before nodding, and I feel instantly remorseful. It's not their fault that I just figured out that my fake fiancé had a woman in his bedroom last night and now he's fucked off to God knows where, probably taking her somewhere where I can't interrupt their fucking.

"Sorry, guys. I'm just not feeling great." Which isn't a lie. My temple hasn't stopped pounding all day. The bruise is covered by carefully applied makeup but the anxiety just keeps coming. If there's anything good about Matthias being away it's that I won't have to worry about hiding that from him.

"Clarissa," James says, with a gentle smile, "there's a guy here to see you. Um, he... is on the sidewalk on a bike... and a piano. And no, I'm not kidding."

That actually makes me laugh because James grew up in Harlem and only just moved out of a shoebox in a five-floor walkup with his girlfriend; he's seen and heard almost everything, and nothing surprises him anymore.

James had just won the Up-and-Comer title in the Neat bartender awards when I read about him in a magazine a few weeks after moving to New York. He'd mentioned being between jobs while he looked for something that could provide constant inspiration.

When I showed up on his doorstep six months ago with nothing but an idea and no money, he talked to me for five minutes before agreeing to embark on this crazy journey with me.

"Oh, great! I've been waiting to see him." I pick up the phone to text Matthias to ask if he wants to come and watch the audition with me. But then I remember.

James lingers in the doorway, waiting for me. "Matthias said he's bringing back a bottle of Macallan M for me from his trip," he says, as if reading my thoughts.

I eye him. "You... talked to him?"

He nods, unaware of the turmoil churning inside me. "He texted. He sent me a bunch of pictures from his flight as well. Crazy."

So... he *can* text. Just not to me. Good to know.

On the third night in a row in Matthias's apartment alone, it's also the third night I haven't been able to sleep. Well, not completely alone. Marika, his housekeeper, has been around here, but when I'm home, she's mostly asleep in her room.

It's just the third night without *him*.

He hasn't answered any of my messages, only texting around three a.m. each night to make sure that I've arrived home safely, although I'm sure that he is getting reports from Kevin.

"This is stupid," I finally say around four-thirty a.m., and kick my blankets off. I'm suddenly ravenous. My appetite must be coming back after...Patrick. After three days of having had my lunch brought to me, I've barely eaten much more than a Caramello Koala since Matthias left.

Wandering in a house that isn't yours at night time is a strange experience. Night already distorts everything, and not knowing where everything is just makes it feel like wandering about a magic fun house in the dark.

I make it to the kitchen; it's a giant expanse of drawers, appliances, and ovens and stoves. I haven't seen Matthias cook here once, but maybe when he's not busy chaperoning me at the club, he cooks up a storm for himself and... whoever else.

Tar fills my stomach.

I hate the thought that he's with someone else. I fucking hate it.

And I shouldn't, but I do.

How I fell into this predicament I don't know.

Matthias is smooth, *too* smooth, everything he says comes with a smirk behind it. One that too many women have fallen for. I've watched it happen all my life. What made me think it was any different with me? Who the fuck do I think I am?

My stomach rumbles in the silence and I shuffle over to the fridge, opening it to see it filled with ingredients for sandwiches and simple meals.

Great.

Except I can't cook for shit.

Maybe a glass of warm milk, then?

I grab the jug of milk and go looking for a mug.

I'm impressed by the layout of the kitchen; everything is stored intuitively. Everything is exactly where you think it should be.

I find the drink ware cupboard and pick a porcelain cup with a pretty wildflower pattern on it. Pressing a minute on the microwave, I watch as my milk make its first turn on the glass plate.

Despite the not-yet-feeling-like-home surroundings, the small domestic task comforts me, and I hum a little tune under my breath as I walk back to the fridge to put the jug away, a little swing in my step.

But as I turn back to the microwave, a dark figure emerges out of the shadows.

"Hi, Clarissa."

Twenty-One

MATTHIAS

HER SCREAM PIERCES MY eardrum and I wince as she freezes, the milk jug slipping out of her hands. We both watch as it falls in slow motion, crashing onto the floor, the thick white liquid spreading all over the floor.

We both watch for a few seconds, before I finally speak up.

"Nice," I say.

She clasps her chest and takes a few deep breaths before she gasps, "What—"

"—am I doing here?" I feel the corners of my mouth twitch. "Really? Even in my own house?"

Her eyes narrow, a coldness creeping in that wasn't there before. It makes me instantly regretful that I'd scared her. I just hadn't been able to wait any longer to say something. I'd just walked into my apartment when I saw her come down the stairs and watched as she'd wandered around my kitchen. It had made me smile, seeing her slowly relax, feeling more at home. The soft humming had been my undoing.

The humming, *the little sway of her ass*, it was the reason I'd come back.

To see her, to hear her...

To feel her.

Taste her.

It takes everything I have not to grab her and take her right now. It might seem like a natural end to three torturous days of missing her, of fantasizing about her, of deciding that I was going to say 'fuck it' to all the things I think I should feel for her, but I have no idea what her feelings are.

The coldness in her grows into a scowl that stretches over the entirety of her face. It seems like an overreaction to scaring her.

"Oh, it's your house now?" she says, her voice dripping with sarcasm. "I thought it was just somewhere you stashed your fake fiancée."

She pushes past me, her body warm through the silk robe she's wearing. My mouth waters, wondering if she's naked underneath. And arousal rushes down to my groin.

My hand grabs around her forearm, holding her in place.

"What are you talking about? Why are you so mad at me, Rissie?" My voice is low as I lean in to whisper against her ear. "What did I do now?"

Her jaw tightens, her cheeks twitching with anger. Under my touch, her arm flexes, ripples. "I guess we didn't make a rule about you fucking around. I just thought you could actually act like a fucking human."

I feel the molten arousal ice over, temporarily held back from erupting over and consuming us both in a fiery inferno from which neither of us will emerge in one piece.

"You're going to need to be clearer; what are you implying?" My voice is tinged with an undercurrent of warning. I don't take kindly to be accused of something I haven't done. That's why I live as brutally honestly as I can. People aren't used to the truth, having been living in a fog of lies their whole lives.

But that's not me. If she wants to blame me for something, she better tell me what it is she thinks I've done.

She shrugs, like she doesn't know that she's skirting dangerously close to crossing the line with me. "I'm just saying, you don't have to take the first plane to fuck knows where, if you want to have a 'guest' here. I would've happily gone somewhere else, you're the one who wanted me to move here, remember?"

"What. Guest? Spit it out, Clarissa."

She squares her shoulders and stares me down. "I'm talking about you. Fucking. Next. Door. To. Your. Fiancée's. Bedroom."

What? Has she gone fucking insane. "When do you think I did that? Because it's news to me, Clarissa."

For the first time, she stumbles. Maybe she expected me to confess to this imagined slight against her, but I'm not taking any flack for something I didn't do.

"The other night. Before you left. When I knocked on your door, you took a while to answer and when you finally did, you were panting, and you barely opened the door, didn't even want to talk to me." Hurt taints her voice, and I want to clasp my hands over my ears. It hurts to hear.

"I was naked, Rissie!" I shout.

"Thanks for making my point, asshole!"

She tries to shake me off her, but I swing her around so that she's facing me dead on. She kicks her leg out and catches me square on the shin, sending a sharp pain through my leg.

"Stop fighting, would you? I'm trying to talk to you!"

"Well, I really don't want to talk, except to say, 'fuck you, Matthias'. I can't believe that even you would act like this? Have you no fucking heart?"

In her flailing, I manage to grab her other hand and anchor it against me. "Clarissa! Stop fucking fighting! Do you want to know what I was doing that night? I was in the shower jacking off. Over you, for fuck's sake! You interrupted me just as I was about to come while I was fantasizing about you sucking my cock!"

She instantly freezes, her eyes blinking. "What did you just say?"

"You heard me. God, you have been driving me crazy since the day we ran into each other again at Leanne's place. Trust me, I don't have any time to even be thinking of fucking anyone else. Just you..."

"Matthias..." she whispers.

It hurts that she would think that I did this, but I can't blame her. I left and have barely said a word to her in three days. "So, no, I wasn't sleeping with anyone else. I had to leave because all I wanted was to ravage you. But leaving didn't do any good, it was no use, Clarissa. Damn... what have you done to me?"

And the dam wall breaks, and there's no holding back anymore.

I yank on her arms and crash her against me, my face burying in her neck, breathing her in.

Fuck.

I'm drunk on one breath.

"Matthias," my name comes out, choked.

I curl one hand around the back of her neck and pull her against my mouth. She returns the kiss, crushing her lips against mine just as desperately.

My itch for her only grows.

I can think of nothing except how I never want this to end.

"God, Clarissa..." I moan against her mouth, her hair falling out of its bun and cascading over my hand, silken strands binding me to her.

"Oh, excuse me!"

The voice throws a bucket of cold water over us, and I look up to see Marika standing in her nightgown in the kitchen with us.

"I'm so sorry, Mr. Baxter, I heard a sound, and I just thought I should check it out. Let me go grab the mop."

I hold up a hand to stop her, taking a moment to breathe, my mouth still against Clarissa's neck. "No, it's absolutely fine, Marika. I'm sorry we woke you. Go back to bed. I'll take care of it. It was just an accident."

She gives us a lingering look, as if to make sure Clarissa is okay. It's a kind gesture that I will always remember. As soon as Marika turns to go back to her room, Clarissa yanks her hand out of mine and runs away, covering a sob with a hand over her mouth.

I'm left standing in my kitchen in the middle of the night, my cock so hard it's making me weep. I touch my hand to my bruised lips. This mouth that has taunted her, telling her I hate her, just begged her for so much more.

Go.

Matthias, go, for fuck's sake, what are you waiting for?

The image of her eyes thawing in that moment when I confessed what had really happened that other night, etches itself into my mind like a firebrand. And I know what I have to do.

Fuck it all to hell.

I storm after her, running up the stairs, thinking about what I'll say when I see her.

She's at her bedroom door when I get there, stopping, her fingers touching her bruised lips just as I had seconds ago.

"Clarissa. My sweet little hellion," I whisper. "Don't torture me. Please. I can't take any more."

She holds her hand out to me and steps backward into the room, urging me to follow.

I'm almost scared to touch her, scared she'll catch fire on the fuel of my fantasies about her for the last ten days.

Our fingers grasp for each other's and I inch my hand higher and higher, until my fist is wrapped around her bicep even before I fully enter the room. I kick the door shut behind us and spin her around and press her against it.

In the fading moonlight, her mouth glistens as she runs her tongue along her bottom lip.

"God, Clarissa." I pull her toward me, nestling her against every inch of my body as I kiss her again.

Knowing that this time, I'm never going to stop.

Her bottom lip shakes, and I bite down on it, marking it.

"Do you have any fucking idea how much you drive me crazy?" I moan into her neck, "Like I'm burning alive from the inside out."

"What are we doing?" she mutters, tilting her head, pressing her face against my hand.

"Shhh, don't think," I answer, as I lead her over to the couch in her room. Sinking into it, I tug on the belt of her robe. The sides of her robe fall open, baring her to me.

I hold my breath as the light falls on her.

She's wearing nothing but a pair of black cotton panties.

And it almost kills me.

Something about the simplicity of the black panties against her porcelain skin makes her look even more unearthly. "You are a fucking goddess. What's a goddess from hell called?"

"I don't know," she murmurs, her hands coming up to pull the sides of her robe back together.

"Drop your hands, little hellion. Don't you dare cover yourself from me."

She drops her hands down her side, her chest heaving.

I'm so fucking hard, my cock feels like it might just shatter into pieces.

"Take your robe off for me, darling."

She hesitates for a moment, biting down on her bottom lip as if she's trying to hold back her nervousness.

"Let me see you. Let me see the body I'm going to be worshipping."

Something in my words emboldens her and she shimmies out of the robe. It falls in a perfect shimmering pool at her feet.

"Come here." I hold my hand out to her, and she takes it as I pull her to straddle over my lap.

My hardness presses up against her heat, still covered by her cotton panties. She lowers her head and, for the first time, she kisses me first. My hips come up to grind against her, she meets it by pushing down on me with a moan.

Am I seriously dry humping my brother's ex-fiancée right now? Yes.

And if this is all I ever get with her, I'll cherish it for the rest of my days.

But it's not enough.

Something tells me it will ever be enough.

I grab her and pull her down onto the couch, my mouth still locked on her.

"I want to fuck you so bad, Clarissa. God, so fucking bad. But I first... I want to watch you come on my face. I want to hear you call out my name. Are you ready?"

A little moan and grind of her hips against me is all the answer I need. I crawl down her body. Laying little kisses along her flat stomach, her skin searing hot under my lips.

She settles against the couch under me as I slide my hands under her, cupping her ass in my hands as I reach her stomach.

She's wet.

I know she is, I can already smell her arousal.

Smell the sweetness waiting for me when I get to her pussy.

I can't even count the hours I've imagined seeing it for the first time, tasting her, sliding myself into her.

My lips catch in the valley between her pussy and her inner thighs.

"Oh..." It's the first real sound she's made. And if it's even half of what she's going to sound like with my cock fucking her I am going to fucking die.

"Easy, hellion, I'm going to take care of you. You don't have to worry about a thing. But that doesn't mean I'm not going to tease you first."

It's a big claim. I don't know if I'm going to last much longer, without driving my throbbing cock into her.

But I can try.

My fingers hook into the straps of her panties and gently slide them down her legs, kissing every inch of uncovered skin as I go.

Her pussy is fucking perfection.

I can't stop myself as I gently part her lips and slide my tongue into her glistening pussy.

"Oh my god," she gasps.

"Yes," I murmur against her. I want every decibel of her pleasure. "You don't hate me so much right, do you?"

I pull my tongue out and drag it slowly all the way up to the lower end of her clit. And then down to the bottom of her pussy. She shivers. Teasing her, I do it again and again

"Matthias, fuck...God, I hate you so much." She wriggles down onto the couch, a silent beg for more of my tongue on her aching clit.

She can wait.

I can't stop tasting her.

She tastes like the sweetest secret. This perfect little cunt hidden to everyone but me.

She is walking desire, pure lust, through and through.

I lust for you too, darling, I paint with my tongue against her pussy, making her groan.

Locking my eyes with hers, I slide a finger all the way inside her.

Fuck.

She's so fucking tight.

It's my undoing.

I finally press my tongue flat against her clit, and she groans, her hands instantly coming down to clasp around my head, pushing me down as I fuck her little pussy with my finger, and lick her clit over and over and over.

"God, I need to come..."

I should tease her more. I should make her beg. I should make her promise that she's only ever again going to come for me.

But I can't. I need it.

I crook my finger against her, looking for her G spot.

There.

I press against it and she screams, my mouth wrapping around her clit, sucking on it hard until she comes.

And fuck does she come.

She climaxes so fucking beautifully; her scream carrying the room as her whole body contracts and then shakes, over and over.

When she finally comes down, her wetness drips down my hand, coating my lips with her nectar, I sit up, unzipping my pants and freeing my cock. I'm surprised it hasn't fucking broken by being held prisoner in there after what just happened.

"Ride my cock, my little hellion."

She clamors over to me, and takes the condom I've retrieved from my pocket.

"Put it on me."

She swallows, nervous, but her eyes are dark with arousal as she rips open the packet and then places it at the tip of my cock.

After a pause, she rolls it down my cock.

It sends a shiver through every corner of my body.

I grab her hand and drag her up and over my body. She straddles over me and I pull her down to kiss me as I push up with my hips and drive my cock into her.

My entire body screams.

"God...my little hellion..." I moan as she settles onto her knees on either side of me.

And I fuck her.

I know nothing but that my cock is inside her sweet little cunt. And she wants it. She wants me.

Her hips grind down in circles as we fuck each other.

Our gasps drenching the room with our desperation for each other.

"God, yes, take my cock, darling."

She whimpers against my mouth, her wetness making her pussy slick against me.

I'm so close. I've been holding off on coming for almost a week now. Not wanting to come without her. And now she's here. With her pussy wrapped around my cock as I watch her ride me. I lean back, fucking up into her, my hand on her hips as I help her take me deeper.

My breath shallows as I bite back a moan. She reaches back, bracing against my knees as we rock.

"God, Matthias... oh, please..." she moans.

"What, please, darling?" I pull her mouth down to kiss me.

"Please.... please, I need to come..." she whimpers against my mouth.

"Again? You greedy girl..."

But I need it too. I need her climax more than I need mine. I reach between her legs and pinch her clit.

And she completely unravels, writhing, coming on my cock, milking me until I have no choice but to join her.

I reach for her head so I can kiss her as her cunt ripples around me and my balls squeeze so hard, I can't breathe as I jerk inside her, coming with a shuddering groan.

"Fuck, oh god, darling...What have you done to me?"

Stars flashing in front of my eyes in front of me as I fall back against the couch, her pussy still pulsing around me, as she breathes, ragged and shallow against my chest.

I drop a kiss on her forehead, and wrap my arms so tightly around her, I don't know where my breath starts and hers ends.

Long after our chests have stilled, and the sun has lifted from the horizon, she finally moves, pulling away from me.

She gets to her feet with a loud gasp, picks up her robe and runs to the bathroom, closing the door behind her.

Leaving me on the other side.

Making me wonder... if I'll ever have her in my arms again.

Twenty-Two

CLARISSA

I CAN'T BREATHE.

God, I can't breathe.

I grip the side of the tub and try to drag the breath into my lungs, but it's like nothing moves past my throat. My heart thumps in my chest, sweat dripping from every pore.

Breathe, goddamit, you have to fucking breath, Clarissa.

I grab the bottle of bottle wash on the side of the tub and fling it at the dressing table.

The mirror shatters into a million pieces, just the way I want it to, trying to shock my brain out of the anxiety attack that has just sprung on me.

Breathe.

Why can't I just breathe?

Waking up and seeing Matthias's arms around me triggered something in my brain and cranked it into overdrive.

Still in the fog of sleep, I was trying to think of the last time I woke up with a man's arm around me... and then I did.

And now I can't fucking breathe.

My anxiety medication is in the drawer on my nightstand, and there's no way of going out there without him seeing me like this.

And he can never ever see me like this.

My brain pulses in my skull begging for oxygen, and I crumple to the floor, hugging my knees as I gasp.

To no avail.

There's a thumping on the door.

"Clarissa! Clarissa, are you okay?"

I just gasp in response.

The thumping turns into desperate banging. "Open the fucking door, Clarissa! Please!"

But I can't, I can't reach it. And I don't want to. He can't see me like this.

"Clarissa! I need to know you're okay!" The worry in his voice reaches inside my chest and tears at me. I don't want to be the reason he feels this way.

I drag myself to the door, reaching up and turning the knob.

"Matthias..." I groan, my mouth opens and closes like a gold fish... gasping for its last breath.

He reaches through the crack, grabbing my hand, but the door won't open any more, my body blocking it. "Oh my god, Rissie, what happened?"

It's ironic that when the brain over triggers its fight or flight, the first thing that it sacrifices is my breathing. The one thing that will help me.

Stupid, broken brain.

He squeezes my hand, his voice desperate as he says, "Rissie, you need to back up a bit so I can open the door, okay? You can do it, just scooch back a little, just a little, okay?"

I don't want to. I don't want to do anything.

But I do it, for him.

I slide back, each inch feeling as a marathon. The door pushes up against me, and his arm slides all the way through.

"A little more, Clarissa, almost there."

One more marathon, and I slump on the floor, still gasping.

His whole body pushes through and he drops to the floor, lying down on his side next to me, eyes wild with fear.

"What's wrong? What's happening?"

I just stare back at him, fear matching fear. When the panic comes, it feels like it will never go away. And all I can think about is how this will either be the way I live for the rest of my life, or that this is how I'm going to die. Gasping for breath, heartbeats racing to an early end.

"Oh my god, Clarissa. Breathe. God, please breathe."

He moves so that he's behind me, and gathers me back against him, his chest warm, strong against my back.

"Oh darling, can you tell me what's happening?

"Pan...ic... a...ttack..." I gasp.

His chest rumbles with understand, and he squeezes me tighter. "Okay, Rissie. You're okay, I'm here. And I'm not going anywhere, you just concentrate on breathing, okay? Just slow... slow down, one breath at a time. One breath... at a time."

I stop moving, stop fighting altogether, try to disengage my brain and choose to trust my body to do what it needs to do. Finally, my mouth falls open and my diaphragm contracts, dragging air into my lungs.

My entire chest inflates, and my back pushes back against Matthias. He doesn't move, an unmovable wall behind me, bringing me strength.

"That's my girl, one more," he whispers, gently stroking the hair out of my face.

I take another breath.

And another.

Each one is a little easier than the one before it.

"You're okay, I'm here. You're okay. Just breathe," he whispers, over and over and over, rubbing his hands all over my body while trying to make the oxygenated blood pump around my body again.

Somehow, it works, and after about twenty minutes I feel human in my own skin again.

Finally, I pull away, sitting up and take one long, satisfying deep breath.

Matthias gently touches my arms and guides me back against him. "You, okay?"

This time it's a question. Now that he's no longer having to reassure me, now he's reassuring himself.

I nod in answer.

"You want to tell me what happened?"

I wait a few seconds to answer, knowing he deserves to know.

My shoulders lift once and fall. "I had a panic attack. I get them sometimes." White lie. I get them *all* the time.

His head tucks itself into the crook of my neck, his breath against me, warm, comforting. "What caused it?"

And then, I don't know why, but I laugh. I laugh so hard I feel his body shake from my body shaking. I can't see his face but I can only guess that he's looking at me like I'm fucking crazy and I don't really have an argument to counteract that. So I laugh.

Because two things I didn't want to happen, just happened in quick succession.

I never wanted to be one of the women that Matthias bedded.

And I never ever wanted him to know about my anxiety.

Ever.

Don't tell God your plans, and all.

When I finally stop, I turn to face him. He's a little less frantic looking, but concern still clouds his eyes. "I don't really know what caused it. I have some triggers that I know about. And sometimes they just come out of nowhere." I don't tell him that one of those triggers is my father, another is confrontation. And the last, is the mere mention of a certain Baxter.

I just thought that I had it under control.

But waking up with him, remembering the way he'd looked when he came, like if he had to choose, I'm the only woman he'd want to be there with him in that moment, quivering under me as we climaxed together must have scared me. The bruised part of my brain took control and in the space of just a few minutes, as I laid there in his arms, made me think of every scenario where this was going to end badly for me.

"Run," my brain had yelled, but I had nowhere to go.

And now he's seen me at my worst. I can't imagine much worse than losing control in front of Matthias Baxter.

A hot, fat, ridiculous tear falls down my cheek.

"Hey, hey... why are you crying?" he says, gently.

Another tear chases the first. "Because I didn't ever want you to see me like this!"

He exhales, and wraps his arms around me even tighter. "Why?"

Seriously? He's asking me that? "You're kidding me, right? You think I want anyone to see me like this? You think I like being this weak?" My sobs echo around us, the bathroom acoustics working against me to hide my emotional state.

He pulls away, crouching to make sure I'm looking at him. "Hey, Clarissa! This isn't a weakness; it happens to countless people around the world."

"Well, I don't want to be one of them."

He lets out a sweet chuckle at my little sulk. "I know. But it's okay that you are. I'm sure it makes life so hard sometimes, and I'm sorry for that. But tell me how I can help you, okay? I'm here."

He pulls me into his arms again, and it comforts me, but I don't want it to. Because in every single one of those scenarios that flew through my brain, none of them ended in us being together for too long. I can't get attached to him comforting me because what will become of me when he's not here anymore?

"I need a bath," I say, once I'm sure it's over.

He gets up and presses a button on the rim of the tub and water flows out of the faucet over the tub. Then he leaves and comes back with a Caramello Koala.

He drops a soft kiss on the top of my head as I take it from him. "I'll be out on the balcony when you're done. Take as long as you need."

Even though I want to, I don't ask him to stay.

***

I finally emerge from the bathroom in a cloud of steam, slightly refreshed, fingertips pruny from sitting in the tub. I'd spent the whole time traveling my hands over the part of my body Matthias had touched.

Locking in every little caress, every thrust, every kiss, every look...

"Orange juice or coffee?" Matthias asks, poking his head into the bedroom from the door that leads out onto the balcony.

"What's all this?" I say, following him out, looking at the spread of Belgian waffles and fresh fruit he's laid out on a small picnic table.

He pops the cork on a bottle of Veuve Clicquot. "It's breakfast. Let me guess, you never eat breakfast."

He's got me there. Even before I started working nights and don't wake up until almost lunchtime, I didn't eat breakfast. "I ate a Caramello Koala. Does that count?

He crooks his finger and it sends a butterfly wing flutter through my body, reminding how it felt when he did that action inside me. I wander over, even wearing my robe, it feels like he can see through it, right through me.

The crooked finger tilts my chin, angling my eyes up to meet his. Then he kisses me. A soft dropping of his lips on mine followed by the trace of his tongue along my bottom lip.

"Yup, definitely Caramello Koala-y."

I giggle, he has me giddy. "I told you. You better get used to it if you—" I clamp my mouth shut.

"If I'm going to keep kissing you? I intend to."

Why does he have no trouble talking about us having a future? Why isn't he ridden with anxiety about the line we've crossed? The answer my head gives me doesn't help. "You intend to keep kissing me, huh? That's bold of you to assume I'm going to let you."

He grins and pours the champagne into two glasses, half way. Orange juice fills the rest of the glass. "It's the least you can do. Considering you won't share your Caramello Koalas and I actually like them, I guess I'm going to have to be content with tasting them on you. Maybe you actually planned it that way." He hands me a glass and I accept it, taking a little sip.

"Me? I would never be so scheming. How could you think that about me?"

I catch him glancing out of the corner of his eye to see if I'm being serious or not. It's too hard to keep a straight face, so when he sees me grinning, he throws his head back in a giant belly laugh.

"Phew, okay, you're joking. I thought your brain had gotten waterlogged after being in the tub for too long."

"My brain could use a little water boarding. Get it to start behaving." I mime shoving something under water.

Instead of laughing, his eyes fill with warmth.

"You know, Rissie, I never thought I'd say this, but you're an incredible woman." He takes a plate and spoons some fruit onto it.

"Well, that's just because you never knew me." And I don't regret saying it. It's not an accusation, it's just the truth. And he had no reason to get to know me. "And I never knew you, either," I say, with a shrug.

He's silent as he picks out a strawberry from the bowl and lays it on the plate. "Well, let's get started now. How do you like waffles?"

"Um, I don't. The fruit is fine." I don't want to tell him it's because it's takes work to look like I do. Some things shouldn't be public knowledge, like they say, you don't want to know how laws and sausages are made.

He doesn't let me get away with it. "Clarissa, when you were little you loved waffles."

Maybe he actually knows me too well. I do love waffles, and in the few times a decade I allow myself one, I want it dusted with confectioners' sugar. And when I say dusted, I mean, I want it to look like a snow storm hit. "Fine. I'll have one then. And don't skimp on the sugar. And some syrup, if you have it."

"You want syrup on your Belgian waffle?" He lowers his voice. "What? Are you trying to get us beat up by a Belgian?"

As if we're sitting in a crowded restaurant, I lean in, dropping my voice conspiratorially. "Shush, you don't have to announce it. If you don't have any, just say that, and we'll go and steal some from the condiments display at the 711."

He guffaws, "Nobody does that..." But when I don't respond, he stops and shakes his head, eyes sad. "No. Oh, Clarissa. There's no shame in it, but I once saw you throw away a whole plate of foie gras because you didn't like the color."

I know I did. But I can't imagine doing that now.

He plops another waffle onto the plate, dumping an entire whole tablespoon of sugar on top. I don't stop him.

"Is that okay?" he asks, handing the plate to me.

I'm shy as I take it, unaccustomed to be taken care of. "Delicious. Did you make these?"

He nods. "I sure did. I went downstairs, saw Marika and said, could you please make me some waffles and freshly squeezed orange juice. And then I brought them up here."

I take a bite and mumble around my full mouth, "That is not the same thing."

He pops a grape into his mouth and crunches down on it. "Ahem, ingrate, I made them appear, didn't I? Don't get caught up in semantics."

I giggle, hungrily shoving a forkful of waffle into my mouth. A plume of sugar wafts, and I reach up to brush it off my face.

Matthias pushes my hand away and runs his tongue along my lips before dabbing at my face gently with a napkin.

It's a sweet moment that makes that spot between my legs throb.

I clear my throat, and take another sip of my mimosa. "You're going to make the Koalas jealous."

"Good, think how I've been feeling watching you suck those things down."

Heat flares in our shared look, and I have to look away before I feel consumed by it.

We eat and he asks how the club has been the last few days. We're coming into our fourth full week of being open and it's going better than I had imagined. He laughs when I tell him about how the piano guy showed up and almost everyone in the neighborhood has come to ask when he was going to be there.

"You know, I wish we could get his piano inside, but I'm not sure how we could swing it. It should look gimmicky but it's not."

"Let me have a look at the club tonight. Maybe we can sort something out," he says. As if it's the most normal thing in the world for him to just find a solution to every problem I have.

"He said something strange, he said that his fee was 'sorted.'"

Matthias doesn't say anything, just pops another grape into his mouth. It's a suspicious silence though.

"Matthias, what do you think that meant?"

"I think it means that his fee is sorted." He holds up the sugar bowl. "Some more?" It reeks of distraction, I should know. It's my favorite method of evading.

I knew it. "What did you do?" I ask my tone accusing.

He grins. "Nothing, I asked a friend for a favor. And now you have a great entertainer and he's getting his name out there."

"*And* you're paying his fee." Unbelievable. But also, unbelievably sweet.

"Eh, let's just say I'm providing financial compensation for him doing you a favor."

I think about arguing, but judging by the way his jaw is set, it's just going to be wasted breath. I'll pick a time when he's feeling more amenable to me arguing with him. "What about you, what did you do in the last few days?"

"I'm looking for a farm. Well, a ranch."

I didn't expect that. "For Baxter Enterprises?"

He shakes his head and wipes his mouth after taking the last bite of his food. "Nope. For myself. It's just something I've been thinking of but... well, since I was getting out of the city, it was as good a time as any to look at some of the places I've been thinking about."

He pours a little champagne into his glass and swirls it around. "The longer I live in Manhattan, the longer I realize I need a place to get away from Manhattan. Damien has Baxter winery in Barossa Valley. Kylian has his island in Ko Kaeo, Thailand. And even though Kingsley's least favorite thing is leaving the office, even he has a place just out of Edinburgh to get away when the doctor tells him he needs to take a break. I have properties in Houston and Chicago, but those are mainly because I don't like staying in hotels long term when I'm there for work. I've just been so busy since I moved here, I haven't really had time to turn a place into a home. A place I can fly to just for the weekend, you know?"

"Sure." I imagine everyone wants that, but not everyone has that luxury. Even if it's just the luxury of time.

He seems a little sheepish that he talked so much, but I wish I could tell him that I liked it. I like listening to him, I like learning more about him.

"Did you ever go to Baxter Winery?" he asks.

"Damien never invited me." I answer.

"Clarissa, I'm sorry. He should've been better to you than that."

I wave his words away. "It's fine. We... should never have gotten into the arrangement, I see that now. We were so naïve making that decision, when we didn't even really know who were as people yet, let alone what kind of people we wanted to be in the future. We both were hyper-fixated on what we both thought we wanted out of life. Turns out we were both wrong."

"You don't have to answer this but..."

I already know what he wants to know, I'm just surprised he didn't know.

"Yes. We slept together once." I rub my hand, anxiety rising in my stomach, but I know this is a conversation we need to have. "You're not going to like me very much after this. We came home from a gala and he had had a lot to drink. We were joking around about something, and we ended up kissing. And then it just happened, even though I knew that if he was sober, he would never have gone through with it. It was stupid. And instead of it making us closer... that day was when he started pulling away. He never blamed me, but I think he didn't want to give me the wrong idea. He didn't have any romantic feelings for me. Anyway, he broke it off a month after that."

It must be a day for long speeches, my throat is dry once I finish. Or maybe it's wondering how Matthias is feeling after knowing the truth.

But he surprises me. "He should've been more upfront with you, maybe you two could've ended up as still friends. He's not a bad guy, you know."

It might be a while yet before Matthias is going to be able to convince me of that. But for the first time in a long time, I'm seeing my part in the whole debacle more clearly, and realizing that it was actually better that it never did play out.

For more reasons than one.

I wipe my hands with a napkin, and fold it, placing it on the tray. "You know, you never gave me a full tour of this place."

"You're telling me you haven't gone snooping yet?" he laughs.

"Rude!" I poke my tongue out at him "I've either been sleeping or at the club, thank you very much."

"Well, then, let's go, Rissie."

Without telling me, I know this place must've cost over $75 million, which is like petty cash for Matthias Baxter but it takes my breath away. The interior of this place was obviously built with Matthias in mind. Half of the apartment is an open plan, with a living and dining area that boasts sitting places and a view of the entire city through floor to ceiling windows. The kitchen runs along one side of the apartment, with bar seating enough for ten. He has a few pieces of art around. One piece, that I recently heard went for almost $300,000, is right there in the middle of his living room. I guess that tells me who that anonymous buyer was.

"I brought this piece from London," he says, when he sees me looking at a bureau. "It used to be my great-grandmother's."

"It's beautiful." I can smell history emanating from the whorls and grooves in the wood.

"If you want to see beautiful, come see my office."

He pushes on what I thought was a wall. It opens into another room that has a large desk that also points out over the same view. What really catches the eye, though, are the floating wall shelves and display cases in the middle of the room. And on them, hundreds and hundreds of toys.

What in the world? "Matthias, it looks like an adult version of Toys R Us in here."

"Right?" He sounds excited rather than insulted. "That's exactly what I wanted it to be!" He picks up a little plane off the middle shelf and waves it in the air a few times, and then lets go. It whizzes around the room until it lands right in the middle of his open palm.

He puts it down and grabs a toy car and does the same thing, letting it go on the floor. It does a few laps around and then ends up at his foot, like a loyal dog. He claps and laughs with joy.

"You're thirty-six years old."

"I know!" he beams. "Think how many more years I have on this earth to play with them! Can you imagine how many other thirty-six-years-old guys wish they had this many gadgets?"

"They're *toys*."

He shakes his head and walks over to the display cabinet. "Look at this." He reaches for a little contraption that he points at a nearby sheet of paper. There's a click and today's date is stamped in the corner. He presses a different button and points. The time appears.

I'm impressed. I take it from him, turning it over in my hand. If I didn't know what it was, I would just think it was a normal ink stamp. "That's ingenious."

"And you can't tamper with the date. That's the tech we've been trying to perfect. Everyone thinks everything is digital these days. It's not. We're hoping to launch in four months," he says with a conspiratorial grin and presses a finger to his lips. "Baxter holds the patent."

"You're going to make a fortune." I shake my head, in awe of the collection that he has here. "What is all this, though, really, Matthias?"

He shrugs and touches his finger to something that looks like a pad of paper, but when he touches it, it comes to life. "I like innovation. I like people who think out of the box. I like solving problems."

"And you like making money off it," I say wryly, then worry he'll take offense.

"Guilty," he admits, "but that's not it. I like things that help people in their lives, and I like it even better when the design is both beautiful and functional. A cross section of necessity and beauty."

"That's.... actually... deeper than I'm going to give you credit for," I laugh and he pulls an offended face.

But it's true. If I keep scratching, I can't help wondering what I might find under that exterior.

A phone buzzes and for a moment I freeze, wondering if it's mine, but he just looks at his Apple Watch and then grimaces.

"You should get some sleep; Paula wants to talk to us at one p.m. Is that okay with you?"

I tell him yes, and he sends her a voice memo. "I'm having her come here. I think I'm going to work from home this morning. Someone tired me out last night."

Before we leave, he goes over to his desk drawer and pulls something out. It's long with something that looks like a claw on one end.

"What in all that is good and holy is that?"

He grins and pulls on the end, and the handle pulls out, like a telescope. He reaches it behind his back and starts dragging up and down over his skin. "Oh yeah, that's the spot. It's a backscratcher. This isn't one of my fancy toys. Kylian bought a bunch at a market and gave one to each of us. It might actually be my favorite of all my gadgets. That's why she gets to sit at my desk."

"'She?'" I ask, eyeing the stick when he pushes down on the end to compact it again.

"Aw, now, don't get jealous, she's just a hand. One that brings me great joy, but a hand, all the same. Maybe if you two spend some time together, you could bond over which one of you has a hand that brings me more pleasure."

"It's a hand that's going to be found giving you a prostate exam in a minute."

His laugh echoes through the house as he leads me to his bedroom. His hand feels warmer on the small of my back by the second and when he falls into step behind me, his face in the crook of my neck, my insides melt into a puddle.

"Your skin is so soft, darling," he murmurs, leading me over to his bed.

Pulling the sheet back, he sits me down on the bed and lifts my legs up onto the mattress. The bed dips as he climbs over me. For a moment I wonder if he's going to lay on top of me, but then he rolls over into the bed on the other side.

Propped up on one elbow, he lowers his head down onto mine, kissing me, softly at first, then it grows deeper, more urgent. One hand tugs at my silk belt; I'd just put the robe back on after my bath. I liked the way it felt against me, almost like I was wearing nothing at all.

As the robe slides off my torso, he pulls away to gaze at me.

"Fuck, you're so gorgeous. Like a marble statue of Venus."

A low growl rumbles through his body as he nuzzles his face between my breasts, his hand sliding down my body, covering every inch of my skin, leaving a trail of heat and goosebumps.

"Spread your legs for me, darling," he whispers into my ear, and my legs move apart, making room.

"Good girl. You like how I make you come, don't you?" His fingers dance between my legs, barely touching me, making my back arch for him. "You like me playing with this sweet little pussy, don't you?"

His words play with all sense and reasoning in my head. We shouldn't be doing this again. We both know this shouldn't be happening.

"Yes," I answer, despite the warning bells in my mind. There's nothing else to say. I want him to touch me, I want him to make me come, I want him to watch what he does to me.

A chuckle escapes his lips as he drops his mouth down over my nipple, circling it with his tongue as he slips one finger between the lips of my pussy, making me gasp. I know I'm already dripping for him, have already been anticipating this since we started walking back to the room. And I came ready.

How can he do this to me with just the slightest of touches?

He teases me for a few minutes, running just the tip of his finger up and down my labia, promising to dip into my pussy but then pulling away. One time he circles my clit, slowly drawing the circles closer and closer to my clit, then moving away at the last moment, making me whimper.

"Have you ever begged before, darling? Have you ever begged to be fucked before?"

I shake my head, knowing my eyes must be begging in their own way.

"It's okay, I won't make you beg me today, I'm going to make you come soon, but one day, one day, you're going to crawl to me, pussy dripping, eyes glistening, body trembling, begging me to fuck you so hard, you forget your name. I want you to remember that. Remember that one day you're going to fucking be reborn on my cock."

His words do more to me than any other man has done to me with his touch.

Before I can respond, two fingers stretch my pussy, and any response I had flees from my tongue.

He bites down on my nipple as I arch into him. The sharp pain is like a direct lightning strike straight down to my clit. Pulsing as it begs to be touched.

"Matthias."

He pulls his fingers out of me, and I whimper at the emptiness. The deprivation of his touch makes my chest tighten, just for a second, before he thrusts them deep into me again, his palm slapping up against my pubis and his thumb grazing my clit.

"My god..." I gasp, my body primed for orgasm.

Teeth drag over my nipples, the sharp pain dangerously delicious. "You're going to be needing to yell the right name if you want to come, little hellion."

"Matthias...God, Matthias..."

He chuckles, his hot breath washing over my chest. "Two names? Darling, we're going to have to work on that. But not tonight, all I want is to watch you come."

He pumps in and out of me, only letting the pad of his thumb stroke over my clit every few seconds. Each time, I inch a little closer toward my climax.

I'm losing my mind.

I know nothing but what's happening with his hands on me, and his mouth on my nipple... and what's about to come.

"You are drenched, darling," he whispers, hoarsely, his voice about as drenched with lust as my pussy.

But when I think he's going to keep fucking me with his hands at this maddening pace, he positions his finger into a V, sliding them on either side of my aching spot, and then presses them together, pinching my throbbing clit between them

And I fucking lose it.

My body arches almost into a full back bend as I writhe against him, my climax explodes, and a molten hot pleasure spreads through my entire body. In the distance, I hear someone scream his name. It's probably me but all I know is my entire body is flooding with intense pleasure as he keeps stroking my clit, pushing me toward another orgasm even before this one is over.

"Come again, darling, I know you have more in you. Give it to me," he urges me.

He bites down hard on my nipple and presses his thumb hard against my tender spot, pushing away any remaining resistance.

"God..." I groan.

His hand pulls away. "What did I say about who you should be calling out for?"

The disappointment makes me scream, "Matthias... Matthias... don't stop."

He laughs as he lowers himself down my body and rams his tongue inside me. The sound of his sucking my wetness out of me makes me feel so fucking dirty. "You taste like fucking heaven. Give me more, come on, my little hellion..."

His tongue returns inside, and he grabs my hips and pushes me harder against him. Clenching, I fight my orgasm, not sure if I can handle another one.

And he knows.

Pulling his tongue out, he grinds it against my clit as he rams two fingers inside me.

There's no warning as an almost painful pleasure, a white-hot electrical current, shatters me.

Matthias pulls his fingers away, but he doesn't stop licking. His tongue curls inside me as he laps at my trembling pussy.

"I'm not going to waste a drop," he murmurs, the vibrations making me jerk. My body is like a live wire, sensitive to everything.

Finally, he crawls back up my body and pulls me against him, stroking my back as my breath slows.

"Get some sleep, little hellion. Trust me, you're going to need it if you're going to marry me."

And even though I don't know what that means... don't know what any of this means, my body is spent and I fall asleep, his heartbeat in my ear, his scent infiltrating my dreams.

Twenty-Three

MATTHIAS

SHE SLEEPS FITFULLY, AND it breaks my heart.

I don't know what's going through her head as she lays there, her face scrunched into a frown, letting out an occasional groan or whimper. And not the kind that turns my cock into steel. This one cuts at whatever armor I have left around my heart.

I wake about an hour after I make her come and don't have it in me to move in case it wakes her. Fitful sleep is better than nothing.

But when my phone buzzes, I know I have to check it. It's in the middle of the workday, and if there's an emergency, I'm going to have to take care of it.

But it's not, it's a picture of Patrick, making his way to his office for the first time since I smashed his face in.

Just seeing him rises the bile up my throat.

I send a message back. *I want to know what deals he's working on right now and all of his clients. I'm going to make him bleed out of his bank account as well as his fucking face.*

I haven't done anything yet because I wanted to lure him into a false sense of security before I disemboweled him from the inside out.

Done, boss, comes the response. And I know it's as good as done. I pay Dmitrik a lot for my intel and I expect to get my money's worth.

Clarissa stirs next to me, so I put down the phone and curl up around her, laying an arm over her waist.

I might not have been able to protect her from the first attack, but I'm going to make sure that if he even dares breathe the same air as her, he's going to find his lungs on the outside of his body.

"Sleep, darling," I whisper.

***

The meeting with Paula goes as well as can be expected.

She is going to leak to the press tomorrow that we're together and then on Friday, release a press release confirming our relationship and announce our engagement.

Which means I need to tell my brothers.

We've agreed not to tell Gerry or the board, and just act as though this is real. But my brothers deserve to know the truth, and they deserve to hear it from me.

Clarissa sits like a statue next to me while we talk about this, and even when I reach out to touch her, she doesn't squeeze my hand back.

I understand.

It was hard enough when this was only a business transaction... but we've made it more than that. And what that more is, it's God's guess. Neither of us knows, that's for sure.

I think I know how my brothers are going to react, but we've always respected what the others have decided to do in the running of our respective divisions.

Even in the case where our leadership jurisdictions have crossed, we've allowed the one we think has the most knowledge in the field to have the most input. And it's the same when it intersects with our personal lives.

We supported Kylian when he decided to keep his personal business with his best friend when it could've done amazing things for us at Baxter Enterprises. But he built that business up from the ground into a billion dollar streaming service without help from any of us and we don't have any ownership over what he does on his own time. And the board will just have to understand that.

And when Damien broke it off with Clarissa, despite her threats, to reconnect with My-Linh, I'm the one who drove him to Clarissa's apartment.

And now I'm supposed to tell him that she's the one I've decided to use to rehabilitate my image for the sake of the IPO. They're going to think that I've lost my damn mind, having always been her biggest hater.

How do I tell them now that maybe I was wrong all along?

"So, we'll release the statement of your engagement on Friday. And then the Monday night after that, at the Doctors Without Borders gala, you'll have your first public appearance. Is that okay?"

"Do we have a choice?" Clarissa finally speaks.

Paula gives her a friendly smile. "I don't want to ask you to do anything that you don't want to, and we can discuss anything you're not comfortable with. But in terms of our timeline for the IPO and your immigration application, we need to get it going as soon as possible."

"It's fine," Clarissa replies with a weak smile, looking like it's anything but fine.

And I wish I could take her apprehension away, but I can't even resolve my own.

"We're going to get through it together," I say, trying to reassure her when we're alone.

And for now, that's the only thing I can think of that helps.

Wednesday night at the club is crazy. I don't show up there until almost eight thirty to catch up on some work, but when I get there, the line reaches far down the street. Considering how many people can fit in Malt, some of these people are going to be out here for hours.

Good for my girl.

She's worked so hard, not just in the last few weeks, but to set this club up for success in just its first month.

She knows what she's doing, and I never should've doubted that.

The whole night is one of the club's most successful nights. I surrender my seats at both her table and at the bar and make my way to her office.

There's no extra information about Patrick yet.

But I'm in no hurry. I want the job done well.

At one a.m. when I think the crowd might have died down a little, I go out to the clubroom. She's talking to a couple at her table and I wander over, making sure not to approach until she's seen me.

She looks exhausted but happy and it makes my heart sing.

Tired is okay, *tired* is worth it when her face beams like this, most of the worry from the earlier meeting with Paula seemingly dissipated, making room for her excitement about how her evening has gone.

"Matthias," she says, holding out her hand to me. "Come meet Marisa and Annette from Heard It Here." She names an entertainment blog popular with the younger crowd. Their presence on TikTok and Instagram command a following in the millions and a single good review can sell out products in minutes, and extend waiting lines around the block.

Them being here and seeing the club on a night like this is an incredible opportunity for Clarissa and Malt. So, I do what I do best; I charm them.

"Hello, it's so lovely to meet you. I'm Matthias."

"Of course," the woman Clarissa introduced as Marisa says, beaming and patting the empty seat next to her. "Do you come here often?"

Clarissa shoots me a look, wondering how we should act. The leaks about our relationship should be out now. But this wasn't part of the plan.

Paula couldn't orchestrate this moment if she pulled every favor she had in the gossip channels. This is a chance encounter, and that counts for gold in the gossip industry.

There's no time to check in with her though, so I make a snap decision.

Tipping my head at Clarissa to suggest that we're going to go with it, I settle into the offered seat.

"Actually, it's a funny story. Clarissa and I go back. We grew up together. Spent our entire childhoods together. And now, well, I'm hoping I can spend the rest of my life with her."

Clarissa's her eyes momentarily widen and then she plasters a smile on her face.

Too much, Clarissa. She quickly corrects herself and tries again; this time she looks genuinely happy to be engaged

"Oh! Wow, I had no idea!" Marisa exclaims and even in the dark, I can see the cogs turn in her head as mentally takes notes for her next post, no doubt, announcing our engagement.

"Well, we've been trying to keep it out of the papers," I say, leaning in like I'm letting her in on a secret.

"Oh, of course, I understand," she nods, careful not to make the outright promise that she's not going to blast it on every channel her brand has.

"But, to answer your question, oh yes, I come here every night. And you know, I've gone to a lot of bars. This one is my favorite, the music, the drinks, the service. It's the whole package, old world charm with a modern atmosphere."

I might not be Paula, but I know how to deliver a sound bite, a quote when I need to.

"And let me tell you this"—I lean in, almost whispering in her ear—"I'm going to put my money down right now, that this place is going to be the hottest spot of the summer and win a few Eat awards. Clarissa and the team have a lot of amazing things in store. Don't you think?"

Always make them verbally agree, it cements the idea in their head.

Any negotiation book will tell you that.

Keep nodding, and they'll nod along, and when they think back on the meeting, all they remember is how they felt, and that it was positive.

I end my little speech with a smile that could make the Empire State Building look like a night light.

She beams back in response. "Well, we certainly had a good night. The music was phenomenal. I hadn't ever heard the band before."

I lean back, nodding. "Oh, if you're here for the music, well, I'll let the owner tell you. I'm sorry, I'm just so excited." I laugh and gesture toward my new fake fiancée. "Darling, tell her about tomorrow night."

Clarissa grins, the mood of the conversation infectious, and she clasps her hands together. "We have a really special guest tomorrow. You actually might have seen him around. It's Tyson. With a T." The name is ridiculous, there's no arguing against that, but it fits him. What else would you expect of a guy who rides around Manhattan pulling a full-size piano behind him?

Annette claps her hands together, speaking for the first time. "You're kidding me! Not the guy who has singalongs in the park."

Clarissa nods. "One and the same, but that is only one aspect of his talent. He is going to blow your mind. His voice sounds like he was raised in a club in New Orleans, so, so soulful."

"We look forward to it," they both say in unison and then laugh.

"We'll reserve a spot for you," Clarissa delivers smoothly. "We're actually all booked up but my table is still free. That is, if Matthias doesn't mind sitting at the bar for a bit."

I pretend to be shocked, and then break out into the friendliest smile I can muster. "Of course. But only if I can buy you a round of drinks."

"Of course," Marissa twitters, and the two ladies share a look as if they're in on a joke that we're not privy to. What they don't actually know is that we were the ones telling the joke the whole time. "We can't wait to come tomorrow. This place is amazing. It's just so nice to see someone run this place who has a true vision."

We have them.

I get up and press a kiss to Clarissa's temple, whispering into her ear, "Good job."

She turns toward me, gratitude in her eyes, and it fills me with an emotion I can't name. Time to step back.

"Well, ladies, I'll leave you to it. I think there's a cognac sitting on the bar that needs to my attention. I'll see you later, darling."

I walk away feeling six eyes on me.

But I only care about Clarissa's.

"James. Impress me," I say, sitting in my seat, twenty feet away, but I can still hear her voice through all the noise.

She falls asleep on my shoulder in the back seat of the car as soon as Kevin turns into traffic. Somehow, I'd convinced her to leave the cleaning to her crew. After a night like tonight, she could afford to tip them a big bonus, while she gets some much-needed rest.

Even then, she's chattered excitedly, at a mile a minute, as she emptied the till and added the money to her locked bag to take to the bank tomorrow.

"And even with the extra ice order, we had to get four more bags! I never thought that I would own a business that would go through sixteen forty-pound bags of ice in a night! James said that with that much, it might actually be worth it to get an ice machine! He said he had someone he might be able to talk to! Oh, wait, that person is the person you introduced him to. Do you really think that Jaxon can help us get an ice machine for a good deal? And then the girls sold almost twice as many cigars as we did on opening night and I thought that was pretty exciting. And I think with the ladies from Heard It Here coming tomorrow night then—"

I'd cut her off, laughing. "Darling, take a breath."

She'd stopped and given me a grin. "Sorry. I'm just so excited, I don't think I'm going to get any sleep tonight."

Thirty seconds in the car proved her wrong.

But this time, her sleep is peaceful, a soft smile on her lips.

I wrap an arm around her, pulling her tightly against me so that her head doesn't bobble from the car's movement.

She murmurs, "Are we there?"

I brush the hair from her face. "No, darling, we're not. Just get a little more sleep."

"I wasn't sleeping," she murmurs, most definitely sleepily.

"Sure," I chuckle. "Go back to not sleeping."

She opens her eyes long enough to say. "It was a good night, wasn't it?"

"It was the best night ever. I'm so proud of you."

A soft kiss on her forehead elicits a sleepy gurgle from her before she's silent again.

"Can you drive around the block a few times?" I say to Kevin, trying not to wake her up.

He nods silently to me in the rear-view mirror.

The city flies past the window with her body against mine. It looks so different tonight. This place that I know like the back of my hand, my city, my home.

With my girl.

I groan inwardly at my own idiocy.

This can't continue. It has all the makings of a volcanic eruption that is going to level everything in its path.

But if I can sit right here for another moment with her, then it might be worth it to raze the planet to the ground.

A text message comes through and I watch the letters scroll past the screen.

Damien: Let me guess, you're not even going to show up to our meeting? Ditching us last week, and already late tonight? Are you even our brother?"

Fuck.

I'd totally forgotten about the weekly meeting after all the excitement of the night.

And I was going to tell them tonight about Clarissa. If they don't find out from me, they're going to read about it online tomorrow.

Kevin slides into the curb.

I cherish the last few moments of just her and me in our bubble and gently touch her face to wake her.

"Home now, Rissie. Wake up."

She growls and rubs her eyes. "I wasn't sleeping. I was resting my eyes."

"Sure, Rissie," I say as I help her out of the car and into the building. I prop her against the wall of the elevator and she leans her head back, eyes closed.

"More eye resting?" I tease her.

"Yup. See? I'm not asleep. A sleeping person couldn't answer you."

Her lightheartedness is like a balm to my heart. "You can sleep when we get home and I get some food into you. Did you even drink anything all night?"

She opens her eyes, looks shifty, and clamps them closed again. "Actually, I am sleeping. I can't answer that."

"Hellion."

"Manwhore," she spits back.

"Guilty."

I can see she's trying to think of a comeback when the elevator comes to a smooth stop and the doors open.

She's about to step off the elevator when her eyes go blank.

And then her face floods with fear as I turn to see what's she's looking at.

Before I can step in front of her, he says, "What the fuck are you doing here?"

Twenty-Four

CLARISSA

I THINK I'M GOING to throw up.

The retort I was about to fling at Matthias after he admitted being a manwhore chokes me.

"I said, what the fuck are you doing here?" Damien shouts, his face red, the grin that he had when the elevator doors opened, sliding off his face into an angry mask.

"Damien. Wait," Matthias says, stepping in front of me.

"Wait for what? Don't make me ask again."

I take a step back into the elevator, my back up against the wall. Past Damien, I see Kingsley standing there, his face frozen in shock. But if Damien is usually quiet, Kingsley is practically mute. A man of the fewest words I've ever known.

"Damien, easy. Let's go inside," Matthias says, extending his hand behind him. What for, I don't know. Is he trying to take my hand? Does he want Damien to actually kill me?

"What the hell am I waiting for?" Damien roars.

He tries to rush past Matthias, his finger pointing at my face. "Clarissa, I told you to stay the fuck away from me and my family. You soul sucking, fucking bitch!"

Matthias shoves his brother, and Damien stumbles back into the apartment. "Hey! I said take it easy. I'll explain everything, but you need to calm the fuck down, okay? I'm not going to let you talk to her like that."

Damien's face blanches, then flashes red again. "I'll talk to her any way I want. In case you want me to remind you what she did to me. To *us*."

"I know. You don't need to remind me. But... we're going to need to put that in the past, Damien. Because, Clarissa are I... we're getting married..."

Well. So much for breaking it to them gently.

Matthias turns to me, his eyes softening to reassure me, checking on me, taking charge.

"I'm sorry, what?" Kingsley finally speaks up, while Damien stares at Matthias.

"I said Clarissa and I are getting married. It's going to be announced on Saturday, Paula leaked that we're dating tonight."

Damien clenches his fists and hisses at me, "What the fuck are you doing to him?"

"I'm not—" I speak for the first time. "This isn't anything like that."

"Then what the hell is it?" He pushes his face up into Matthias's face. "You hate her, Matthias. You've always hated her."

"Well, yes, I did." Matthias agrees as he takes a step back to stand next to me. Maybe it's for a united front, but frankly, I was okay with him shielding me from Damien,

Damien, who's always just waiting to erupt.

A traumatic childhood, so many pressures from his job, with no outlet, left him angry, brooding, and unreasonable when he was with me.

He's never hurt me, but his anger is intimidating.

Matthias continues, "But I don't anymore. Look guys, we'll talk about this inside. It's for the best, I promise."

Damien narrows his eyes. "You're making a mistake."

"I'm sorry, I don't think so." I'm not sure I don't agree with Damien about this. Maybe we have made a big mistake.

My ex snickers as he glances back at me with hatred. "Trust me, you are. You don't know what she's capable of."

Somehow, Matthias remains calm as he responds. "I think I do."

His composure lends me temporary courage. "Damien... I promise you, it's not what you think."

But all it does is stoke his fury. "I'm pretty sure I told you that I never want to see or hear you ever again. So, your promises are worth fuck all to me, Clarissa. I don't know what spell you've put on my brother, but you listen to me, I'm not going to let you do to him what you did to me. Do you hear me? If I have to spend every last fucking dollar, every last second I have, I'm going to make sure he doesn't fall into the same trap I did."

Matthias holds his hand out, pushing on Damien's arm. "Okay, that's enough. I said stop it."

Damien hisses again. I've never seen him this angry, not even when I screwed up his life. "You're going to choose her over me? Really?"

"It's not about choice, it's about doing what's best for us. And what's best is us getting married."

"Do you love her?" he flings the question like a weapon.

Matthias stiffens.

"I said, do you love her?" Damien looks from Matthias to me and back to his brother.

"Damien..." Matthias says, his voice tight.

"Answer the fucking question, man! Are you marrying for love?"

Matthias doesn't even look at me when he answers. "No. This isn't about love. It's about business." The answer is clear, simple. Of course that's the answer, I never expected him to answer any differently. But it stings, it more than stings, it slashes at me.

He reaches out to touch me, but I duck out of reach. "Clarissa—"

I don't hear what else he has to stay. The air feels like incense burning my lungs, choking me.

Fuck.

No. Not now.

I can't.

I can't do this in front of them. Not Matthias, not again. And definitely not Damien.

My cells suck in whatever oxygen is left in my blood and with two hands, I push on Matthias's back, shoving him out of the elevator and pressing a button on the elevator floor panel.

Matthias realizes too late what I'm doing and by the time he turns and tries to step back into the elevator, the door slam shut.

Breathe.

You can breathe, Clarissa.

But the claustrophobia kicks in and I dig my hands into the gap between the elevator doors, willing them to open, to let me out.

By the time they open in the lobby, I'm drenched with sweat, each breath feeling like a fight to the death. And I'm on the losing end.

I run out to the street, flagging down the first taxi. Collapsing on the seat, I say, "Drive. Anywhere, just go."

And close my eyes, willing for escape.

"Miss. Miss, we're here."

I jolt awake and stumble out of the cab and out onto the street outside of Malt.

"Hey."

Matthias.

It momentarily awakens me.

I never get used to seeing him. He's a god, a goliath. Physical perfection. Emotions destroyer.

"What —"

"Really? Are we still doing that?" I can't tell from his voice what he's feeling right now.

I shuffle on my feet. They're still aching from being on them all night. My eyes burn in my head, but I don't think it's from fatigue. It took an hour of driving around New York for my anxiety to ease enough for me to give the cab driver the address to the club. I'm so tired and can barely stand.

"I had to leave. I didn't want to hear what he was saying."

Matthias nods. "He was out of line."

"He said I was going to ruin your life. You didn't argue. I didn't know if you agreed or not. So I thought I'd make it easy for you."

"You didn't know if I agree that you're going to ruin my life or not?" His voice is light, smooth, nothing in it to tell me what he's feeling.

He steps toward me, and presses against me until even the thinnest sliver of light wouldn't be able to squeeze between us. "Clarissa, I asked you a question. Do you think I think you're going to ruin my life?"

"I don't know," I whisper, scared it might scare him away.

"Do you want to know the answer?"

I don't.

I don't think I can stand to hear any more truth tonight.

He grabs me by the shoulders and pushes me down into the alleyway. One more step and we fall into the shadows of the buildings.

Pinning me against the wall, his face moves to within an inch of mine.

"Ask me the question, Clarissa. You know you want to know."

This close, I can't say no to anything he asks. "Matthias, am I going to ruin your life?"

The palm of his hand cups my cheek, and I forget when there was a time when I didn't want him.

"Darling, my sweetest torture, hellion of my heart, you already have."

Then he kisses me like there is nothing in this world but us.

Desperately, ravenously, painfully.

Like he's trying to suck the hurt out of me, and breathe me back to life, forever branded by his breath in my lungs.

"You have already ruined me," he growls roughly against my ear. "There is nothing that came before you, and there's nothing that's going to come after. I don't know how, and I don't know why, but in the last few days, you have become my everything." His thumb leaves an imprint on my cheek when he grips my face, pulling me in for another kiss. "Nod if you understand, Clarissa."

But I don't.

I don't know if I believe him, and I don't know if I want to.

I don't know what it means. I don't know what it means for now and I don't know what it means for the future.

This was never supposed to happen.

These declarations, these kisses, these promises. They were never meant to happen. That's why I thought I would be safe with him. The one person I never ever had to worry about complicating our relationship. But now, I don't know how to return to a time when I wanted anything but Matthias's mouth on mine.

He pulls away, his eyes deep and dark. "Tell me you believe me."

I shake my head. I can't.

He kisses me again, this time like he's punishing me, the taste of blood spreads in my mouth as his lips crush mine, his tongue ramming into my mouth, sweet, the lingering of cocktails he'd had at the bar.

He moans against my mouth, "You're going to be the fucking death of me, my hellion."

And my resolve crumples into a pile of ashes in the inferno of our arousal.

He takes my hands and pins them over my head against the paint chipped wall, pressing his hardness into my stomach.

"Feel how hard you make me? Feel how you drive me fucking crazy? Do you think anyone has ever made me feel this way? Do you think I've ever stayed in bed with another woman while she slept next to me? Wondering what she's dreaming about, if it's me she sees?"

He pulls away and stares at me, his other hand pulling at my dress, bunching it around my waist as he unzips his pants.

Wetness pools in my panties, my body cleaving to the idea touching me.

"Do you think any woman drives me so mad, I can't even wait to get her inside to fuck her?"

He yanks my panties aside and drives his fingers inside me.

"Matthias..." I moan, my legs stepping apart to make room for him.

"Good girl," he murmurs huskily, watching my face as he slides a second finger inside me, fucking me. "So wet already, my own little hellion, waiting for me to fuck her right here. Right now."

"Fuck... yes," another moan falls out of me. His words ignite a fire in me that blazes hotter than anything I felt I could withstand. I meet his fingers with a grind of my hips. I want to touch him, but his hands still pin mine over my head, and it makes everything more intense.

"You ready?"

"Ready?" I say through gasps, as his fingers curl inside me.

"Ready for me to destroy any doubt you ever had about me out of you?"

He lets go of my hands and there's the faint sound of a foil wrapper tearing. I rest my head against the wall, waiting.

He lifts me up by my hips, hands gripping at my ass as he pulls me to him.

"Wrap your legs around me, Clarissa. Take my cock like a good girl."

He slams me back against the wall and in one movement slides into me all the way, into the hilt. I'm so wet my thigh thighs slick with want, his cock still stretches me almost to my limit.

"Oh, god..." I moan, my pussy contracting and relaxing around him, making room for him inside me.

Sounds from the street mix with our breaths, he kisses me, and it's like all other kisses in one. My legs pull him in tighter as he pulls out and slams back in.

The look in his eyes rake at my heart as he fucks me, without rhythm, with total abandonment.

"Yes, darling, god, you feel so fucking good. My cock belongs inside you, doesn't it? This perfect little cunt was made for me. Ruining me. Fucking with my mind, fucking with my life. Ruin me, darling. Make me yours, you sweet demon from hell," The words all roll into one. He thrusts into me with such force, I forget to breathe.

I forget what it was like to be touched by any other man.

I forget what it's like to hate him.

I forget what it's like to want anything but to come with him.

"I'm so close," I murmur against his lips and he pulls away.

"Me too, darling. Come with me. Watch me, watch me come and I dare you to tell me that I'm not yours. And that not I'm yours to ruin."

His hands grab at my ass, lifts me higher as he grinds against me. My clit burns as the friction of his thrusts pushes me over the edge.

"Fuck... Matthias..." I cry out.

"I'm yours. Tell me you believe me."

My head bangs against the wall as I shake, my orgasm shattering every cell in my body.

He lets go of my hips with one hand, and grips my chin, forcing me to watch as his eyes glaze over and his entire body shakes against me.

"Say it, Clarissa..." he gasps. He drives one last time into me, shuddering as he comes. "Ohhhh, fuck."

"I believe you, Matthias..." I whisper as he grunts out his climax, "I believe you."

My legs give way under me and my body threatens to slide to the ground.

"Easy." He lifts me back up, his cock still deep inside me. "Stay. Don't move. Just stay."

With heavy breaths, his head falls onto my shoulder. He whispers my name over and over as tremors wrack through our bodies.

The pressure of his body pinning me to the wall grounds me.

It grounds me in the moment and grounds my mind back into my body.

Or else I could just float away.

"Did you mean what you said? That I've ruined you?" I ask.

He doesn't answer, he just stands there until we unwind our bodies and our breaths slow as one.

Finally, he sighs and lowers my legs to the ground.

Picking up my purse, he rifles inside for the club's keys and leads me to the back door of the club and inside.

"Come with me."

So few words. So unlike him.

I follow him inside and he lifts me onto a bar stool. Eyes never leaving mine, he takes off his and shirt and then, gently, dabs the shirt between my legs. It takes me a moment to realize he's cleaning me up, thoughtful, unprecedented.

When he's done, he leans down and presses a kiss to my inner thigh and lays his head on my lap. He's so tall, he's almost at a 90-degree angle, but it's the most intimate moment of my life.

"I'm sorry if I got carried away," he says quietly.

My hand lies on his head, stroking his hair, tucking it behind his ears making him let out a happy sigh. "You didn't. I didn't want you to stop. Not for a moment."

He nods against my leg. "Okay. You'll always tell me?"

"I promise."

H stands up, leans in and kisses my bruised mouth, and then goes behind the bar. I watch him make himself at home in my club, pouring a glass of Remy Martin XO.

"Take a sip," he says, holding it up to my lips. I open my mouth and let him tip some into my mouth, my eyes never leaving his face.

He pulls the glass away from my mouth and then pours some into his. I watch, mesmerized by him, his eyes, his lipstick-stained lips, the way he holds the glass, the way his eyes never leave mine, as if it would kill him to look away.

He pulls the glass away from his mouth and suddenly his mouth is on mine, his lips and tongue gently prying my lips apart as he lets the cognac from his mouth drip into mine. We share it back and forth in a moment that is the most sensual experience of my life. Two "mosts" in a matter of minutes. He's going to ruin me, not the other way around.

Ending the kiss, he falls to his knees and pulls me to the edge of the bar stool, my ass almost hanging over the edge as he drapes my legs around his shoulder, his mouth on my clit.

"Lean back on the bar, darling. Let me worship you."

Without thinking, my shoulders roll back, my elbows come up to prop myself on the bar as he drags his tongue along the opening of my pussy.

With one hand, he holds me open and he licks me for what feels like hours, bringing me to within an inch of my life before he pulls off.

"So sweet. The only thing I ever want to taste again for the rest of my life. God, you have no idea how delectable you are, do you? You have no idea."

All I say comes out in moans and soft whimpers as he tortures me.

Pleasure builds both in the pit of my stomach and the small of my back. A little knot that grows and grows. He presses the tip of his tongue against my clit, barely moving, pulling away whenever I try to press against him, needing more.

"Patience, darling. Patience," he teases, before returning his tongue to my aching clit.

I feel like a goddess, worshipped, adored. Like his whole life exists to pleasure me, like my whole life exists to let him.

Finally, his tongue moves against me, my breath stills, anticipating.

Waiting, wanting, silently begging.

"Yes, Clarissa?" he murmurs against my labia.

"I need to come. Please."

He pulls back, looking up at me, his face glistening with my arousal. "Do you want to come on my face or my cock, darling?"

I don't hesitate when I gasp, "Your mouth. God, make me come with your tongue,"

"Your wish is my command, darling."

He pushes my legs as far apart as they will go and buries his face into me, driving a finger inside my cunt as he laps at my clit.

"Fuck... fuck..." I groan, my whole body splitting apart on his tongue.

"More, darling, more..." Lips wrap around my trembling clit, sucking hard, urging me to another climax. And all it takes is another finger inside me to make me fall.

Hands in his hair, I grind against him, making him growl with approval as I burst at the seams, groaning his name.

When I finally start to come down, a purr of contentment escapes me and he chuckles as he gets to his feet, kissing me, spreading my wetness over my lips and onto my tongue. Somehow, it's even more intimate than when he dripped the cognac into my mouth.

"Okay?"

I nod, shyly.

He chuckles, sliding a finger over my wetness and bringing it to his mouth. "A shy demon from hell? I didn't know there was such a thing."

I didn't either. But there are an infinity of things I didn't know until now.

He grins and tips the rest of the content of his glass into his mouth before grabbing the bottle off the bar.

"Let's get drunk, darling."

Twenty-Five

MATTHIAS

WE GET SO DRUNK that if someone asked my name, I could probably tell them it starts with the letter M but that's about it. We drink and talk and laugh, reminiscing about the past and learning about who we are as adults.

"Remember that time you fell out of a tree when your mom told me to come to tell you dinner was ready? What were you doing?" she asks.

I shrug. "Same thing I was always doing. I was spying on the Hamilton girls next door in the pool."

She pretends to gag. "You are so disgusting."

"Guilty."

"Okay, your turn," she asks, playing with the empty glass, spinning it around on the floor.

"I know everything about you," I say.

She rolls her eyes. "Prove it, sure I like Caramello Koalas now, but what did I like when I was a kid?"

I roll my eyes in response. "Come on, give me a hard one!"

"Stop stalling," she laughs, pouring about $20 worth of Grey Goose XV vodka into her mouth, ignoring the drops that slide down her cheek.

Sliding my hand up her bare thigh, I revel in the knowledge that I can just reach out and touch her. "You liked boysenberry ice cream and Diet Dr. Pepper."

She looks surprised. "How did you know that?"

Her voice brings a smile to me face and I kiss her gently. "Because I have eye balls! What did *I* like?"

She scrunches up her face. "I have no idea."

I steal another kiss. "*You* lose. Your turn to go pick a bottle."

She gets up, pads over in her bare feet, staring at the wall of liqueur bottles that now has some holes in it. "James is going to kill you," she warns me.

"Kill me? You're the one who picked the Watenshi Gin. It took him over three weeks to find one, and he had to drive to Rochester to get it."

She gives up and reaches for the closest bottle, a bottle of Jagermeister. "How do you know that?" she says, skipping back to our little oasis in the middle of her clubroom floor.

I pretend to gag as she pours some into my mouth. "We're going to be really sick tomorrow."

"Good." She takes a drink and makes the same face I did, making me laugh. "Answer the question. How did you know how James got this bottle?"

I put the lid back on and return it behind the bar. "He told me," I say, grabbing a bottle of Kopke 380th Anniversary Tawny Port.

"He didn't tell me."

I grab some port glasses and join her again on the floor. "Well, did you ask him?"

She looks so cute trying to think. I grab her hand and pull her into my lap, nuzzling her neck from behind. "It's okay. You're pretty. And you smell like figs and vanilla. And sometimes supermarket chocolate."

She pulls a face. "That makes up for me being a cold hearted bitch?"

I nibble at the crook where her neck meets her shoulder, little nips that make her yelp when I do it too hard.

She pivots in my lap, trying to glare at me. "Um, excuse me, did you hear me? I said, *'that makes up for me being bitch?'*" she repeats.

"Oh, I *heard* you, Rissie."

Growling, she grabs the glass out of my hand and takes a drink. "And what are you going to say about it?"

I sigh. "Well, I can't speak for other people, but yes, being cute and smelling like Dior makes up for you being a bitch."

"Hey!" she yells and punches me in the arm. "I'm not a bitch."

I take her hand and kiss the palm. "Rissie. Come on."

Her nose scrunches up, then she pouts, her shoulders drooping, leaning back against me again. "Well, I'm trying not to be."

I laugh. "Are you?"

She spins around and her hand meets the back of my head in a karate chop.

"Oowwwwwwwwwwww," I moan in exaggeration. "Not only are you a bitch, but you're violent too!"

"Good. You show everyone your bruise and tell them if they don't bow down to my bitchiness, I'll karate chop them, too. And maybe even kick them a little. But just in the shin."

Finger tips lingering on the nape of her neck, I blow gently, a shiver scattering over her body. "Scary. I take it back. You're not a bitch, Rissie."

"That's right," she gurgles happily.

"You're *Queen Bitch*!"

"Matthias!"

I hug her to me, enjoying the feel of her wriggling body against mine. "Come on, I'm just saying you know what you want and you make it known. And usually what you want is the right thing. But when it's not..."

"Yeah?" she says, a hint of hope in her voice.

"Well, then you're really a bitch."

She sighs and looks down at her hands. "Fine, I'll try harder."

My finger comes up to tickle her cheek. "Why, Rissie? Did I tell you that I don't like it?" She shrugs. How does she make even that look cute? "I didn't. I don't want you to change a damn thing about yourself."

That seems to placate her and she thinks about it for a moment. "Good. Because I don't see myself changing."

"But you already have. Look around you. Look what you've done. Would Clarissa of a year ago have been able to do all this? Clarissa from six months ago?"

"No?" she sounds unsure, not knowing where I'm going with the question.

I smile and kiss her on the forehead. "Of course, she could have. She *did*. You did. That was a trick question."

Her head rests against my shoulder and she looks up at me, giving me a grateful smile. "But it was really hard. It *is* hard."

"I know, darling. I know."

Thoughts still running through her head, she unwraps a Caramello Koala from the tray of snacks we pilfered from the kitchen. Breaking off the head, as is her ritual, she pops it into her mouth. Then she reaches behind her toward me. I open my mouth and she drops the other half inside.

"Hmmm, thank you," I mumble with a full mouth. "Wow, who are you? Is this an imposter? The Rissie I know would never share her Caramellos."

Her fingers reach back and to play with my hair as she says, "I'm just trying not to be a bitch, remember?"

I test the theory and reach for another koala from the plate.

She grabs a handful of my hair and yanks.

"Ow!!" I playfully yell, "I'm calling the police! Tell them I'm being attacked by a bitchy notbitch!"

"Go ahead, they'll side with me. I'm pretty, remember?" Her eyelids flutter prettily as she says it.

My arms come back around her middle and I hug her as tightly as I can. "Yes, darling. You're pretty."

She giggles happily, drunkenly, and does a little dance as she unwraps another chocolate.

My heart almost bursts with contentment.

I don't know how we got here.

But I don't know the way out, and I hope she doesn't find it either.

Twenty-Six

CLARISSA

"Ow."

I think I'm the one who says it. I don't know for sure. My eyes aren't open and I never, ever want to open them ever again.

"Matthias?" I say after a while when I don't hear him respond. It sounds like a yell to my ears, but it's probably just a murmur. It's hard to yell through a mouth that won't open without cracking. Somehow, I roll over onto my side, feeling the wooden floor creak underneath me.

Wow, how drunk did we get? And how drunk am I still?

"Matthias?" I say again. But there's still no response.

I'm going to have to open my eyes, aren't I?

Maybe I can just lie here forever.

I can work from here.

They can set up the tables around me, I can wave to guests from here, and now and then, the cleaners can turn me on my side and mop under me.

It's settled.

Here. *Forever.*

Shit, except... now I need to go to the bathroom.

Now I really need to know where Matthias is. He needs to push me to the bathroom.

"Are you there, Matty, are you there?" I call him by the nickname I only dare to call him when we're both blind drunk.

Still no answer.

Maybe he's dead.

I wouldn't even blame him.

If I had a choice, I wouldn't want to live through this either.

"Good morning!" I finally hear him say, in a voice that can only come from beyond because there's not a chance that he sounds that chipper after last night.

"Ughhhhh-uhhhh," I groan. Maybe it's better if he doesn't speak.

"I'm going to need to put that through google translate," he jokes.

"I said... 'Shut up. Headache.'"

I feel him move next to me, and put something in my hands.

"Whadis?"

He squeezes my hand around the object. "It's a bottle of water. Drink it. I'm going to get something greasy for us to eat."

"Ughiwannaleepaneverwayup." I don't even know what I was trying to say there. But apparently, he doesn't have the same problem.

"Well, you can't sleep and never wake up. I'm too busy to organize your funeral right now, in case you haven't heard, I'm supposed to get engaged and I'm not in the mood for looking for another woman who can actually hold her liqueur."

"Dieasshole."

"You're right, you're not a bitch at all." He kisses me on the cheek, jumps to his feet and leaves.

Over the course of however long, I manage to sit up, lie back down, sit up, and fall back down again, but it must be at least twenty minutes because Matthias knocks on the door and there's nowhere in the West Village where you can get breakfast in less than twenty minutes.

I contemplate letting him stay out there, but at some point, I'm going to want to eat whatever greasy thing he's brought back. "Coming. Geez, why didn't you take the keys?"

I pick up his shirt that still has my scent on it, wrap it around me and make my way to the front door, hoping that no one else will be around.

"Next time, take the damn key, Matthi—"

I stop.

It's not Matthias.

"Hey Clarissa, looks like you started the party without me."

Nine months ago

"Clarissa. Are you crying? Oh, my dear, come here. Tell Uncle Gerry what's going on. Is this about Damien?"

I don't know where he came from, but it's actually comforting to see a familiar face at the bar. Not only because the bartender has threatened to cut me off.

"He needs to pay, Gerry. He can't do this to me. No one messes with a Masters!" I quote my father and thank him for instilling me with a sense of familial pride.

He gestures to the bartender to bring me another drink. "I know, dear, I know. And what are you going to do about it?"

"What can I do? He's a Baxter, I can't touch him."

Gerry pats my hand and slides his chair a little closer, a smile on his face. "Well, I'm a Baxter too, sweetheart, or have you forgotten that? In fact, I'm the most powerful Baxter. And I'm not going to let my nephew do this to you. You deserve better. So, we're going to have a drink and talk about what can be done, okay? And maybe we can

*come up with some ideas on how to make sure that he doesn't get away
with this."*

"You think so?"

*"Oh, sweetheart, if you and I put our heads together, there's noth-
ing we can't do."*

Present Day

Gerry.

Gerry Baxter, the man behind my downfall.

The Baxter that triggers my anxiety and reminds me about every
mistake I ever made.

What is he doing here?

I move to close the door in his face but he stops it, sticking his
foot inside my club. Like a slug, he drags his eyes over my body
making me feel even more exposed than I actually am. My arms
wrap around my body, trying to hide it from him. But is there
really any point? He's seen it all before.

"What do you want, Gerry?" I ask, my voice teetering on the
tightrope between fear and anger.

He smirks, enjoying my obvious discomfort. "Well, I've been
trying to call you, sweetheart. Call, text, email... but you haven't
responded. I was getting worried about you."

"Well, I'm fine." No thanks to you, you slimy fuck. "You can go
now."

He edges his foot further inside, opening the door wider. "We
haven't really had a chance to catch up at all. Do you really want to
do it here, in front of everyone? Dressed the way you are? Especially considering that you're about to be announced to be engaged
to my nephew. Again. To a different one this time. Imagine my

surprise when I heard the news. I thought you and I were in this together. So, invite me in and I'm going to make this as quick and as painless as possible."

I step aside.

Because that's what I want.

All this to be over.

Quickly.

I couldn't care less about the painless.

I close the door behind him, checking the curtains for any gaps. "Make it quick, Gerry."

"I have plenty of time. You can tell me what you've been up to since the last time I saw you wearing only *my* shirt."

I want to throw up, and it has nothing to do with my hangover. I never, ever want to think about that night ever again, or anything that came after it. Not the plan to blackmail Damien, not the deals we made with each other, not that drunken night, not the aligning with the most disgusting excuse for a man I've ever known.

How Gerry can come from the same stock as the other Baxters will never cease to amaze me. While the Baxter boys, their father and grandfather, are intelligent, hardworking, talented, Gerry is nothing but a snake in the grass waiting for an unsuspecting ankle passing by.

And I was that ankle, desperate, stupid. So stupid.

"Get to the point or get out," I shout. I certainly don't have to worry about being a bitch to Gerry.

He pins me with a smug look. "Well, I happened to be in New York, and it's a good thing too, since a very interesting memo came across my desk. You and Matthias. Well, color me surprised. So, after all this time, it looks like you are still working at getting revenge against the family after all. And all without me. I'm hurt, sweetheart."

I can never ever hear the word "sweetheart" without wanting to gag. "I'm not getting revenge. This isn't what this is about."

He leans in, his overpowering cologne choking me. "I don't believe you, Clarissa. You forget, *I know you.* I also remember me being there for you through all of it. Comforting you. Giving you everything that my nephew had not. My time. My *bed...*"

"Stop! Please. just stop. Just tell me what you want!"

My stomach churns, I need him to leave. I cannot have Matthias coming back while Gerry's here. Knowing the way they all feel about their uncle, I don't know if Gerry will make it out alive.

"Oh, I just wanted to remind you who was your friend when no one else was, and that maybe one day, I'm going to need you to return the favor. Because the only thing that's important is the best thing for Baxter Enterprises. And that, I think we can all agree, is me."

He has no shame. I guess that's easy if you don't have a conscience.

"Anyway, I'll let you get back to your fiancée duties. I do remember how you were so good at that. And next time? I suggest you *answer* my calls. I'd hate to think what would happen if everyone found out how you're making it through the family. Sure, they know about Damien and Matthias... but what about me?"

I grab my stomach, I'm going to be sick. But he's not done yet.

"All this could go away, if you choose the Baxter man you're supposed to be with, sweetheart. Me."

He opens the door and leaves, humming a tune under his breath.

I grab the wastebasket behind the hostess's desk and heave.

And wonder if I'll ever be able to repent for my past.

Twenty-Seven

MATTHIAS

I DON'T HEAR FROM my brothers after I storm away from the apartment. Or rather, I have no idea if I hear from them or not. I didn't answer my phone, I didn't even look at it once Clarissa showed up at the club.

I wanted to make it clear to Clarissa that we're in this together. That there is something real between us, and my family's ire isn't going to stop me finding out what that is.

But you can't hide from reality forever, and when I leave to get some food for Clarissa, I check my phone to see more than fifty messages and voicemails waiting for me.

Good.

They deserve to stew. I'm not sure I'm even ready to hear what they have to say now.

Being unplugged gave me time to spend with her, focus only on her. And for a little while, we were without inhibitions, without the baggage of the past, without answering to anyone and anything. And it had been the most fun I'd had in as long as I can remember.

She is intelligent, smart as a whip, with a sting just as fatal. She can talk on any topic I bring up, sometimes to test her knowledge, sometimes just wanting to know what she thinks about things. She took to business fast, probably helped by growing up in a family with a fortune of almost 80 million dollars and being twice engaged to my brother. She might not have sat in on board meetings, but she'd listened and learned. And now was using it to run her business.

Last night, she'd talked about dreams for the club, for the future, with a gleam and glint in her eye, and made me wish and wonder whether or not I'd see them come to fruition.

And when I talked about mine, she listened, asked insightful questions, and I couldn't help wondering if she was seeing herself in them as well.

Somehow, she had gone from a dark mark in my family's past, to a shimmer, not yet taking form, in my future.

And how it happened, I may never know.

I only know that now, having only left her side five minutes ago, I ache to be near her again.

My brother was a fucking fool.

He is so happy now, but could he have actually had a fulfilling relationship with Clarissa if he'd just opened himself up to it?

Jealousy streaks through me like a lightning bolt.

The thought that my brother had once touched her irrationally burns.

I've been jealous of my brothers before, but not over women. Until now, we have never shared even a glance at the same woman. None of us were ever interested in relationships, which made it easy never to fall for the same woman.

But it turns out... it just took the right woman.

It took Clarissa.

I order two breakfast burritos and coffees. And step outside to go through my messages.

Voicemail and texts from Kingsley and Kylian. Not surprisingly, there's nothing from Damien.

Kingsley's messages only say to call him. That we need to talk.

Kylian's messages are... well, Kylian-ish. Ranging from *"What the fuck, dude?"* to *"Tell me something about yourself that no one else would know so I know it's really you"* to *"What do you think your smooshed together name is going to be "Mattarissa? Clarrias? Your children are going to be so confused when they see their Uncle Damien's photos with their mother."*

None of it helpful. But he rarely is. God gave him a brilliant brain with the worst case of adult ADHD I've ever seen in person. He's like an energizer bunny on meth. Brilliant and bouncy.

I dial Kingsley's number. Maybe he's still in New York, who knows. It's eight a.m. in Hong Kong and Kylian's probably already in a morning meeting.

Do I know what I'm going to say? No. Is there anything he can say that might change my mind? Maybe before Clarissa and I slept together. Now? I can't imagine a single thing.

He picks up on the first ring and the conversation goes as well as any reasonable person might have expected. A lot of *"do you know what you're doing"* and *"I don't think this is the right thing to do even for the IPO. We can work something else out."* But the one that is hardest to handle, and the one that I've been telling myself since this whole business started is *"You can understand why Damien's not going to be okay with this."*

I do understand.

But just as I understood when he decided to follow his heart, I'm going to expect that he does the same for me.

I hang up with Kingsley with the promise that the four of us will talk soon.

Although I don't know what else can be said.

I know them as well as they know me. None of us have ever been convinced to change our mind once it's been made up, and I made it clear my mind is stuck on Clarissa.

I grab our order and walk back to the club; the sunshine beating down on my head, helping to dissolve some of the alcohol I consumed last night. I think about maybe taking her upstate to see the

ranch I'm thinking of buying and it adds a spring to my step. I turn
the corner and something I see makes me stop.

No. It can't be.

A man looking curiously like Gerry is getting into a car outside
the club.

I know he arrived in New York last night for a board meeting we
have tomorrow, but there's no reason for him to be here.

Maybe I'm more drunk than I think I am. I take a sip of my coffee
and hurry my step so I can see Clarissa again.

"Have you talked to your brothers?" Clarissa asks later in bed after
we get home from the club. We'd showered together, and after a
lazy fuck under the water, me sitting on the shower bench and her
riding me, we'd come to my bed.

Legs intertwined, I spoon her, burying my face in her freshly
washed hair. She'd murmured the question, eyes closed, face resting on the pillow, so I know sleep is coming soon. I could wait until
she falls asleep but I think it's fair that she knows what's going on.

"I talked to Kingsley."

"Not Damien?" she murmurs.

"No."

I think she's asleep when she mumbles again. "Kylian?"

"Kylian is no help in this situation, he just wants gossip."

Clarissa giggles, the vibration speeding through my body. "I always liked him the most."

"He's easy to like."

She sighs. "He doesn't think the same about me."

"Good. Less chance of him stealing you away."

She pulls my arm against her stomach. "I would go, too. He's hot. But he and I are closer in age, and I want a sugar daddy."

"You're sassy tonight."

She giggles again, playing with my fingers. "Get used to it, Mr. Baxter."

A kiss against the back of her neck makes her sigh. "I hope I never do, future Mrs. Baxter."

I can't see her face, but I sense her eyes opening.

"Are we really doing this?" she asks, more awake.

"Try to get out of it. Go on, just try." I dig my fingers into her side, eliciting a squeal, and she wriggles, turning over onto her back, looking up at me.

But the smile on her face quickly fades.

"Hey, what's going on in there?" I whisper, gently stroking her head.

"What if Damien never comes around?" she asks, echoing the same thought I've had since he found out about us.

"Then he doesn't." It's as simple as that. But I can't help the gnawing feeling of guilt in my chest. It's not as simple as that at all.

She shakes her head. "I can't let that happen. I know how close you all are. That will kill you. And it will probably kill him as well."

I kiss her, hoping to assuage her worry. It's not her problem to worry about, it's mine. "It's not going to happen."

"How can you be so sure?"

I don't tell her I'm not sure. We've never been tested like this before. But I'm an optimist and I choose to believe my brother will come around. "Because, like you said, we are all so close. It's not going to happen. I won't let it. Okay? Don't worry about it. I charmed you, didn't I? Damien's going to be a piece of cake."

She turns back onto her side, and hugs the pillow. "I know why he hates me. I get it. I'd hate me, too."

"No one hates you. Really. They're just really mad. He'll get over it. Damien's not vindictive." That, at least, is the truth.

"No, but I am. Toward him anyway," she admits.

"So... win him back?"

She wriggles back against me, her ass grinding against my groin. It instantly responds. "How do I win him back?"

I groan into her chest. My body is ready for hers whenever she wants. "I don't know, but definitely not by what you're doing right now!"

She laughs and turns back to rest her head on my chest, her hands dragging down my body to wrap her fist around my already hardening cock.

"Careful, hellion. Don't start something if you want to sleep."

She drags her tongue along the line of my neck, whispering into my ear, "Maybe I want to help you sleep."

"Then by all means, don't let me stop you."

I lay back and let her stroke me, whispering to her all the things I want to do to her, and when I come, it's her name on my lips.

Twenty-Eight

CLARISSA

SOMEONE IS WHISTLING AT me.

It's James.

James, my own bartender, has his fingers in his mouth and is letting out an ear-piercing wolf whistle.

"Woo-hoo, look who made it into the papers!" he holds up his phone and reads off it. "'Baxter and Masters are the newest hot couple on the New York dating scene. Which begs the question, is New York's most eligible, self-described, lifelong bachelor finally off the market? What will this do for the Kids & Care share price when it goes public in a few months? In the wake of Baxter's recent scandals, there was talk of postponing the IPO. We don't have the answers, except to tell you that the two make an enviable couple.' Shall I go on?" James asks, taking a breath.

I don't know why, but I bow. The ridiculousness of the article, as well as how my employees are acting, makes this all seem like a circus.

I'm no stranger to the tabloids, but no doubt, this is going to be fodder for a while. Socialite dated her ex's brother? It's the stuff of gossip dreams. Maybe that's why it's perfect for Matthias, something to take everyone's mind off the last time he was in the papers.

James grins, but then turns serious." Hey, Boss, I just realized that you might think that it's one of us who talked to the papers. It wasn't me and I can't imagine it was anyone else, either."

As I hang my jacket on the back of one of the bar stools, I eye James, making him squirm. "You think these stories are true?"

I take turns staring down each one of my employees.

None of them speak up.

Hell, I really am Queen Bitch.

I laugh to break the tension. "Guys, relax. Look, you've seen him around., So yes, we're... whatever the word is... when two adults spend some time together. But yes, please, anyone comes asking questions, we'd really appreciate if you tried to be discreet as possible. It's nobody's business."

Unless you literally leak it to the tabloids, the traitorous bitch in my head says.

"Sure thing, boss," James answers, and everyone else makes noises of understanding.

I go to my office and sink into my chair, and pull my phone out of my pocket. Since my run in with Gerry yesterday morning, I dread every message, every call that comes in.

Fuck him.

He was the biggest mistake of my life. How much longer am I going to have to pay for it?

I have never thought of myself as naïve before; I know how to look for signs of people trying to take advantage of me for money, for sex, for my family... but using me to try to organize a mutiny on his whole family? That's not something I ever knew to look out for. Damien had complained about Gerry since his grandfather passed away, telling me about how all Gerry wants is to maintain his role as CEO, but I had never thought he'd use me as a pawn in his game.

How long is he going to use one drunken, desperate night against me?

I don't want to know what Matthias will do if he knows what happened with Gerry. I don't want him to know just how far we plotted, how much we reveled in the thought that one day we were going to take them all down.

Desperation and hate rots you from the inside out, and I only felt it for a short amount of time. Gerry has lived with it since the day he realized that his father would always prefer his brother and his brother's children over him.

And he had been fighting it since.

Low life scum.

My phone buzzes. It's Matthias. There's no hiding how wide I smile, or how the thoughts of my predicament fade in the light of him.

It's a picture of the view from his office.

Matthias: Want to go for a ride?

Me: Is that a proposition, Mr. Baxter?

Matthias: You are insatiable, Ms. Masters.

Me: Only for you, Mr. Baxter. But I'm going to have to take a raincheck. The news of our relationship is starting to spread. The guys at work pretty much laid out the red carpet for me.

Matthias: Nice. Hope they leave it out for me. I'll be there a little late tonight. Have to catch up on some work. A hellion has been sucking me of my lifeblood lately.

Me: As far as I can recall, Mr. Baxter, I have done no such sucking of the kind.

Matthias: Would you like me to stop burying my face between your legs so you can get to sucking?

Me: Now, now, no need to be hasty. Go to work, Manwhore.

Matthias: Only a manwhore for you, hellion. Only for you. Miss you, can't wait to see you tonight.

I hug the phone to my chest, smiling like a fool.

Smiling because of a text? What am I, a teenager?

No, because teenage me never felt this way. Not adult me either. And who knows if I'll ever feel like this again when this is all over.

***

As predicted, the club is packed after Paula's press release announcing our engagement. She'd made a point to subtly refer to me as "local business owner of the recently opened whisky and cigar club, Malt."

Thanks, Paula.

It hadn't taken long for our website to crash after Heard It Here's posts went live, and for the line to start building an hour and a half before we opened.

Matthias is an A-list celebrity in New York, despite his playboy ways, or maybe because of them. His generosity in spirit and with his money has always made him a favorite celebrity to spot around the city.

So, the promise of an almost guaranteed glimpse of him at the club is too much for even hardened New Yorkers to ignore.

Time flies by as we try to make sure everyone there is happy, and it's all hands on deck. We call in James's bar apprentice, and a friend of his drops by to help as well.

We rotate people from the bar to the tables as fast as we can, but it's Friday night and people don't have to worry about going home early.

I'm rushing out of the office when I feel two hands grab my waist. "Hello, darling."

I stop for a moment to melt against him. "How are you doing, darling? It looks a little busy," he jokes.

I shake my head, eyes wide. "It's been crazy. But also so much fun," I admit to him. As busy and chaotic as it's been, filling this club is why I opened it in the first place.

He tucks an errant hair behind my ear and smiles. "No kidding, the line's still weaving around the building."

I pull his arms around my waist and let myself rest against him for just a few more seconds. "Well, can you blame them? There's a very special guest here tonight!"

He primps, lifting his chin. "Guess I better go out and appease your masses."

I look at him, confused. "Oh, no, I mean the band. They've been a big hit here since they came last week."

"Wench!" he shouts and pinches my ass. "Should we practice a kiss for your public?" he murmurs against my lips. I don't even have a chance to reply before his mouth presses on mine, and I forget that I have an entire building of people needing me.

I was never a good sleeper. Someone said something about it being because women always have a million things running through their head. But I've never slept as well as I do next to Matthias.

The morning after the announcement of our engagement, I refuse to leave the cocoon of the bed, having gotten six straight hours of sleep for the first time in... ever.

Matthias pulls the blanket off me some time around nine-thirty a.m. and I kick the bed like I'm the last leg in a freestyle relay competition.

It takes half an hour, two espressos and multiple promises and threats until I finally agree to get up. All he tells me is to take a shower and get dressed. The lack of details means I just waste more time trying to decide what to wear.

"But can't you give me a clue?" I say, standing in front of him in nothing but a lace thong, hoping I can distract him into giving me more details.

"It requires clothing. Kind of. Hurry up!" He slaps my ass as he walks by, taking my espresso cups back into the kitchen.

Figuring that it's Matthias, and it could actually involve jumping out of a plane, I decide on a comfortable but still stylish pair of The Row beige wide leg pants and an off-the-shoulder chocolate angora sweater. The two are staple wardrobe pieces that have gotten me through months of no shopping. As frivolous as it was, shopping, or specifically, buying designer dresses, always made me feel beautiful.

I put on the outfit and make sure that it looks presentable. There's a loose thread on the sleeve, but I just tuck it into the armhole and it's as good as new. Almost. And comfortable. This way, even if I die from whatever activities he has planned, I'll still look good.

We've been in the car for almost ten minutes before he tells me where we're going.

"We're going to get you a dress for the gala on Monday night," he says with a grin.

How did he know? How did he know of all the things we could do, this would be the one I'd want to do the most?

When I don't say anything, his smile falters, and he nervously says, "I didn't know if you had anything you wanted to wear to the gala, but even if you did, I thought you might want something new, anyway."

I shake my head, touched. "I don't have anything. Is there something you'd like me to wear?" The thought of him picking a dress for me that pleases him thrills me.

The smile is back. "I'm glad you asked! There's a designer I've always loved. Ravel. I don't think I've seen you wear him before. I know him, actually. Weird fellow. Can't see past the end of his nose, but he makes a mean couture dress."

I reach over and squeeze his hand. "I love his designs. Thank you so much. This is the perfect outing. Definitely better than jumping out of a plane."

We fall into a comfortable silence, me leaning against him in the car while he checks his work emails.

"Shit," he hisses when we're almost at the Ravel showroom.

"What's wrong?"

He grimaces, rubbing his head. "I... have to do something. Do you think you'd mind going ahead of me? I really need to take care of this, but I'll join you later. I'm so sorry."

Something's caused a tightening, a pinching of his face. Whatever's going on, I don't think he'd be able to think about anything else until he takes care of it.

"Um, sure," I say, not wanting to make this more difficult for him.

"I won't be long," He pulls out a credit card from his wallet and hands it to me. "Here's my card. Go crazy."

"Are you sure?" I turn the card over in my hand. *Matthias Baxter* is embossed on one side.

"Never surer of anything more in my life. I actually ordered you your own card, but it hasn't arrived yet."

He jumps out of the car before I can say goodbye, evidently already preoccupied with his issue.

I'm disappointed that he's not coming with me, but I know that he has spent so much time with and *for* me lately there must be so much he needs to catch up on. He's been basically clearing his schedule every night to be at the club, and wait there until at least two-thirty a.m. just to make sure I get home safely.

Kevin drops me off in front of the Ravel entrance and I get out, wiping my palms down the back of my pants. I don't know why I'm nervous about going in there.

A designer showroom is my domain. I've probably spent more time in one than in my own apartment. But throwing money around is apparently a muscle, one I haven't used in a while.

I step inside.

It's your standard showroom. By that I mean that there is nothing standard about it. Ravel has chosen a minimalist décor, a soft pink, allowing the sparsely displayed clothes to stand out.

In the back, there's a showing area. Giant gilded mirrors adorn three walls, with a stoop in the middle for modelling and taking measurements for tailoring. I spot a dress on a mannequin near the back, and I start to make my way over when a salesperson steps in front of me, essentially blocking my way.

"Hello, Miss," she says with zero warmth.

"Good morning." Show. No. Fear. It's one thing to walk into a store knowing that they know you can buy and sell them with a dial of the phone. It's another to prove to them that you belong there.

"I'm here to look for a dress for an event on Monday," I tell her.

She snickers. *Snickers out loud.* "Left it a little late, haven't we? We're not going to be able to do much with it," she sneers, looking me over.

No fear, Clarissa. "That's fine. I can make it work."

"We'll see."

She eyes the loose thread on my sweater and it makes me painfully aware that this design was released two seasons ago. A little wave of her hand and another sales assistant comes walking over.

"Donna will help you. I need to return to my other customer." She gives me one more derisive look and stomps off.

Donna isn't any more thrilled to be serving me than the first woman. I ignore her as much as I can and walk over to the dress I'd eyed from the front of the store. "I'd like to try this one on please."

Donna smirks. "Miss, I think that's not going to really work for you."

"I'm sorry, did I ask for your opinion?" If she wanted to tangle, I was here for it.

The direct confrontation makes her blink. "Yes, miss. What size would you like? A size ten?"

There's nothing crueler and more passive aggressive like a sales assistant with a tape measure.

"I'm a size four."

The other salesbitch returns while her customer goes into her prepared fitting room, looking at me like I'm inconveniencing them. "Miss, we are actually going to be closing for a lunch event. Is it possible for you to come back later?"

Lunch event.

Lunch event is code for, "you're too poor to shop here, and we don't want to bother with collecting clothes for you and having to put them back."

The two of them step in around me, closing ranks.

And the last of the excitement I had about coming here disappears. This is not any fun, and I don't want to be here for another second.

But I'm not going without a dress.

I gesture at the one hanging in front of me again. "I want this one in a size four. I don't need to try it on. Just wrap it up, please." I hold out Matthias's card and the boss salesbitch practically rips the card out of my hand and stomps off.

I'm standing by the door for almost ten minutes before she comes back, without a dress.

"Miss. This isn't your card." She doesn't frame it as a question so much as an accusation.

Fucking hell. "No, it's my fiancé's."

"It says it's *Matthias Baxter* on it."

I've hit a limit of dealing with her confrontational manner, all I want to do is take Matthias's card back, go home and hide in the cocoon of our bed again. But I have to try one more time. For him. "Yes, that's because he's my fiancé."

The two ladies look at each other and then burst out laughing. But there's no mirth in the laugh, it's empty and cruel.

"I don't think so," she says. "Mr. Baxter is a regular customer here, and I've never seen you with him."

My lungs tighten, and humiliation laces each breath. I put my hand on the counter. "Please. I need this dress. Please, just call him and he will approve the purchase."

She lifts her chin, her harsh features angled in the light giving off a matronly air. "No. I won't be bothering Mr. Baxter. I suggest you leave right now, and we won't report you to the police for credit card fraud."

A security guard steps in behind me before I can even tell her how wrong she is. "Miss?" he says, firmly but not unkind.

It's the nicest thing anyone's said to me since I stepped into the godforsaken place.

I pull at my collar, it's getting hot in here.

And I can't remember the last time I took my psych meds.

Stupid. Stupid Clarissa, getting too caught up in her happiness to take care of herself.

"I... didn't steal the card," I hiss as the sweat drips down my back and I struggle to swallow. Finally, when I don't think I can stand their looks at me for another moment, I flee.

Luckily Kevin's found a close parking spot, and he's Kevin's leaning on the car with a book.

I run over, climbing into the car without a word.

"Ms. Masters? Are you okay?" Kevin asks through the window.

I shake my head and bury my face in my hands.

This isn't a panic attack.

This is pure, unadulterated humiliation.

Outside, I see Kevin pick up his phone. Frantic, I roll down the window and shake my head. "No! Don't tell him."

Kevin gives me a pained look. "Ma'am, I have to. He'll be so upset with me if I don't."

But I don't care anymore. I roll the window back up and slump against the car.

All he'd wanted was to do something nice for me, and somehow, I've managed to even screw that up.

Twenty-Nine

MATTHIAS

"This is Matthias Baxter," I say, answering the call, ignoring the angry looks from the other people in the meeting. They wanted to call an emergency meeting on a day that I've cleared to spend with Clarissa, then they can wait for a few minutes.

"Sir, I am calling from Ravel to tell you someone came into the store using your Centurion Amex card. We blocked the sale and confiscated the card. Would you like me to courier it over to you?"

Confusion clouds my head. Only one person would be using my card, and she's supposed to be at Ravel. There must be a mistake. "Are you telling me that a woman came in trying to use the card and you took it away from her?"

Silence. "Er, yes. We didn't think that it was an authorized."

I take a moment before I answer. "I'm coming down. Don't leave."

"Yes, sir. Of cour —"

I tuck the phone in my pocket and stand up. "We're done here."

"Respectfully, Matthias, we're not done. There's still a lot to discuss about you and Clarissa."

I face the five members of the board who decided to ambush me on the closest thing I have to a day off. One of them being Terry Masters, Clarissa's asshole of a father.

I've been tempering my annoyance for half an hour while they talk at me about all the reasons they think my engagement to Clarissa is a bad idea. They have conveniently forgotten that the whole reason I even considered this solution in the first place is because they had given me a veiled ultimatum: fuck up the Kids & Care IPO and you're done.

"I'm leaving, but please, by all means spend your Saturday discussing something that's already happened. I'm doing it for the good of the company since you all decided that it was so important that people pay attention to my reputation rather than the work I do. So, I've appeased you once, you don't get a say any more. Now, if you will excuse me, I have to attend to my fiancée. Because, unlike some people at this table, I actually care about how she's doing."

As I make it to the door of the conference room, I twist around, glaring at her father.

"You and me, we're going to talk, Terry. And you're going to have a lot of explaining to do."

I run out of the office and jump into the first available cab before it even has a chance to come to a stop.

"The Ravel showroom. Make it fast and there's a $500 tip for you."

I pick up the phone to call her, but there's no answer.

Kevin picks up before the first ring is over.

"Kevin, where is she?"

"Sir, you need to come here quickly."

I roll out of the still moving cab when it pulls up outside of Ravel. Kevin is standing by the car, pretending he's not looking in the backseat window, but he's been with me for too long to fool me.

A quick glance at him as I run to the car is enough to tell me I'm not going to like what I find.

He opens the door for me and I climb inside.

She's sitting, back straight, staring out the window. I rub my arms, goosebumps trailing forearms. It shouldn't be cold in here, but it is.

"Clarissa."

She doesn't say anything, doesn't move. Like she's turned to stone.

"Are you having a panic attack?" I ask, but this feels different.

This time she shakes her head.

"What happened, darling?"

She looks at me, no, she looks *right through* me. "Nothing. I don't think I'm going to get a dress for the gala from here. There just wasn't anything I wanted."

My heart aches, the pain in her voice is the only give away that something's wrong. "We can go after you tell me what happened. Did they say something to you?"

"No," she says, so quiet I can barely hear her. "I don't think I want to get a dress."

"Clarissa, there may be lots of things I don't know about you, but I know you're not going to say no to a new dress. What happened? Is it because they took my card? It's okay, we'll get a new card."

She just shakes her head.

Fine. I'm getting to the bottom of this.

I grab her hand and drag her out of the car and into the showroom.

Two women make a beeline for me, then immediately stop when they see I'm not alone.

"Mr. Baxter, what a surprise," one of the women I've seen here before greets me. I recognize her voice from the phone. "Good morning," she adds.

"Is it? I mean, I get the distinct impression that it's been a pretty shitty morning." I pull Clarissa in against me to send a clear signal: this woman is with me.

Clarissa doesn't say anything, just lifts her head and stares at the sales assistant.

That's my girl.

"I sent my fiancée here so that she could find a beautiful dress to wear to a charity function on Monday but, well, I don't see her with a dress, do you?"

The two women look at each other, neither saying a word.

"And then I get a call about my card. I want to know why you didn't put the sale through when my fiancée used it."

The older woman finally speaks up. "Well, when Miss..." She looks around, panicked that she doesn't have my name.

"Masters. My fiancée's name is Clarissa Masters. You didn't ask for her name when she came in here? Shouldn't that be standard when someone comes in here wanting to spend thousands of dollars on a little bit of fabric?" I'm holding back, but it's not going to last forever.

Just seeing the way they're scrambling is boiling my blood. They fucked up and they know it. They're not sorry yes, but they will be.

"Clarissa? Did either of these ladies ask for your name?" She shakes her head. "Well, that's awfully rude, don't you think?"

"We're sorry. Ms. Masters."

"Good." I step back so I'm level with Clarissa, so they see we're in this together. So, they'll see the way they treated her is the way they treated me. And whatever they did to make her feel this way, they're going to pay for it. "Now, darling, why don't you show me the dress you wanted to buy?"

She just blinks, eyes still crystal clear, giving away nothing. I feel sadness and anger at once.

Hand curled against her neck, I pull her in close, lips brushing her ear as I say, "I'm here, Rissie. Nothing's going to happen to you now I'm here. Let's show these snobby bitches how to treat customers. You in?" Her temple rests on my lips and then I pull away with a reassuring nod.

Through the showroom, she leads me until we're in front of a mannequin wearing a rose gold, floor length gown with crystals embroidered all over the skirt. The straps hang off the shoulder, and when worn, the bust would fall right at the swell of her breasts.

"It's stunning. Let's try it on you." Still keeping her pinned to my side, I crook my finger at the two women hovering a few feet away. "Would you mind getting this one down for my fiancée? Also, she looks parched to me. We'd like some Cristal."

The woman trip over themselves and each other trying to run out back to grab the dress and our drinks.

"Ma'am, you said a size two?"

Next to me, Clarissa snickers. I'm glad to hear her respond. "I believe *you* said I was a size ten. So, you're the expert. Why don't you get for me what you think is best." Her hand squeezes mine, and I know she's feeling better.

I kiss her cheek and say, "You've fought worse than this, my sweet demon of hell. You can snuff these bitches out with your pinky toe."

The dress and champagne arrive at lightning speed, and the sales assistant slides open the curtain of a dressing room and hangs the dress up inside.

"Ma'am, would you like to try it on?"

Clarissa glances at me, still lacking that last morsel of confidence she needs. I nod reassuringly. "I can't wait to see it on, Clarissa."

She fiddles in the dressing room for a few minutes, but finally, in a voice sounding more like herself, she calls out, "I'm coming out."

I hold my breath.

Since we've been together, she's been dressed in a variation of the same outfit for work, an elegant ensemble of shirts and skirt, and the occasional black dress. At night, in bed, she's either naked, in a silk robe, or in one of my T-shirts.

It's been a long time since I've seen her dressed up, and when I last did, I wasn't actually looking.

I was so blind.

The curtain rings rattle as she pushes through the hanging fabric, and my heart skips a beat.

"Up here, Clarissa," I say, pointing to a raised stoop in the middle of the dressing area, surrounded completely by mirrors. She strides over, completely comfortable in the garment.

As the saying goes, she doesn't wear the dress, it wears her.

She's molten sex and feminine elegance in motion, the hint of the length of her leg as she takes each step is breathtaking, the fabric as light as a whisper over her décolleté, hinting at the fullness of her breast. Her waist is accentuated by the most delicate pinch of the seam.

I can't help but beam with pride.

To know her. To be with her.

Venus in stone, except now she's living, breathing, perfection.

It's too bad she won't be wearing this dress.

"What do you think?" I turn to the two sales assistants.

Now they trip over their tongues.

"Oh, she looks absolutely beautiful, stunning, sir."

I stop them by holding up my hand. "No, don't tell me. Tell *her*."

The younger one blinks and looks down at the floor as she mumbles, "Ms. Masters, the dress looks amazing on you. Like it was made for you."

Clarissa says thank you, but she's looking at me.

I turn to the older one and say, "I need a pair of scissors, please."

The poor woman blanches but thinks twice about refusing. It's the smartest thing she's done thus far.

Less than a minute later, a pair of fabric scissors is placed in my hand. I close my fingers around it, enjoying the feel of the weight in my palm.

Clarissa watches me closely, as if she knows something's about to happen.

"Thank you for the scissors, and now, ladies, I'm going to have to respectfully ask you to leave."

"I'm sorry, sir?" the older one stammers.

"Get. Out."

"Sir?"

My eyes bore deep into their faces, making sure to burn mine into their memories of this moment.

"I said, leave. Unless you want to hang around and watch while I fuck my fiancée right here in the middle of your showroom floor. Your choice."

Their mouths fall open, spluttering, cheeks blazing red

"What are you worried about? You think Ravel is going to mind? Do you know who owns this building? Do you think he's going to tell me that he's not happy with how I treated his employees who made my fiancée feel like shit? Basically treated her like a criminal?" Anger leaches into every cell. "So, I'm going to say it one more time. Get. The. Fuck. Out." Balled up fists by my sides turn white, "Now."

They scramble, shoes slipping, sliding on the floor as they flee out of the door. And when it closes behind them, I turn to her.

Resplendent in her dress, I'm almost loathe to ruin the illusion.

"Matthias."

"Yes, darling?" I say, the anger gone now that they're out of my sight, but the intensity of my emotions is still there.

For her.

All hers.

I walk up to her, circling her as she models the dress on the stoop. Her neck invites my touch, and I run a single finger up from her décolleté to her lips. God, I'm so obsessed with her neck. The little stretch of skin between her neck and shoulder is where I want to be reborn, live for the rest of eternity.

"Do you have any idea how fucking beautiful you are? Do you have any idea that it's a privilege to be near you? Do you know that there's never a single moment when I'm not thinking of you?"

"Matthias," she says again.

"Yes, my darling?"

Her bottom lip dips where her teeth bite into it. "Did you mean what you just said? About fucking me here?"

I'm almost scared to touch her, she's too good to be tainted by my hands. "When have I ever said something I don't mean?"

I kneel at her feet, pulling on the hem of the dress, and make a single cut with the scissors.

She watches, as I grab a hold of the two sides of fabric I've just separated, and tear them apart.

The sound of the fabric ripping is oddly satisfying. All the more because I enjoy the sight of the ruined dress in my hands. I keep tearing all the way up the skirt until it meets the bodice. I grab the straps and separate them from the dress with a snip of the scissors.

"Careful, don't move," I whisper to her as I slide the scissors down the middle of her breasts, slicing at the bust until it hangs lifelessly on either side of her body.

My pulse roars in my ears as it rushes to my groin. I walk backwards until I reach the armchair and settle into it, taking in the view of her standing there in a destroyed dress, eyes trusting me all the same.

Under my intense gaze, she starts to feel self-conscious, though, her hands coming up to cover her body where she can.

Good. I want her to feel it, and work through her emotions.

"Take off what's left of the dress off, Clarissa."

"I can't."

"I wouldn't ask you to do something you couldn't do."

She glances at the front of the store. "What if someone comes in?"

"Then let them. It's their lucky day. Take the dress off, darling, let me see you."

Nervously, her hands fidget with the neck of the fabric, and then, eyes locked on mine, she slowly shimmers out of it, until it's a pool of shimmering rose gold and crystals at her feet.

She's topless underneath, with only the thin red thong covering her.

"Turn around."

Teetering on her heels, she spins slowly, giving me a chance to take in every single inch of her until she's facing me again,

"Now take your thong off."

Her skin glows pink. "Matthias..."

"No? Are you scared to show yourself to me?"

"No... I..."

"Take it off, Clarissa," I say, gently but firmly. I'm going to walk her through this experience, until she breaks and is put together again.

Her slender fingers find the straps of her red G-string and she slides it down her legs and steps out of it.

"Turn."

She's already starting to before I say it, her breath growing heavier, her center of gravity lowering as she gives in to my commands.

The air weighs heavier with my arousal, but it's more than that. It's want, it's need. It's a craving for her that I've never been able to quench no matter how many times we have sex.

When she finally faces me again, I get up, walking over to her to tilt her chin with the crook of my index finger, and lay a soft kiss on her lips.

She shivers and her eyes flutter closed until I pull away.

"Listen to me. Now you are beautiful. Just you. Nothing in this fucking place can compare to you. Do you understand me? All this is just a fucking insult to my eyes because it hides me from you, and I want nothing but you, wholly, completely, untouched."

I return to the chair, lean back, unable to look away from her.

"Do you ever touch yourself, Clarissa? Do you ever play with that sweet, perfect cunt and make yourself come?"

"Sometimes. Not much." She flushes with embarrassment.

"Where do you do it? In bed? In a chair?"

Her face blazes scarlet. "The shower."

"Show me. Stand there, in your heels, naked, and show me how you touch yourself. For me."

She starts to protest but stops when she sees how I'm looking at her.

Hungry. Starving.

"For me, Clarissa. Not for you. For me."

Her fingers, tentative and trembling, lift to the curve of her neck, and she slides them down to flick at her nipples. Soft flicks as they harden under her touch. She doesn't linger for too long.

Her right hand walks down the length of her stomach until it rests on her pubis, her fingers gently fluttering over her pussy.

"Spread your legs, baby, spread them so I can see how wet you are."

She complies, taking two little steps outward, her pussy already glistening under the showroom lights, the mirror showing me every angle of her, every curve.

Her tongue flicks out, running along her bottom lip, and then she slides one finger between her legs and inside her.

God.

"Oh, darling, you are so fucking gorgeous. Touch yourself, show me what feels good to you."

All I want is to take out my cock and jack it, but this is about her. I have to remind myself that this is about her.

Legs spreading a little more, she lowers her hips, one hand flicking her nipples hard as she circles her clit, a moan bubbling over her lips.

I don't know if it's the lights or from her fingers, but a soft sheen makes her face glow as she circles her lips.

"Matthias?"

"Yes?"

Her voice is thick with the need to come as she asks. "Do you like what you see?"

My girl is getting braver. "If I would do nothing more with the rest of my life than watch you make yourself come, I would die a happy man."

She chokes back a groan, but her hand moves faster between her legs, alternating between pumping her fingers into her dripping cunt and rubbing her clit.

The rhythm of her breath tells me she's close.

"Come, darling, come for me. But don't you dare take your eyes off me."

She obeys. Perfectly, devastatingly beautifully, she strums her pussy until she's at the edge and then reaches back up to her clit, flicking it fast as I watch her entire body contract and shudder.

"Oh god, fuck... Matthias..." she moans as she loses herself to the orgasm.

My breath mirrors hers as her mouth parts in a stunning tableau of pure pleasure as she breaks. I rush up to her, pulling her shaking body to me as her legs look like they're about to buckle under her.

"That was... my sweet torture. My perfect girl, my desire, my salvation." I whisper, the emotions unable to stop spilling out of me.

They hurt her.

And now I have to make her whole again, remind her that this world will burn before I ever let anyone cause her any pain again.

She whimpers against my neck as she steadies.

I pull her hand to my mouth and hungrily suck her cum from her fingers.

I'm so fucking addicted to the taste of her.

Eyes still glazed over, she slowly undresses me, taking charge.

Bolstered, emboldened by her own orgasm, she fears nothing now. I wonder if someone walked through those doors, would she'd even stop.

One by one she unbuttons my shirt, and slides it off my shoulders. Her fingers find the hem of my undershirt and she lifts it over my head.

Soft kisses fall on my chest and stomach as she lowers herself to the floor, unbuckling my belt and pulling my pants down.

She taps on my legs, gesturing for me to step out of them, then she prompts me to take my shoes off.

"You're overdressed," I joke in a shaky voice as she stands up. "You're still in heels and I'm naked."

"I can take them off," she says with a smirk, knowing full well I want nothing of the sort.

Her hands reach down, grazing the tip of my aching cock. I must be dripping already, the precum oozing down my cock just from watching her.

She pumps my cock a few times and then lifts her hand up to her mouth, dragging her tongue along her palm, tasting us both on her skin.

It's so fucking sexy, I almost explode on the spot.

"I need to fuck you," I growl, pulling her to me, crashing my mouth on hers until we're both gasping for breath. "I want to be inside you. I need to come inside you, darling."

She knows what I'm asking, and she replies with a nod.

The thought of exploding inside her incinerates the last of my restraint. I spin her around and bend her at the waist, roughly kicking her legs apart. In one rough, brutal movement, I slam into her.

The force almost propels us off the step, but I grab her hips to grind back onto my cock.

"God, your pussy is sweet, torturous perfection. You are my heaven and hell." I mean every word.

I pull all the way out, wanting to feel her pussy take every inch of my cock all over again.

And I do it over and over and over, pull out all the way and then ram back into her, her pussy barely having time to recover, pulsing, aching, trembling as I thrust into her.

I grab her arms and lock them behind her back, reaching for her head, lifting it so she can see us in the mirrors.

"Watch me fuck you, little hellion. Watch how you make me lose control. Watch me fuck you like I've never fucked anyone. Watch me come for you, and only you, darling."

One hand keeps her hands pinned to her back, the other slides under her to her clit.

It's hard under my touch and I stroke it until I feel her cry out and squeeze around my cock, coming on me.

And then I do it again. Keeping her locked to me as I push her to her third orgasm, until she can barely breathe, begging me to give her mercy, then and only then I let go of her arms and grab her hips as I fuck her. She's watching us through hooded eyes and I drive into her over and over, using her cunt for my pleasure and mine alone.

Making her mine.

Making me hers.

"Oh god, I'm going to fill you up with my cum, little hellion. Yours. God, I'm yours."

I grunt and erupt inside her, as my orgasm rips through me like brush fire, burning everything in its path, uncontrolled. Her whimpers fill my ears and I wrap my arms around her, pulling her upright as I bond her to me, my teeth digging in her shoulder as I leave nothing behind and give her everything.

"Darling, my girl, my love, my everything," I murmur, no sense of anything around me but my cock buried inside her, spent.

At some point, we collapse to the floor, our cum dripping onto the floor and onto the wrecked dress under us.

We curl against each other, two halves just trying to be whole.

"How do you feel?" I ask once my soul has returned to my body.

"Well, I don't think I can come back here, but not because of the bitches." She chuckles.

"Fuck this place, Rissie. It doesn't deserve you. When you think of Ravel, I want you to remember you and me, what we did together. And that's all, okay?"

She nods, her head moving on my chest, probably listening to my heart beat for her.

"What the fuck is going on here?"

A male's voice booms and we look up to see Ravel standing there, hands on his hips as he takes in the spectacle of us naked in the middle of his showroom floor.

Clarissa scrambles to cover herself while I laugh, rolling over onto my back, in full post fuck splendor.

"Well, hello there, Ravel. How are you doing?"

He splutters, but doesn't look away. "Explain yourself, Matthias. You can't just come in here and kick my staff out."

I stand up, fully aware my still half hard cock is pretty much waving at him while Clarissa gathers up the dress to cover her and stands behind me.

"Really? And your staff can insult my fiancée and refuse her service, refuse my credit card?"

He turns white under his fake tan and he spins around to look at his two sales assistants, who for the second time that day, realize too late that they're dealing with the wrong person. "I'm sure it was a mistake, Matthias."

"Really Ravel? You're lucky I'm not making you and every person here get down on their knees and beg my fiancée for forgiveness. I suggest you find a way to make it up to my fiancée." I look around. "I'd hate to find a new tenant for this place. But I will."

I pull my clothes on, pants, T-shirt, and then drape my shirt around Clarissa's arms. Leading her out of the showroom, I throw the ruined dress at the women's feet.

"It's a nice dress, but I've seen better. I think we're going to go somewhere that actually appreciates our business."

I open the door for Clarissa, who walks out with my cum dripping down her legs, and her head held fucking high.

Thirty

CLARISSA

WE'RE ON A PLANE to Milan.

We're on a plane that Matthias is flying, to Milan.

From the showroom Matthias had had Kevin take us straight to the airport, where the company jet had miraculously appeared. Or at least, where it had been summoned while Matthias was madly texting, his hand on my inner thigh as I rested in the car.

At one point he'd cryptically started a strange conversation about how personal security is so important, and did I make sure that where I kept my passport was secure.

I told him, "Well, I keep it by the nightstand in our bedroom. If that's not a safe place then you need to tell me now."

I didn't even put two and two together; I was too busy reliving every second of what happened at Ravel, what was done and what was said.

So when we arrived at the airport, there was a bag of my clothes, my passport, and my toiletries that appeared on the plane, ready for an impromptu trip to Milan.

"We'll find you a dress there," he says as he clicks his seatbelt in place.

I admit I pull mine tighter than usual. "Are you sure you know what you're doing?" I ask, looking at all the buttons and levers, tucking my arms in against me so I didn't inadvertently touch something and eject us both out of the damn plane.

He doesn't say anything as he's busy reading something off the dash and scribbling something in a notepad. "Of course, I got my commercial pilot's license when I turned twenty-two," he says, tucking the notepad into a side compartment of his seat. "And I've only ever almost crashed one plane," he jokes. "Two if you count iffy landings. But I blame the ground at our winery in Barossa Valley. We hadn't had it properly laid yet. Totally not my fault," he says defensively.

"So, whenever you say you hopped on a plane..."

A wide grin stretches from ear to ear. "I mean, *I* hopped the plane there, so to speak." He hears something on the radio and responds. "Ready?"

The trip is eye opening; Matthias goes into great detail about all the controls, and I retain the grand sum of zero of any of it. But I do remember all the sites he points out to me as we leave the clouds and drop down over Italy.

I sit, awestruck when he lands the plane.

"I'm still alive." I sound surprised because I am.

He throws his head back and laughs.

It fills up every cracked and broken part of me.

"Come on, I'm famished. Someone sapped every last ounce of energy from me." He winks. "And I need to eat something so she can do it again."

I wonder if he picked Milan for any particular reason other than because it's the fashion capital of the world. Or if he knows that it might as well be my second home, and after what went on a Ravel, my comfort is highest priority.

I used to come here for every fashion season. Sat on countless runway shows, met all the designers, including ones that would become some of my favorites. It's what made today's experience at Ravel all the worse. It was a reminder of how far I've fallen.

Being just a normal person was never on my bingo card for my life. But maybe, that's just what I am now.

Yeah, a normal person whose fake billionaire fiancée just flew his own plane and landed it in Milan.

Well.

Guilty, as Matthias says.

Matthias checks us into the Four Seasons and collapses on the bed until he pulls me into the shower, washing off the remnants of the most incredible moments of my life.

His fingers tangle in my hair as he washes my scalp, massaging the tension from my head. Afterwards he gently brushes out the knots as we sit on the side of the bed.

"Is that okay?" he asks, uncharacteristically nervously, handing me the brush. "I've never done that before."

It thrills me to no end that, finally, Matthias Baxter has done something with me he hasn't done with another woman.

And no one can ever take that away from me.

Despite the time difference we sleep until the sun peeks through the curtains.

"Get up, sleepy head," I'm unceremoniously awakened the next morning by a pillow straight to the head.

"No. Sleep," I murmur pulling the blanket up over my head. Last night was the first time I was away from the club. But when I called after I got off the plane, the team seemed confident that that they could take care of everything. James and Clementine had been kind enough to answer all of my incessant questions as well as give me updates complete with their own special brand of commentary. They both mentioned how the club was packed, and that some people seemed a little disappointed that neither I nor Matthias were there but that was quickly replaced by genuine enjoyment.

Knowing that had helped me finally fall asleep.

Even if I felt a little... *something*... at knowing that they were doing okay without me.

"Hey. How did it go last night at the club?" Matthias asked, as if reading my mind.

He's been doing that a lot.

"They said it was fine," I reply, emerging from the blanket. "I guess that's good," I say, lightly.

Matthias bites back a smirk and touches the side of my face. "It's just one night. You've worked hard to get it to the point where you can step away and know that everything will be taken care of."

"I didn't say anything," I say in a tone that can only be described as sulky. "Um, is that coffee?" I say, pointing to the mug sitting on the nightstand, trying to deflect.

He laughs and hands me the coffee cup while shaking his head.

Instead of staying at the hotel for breakfast, we decide to go for a walk to Pinacoteca di Brera to take some photos, and spend an hour at the Brera Botanical Gardens, just enjoying the warm morning before it gets too hot.

Hand in hand, we talk about everything and nothing. Making plans that may never come to be, about all the time we wasted hating each other, but knowing maybe we had to go through that, to get here.

But we don't talk about how we feel.

We don't talk about how he called me "my love" at Ravel.

We don't talk about when this all becomes real, and whether any part of it is still fake.

He takes my hand and pulls me up from the bench we've been sitting on, taking a break in the shade. "Come on, we have to be at Cavelli House in half an hour. Maybe we'll actually get a dress for you today, and I don't even have to fuck you in public to get it."

The experience at Cavelli House is the polar opposite of what happened at Ravel yesterday.

Even before we arrive, we see a whole entourage waiting for us at the entrance. The car barely stops before the door is flung open and two hands reach for me and pull me to my feet.

"Bella, you are perfection. You could go dressed in just a garbage bag, no? But that won't do, we will make you look even more like a goddess. A goddess with a stylist, okay?"

Matthias is just a blur of blue as I'm swept inside the studio.

After a parade of stunning dresses, I finally pick a turquoise one that makes Matthias's eyes melt when he sees me in it. As the seamstress pins my waist and hem, Matthias watches, his espresso cup hovering two inches from his mouth. And something tells me, he's going to be showing his appreciation in the form of his mouth between my legs when we get back to the hotel. He's addicted to making me come with his mouth, and there's not a single problem I have with it. Under his touch I've felt a new feminine energy bless my body and every movement I make feels more fluid, elegant.

"The dress will be ready by this evening?" Matthias confirms for the fifth time.

"Bello, have I ever disappointed you before? Sì, it will be delivered to your hotel tomorrow morning before you leave."

He takes my hands, "Bella, it was a privilege to dress you. I cannot wait to see you all over the pictures tomorrow."

We kiss on both cheeks.

Matthias pulls me away with a growl. "Okay, that's enough. Hands off, Gio. Don't make me steal your material scissors."

"Ah, no, do not joke," he says, paling.

We can't help laughing at his reaction as Matthias helps me into the Maserati that somehow materialized sometime during the night.

I don't insult him by asking where it came from. Money makes things appear seemingly out of thin air.

He sits, his hands on the steering wheel without moving for a minute, then he runs his hand through his hair, looking nervous. It's funny to me that I can make him feel that way. Finally he says, "I have some college friends here, would you, um, would you be okay with meeting them? You don't have to, I just thought you might be sick of just being with me."

Friends. Meeting. If we're really going to go through with engagement, I guess I'm going to have to meet people as his fiancée.

Might as well start now.

"I'd love to."

"Really?"

His surprise surprises me. "I can meet people. I've been known to know how to use cutlery and say excuse me when I burp and everything."

"It's not that. It's... well, I don't know."

"Matthias Baxter, are you feeling nervous right now?" I poke him gently in the side and he pretends to squeal in pain.

"Ow! Shut up. Let's go then, 'goddess,'" he says in Gio's accent and speeds away.

***

Matthias's friends Anna and Dom, or Domenico, are just about the most wonderful people I've ever met.

Both professors at the university, one in art history, and the other in anthropology, everything that comes out of their mouths is fascinating. They share stories about their crazy adventures without sounding as though they are bragging; if anything, they try to one up each other in their roasts of each other and self-deprecation.

When we get to their apartment, I'm surprised to see that a dining table has already been set out on the balcony with a tray of antipasti already laid out, and a bottle of Chianti in a rustic ice bucket against the wall.

"Clarissa! What a beautiful name. It means 'light,' yes?" Anna says, enveloping me in a big hug.

"It does," I beam, unconsciously emulating my name's meaning. But it's not hard. Anna is effervescent and friendly. Dom lets his wife take the lead while hanging back and catching up with Matthias.

"Sit, sit. We have some cotoletta with insalata coming. Is that okay? Sorry, Matthias did not give us much time or details," she says accusingly and punches him lightly on the chest.

"I was testing your hospitality skills, Anna," Matthias teases. "Come on, Rissie," he says, guiding me to the balcony.

The view takes my breath away.

I don't know how they can afford this place on professors' salaries, but then I remember that Matthias met Dom at Eton so his family probably has money. The decor is simple but elegant. Probably helps that Dom is an art history professor,

I sit back and listen to the three of them catch up. From what I can tell, it's been almost six months since Matthias has been back in Milan. He makes a joke about being the only one of his brothers actually doing any work and gives me a little wink.

The little gesture lodges into my heart. It's intimate and playful and I don't know what to do with it. It's hard to not replay the way he'd called me "my love." Yes, it had been during sex, during an experience that elevated our relationship but Matthias has never misspoken in the entire time I've known him, and I don't just mean in the last few weeks. He talks a lot and a lot of what he is saying is joking but in the tiniest twinkle of his eye, I know everything he says has been turned over in his head.

And the day that he says something that hurts me, I know he'll mean that too.

"Anna, tell Rissie how your scum of the earth husband here stole you from me."

The three of them dissolve into howls.

When she finally catches her breathe, Anna cocks her head at Matthias. "As far as I remember, I met Dom because Matthias was trying to hit on my roommate. He spent one night with her and never saw her again, and I had to deal with her asking me a hundred times if she could tag along with me and Dom just in case she could run into him."

Matthias drops his mouth open in an exaggerated shock. "I remember nothing of the sort. Don't listen to her, Rissie, she lies. She's not even Italian. I heard her sound like a valley girl one time over the phone when she thought no one was listening."

Anna opens her mouth and a string of what I can only imagine are very Italian curses spews from her mouth. She grabs a bread roll out of the basket and pelts Matthias with it.

He guards his face as he shouts, "Rissie! I'm dying, tell my family I loved them all! Actually, no! Tell them I loved all but one of them and let them try to figure out which one it was."

I laugh so hard I choke on my wine, and Anna has to stop attacking Matthias to pat me gently on the back.

"Clarissa, no, don't die over him. He's not worth it. I'll introduce you to some Italian men. And you will forget this blond manwhore in no time."

Dom watches in amusement as Matthias brushes the crumbs off his shirt. "Excuse me, my name is *Matthias*. That's an Italian name."

Why do you of all your brothers have an Italian name?" Dom asks, lips twitching.

Matthias shrugs. "How would I know, perhaps because there is actually reason to believe that my mother had an affair with an Italian winemaker around the time I was born?"

The look that Anna gives him is full of sisterly affection. "Maybe, I'm not sure why that is, but you definitely sunburn like a ginger Englishman."

"I do not!" Matthias pulls his shirt sleeve up and it shows an angry red tint that has appeared just from sitting out on the balcony for half an hour. "Never mind."

The rest of us laugh so hard we drown out any protests that he makes.

We follow up lunch with a game.

Chronology, they called it, where you have to line up cards that represent human events based on when they happened in history. The first to ten correctly placed cards wins.

When Dom, Matthias and I all reach nine correct ones at the same time, the competitiveness boils over into some pretty colorful trash talk.

"Matthias, if you paid as much attention to history as you did any ass that walks by, you would've won by now!" Dom taunts him.

But Matthias doesn't let that slide. "Hey now, Dom, if you paid attention to material that you stole off Wikipedia for your lectures, maybe you wouldn't be trying to make me look bad in front of your wife." He adds, "Who you stole from me."

"You tell him, Dom!" I yell, in support of any one but Matthias.

"Don't you talk, as far as I can remember you cheat," Matthias says, a grin on his face.

"Okay, to win the title of reigning Chronology overlord, Matthias, when was the Great Wall of China finished?" Dom reads off the cards. Matthias's face turns serious as he thinks then his entire face scrunches up and he folds, banging the table. "I'm going to guess it's between 200 BC and 175 BC."

A grin dances over Dom's face and he throws that card down and yells, "And you are wrong!"

Everyone but Matthias jumps up cheering, while he groans and drops his head into his hands.

Dom grabs another card off the pile. "Okay, Clarissa - when did Vincent Van Gogh... die?"

I grin and jump up, do a silly little dance, which I have never ever done in my entire life. "Why, Mr. Art Professor, that would be in 1890, so between these two," I point at the1860 and 1912 cards.

We all wait, breaths held, as we wait for Dom to give the answer.

Finally, he hands me the card, "Congratulations, Clarissa Masters, you are the new champion of Chronology, unseating our current champion, Matthias the loser!"

Anna jumps up and gives me a hug, cheering as Matthias protests, but with a smile on his face.

The men put the game away while I help Anna carry the plates into the kitchen. She tries to wave me away when I grab a tea towel to help her dry the plates, but I insist.

"You two are good together," she says, after a few minutes listening to the music streaming through the speakers.

"Why do you say that?"

"I tend to say what I think," she laughs.

I let it sink in, and can't help wondering how many other women she's said that to. Maybe this is where he brings women when he wants them to like him. I inwardly laugh, Matthias has never had trouble getting women to like him. If anything, I'm probably the one he's taken the longest to break in.

But he has most certainly broken me in.

I don't know what that says about me or him.

"He let you win, you know. Matthias never lets anyone win. He beats my kids at every game he plays with them. My daughter is five years old, by the way."

I frown. "He didn't let me win."

Her lips curl into an ironic smile. "Trust me, he knows exactly when the Great Wall was finished. I've played this game with him a lot."

I lean back against the wall as I wait for her to hand me the next plate, letting her words sink in.

"You know how Dom and I ended up together? Trust me, it wasn't easy. We had a lot of problems. Lots of missteps, lots of hurt feelings. And we're both competitive, we make Ronaldo and Messi's rivalry look like a fight for a toy on the playground. But at some point, we both said, *'hey, what are we doing here? Are we just wasting time together or apart? Because I love you and I want to be with you.'* And we have to stop letting our own shit get in the way of us being together. And here we are. But it takes a lot of compromise and a lot of forgiving and forgetting about the past." She takes a breath, leaning on the sink, looking at me thoughtfully. "We chose to trust."

I listen to every word and it makes me adore her even more. The way she speaks, clearly and concisely, simply, real. But what I'm supposed to do with it in my own situation? I don't know. There's a lot going on that I'm not sure we can overcome. Not the least of which, the things I've done in the past.

She grabs the wine glass and carefully rinses them. "Yes, he trusts you."

"How do you know?"

"Because he's never brought anyone here before. When he called and said to Dom, 'I'm bringing a friend,' *I knew*. You were going to be special. And I wasn't wrong."

I want to believe her. "What's so special about bringing me here."

"He's getting our approval. He has it, Clarissa."

We clean the rest of the plates in silence, each lost in our own thoughts. When we're done, she takes the tea towel from me to hang up on the rack, and hugs me again. "You can trust him, too."

They send us home with bottles of homemade limoncello and a promise that they'll be in New York soon. And many, many things for me to think about.

***

He slides into me slowly, deliberately, torturously.

Wrapped around his waist, my legs pull him in, urging him deeper. "Please..."

He's been teasing like this for an hour.

My pussy hums with the need for release.

"They liked you; my friends liked you," he whispers as he pulls out again, making me whimper at the emptiness. "Should we invite them to the wedding?"

"Whose?"

He bores into me with his darkened eyes. "Ours, Clarissa."

"Our real one or our fake one?"

It has to be asked.

But he doesn't argue, just sucks on my neck for a moment as he presses into me. Inch by inch by inch, thrusting in the very last moment, pushing himself to the hilt before pulling out again.

"When are you going to realize there's nothing fake about this?"

He finally lets me come, my entire body splitting apart from the pleasure, the sensations long overdue, and I burst out crying at the release.

Once he catches his breath, he pulls me to his chest.

"It's all real, darling. Did that feel fake to you?"

We both spend the plane ride back catching up on work. He isn't flying this time, hiring a pilot to take us and the company plane back to New York. He sits in the chair opposite mine, our legs tangled together as we reply to emails and phone calls.

Half way through the flight, I get an alert on my phone.

"Playboy billionaire Matthias Baxter set to marry Baxter Enterprises Board Chairman's daughter Clarissa Masters."

Fuck.

Fuck, fuck, fuck.

That is not what I wanted at all. The tabloids must've done some digging all on their own. I could handle the mention that I used to be Damien's fiancée. I could take everything that came with that implication, because it's the truth.

But I did not want my name tied to my father's. I knew it eventually would be, but not yet. Just... not yet.

I throw the phone on the table between us and Matthias frowns, pulling the phone away from his ear, mouthing, "You okay?"

I just shake my head, and get up to sit at a neighboring seat so I don't interrupt his phone call.

Even 30,000 feet up in the air, I can't escape him. Even if I can run from my past, I can't run from my bloodline.

"I'll call you back later," I hear Matthias murmur into the phone and then he's right there, kneeling on the ground next to me. "Hey, what happened?"

I turn the phone to him and he reads, lips instantly pursing.

"Fuck them, Rissie. One day, it's just going to be Clarissa Masters, wife of Matthias Baxter. And we're going to deal with your dad. You know that right? You know I'm not going to let this go."

"I don't know what you can do? He's the chairman of the board."

He squeezes my knee. "Chairmen can be voted out. And maybe it's time anyway. With Kingsley's CEO vote coming up... maybe it's time to clean house. But don't worry, okay? We're going to be okay."

I just nod.

And which I could tell him about what's worrying me, and it's not just my father.

But he can't know. He can never ever know.

Thirty-One

Matthias

Clarissa to be dropped off at the club so she can jump right into work when we land late Sunday afternoon. I watch her through the car window as she walks down the side alley to the back door of the club, and instantly yearn to follow her.

But I have to content myself knowing I'll see her in a few short hours, and that maybe she could use a few moments to miss me.

I'm in my own office ten minutes later, with Hannah waiting at the elevator when I get off.

"What are you doing here?" I ask her surprised to see her there. Apparently that question is catching.

"You're here, I'm here."

She doesn't follow me into my office, just returns to her desk, clicking away on the computer. She could be playing solitaire for all I know.

I scroll through my emails, stopping when I see one from Dmitrik with the subject: *Patrick Linzer*. Finally. I open it and I'm instantly disgusted. It's filled with over a hundred scanned documents, covering every aspect of his life. As I open each one, my anger rises.

When I'm done going through them, I send off an email to Dmitrik, and wire his fee with a 50% bonus. He's gone well above and beyond. And now I have what I need to bury the fucker.

Then maybe once and for all, the haunted look in Clarissa's eyes when she thinks no one is looking can fade for good.

Limos line up along Fifth avenue clogging up traffic all the way down to Columbus Circle.

Why people with money have to ride in excessively long vehicles, stopping traffic in Manhattan, that hardly has free-flowing traffic as it is, is your guess as well as mine

Our car finally reaches the entrance of the Plaza, I jump out and run around to Clarissa's side of the car. When she emerges, the night fills with the flash of camera bulbs. She smooths her hand down the front of her dress; I catch it and kiss her palm.

"You are a vision, darling."

She's used to these events, having organized a bunch of them herself, as every society woman has. But this is her first time as Matthias Baxter's fiancée in his home of New York.

This isn't Sydney.

New York City is a vulture's nest and they're always hungry.

My hand locks onto the small of her back as we make our way inside to The Grand Ballroom.

"Come on, let's get you a drink," I whisper, hoping the sound of my voice can act as her anchor.

Over the last week, I've caught her a few times on the precipice of an anxiety attack, and the best thing I've found is to try to ground her in an action. Sipping a drink helps, as well most simple but physical tasks with her hands.

On our twenty-foot walk to the bar we're stopped three times. Old socialites fawning over her, pretending they're not judging every last thing about her.

It makes me sick.

Thankfully, Kaine Ashley and his wife Jade find us at the bar. Jade is like the New York version of My-Linh, sunshine and sweetness.

She puts Clarissa instantly at ease, and it makes me wonder if My-Linh will ever welcome Clarissa the same way. I wouldn't blame her if she didn't, though.

My conversation with Kaine falls naturally into business, and we talk about the problems we've met with a joint project we're working on. In the corner of my eye, I see Jade pull Clarissa aside to chat. Eventually they wander away, but as long as she's with Jade, I don't feel a need to chase after her. It's been a while since Clarissa has been in a place like this, and with all the things that are happening with her, at any point someone could approach her with a topic she doesn't want to talk about and I'd prefer to be there to run interference if she needs it.

Kaine is about as talkative as Kingsley is, so once the work part of our conversation comes to the end, we make small talk that soon fades to a comfortable silence. I'm happy to see him though. He's so different to the man I first met ten years ago. We were both so green back then, but him especially as he had come from a different upbringing all together. He was forever hiding behind a hoodie to spare the public from seeing the scars he'd obtained in the house fire that had taken his family.

Under the love of Jade, he has grown into a powerful man to match the business mogul. Three kids later, Kaine and Jade are a constant but positive influence on the scene in New York City.

I'm about to ask if he wants a refill on his drink when I feel a third person joins us.

Even without looking my skin crawls.

"Gentlemen." Somehow Patrick interrupts even though Kaine and I aren't even speaking. "Lovely night, isn't it."

Kaine has no control of his face, so he just lifts his drink to me and walks away.

"Thanks, man, I'll return the favor sometime," I shout after him, feeling no need to maintain any semblance of civility with Patrick.

I had little respect for him, even before I saw him hit Clarissa. Now that I've read about his professional and personal exploits, I wouldn't dirty my shoe stomping on his slimy face. "What do you want?"

"I just came over to say hello. We're practically brothers, you know," he sniffs, and whips his nose on his sleeve. He's probably ten drinks in, making him stupider than usual.

"I have enough brothers. See you, Patrick." Just seeing him reminds me of all the things I'd read about, and it wouldn't take much to reach out and snap his neck. But I'm not interested in a quick death. I want to watch the life drip out of him drop by drop. While I watch. Swilling a glass of Louis XIII in his honor.

"I'm just saying, I see you're engaged to Clarissa now. First Damien, then me, now you. We might as well be brothers, all sharing that slut."

I grit my teeth.

He's baiting me.

And if I bite, I'll have let him win. And I owe it to Clarissa not to let that happen.

"Actually, as I hear it, you were never even in the running. You forget, I saw you, Patrick." I spit out his name like its rancid wine. "As I recall, you were so desperate that she wouldn't sleep with you, that you weren't above trying to force her. That's not very gentlemanly of you." I take a sip of my drink, taking a beat to calm down. "At least my brother and I closed the deal you never could. Maybe that's why our name is on the banner over there"—I point to the sponsors banner with the Baxter logo on it—"and you had to beg for an invitation."

His face crinkles into an ugly mask. "You asshole. You think you're so slick—"

"Actually, no. I don't. I just think I'm not a shit man. I got my woman and took care of her. While your face still carries the shape of my fist. Do yourself a favor, stay the fuck away from the both of us."

His nostrils flare and steam. "You're going to regret ever coming here, English scum, you should've finished me off when you had the chance."

I lean in, although he smells like a fucking brewery. "Don't worry. I'm going to. You just keep drinking. It's going to take the edge off the hurt you're about to experience." I'm about to walk away, but then I decide to deliver the final strike. "Oh, and one more thing, Patrick, you should call that immigration agent you bribed to reject Clarissa's application for a green card so she'd be forced to marry you. I think you're both going to need to get your stories straight..."

As I walk away, he's practically foaming at the mouth. That makes two of us both, but at least I can keep control of my anger.

I scan the room for Clarissa.

She's standing with Jade and Kaine, waving her arms excitedly in the air as if she's describing something. It could be anything, the club, the trip to Milan. Hell, it could be her box of Caramello Koalas for fuck's sake. Whatever it is, she's holding their attention. Even Kaine is watching her while he rests his hand on his wife's back. Jade alternates between listening intently to Clarissa, to turning to her husband, giving him a little smile, sometimes reaching up to touch his cheek.

It's a picture of perfect happiness, and it makes my heart ache in a way that should make me want to run. Instead, I rush over to join them, I have to get Clarissa out of here before she runs into the pond scum. But she also deserves a moment to shine. She worked so hard to get ready for the night, and after everything that happened at Ravel, I wanted her to revel in the attention.

Not a single man, Kaine excluded, walked by without fixing his eyes on her. Every woman watched her with envy.

And, at least in this moment, she is mine.

"Kaine, I'll be remembering that betrayal," I say, lifting my glass to my face.

He bites back a smirk and buries it in his wife's hair.

"What happened?" Jade asks when Clarissa finishes her story, and not a second before.

Kaine and I share a look. "Jade, your husband owes me big, that's all you need to know. Remind me, okay?"

She just laughs and tugs on Kaine's arm so that it reaches all the way around her back so that his hand rests on her waist.

"You, okay?" I murmur against her ear, taking a deep breath of skin.

Clarissa beams at me. All the apprehension from when we arrived seemingly gone.

Jade grabs another glass of champagne from a passing tray, and says, "Clarissa was just telling us about your trip to Milan. I adore Milan."

"It was just a quick trip. We had to pick up this old thing," I gesture to her dress with a wink

We chat for a little longer, but I'm getting antsy.

I excuse us and pull her to the side. "You ready to go?" She seems surprised, but I don't really want to explain. "I'm just feeling exhausted. You've tired me out, hellion."

She nods, "Of course. I'll be able to go home and change before I go to the club."

"No, darling. You're not changing out of anything. You need to be seen wearing this all night. I'm sorry I'm pulling you away, I just have a throbbing headache." It's not a lie.

She frowns, it quickly gives way to a glint in her eye though and takes my hand. "Come with me."

I don't ask, just let her lead me for once.

We walk down a hall way, past the cloak room and then into the adjoining empty ballroom. It's dark and the chairs are stacked along the wall. No one's using it tonight.

Without a word she pushes me against the edge of the raised stage.

Then anchoring my body with hers, she kisses me, grips my head as she crushes my mouth, her lips smearing her lipstick against my mouth.

"Wow," I whisper against her mouth. While she is more than wanting, needing when I've initiated sex, she's never been the one to make the first move. She signals she's interested with nothing more than a grinding against me with her ass, or holding a kiss too long. But nothing like this.

"Shut up for once, Mr. Matthias Baxter," she whispers hoarsely and then falls to her knees.

Despite looking like a fucking queen, she's the one kneeling at my feet, her dress billowing around her like a pool of liquid gold.

She fumbles with my zipper and reaches in for my already-hardening cock. The anticipation pulses like a drumbeat, faster and faster.

After everything we've done, my cock hasn't been in her mouth yet. I could tell that her experience with sex hasn't been as *extensive* as mine, and I wanted her to initiate her sucking my cock when she wanted to.

And apparently, she wants to now.

She wastes no time, and licks the head of my cock with the tip of her tongue.

"God," I hiss, my cock twitching at the touch.

My reaction burns away the last of her reticence, and her mouth slides down over my cock.

Pressing against the underside of my hardness, her tongue strokes the seam running along the length. Her lips stretch as she struggles to navigate the thickness of my cock that is now inching towards her throat.

Frustrated, she pulls off and makes a soft needy sound, her hand gripping on the base of my cock.

I lift her chin so she's looking at me, can see what she's doing to me. "Easy, darling, just take it easy... there's no rush. It feels so good already," I encourage her.

If I died today, I'd be a happy man, having had her mouth wrapped around me.

She nods, and tries again. Rolling her tongue over my tip, her saliva with the precum already pooling. My body can't refuse her, it reacts to her without my input.

In this case, we agree.

She presses her pursed lips against me; they spread, sucking tightly around my cock as she pushes her head down.

I'm going to fucking die.

My hand runs through her hair, pulling at the hair clip, letting the curls fall down to frame her face.

She pulls off to take another breath, then returns her mouth to my cock, taking a little more of me each time.

I stroke her cheek, focusing on her breathing and almost forget mine in the process. Her jaw relaxes, taking me almost all the way.

"Good girl, take this cock. It's all yours. You've made it yours forever."

It spurs her on and her movements quicken, each stroke making my eyes roll up into my head.

I grip her chin and lift it to look at me, those big beautiful eyes trusting me.

"Make me come, darling."

She nods, her hand gripping me more tightly as she shifts higher up on her knees so she can angle her throat, taking me deeper.

Her mouth strokes me over and over as she quietly gags on my thickness.

"Don't stop, god, you feel so good my little hellion, kneeling there in your designer dress, gagging on my cock. You're perfect for me, did you know that?"

The climax explodes like a supernova in my chest and spreads all over my body, I grunt as my cock hardens almost painfully and I pull out, gripping my cock and jack it into her open mouth.

The cum ribbons on her mouth and cheeks.

"You're a vision, darling."

A goddess on her knees bringing me to mine.

She collects the cum on her face and licks it off her fingers with a satisfying purr.

I groan. How can that look so fucking hot?

I lean back on the stage, headache gone. She pulls my hand away and licks my cock clean, making me jerk, before tucking me back into my pants. Then she stands, fixing her hair as she says, "Ready to go, Mr. Baxter?"

I laugh and pull her close, sucking my cum off her tongue.

Thirty-Two

CLARISSA

IT'S THRILLING TO LEAVE the empty ballroom, still tasting Matthias's cum on my tongue and knowing he tastes it as well. I stand in the warm night air in front of the Plaza waiting for him to return with the car, my feet aching from the new shows. My mind wanders, thinking about all the ways he's going to fuck me in the dress, when someone grips my elbow.

"You look pretty. Wearing that dress for anyone in particular?" Gerry slithers into the space next to me.

The urge to be sick slams into me like a runaway truck. "Yes. Myself."

He snickers, his hand clammy, still grabbing my bare arm. "Always such a sassy little mouth. Even when you were in college, you would come to my house parading around in those little shorts. Were you hoping I'd fuck you?"

If I wasn't surrounded by people coming in and out of the hotel, I'd have kneed him in the groin and punched him in the face. "You're drunk. Get away from me."

An older couple I recognize from the gala gives me a friendly wave as they get in their waiting car. "Good night, Clarissa."

I wave back with a nod, not trusting myself to speak.

Next to me, Gerry snuffles like a pig digging for truffles. "Sweetheart, I think it's time I called in those favors, don't you think? Before things get a little too hot and heavy with my little nephew?

Wouldn't you rather be seen on my arm, the actual CEO of Baxter Enterprises, rather than just some piddly little regional director?"

"He's ten times the man you are."

"But sweetheart, he'll never be yours. He's a fucking skirt chaser. Fucks anything that moves." My eyes close, trying not to listen to all the things I'd said to myself about Matthias. I don't even see when Gerry spins me around to face him. "Whereas I love you."

What the fuck? Just how drunk is he? "Let me go. He's going to be here soon."

"Good. He and I should talk. He might be promising you everything right now, but that's because you're all nice and shiny. I wonder how shiny he's going to think you are when I can tell him I was inside you before he ever was. What do you think he'll think about that?"

Dread mixes with abject regret, and I have to bite back a sob. "It was a mistake. You took advantage of me."

"Well, you would know all about that, wouldn't you? You did the same to Damien. We're cut from the same cloth, sweetheart. Come to me. I promise I'll treat you the way you need to be treated."

"We have *nothing*," I yell, unable to hold back. "You don't feel anything for me. And I certainly feel nothing for you."

I snatch my hand out of his grip and step away, trying not to make a scene.

His hand grabs my neck and he pulls me against him, snarling against my face, uncaring about all the people around us. "You little bitch. I'm going to make you mine anyway I can. Not that sniveling Patrick, not Matthias. And if I don't, I'm taking you all down with me. Check your phone next week. I'm going to tell you what I need from you to take Matthias down. You better decide right now whether you're with me or not."

I push him away, feeling my dress rip down the side.

I'm about to run when I see Matthias standing there.

"I suggest you step away from my fiancée, Gerald."

Gerry snaps around to see his nephew standing there, his car parked at the curb.

His eyes dark and dangerous.

I can't imagine what it must look like to Matthias, Gerry grabbing my arm, his face all but buried in my neck. Fear lodges in every pore, but I refuse to let Gerry see.

"Hello there, Matthias, where have you been all night? So much for representing our company at the gala. It's a good thing I'm here."

Matthias ignores his uncle and just repeats, "I said, step away from her. And take your grubby hands off her as well. I'm not going to ask you again."

Gerry sneers and then drops my hand and holds his up in surrender. "What's the big deal, nephew? I'm just saying hello to my former-now-current again niece-in-law. She looked a little lonely standing here, while you were off doing fuck knows what, fuck knows *who*." He wiggles his eyebrows at me.

Matthias storms over and wedges his body between us. "We're in public, so I'm not going to do what I want to, or say what I want to, because I, unlike you, put my company above all else."

Gerry doesn't move, staring Matthias down. "Your reputation says otherwise."

"You stupid fuck, if you think that me just enjoying myself does half the damage that your ineptness does to our 'image,' you're about as stupid as you look." He gets up in Gerry's face, no doubt getting a face full of rank breath. "Now, I'm just going to say this one more time, *stay the fuck away* from Clarissa. If you so much as think about looking at a even picture of her in the paper, I'm going to choke you with your own gangrenous pickle for a dick."

Gerry stumbles back, pointing a shaky finger in Matthias's face, slurring, "You little shit. When are you going to realize you're a child playing an adult's game? And you're going to cry like a baby when you lose?"

I watch, breath held. I just want it to be over.

Gerry stumbles away, and Matthias doesn't move until he's sure that's he's not coming back.

Matthias pulls off his jacket and wraps it around me as he leads me to the car.

"Come on, Rissie, let's get out of here."

I grab his wrist, needing to explain. " I don't know what he was doing..."

His arms come around to hug me. "Shhh, it's okay. I'm sorry I wasn't there when he appeared. He's a piece of work."

After standing there safe in the circle of his arms for a minute, he helps me into the car. It's a warm night, but I can't stop shivering.

The clock ticks on the dashboard, like it's mocking me, counting the last few moments I have before I'm going to wake up from this dream.

We spend the next week in relative peace after the excitement of the last two weeks, and we fall into a routine trying to fit our two vastly different lives together.

He comes to the club almost every night, or at least is there when I'm done, to take me home. Sometimes he drives me around the city, letting the sound of the night lull me to sleep. One time I woke up, and he'd been driving around the city for over two hours, his hand on mine, as soft music streamed through the speakers, the wind in our hair.

He spoils me constantly. We never talk about finances again after the day he first kissed me, but he takes care of me in a hundred different ways. He pays for everything when we're together as well everything that I might need at the house. He takes me out for expensive lunches, and when one or both of us are too busy to leave the office/club, we'll meet somewhere for a quick picnic lunch, catching up with a sandwich or salad from one of our favorite places.

As the Kids & Care IPO creeps closer, there's no doubt that it's weighing on his mind. He gets almost no sleep, always coming to bed at the same time as me, but whenever I wake up, he's in his office. The demand for Kids & Care shares haven't bounced back as fast as we'd hoped, and time is running out.

We have another meeting with Paula to time the next step in our "marriage"–the wedding. I have a few more months left here before my visa will run out. Matthias tells me that he's hired another immigration lawyer for me and tells me not to call the old one ever again. Something about having heard disreputable things about him. I'm not surprised, that's what happens when you get a number off a telephone.

Day by day, he and I grow closer.

He knows my drink order, I know his favorite setting on the thermostat, he knows what I want for the club in a year's time, I know about his plans for The Americas region of Baxter.

In bed we fit like laser-cut puzzle pieces. He takes me to new heights; I follow him into the light and the dark, taking everything he wants to give me.

Neither of us broaches the topic of our future. The few times we have, the conversations descend into a rehashing of past hurts. So we cocoon in a bubble that lets no one else in.

And when I wake each morning, I wonder if it's going to be our last.

Gerry's text doesn't come.

And I wonder if that was the plan all along. To fuck with my mind so that I'll trigger my own demise?

Anther date looms, an elephant in our bedroom, Damien and My-Linh's wedding. In a week, he'll have to get on a plane and fly away from me.

And no matter that they haven't spoken since Damien found me here, I know Matthias will swim across the ocean to make sure he's there.

He doesn't speak about them much, knowing it's still a sensitive topic for me, but when he does, his affection for My-Linh is clear.

It's the only time I want to scratch his eyes out.

I hate that he likes her, loves her as a sister. I hate that he smiles when he speaks about her, even if it's completely platonic.

I hate that when he leaves, it will be to go to them.

So, I just sit and nod, letting the words wash over me, trying not to ruin the happiness in his voice when he speaks about his family.

Even now, barely speaking to Kylian and Kingsley, and Damien never picking up his calls, I know in his heart of hearts, he believes that all will work out.

Matthias Baxter is an optimist.

Who would've thought it.

As for me, I don't have family, except for those at the club. And it takes Matthias to show me, I'd walk through fire for them.

And if that's not family, what the fuck is?

Matthias: Lunch? The roof? Too public.

Me: For what?

Matthias: Eating my lunch

Me: You're insatiable.

Matthias: Just trying to match you, little hellion. Be there in 30 minutes.

Me: Hurry up, it's going to *get cold here naked waiting for you.*

I smile as the phone buzzes again and I can't wait to see what names he calls me when I see the text isn't from him.

It's from Gerry. *"Be at the Boathouse in the Park in 30 minutes. Meet me or you'll be sorry."*

And I know my time is done.

Thirty-Three

CLARISSA

DREAD AND SHAME SWIRL in my stomach like a whirlpool of deceit.

I cancel my lunch meeting with Matthias, even though it kills me to.

I go, I go to see Gerry to tell him once and for all, I'm not in this with him. Whatever little sick duo we were, buoying each other up with our own desperation, is over.

I'm not the Clarissa of a year ago.

He's already there, I can see him from two hundred feet away, and I force myself to keep moving forward.

"Hello, sweetheart. You're early. Eager to see me?" he says, raising an eyebrow.

"How is it that every single word that comes out of your mouth makes me want to throw up?"

His smug grin falters for just a moment, but the devil knows no shame. "Because that's what people like. Don't let anyone convince you otherwise. You came to me because you want to feel dirty."

"That's because you *are* dirty, Gerry. I came to tell you, I don't *ever* want to hear from you again. "

He shakes his head and reaches for my hand.

I snap my hand back. "Don't touch me."

"He's turned your head. Where is that firecracker that came to me that night asking for help?"

"I didn't come to you for help! *You* took advantage of *me* in my lowest moment! And I wasn't a firecracker. I was broken."

"And I put you back together."

"No, you stomped on my broken pieces to make the foundation for your very own playground. I might feel like Damien did wrong by me, but he's not the one I hate."

"I'm sorry to hear you say that. Because I told you I'm going to destroy them all. One by one. Starting with your precious Matthias. So, you choose what matters more to you–Matthias the man, or Matthias the Director of the Americas division of Baxter?"

"What are you talking about?"

"Just what I said. It's your choice. I tell my dear nephew, warn him, that his new fiancée is a conniving slut, or you help me take him down. You don't have to do anything more than tell me if you find something that is a little shifty, a little not quite right, something the public wouldn't like to learn about their precious 'most eligible bachelor.' He'll do that on his own. All you have to do is find it."

He's crazy. This isn't just a little familial rivalry, this is about destroying him. "You're out of your mind, Gerry."

"No, I'm smart. You think when you laid in my bed, skirt up around your waist, taking it like a bitch in heat, I didn't keep a little insurance?"

I gasp, covering my face with my hand. He wouldn't.

But he would and we both know it.

"You are vile," I choke out. "Why are you doing this to me?" Nothing is making sense. This is beyond anything that I thought he was capable of.

"Didn't you hear me the other night? I *want* you. I might even love you. And I want to break *him*. Two birds." He leans in, and I can't move. I'm frozen. "I'll be hearing from you soon. You looked amazing in that dress, by the way. Remember what I said. It's your choice, sweetheart. I look forward to hearing from you."

My arms come up around me, hugging me tight. But the cold doesn't go away.

And I'm worried I might never be warm again.

An hour after walking around the city trying to clear my head, I return to the club. There's a paper bag sitting on my desk.

The fragrance of tomato and garlic emanate from it, and I know, without opening it that it's wild boar ragu pappardelle from Via Carota. My favorite. One of the times we went there, they had run out, and I was grumpy for the rest of the day.

Matthias.

Still worrying about me even when I'm not here.

I open the bag to look inside and take out the slip of paper lying on top of the food containers.

A chuckle bubbles out of me despite my mood when I see he's scribbled a picture of a Caramello Koala on it with a speech bubble. *"I can't wait to spend some Koala-ty time with you. Miss your smile and brimstone, sweet hellion of my heart."*

Then there's a crude picture of him eating me out.

I let myself enjoy the moment before I tuck the note away in my desk. And try to figure out which fork of the road I'm going to take.

Thirty-Four

MATTHIAS

"Hannah, where's the—?"

"It's on the desk right in front of you, for god's sake, open your eyes!" she yells back from her desk.

"Wow, is that how you speak to your boss?" I say into the intercom, even though we seem to be doing just fine yelling.

"It is when he's interrupted me for the fifth time"—she comes storming into my office—"in the last hour, asking where something is and the answer is the same every time. Right in front of your face!" She jabs at a stack of papers to the left of me.

Oh, I'm the one who had put it there. "I thought they had an orange folder. Did someone change it? If so, that one wasn't my fault."

She glares at me and then takes a breath. "Can I get you something, sir?" her voice uncharacteristically sweet.

"Well, I'd love a cappuccino?"

Her face takes an air of triumph. "Then get it yourself!" She storms out, slamming the door behind her.

Hmmm. Someone's in a bad mood.

And she's not the only one.

Clarissa hasn't been herself in the last few days. I thought it was just all the things going on with the club, but last night she didn't even want me to come to the club, saying that they couldn't even spare one seat. They'd added two tables, but were very cognizant of not making things too crowded, not want to cram her customers in. It wasn't part of the atmosphere she was trying to create.

So, I hadn't gone, just came to pick her up when she texted to say she was done for the night. She'd fallen asleep and then gone directly to bed without a shower.

We haven't been intimate in days.

And I miss her.

Not the sex, although sex with her is mind-blowing, but I miss the physical intimacy. Her body against mine, skin touching skin. I can't even remember the last time she kissed me.

How do you miss someone who's sleeping in your bed?

I'm going to give her a few more days, and then maybe I'll just take her away on a short trip. New York City can push and push and push on you, until you either turn into a diamond, or a pile of rubble. And either can happen to anyone, at any time.

I can't go away until I come back from Damien's wedding, but I'll take her somewhere. Maybe upstate to see a few more ranches, or maybe west for some beach time. The sun and saltwater are natural healing agents.

My office door opens and Hannah comes in looking even more irritated. But she's here, her professionalism is she's still around, even if she's threatened to fire me more than I've threatened to fire her.

"Your two o'clock is here."

I nod.

It's the first of a series of meetings I'm having today, with Patrick's associates and clients he's in deals with.

And I'm going to dismantle what there is of his business, brick by brick.

Me: Lunch?

Clarissa: I can't, I have a meeting.

Me: I feel like I haven't seen you in days.

Clarissa: That's silly, you saw me this morning.

Matthias: You were on the phone and didn't even wave goodbye to me

She doesn't reply.

I feel like a nagging, lovesick teenager.

Come on, Matthias, you're better than that. If you want to see her, go see her. When have you ever sat around just waiting for something you want?

"Hannah, I'll be back at one," I tell her on my way to the elevators.

It must be a riveting document she's reading, because she doesn't even look up. "Don't come back on my account, by all means."

"You're a gem, highlight of my day, Hannah."

She glances at the yellow highlighter in her hand and throws it at my retreating ass.

I stop by the Vietnamese restaurant that just opened up a block from the club and pick up some pork spring rolls and Vietnamese coffee that I know she loves.

There's a spring in my step that hasn't been there since Clarissa has been distant. I've never been a passive man, taking what I want has always been my wheelhouse.

The front door of the club is open when I get there. They must be working early to get the club ready for my friend, Tyson with a T tonight. I'm looking forward to it; even if I have to stand behind the bar with James, I'm going to be there.

There's chatter in the club when I enter, and I follow it into the main room. She's there. With another man's hand on hers, giving it an affectionate squeeze.

My ears roar with jealousy. What the fuck. "Well, hello."

Clarissa's head snap around at my voice. "Matthias! What are you doing here?" She doesn't sound shamed, just irritated.

I lift the bag of food. "I was bringing my fiancée some lunch, but apparently I'm also interrupting something."

She sits back, her hands slipping out of the other guy's, folding her arms as she narrows her eyes at me. "I *told* you I had a meeting."

"So, I see." I want to slap myself. If I thought I sounded like a lovesick teenager before, now I sound like a jealous husband.

I drop the food on the bar and walk over to the table, Clarissa's eyes following me.

As I get closer, I realize I know the guy. I can't remember his name, but he definitely looks familiar.

"Matthias," I say, extending my hand.

"Hello!" He greets me cheerfully as he takes my hand. "I'm Halifax. We met at Leanne's a few weeks ago, remember?"

Right. I knew he looked familiar. Was that really only a few weeks ago? A little over a month, I think. Time with Clarissa has felt like just a second and an eternity, both at once. No wonder I don't know my brain from my asshole.

I give him a friendly smile. "Of course, Halifax, how are you doing, man? It's good to see you. I'm sorry, I didn't place you. It's a little dark in here." In my soul, maybe.

"It's okay, we were just—"

"I *told* you I was busy, why would you come here?" Clarissa interrupts, her face a swirling dark storm.

Halifax clears his throat and leans away from her as I mouth an *"I'm sorry"* to him before addressing her. "I just came to bring you some food. I know how you forget to eat if I don't remind you."

She slides her chair out, ignoring the squeak of the chair legs on the floor, and grabs my arm, pulling me over to the bar.

"I run a business, Matthias," she hisses, her anger hardly simmering, rather boiling over. Hot, spitting oil.

"I know, darli—"

She throws her hand up. "I wouldn't just barge into your office if you had told me you were in a meeting. It's not professional."

"I'm sorry! Like I said, I was just dropping some food by." That's a lie and even I know it. "I just miss you. I feel like we haven't had any time together for a week. My heart misses its hellion."

There's a thawing of her eyes, and then she blinks and it's gone. "I'm busy. I'm trying to make this club work, Matthias. I spent two days away from it when we went to Milan."

"I know. It wasn't planned, but it all worked out, didn't it?"

"Luckily! And with all the extra traffic from the"—she rubs her temple and drops her voice—"the fake engagement, it's just taking a lot of juggling so that we can fit more people through while keeping up the service that we're being known for."

I want to reach out for her, but the fear of rejection holds me back. "I get it. Can I help in any way?"

She nods. "Yes. When I tell you I'm in a meeting, *please,* respect that I'm in a meeting."

My jaw twitches, she keeps pushing me away, and I don't know how to bring her back. "Fine. I'll go, but promise me you'll eat some of the food."

She sighs. "Matthias."

"Promise or I'm not leaving."

She lets out a little snort and rolls her eyes, and for just a second, it's just us again. I pull her in and kiss her, her scent calming me, her skin against mine, bringing me peace. She leans into the kiss, and everything is okay.

Then she pulls away.

"I miss you," I whisper.

She just sighs, and murmurs under her breath, "Maybe that's something you're going to have to get used to."

Aside from the total cold shoulder Damien has given me since the day he saw me with Clarissa, my other brothers are mostly on speaking terms with me again. Kylian, if anything, he's been around more than usual, but also, as I predicted, he's no help as to how I can get Damien to thaw out. But as someone who is dating his best friend's little sister, and almost got killed in the process, I'm not sure I would take any advice he has to heart, anyway.

Kingsley does talks to me, but only about work, and to remind me to work things out with Damien.

Er, thanks, big bro. I hadn't thought of that.

I've called, texted, emailed, sent messages through Melissa, Damien's assistant, basically everything but carrier pigeon. At this point, I wouldn't rule it out, though.

There's only one more way to get to him.

My-Linh.

Neither of them were at last week's Wednesday meeting. That's the only time one of us has missed a meeting other than when Kylian was lying in a hospital bed. While I wish Damien was returning my calls, I never ever want to experience what I felt when Kylian was hooked up to all those machines.

I call My-Linh and she answers on the second ring.

"Matthias." Just my name. But she answers.

"Hey, honey, how have you been?"

"Um, okay, you know. Wedding's this weekend." Her sweet voice sounds sad rather than tired. And if it's because of me, I don't know what to do with myself.

"I'll be there, My-Linh."

"You will, Matthias?" Her voice lightens, lifts. Hopeful.

"I'm really s—"

"Who is that?" I hear Damien's voice in the background. "Is that him? Give me the phone, My-Linh."

"But..." she starts but never finishes.

There's a scuffle on the other line, and I hear her sigh in the background.

"Why are you calling My-Linh?" Damien growls into the phone.

It instantly makes me defensive. "Why not? She's about to be my sister. I love her. I haven't gotten to talk to her in weeks because you won't come to the Wednesday meeting. And I miss you too, asshole. I wanted to talk to you."

He scoffs, I can see his fucking face all screwed up in that grumpy fuck way that he has. "If I wanted to talk to you, I would've picked up your calls, answered your texts, replied to your email."

"Well, you're really going to love the carrier pigeon coming."

He pauses. "Don't do it." He wouldn't put it past me. It tickles me he knows me that well.

"Come on, man. We need to talk," I urge him.

"Don't call My-Linh again. She has a heart; she might actually answer."

"Bro, it's the week of your wedding, can't we—"

He cuts me off. He doesn't want to hear it. "Come. Don't come. It's up to you. My-Linh and everyone will want to see you. But stay the fuck away from me."

"Dami—"

He hangs up.

Fuck!!

I slam my hand on my desk, and it sends a jarring pain up my arm.

Why can't he just sit down with me for two fucking minutes and help him understand?

People change. *He* changed for fuck's sake! In what universe did we ever think that Damien was going to be the first of us to marry for love? He didn't believe in ever giving himself to someone like this. After the number that our parents did on us with the worst marriage in the history of dysfunctional marriages, the word "marriage" made all of us physically convulse and fall into a drunken stupor.

And now we're here.

Him loving someone so much I know without any doubt if someone hurt half a hair on her head, he would torture them until not a drop of blood was left in their body.

And now, I just want him to know... I know how that feels. I want him to know that my and Clarissa's arrangement, to start out was, was for business, now it's so much more.

My heart hurts. I miss my brother.

And I need Clarissa.

I pick up the phone and dial her.

She doesn't answer my call.

Two times.

Three times.

Four.

Nothing.

"Clarissa. I need to hear your voice. Please," I finally say into her voice mail.

Despondence settles in my body.

And I do the only thing I know how to do when my brain feels fogged.

I run.

I run until the thoughts can't keep up.

Grabbing the car keys, I run down to the building's garage, jumping into the Audi, enjoying the smell of the leather seats. It's a Pavlovian response, reminding me about all the speeds I've reached in this vehicle. Turning out onto Broad Street, I make for FDR drive, weaving in and out of traffic.

The yellow light ahead goads me, and I rev the engine, passing the intersection just as the light turns red.

There's a clearing in the road ahead and I press on the accelerator, swerving into the empty lane, a laugh slipping out, the air cooling as it whooshes through my ear.

Shit.

Sirens.

Come the fuck on.

Fuck that.

I skid between two cars and then swerve into the left lane, rushing forward, knowing there's no way they're going to get to me.

"Let's go!" I shout, adrenaline pumping through.

On the bridge, the traffic moves faster than usual, but not fast enough. Behind me, I can hear the sirens, the cop car following me over to Brooklyn.

The traffic empties into Brooklyn and I make a sharp turn to take me to Downtown Brooklyn,

Fuck!

A crowd of kids crossing up ahead.

I swerve into a side street, not expecting traffic, and slam into the back of the garbage track. The impact jarring all the way through my body.

Behind me, the cop car catches up, blocking me in.

"Get out of the car with your hands up," the voice comes through the car's PA system and I know I'm done.

I climb out of the car, hands raised over my head."

"Hello, officers, fancy seeing you here."

It takes Clarissa almost three hours to come and bail me out, even though I call her almost as soon as I get to the station.

And when she arrives, she looks about as happy with me as the cops.

"What is wrong with you?" she hisses as soon as I'm released.

"What? It was just a car accident. It happens. You look good, by the way. Finally, we get to spend some time together," I say, truly happy to see her.

If eyes could strangle, hers would be wrapped around my neck, choking the life out of me. "Is that why you called me and not your lawyer?"

"Nope, he's out of the country right now. Probably sleeping. So, I didn't want to waste my call on him. You didn't answer my call either, by the way, but at least you checked your voicemail." It sounds accusing, and maybe I mean it that way.

She tries to hail a cab, but none stop. "I've been busy. How many times do I have to tell you that?"

"Until I believe it, Clarissa. Until I believe that after spending every moment together for weeks, now you can't stand to be in the same room with me for two minutes, other than when we're asleep. Something is going on, and just saying you're busy isn't going to cut it." Kevin pulls over and I guide her towards the car. "So come on, I'll drop you off at the club. I have to get ready to leave for Damien's wedding tomorrow."

"Matthias," she hesitates, grappling with something within herself.

"What?" I ask, not daring to hope.

"Nothing. Um, I talked to the police, they said that they're not going to press charges. Pay for the damages, but that's it. I don't know how you managed that, but..."

I kiss her on the cheek before she can stop me. "I told you, I have an adoring audience in every room," I joke. "I thought you would've known that by now."

She looks pained. "You're going to get in trouble one of these days. And I'm not going to be there to bail you out."

I open the car door for her and she climbs in.

"Then, darling, nothing else will matter."

Thirty-Five

CLARISSA.

My anxiety is at an all-time high. It's been growing since the night of the gala and now I can barely get through the day without having at least one full blown anxiety attack.

And the only person who's ever really helped me, the only person I've felt comfortable seeing me that way... is the one person I can't call.

Every day, I curse Gerry for what he's done to me, for what he's done to my relationship with Matthias. But I can't be with Matthias knowing that one way or another, something is about to rock our relationship to the core. Maybe I'm checking out so that when it happens, somehow, I'm still going to be able to survive it.

But it hurts.

It aches knowing he's just within reach, but that he was never really mine.

But I know now, I am his.

Completely, utterly, desperately.

And I always will be.

There's a knock on the door and Clementine calls out to me.

"Mr. Baxter is here to see you."

My body reacts before my brain does and I leap to my feet before I remember that I'm trying to distance myself from him. I smooth my hands over my dress and follow Clementine out, preparing my face for when I see him.

"Hello, sweetheart."

Gerry.

If I had a gun, I would shoot him. Right between the eyes the pop a bottle of champagne to celebrate.

"Please leave," I say, keeping my voice down. But I don't want him here. In this place that had become my safe space.

"I won't be here long, I just wanted to remind you that the time to make a choice is coming. Clock is ticking."

"I told you, I'm not doing anything to help you take Matthias down. He hasn't done anything wrong."

Gerry sneers. "But he will, sweetheart, he will."

He looks around, running his finger along my name on the door. "This is such a lovely place. I think I might book a regular table here. Just think, we'll be able to see each other every night, wouldn't you like that?"

Then he leaves.

And the room swirls around me.

I grab the hostess's podium but it doesn't help. I slip to the ground, my brain forgetting how to breathe.

Thirty-Six

MATTHIAS

"FASTER, KEVIN, FOR FUCKS sake!" I shout, heart frantic.

"Yes, sir, there's a lot of traffic."

"I'm sorry... fuck! I'm going to run." I jump out of the car, it's only another four blocks, the call from Clementine still ringing in my ears, *"You need to come, something's wrong with Clarissa."*

I'd been on the way to the airport, and made Kevin turn the car around.

It's probably another anxiety attack, but she hasn't been telling me if she's been having them since we stopped really talking. She shouldn't have to go through it alone.

My lungs threaten to explode in my chest as I run to the club, pumping my arms, the heat bearing down on my back as I sprint.

"Where is she?!" I yell when I get to the club.

"She's in her office, she crawled in there and won't open the doo—"

I'm at her office door in seconds. "Clarissa, open this fucking door, right now!"

She doesn't answer as I bang on the glass, almost afraid it'll shatter. I look through the window, and she's sitting on the floor with her back against her desk, out of the range of the door. She's not refusing to open the door, she just can't.

I slam my shoulder against it, I can't believe I'm still doing this. I can't believe that so much has changed, yet so much is the same. I take a few steps back and charge at the door.

It swings open and I fall onto the floor next to her, pulling her to me, rubbing her back as I whisper. "I'm here, darling, I'm here. You're okay." She's shaking so hard, sweat drenching her body. "Oh, darling, look at me. Look at me, come on. We're going to get you through this."

She tries to lift her head, but it's too hard.

I gently prop up her chin with my palm, and lean down, level with her face.

"Look at me, there's a good girl." Those dazed eyes reach into my chest and rip out my heart. "Now we're going to breathe together, okay?" I cross my legs so I'm sitting right in front of her. "I'm panting too, see? I ran here to see you. Now we're going to breathe together. On three."

One hand on her face, one hand reaching around rubbing her back. I take a deep breath.

She doesn't do anything, just keeps gasping. Panicked.

"It's okay, Rissie. We're going to do it again. Don't think about a single thing other than breathing when I breathe." I swallow, focusing on her and only her. "One, two, three," I say and then take a deep breath. Her jaw drops a little as she tries to take a deeper breath. "Good! Oh, my love, that was so good. Another one. Come on. One, two, three, breathe."

She copies me again.

"And out," I exhale and she mirrors me. "Again. One, two three, breathe, deep deep deep!"

She copies, her eyes fluttering, trying to focus on mine. Sometimes she slips and starts to gasp again, but then I grab her chin and she focuses. "Such good big breaths, you're doing great, darling. You're really helping me, too."

Slowly, she starts to breathe on her own, her shakes still there but faded to a tremor.

My hand draws hundreds of circles on her back. "Good, now tell me, what are five things you can see right now."

I take her through the grounding exercise, and by the end, her eyes are focused, and she runs her hand over her forehead, wiping away the sweat.

And when she says, "I'm okay," I almost cry with relief. Arms wrapped around her, I pull her to me, hugging her so tightly, I feel her heart beating against my chest, and hope she can feel mine.

"That's good, darling, that's so good," I say, before I choke up. "You're going to be just fine. I'm here."

And we sit there, until the sunlight outside her office window turns into night.

***

"I need you to pack a bag when we get home," I say when we're in the car going back to my apartment later that afternoon so she can rest.

"What?" she frowns. "What for?"

Things have become so hard, I feel like every conversation is a fight. "I can't leave you to go to Damien's wedding worried about how you're going to have another panic attack and I'm not here."

She looks away, training her eyes out the window. "I'll be—"

I slide over until I'm pressed up against her. "For the love of fuck, Clarissa, if you say you're okay, I think I'm actually going to tell Kevin to drive this car right off the fucking bridge. You are *not* okay. And I'm not talking about your anxiety, I understand how hard that is for you, and I think you're doing your best. I'm talking about what is going on with us! Something's happened, and if you're not ready to talk about it, I don't like it, but I understand. And I'm going to give you a little time before I shake it out of you. But you are *not* fine. That was not a normal attack, something triggered you. And I'm not going to be on other side of the world and get a call. I will lose what's left of my ever-loving mind."

Her forehead crinkles and I can't tell if she's frowning or crying. "But I can't go with you. Not to *Damien's wedding*. In what world do you that that can happen?"

I know she's right. But I have my reasons too. I won't be able to enjoy my brother's wedding, and he deserves for me to be present on this most important day of his life. "Please, just come with me and we'll work it out." My tongue darts over my lips, my mouth suddenly dry. "I'll talk to him."

"And the bride?" Clarissa asks. It's the first time she's even acknowledged My-Linh.

"She'll understand." I think she will, I just don't know how I feel about forcing her to.

"Will she?" Clarissa asks, sounded incredulous.

"You don't know her."

She stares out the window, jaw twitching. "No. I guess I don't."

The car parks outside of the building. I link my fingers with hers, and she doesn't move her hand away.

Considering how she's been this last week, that's a win.

"I'm going to wait out here for twenty minutes; if you don't come down. I'm coming up." She starts to protest but then stops when she sees the look on my face. "The second to last thing I want to do is miss my brother's wedding. The last thing is leaving you here without me. And if you think that I can do that, then maybe you don't know me as well as I thought you did."

I turn to the window, wanting to give her space to make her decision. "Clock's ticking, Clarissa."

An unreadable look flashes across her face, but then she gets it under control.

"I'll come. I'll be down in ten minutes," she says, and gets out of the car.

We don't talk on the flight. I work and she sleeps, exhausted from her anxiety attack.

Despite the mountain of work that I need to catch up on, I glance up almost every fifteen seconds to make sure she's okay. At one point she murmurs something under her breath about choices and I wonder if that has anything to do with what triggered her. But she quietens when I tell her she's okay, and she settles in for the rest of the flight.

Kylian meets us at the small airport we fly into after we refuel in Sydney. I hadn't wanted to land the plane on the Baxter Winery property without knowing how Damien's going to react. Kylian waves, his car parked on the runway like he's some fifties movie star.

"Hey, bro!" he shouts, jumping up and down.

My heart swells at the sight of him. I still thank the stars every day that he's okay. He still sends me pictures of his injuries as if to remind him that I'm *"like just soooo lucky to still have his baby brother."*

That's especially true considering if he weren't here, then Damien would be the next baby brother, and that's not going so well.

"Hi, Clarissa," Kylian greets her, friendly but not overly so.

"Hi Kylian, you look well," she replies, voice a little nervous.

"Not really." He shrugs. "I'm just that good-looking."

"Oh, my god," I snort. "I see Kiara's been taking good care of that ego. I'm going to have to have a chat with her. Kiara's Kylian's girlfriend," I explain to Clarissa, although I've been talking about them all for weeks, in the hopes that come the day she has to meet them, she might feel like she knows them.

"Fiancée," Kylian corrects me.

"Shit, I keep forgetting. All my brothers have been tied down. Poor things," I joke, but as soon as I say it, realization strikes. "Oops. I mean... being tied down is the best."

"Ooooh, you're in trouble now. Clarissa, we can drop him over the Barossa dam, what do you think?"

I turn to Clarissa worried about how she's reacting but she is actually laughing. The first laugh I've heard from her in over a week. I smile and slide my arms over her shoulders and she gives me a gentle smile.

"Sure, but how about this idea - we find a church with a really big spire and drop him over that instead?" Clarissa says, ganging up on me.

Kylian laughs, his warmth infectious. "Good idea. Guess that's partly why this ugly fucker keeps you around."

She pats the back of my back as I open the car door for her. "That plus he can't drive for shit."

"Hey!" I exclaim.

In the car, I watch in the mirror as Clarissa looks out the window while we make our way to the Barossa. It's a short drive from the airport, with interesting landscape as farmland turns into miles and miles and miles of vineyards.

It's almost winter here, but it's still relatively warm, the sky clear and the scent of earthiness in the air. I love it here and I'm so jealous of Damien getting to live a short plane ride away. I'm just going to have to find a place of my own.

"Does he know we're here?" Clarissa asks after we're almost halfway there.

"Um, he knows Matthias is coming," Kylian answers, glancing at me. "We weren't really sure what else to tell him."

She nods. "It's okay. I'm just going to stay in the room. I won't come to any of the wedding activities. They won't want me there. And I don't blame them. I'm not here to cause any trouble, Kylian."

"I know. Matthias wouldn't bring you if you were. That much, I believe. We'll work something out."

I reach around the seat and touch her knee, giving it a little squeeze. She puts her hand on mine to let me know she's okay.

When she's not looking, I mouth "thank you" to my youngest brother, who can also be the most mature amongst us sometimes.

Kylian parks the car around the back entrance of the estate and ushers us into one of the rooms. "I'll let you know about what's going on, okay?" he mutters to me. "I'll see you around, Clarissa," he calls out and she gives him a grateful wave.

I feel like I'm being torn a thousand different ways. I want to go see my brothers and soon-to-be sisters-in-law, but I can't just leave Clarissa here. That's not fair. I dragged her here, I can't just dump her to stay in a room the whole weekend.

She laughs and shakes her head. "Your face is like a billboard. You don't play poker, do you?"

I run my hand over my face, hoping to wipe away some of the evidence of my thoughts. "No! And if Kiara asks you if you want to play, say no immediately. She will chew you up, spit you out and feed you to the possums." I sit down on the bed next to her. "I'm okay here."

She pulls out her laptop, and plugs it into the wall. "I came because you wouldn't go if I didn't. So I'm here. If I need something, I'll text you; otherwise, pretend I'm not here. I'm going to be fine. Just go."

I wrestle with myself for a moment and then remember that she's right. Damien and My-Linh are my reason, and they deserve the best of me.

I stand up and smooth out my travel wrinkled pants. "I'm just going to have a look to see who is here, and I'll be back okay? Don't run off with some other man before I return"

She laughs, something about being away from the life that we have in New York has lifted a weight from her shoulders. "Just go, I'm sick of your face anyway. I forgot how good looking Kylian is." She tilts her head, sizing me up with a look. "You think he and Kiara are going to last?"

Her squeals fill the room as I launch myself at her and wrestle her onto the bed, then give her a deep kiss. "I'm going to come back later and finish that thought."

"I'll be waiting."

And when I leave the room, I'm whistling without even knowing it.

Thirty-Seven

CLARISSA

THE VIEW OUT OF the window is breathtaking, and a small and niggling voice almost wants to resent Damien for never bringing me here.

But I don't blame him. We were only ever just friends, and we made a bad decision thinking that we could have a marriage of convenience, that we could live that way forever. It just so happens that he came to that conclusion before I did. And I took it as a slight when I shouldn't have. Falling in love with someone, or not being fallen in love with someone shouldn't feel personal. We've all taken for granted how often it really happens.

I wonder if I would have come to that conclusion without having experienced these last few weeks with Matthias. Or would I have forever thought that wanting, wishing for a healthy relationship born of love, was a pipe dream?

The sun is low in the sky, and it paints an orange hue all over the vineyard. A group of parrots fly over the vineyard, sunlight on their wings. Not *group*. A *pandemonium* of parrots. Only Australians could say that with a straight face, I think affectionately.

I watch them fly off into the sky. Utterly majestic.

I could live here forever.

Checking the time, I call the club and tell everyone that they're going to have to take charge for a few days. When I hang up, my tongue sticks to the roof of my mouth. I'll never get over how dry Australia is. I need some water, maybe there's a bathroom or kitchen nearby.

I crack the door open to make sure the hallway is clear and step outside, almost colliding with my ex-fiancé coming around the corner.

"Whoa, whoops, I'm so—" Damien starts, his face hardening as soon as he realizes it's me. "You have got to be kidding me!"

"What's going on?" Kingsley asks as he turns the corner with the rest of the family. "Oh. Clarissa."

I know it's rude not to answer, but I can't move.

Of all the things that could've happened this was the absolute worst. In the back of the group I see My-Linh and a tall, slender, woman with hair almost all the way down her back turn to each other, mouths dropped open. The bride and her bridesmaid, I'm guessing.

'"What are you doing here, Clarissa? Actually, I don't care. Just leave. Now!" Damien's voice booms over me.

"Whoa, whoa, take it easy, bro," Kylian cuts in, pushing in between his brother and me. "Look, let's just sit down and talk about this."

"Where is he?" Damien growls, eyes still on me.

I open my mouth and sounds actually comes out. "He, er, he went looking for you."

Kylian nods enthusiastically. "And look! Clarissa's found you. See how helpful she is?"

Damien pushes his brother out of the way so he can tower over me. "Shut up, Kylian. Why is she here? Did you know she was coming?"

This time, Kylian isn't as emphatic in his reply. "Um, I wouldn't say 'know'. I mean, do we ever really know anything?""

"Not helping, baby," the tall woman in the back shouts. She must be Kiara.

"I'm trying, Kiki," Kylian says out of the corner of his mouth.

"I think you're failing though," she says, matter-of-factly and I can't help being fascinated by them despite the fact that my ex-fiancé is looking at me like he wants to bury me in the grounds of the Baxter Winery.

"Damien, I promise I'm not here to cause any trouble. Tell him, Kylian."

Kylian shakes his head, covering his mouth. Sure, now he shuts up.

Damien bears down on me, face a picture of anger and disgust. "You don't get it, do you? This almost didn't happen because of you."

His words hurt. "All this"—I wave my hand in the air —"was supposed to happen with us! Or have you conveniently forgotten now that you have someone who'll cater to every whim?" I regret what I say as soon as it's out of my mouth. I'm just angry. And we've never really sat down and talked about what happened.

"Damien, you didn't know...? A small voice in the back finally speaks up and My-Linh walks to the front.

Damien's face falls, softening when he looks at her. "My-Linh, of course not!"

She takes turns looking at me then him. "I think I need some air," she says, and pushes past us so fast, all I sense is a waft of cherry blossom.

"I'll go talk to her," I say, feeling genuinely sorry that I'm ruining her day.

Damien sticks his arm out, blocking me. "The fuck you will. I think you've done enough. Just go." He runs after her, and I see him in a whole new light.

If I had ever run like that from him, he'd just forget he ever knew me.

Kylian sighs. "Well, that went well, don't you think, Kiki?"

Kiara steps forward to touch his arm, shaking her head as she eyes me. "Shush, just shush, baby."

He frowns. "I can't shush. And now I'm in a pickle. We all know I'm My-Linh's favorite and Damien's definitely. Kingsley, you adore me, and Clarissa, it's safe to say I'm your favorite Baxter brother?"

"Get to the point," Kiara says, even though she's smiling at him.

He gives her a little kiss on the tip of her nose before he says, "My point is, should I go after them, or should I stay and wait for Matthias with you guys? I'm his favorite, you know."

I genuinely feel utterly guilty. I don't know what to do, other than go back inside the room, there's no place for me in this conversation. "Go make sure they're okay. I'm fine, I'm just going to go inside and wait for Matthias. I truly did not mean nor want to spoil this weekend as someone you hate. I was just coming out to get some water and it was just really bad timing."

Kylian sighs making his way down the hallway.

Kiara starts to follow but then stops in front of me. "She's my best friend, you know. And I don't have best friends. Never wanted one, never needed one. Until I met her. I've only known her six months but I would die for her. She's the best person you'll ever meet. She'll even learn to like you more than you like yourself. So she doesn't deserve this, not on her wedding, not *ever*. I don't know why you're here, but maybe you should've thought about someone other than yourself for once."

It's only me and Kingsley left. And despite all the years I've known the family, this might be the only time he and I have been alone together.

"We don't hate you, Clarissa. We just don't trust you. And in this family, with everything we go through and all the work that we do, trust is everything." He doesn't break eye contact once. Strong. Unnerved. The opposite of how I'm feeling. "You've betrayed one of us before. It's hard to get over that. That's all. I'll go find Matthias. He should talk to Damien. Until then, I'm sorry, but I think it's best if you stay in your room."

He fixes me with his serious face and then leaves.

I run into the room, face blazing as I shove all my things into my bags. Damien's right, I shouldn't be here. I shouldn't think that I can just appear on his wedding day after everything and think it's okay, even if it's with Matthias.

Tears streaming down my face as I check my phone for an Uber. Shit! It's going to take half an hour to get here. Stupid fucking rural towns!

I fling my phone across the room, tears streaming down my face as I remember the looks on their faces as they saw me.

People who I used to call friends, as close as family.

I peek out the window, trying to figure out the lay of the land and how I can escape, when my phone buzzes. I consider ignoring it, but then I realize it might be the Uber.

It's not.

Matthias: Don't run. Rule no.5, remember? No more running. I'm going to talk to Damien. Kingsley told me what happened. Please. Please. Please. My darling, please don't run from me again. My heart can't take it. I've missed you so much these last few days, I couldn't even breathe. And now you're back. I can't take it if you're gone again.

Guilt drops on me like a two-ton weight, and my legs buckle, collapsing me on the bed.

Kiara was right. I was only thinking of myself again.

When will I learn that life is about more than that?

Thirty-Eight

MATTHIAS

I KNOCK THREE TIMES before there's an answer from inside.

"What?" Damien's grumpy voice growls from inside.

I open the door; he sees me and growls again, his second growl somehow even louder and grumpier than the first one. "Well, that was friendly."

He stares at his feet and then up at me. "What the fuck is she doing here, Matthias?"

"I had to bring her. Neither of us wanted her to have to come. I promise you that. I practically had to threaten that I wasn't going to come if she didn't come with me. But... I couldn't leave her. You would understand if you knew why. Maybe she'll tell you one day, but it's not for me to say."

He gets up from the bed and walks toward the open window. A hot breeze blows in at that exact moment. "My-Linh's crying." His voice is tight, angry.

"I'm sorry. I'll talk to her." I don't know if I should move closer to him, but something tells me he might need some space while we talk.

He lets out a little joyless chuckle. "Good luck. Kiara's barricading the door, Kylian tried to see My-Linh, apparently saying something about him being her favorite, and Kiara whipped him with a bouquet."

I let out a snort. She really is the perfect woman for Kylian.

"You're making a big mistake," he says.

The laugh dies on my lips. "Maybe. But I don't think so."

He tucks his hands into his pockets, not looking at me. "It's not just about the company anymore, is it?"

I shake my head. "No."

"I can tell. I don't think you'd still be doing this if it was."

"I wouldn't. Not knowing how you feel about it. She's different, man. I don't know if she's different because I just didn't know her before, or if she's just actually changed. But she's remarkable. You'd like her."

He purses his lips as he sits back on the bed. "I *did* like her. She was my friend until we... made a stupid decision."

"My-Linh would like her," I add.

He looks at me, unimpressed. My-Linh likes everyone.

"You can't convince me she's changed. People don't change that much. The core of what they want stays the same."

I wonder if he's speaking from a place of experience or from anger. Because I know that he knows better.

"You changed. Did you ever think you'd be sitting in the bridal suite the day before getting married, worried about some woman crying?"

He flinches at "some woman" just the way I mean him to. Before My-Linh, would he have cared if I referred to any woman he was with as "some woman"? Fuck no.

"I don't know how much I've changed," he sighs. "But I guess deep down, I just always wanted to be loved."

There's nothing to say about that. Of all of us, our mother fucked with his head more than the rest of us put together. And that's just been a hole he's always needed filled.

"I know you did, man. That's why I'm incomparably happy that you found someone who loves you like My-Linh does." I sit down on the bed next to him, taking away the napkin that he's shredded into a pile at his feet. "And Clarissa *has* changed. She has. If you saw Malt and how she runs it, you would see just how much she's changed and how hard she's worked. Her staff love her. She makes mistakes, and she holds herself accountable for them, and they respect her for that. You would be so impressed. And proud. I know she's caused so much trouble in your life. In yours more than anyone's. But she was your friend. And I know under all that anger, you still care about her. She made some mistakes. We all have."

He flexes his hands. Over and over and over for a minute. Maybe I shouldn't have taken his comfort tissue away. "Do you love her?" he asks after a long minute.

I don't have an answer.

Not one I'm ready to admit, anyway. Not to him, not to her. And certainly not myself.

"Ah, I guess I have my answer," my brother says.

"What?" I snap.

He tucks his lips over his teeth, trying not to laugh. "I'm just saying you answered my question."

I frown. "No, I didn't. I didn't say a fucking word."

This time he doesn't bother to restrain the laugh. "You did with your face."

"We have the same face, bro!"

He throws his hands up in the air. "That's how I know! That's how I know all of you fucktards. You're my blood and flesh. Literally."

And we laugh. Because what else do you do in a situation like this? I could punch him, but My-Linh will never forgive me if he's got a black eye in all the wedding photos.

Finally, when the laughs fade, I say, "I don't know what I'm doing. I just know that if I don't try, I'm going to regret it for the rest of my life."

He cocks his eyebrow. "So, you thought you'd try it at your brother's wedding, who also just happens to be her ex-fiancé, whom she blackmailed into leaving the bride so he could marry her?"

"Touché."

He sighs, reaches over, and pats me on the back. The simple gesture makes my whole body sag with relief. I haven't wanted to admit how much his silence has stressed me out the last few weeks. I hate fighting with all my brothers. We so rarely do. We've just put so many measures in place, in our personal and business relationships, to help avoid that, that most things can be settled with an open talk.

He lets out a long breath. "I don't trust her. But I don't have to. You do." He searches my eyes for the truth. "Do you?"

"I think so." A part of me niggles, maybe questioning if I can really trust someone after only truly knowing them for a few weeks.

"Find out."

I nod. He's right. And then I ask the question I came here to ask. "Can she come to the wedding? She won't if you don't want her to. She's not a bitch."

Damien snorts.

"Okay, fine, but she's not cruel. *Anymore.*"

He's about to answer when we hear a stampede from the bathroom and look over to see Kingsley and Kylian file into the room, having obviously been eavesdropping and deciding the serious part of the conversation is over.

Damien rolls his eyes at them before saying, "As far as the wedding, it's fine by me. But I'm not the one whom you have to talk to about that. I'm just the groom." He looks serious again. "And it really is up to My-Linh. All of it. If Clarissa's going to be a part of our lives, she has to be okay with it. I love you. You're my big brother. You're literally my flesh and blood. But make no mistake. My-Linh is my heart and soul. You know the choice I'll have to make if she's not okay with this."

I would expect nothing less from him. "No problem, My-Linh adores me."

Kylian snorts and slaps me on the back of the head. "Maybe. But her henchman might not."

"Shit."

Thirty-Nine

CLARISSA

I DON'T REALIZE I'M just sitting staring out the window until there's a gentle knock on the door that pulls me out of my thoughts. It's been almost an hour since Matthias texted; it must've been a long talk for him only to be coming back now.

"Come in."

There's a pause before the door handle turns and it reveals My-Linh standing there with a bag.

"Hi," she says nervously. "I wasn't sure I should come. You probably don't want to talk to me. I just wanted to drop off some drinks and food. I thought you might be thirsty."

"Actually, I'm parched," I admit. "Please, come in."

She holds the bag out to me. I look inside. There are bottles of water and soda. And a bag of Caramello Koalas. She can't know.

"Thank you," I say gratefully. "I'm sorry. I'm really not here to cause any problems. I..... I couldn't be alone. It's hard to explain."

This is a surreal moment. I'm not entirely sure I'm awake. I've spent so much time hating this woman. And here she is, on her wedding day, making sure I don't starve to death.

She shakes her head kindly. "You don't have to explain. I believe you. Can I come in? I don't know where everyone has gone, and Kiara's trying to find someone to play poker with to work out some of her stress so I need to hide.""

I gesture into the room. "You're the bride."

She doesn't sit, just stands next to me at the window, as we watch a little sparrow pick at a rose.

"I won't take up too much of your time. I just have two questions. You can answer or not, it's up to you." I just nod. Her face looks determined. "Why did you do what you did to Damien?"

A long exhale whooshes through my lips. She didn't come to play. And I have no intention of sugar coating any of it. I'm past that now. I can't ever move on if I don't take accountability for what I did.

A deep breath.

"I was a very different person a year ago. I was unhappy. I didn't know who I was. I was cruel and selfish. And Damien had reneged on our deal and I was mad. Back then, I cared how people in our society thought about me. I hated the things that everyone was saying behind my back, hell some of it was right to my face. I couldn't get a date to save my life. I was Damien Baxter's ex. No one wanted to touch me with a ten-foot pole. It hurt my ego in a hundred different ways. So, I hit him where it hurt, his family, his company."

I take another deep breath and glance over at her. Her face is neutral, and she's listening intently.

I continue, "I want you to know that the whole time we were 'together' again, he didn't touch me once. He didn't hold my hand, he didn't reach out and accidentally graze my fingers passing the salt. He didn't help me zip up a dress. He didn't help me out of a car, he didn't even open a car door for me. He didn't touch me one time. We didn't share a bedroom, and barely shared a life. He didn't talk to me about you, he didn't talk to me about anything. He made it clear that he was there against his will. And then one day, he left again. Because it turns out there is one thing he loves more than his company. *You*. I did it because I thought I was never going to find love. That it was a fairy tale. And when he told me he was in love with you, I thought he was deluded. That we understood each other because we both knew that it was a myth. And that one day he would realize that I did him a favor. Because together we could be a good team." I swallow. "What I didn't understand then was that we lacked the one thing that would've made it bearable for a lifetime. What you two have now."

She doesn't say anything, just plays with the necklace on her neck. I recognize it as the Baxter boys' grandmother's wedding necklace. It was supposed to be in their father's care. The only way she has it is if he gave it to her. I'd had my eye on it for decades. And now, I know, the right woman owns it.

I clear my throat, nervous. "And your other question?"

She nods. "Are you doing the same thing to Matthias?"

"No."

The length of the two answers makes us both chuckle, a moment of brevity in a sea of tension.

But I owe her more than that. "Matthias is the one who originally came up with the idea. I need a green card to stay in the States and I don't want to go anywhere else. The person... I was supposed to marry didn't work out." I unconsciously touch the side of my temple where Patrick struck me. The bruise is gone but the ghost of it is still there. My-Linh notices and frowns, but doesn't say anything. "And Matthias, well, you know, he needed a little stability for his reputation, leading up to the IPO. So... he approached me. When he first mentioned it, I thought he was pranking me. But he wasn't. Over time, granted, not a long time"—I chuckle—"something happened between us. And here we are. But no, this is not the same thing. I would never hurt him."

"Okay." That's all. Just one word.

Something compels me to say something else. "Wait, My-Linh, one more thing." I swallow, not sure how to word the next thing I'm about to say. "I want to tell you; I am so sorry. I can't tell you how sorry I am. I had no idea what I was doing, how much hurt I was causing. And I can only hope that one day you and Damien can forgive me. Although Damien"—I roll my eyes and then grin—"can hold a grudge."

She rolls her eyes and lets out an unladylike snort. "Tellin' me." And then she smiles. "Do you have anything to wear to the wedding? We have a rehearsal dinner tonight at my cousin Jasmine's winery, Simpatico Wine Estate, down the road. And then the wedding will be here tomorrow. It would be so lovely if you could come. It's very laid back, you can wear whatever you like. I just wanted to make sure you felt comfortable. I mean, I'm short and stumpy"—we both look down at her short, yes, but anything but stumpy body—"but Kiara's clothes might fit. Just be careful, though. She's still pretty mad at you."

I blink. Is this woman for real?

I was bracing for a screaming match, ending with her kicking me out onto the streets of Barossa Valley. Not this... this understanding and kindness. How does someone become like this? Or is kindness God-given, planted in a soul like the little drop of blue or brown tint He colors into our eyes?

Either way, even though I cannot even aspire to this level of kindness, I'm privileged to be the beneficiary. "You are an angel," I say, genuinely awed. And secretly hope that her good nature will rub off on me.

"Ooh, no, no," she waves her hand. "Don't let Kiara hear you say that. That's what Kylian calls her."

"What does Damien call you?" I ask, curious. I can't imagine him having a nickname for anyone.

She laughs, a deep blush sprinting up her face. "You don't want to know."

"Matthias calls me 'hellion.'" I admit with a snort before I can stop myself.

My-Linh's face stiffens, eyes wide, and then she bends over and howls with laughter, grabbing my hand for support. She laughs for whole minutes. Now and then she screams "hellion" again, reinvigorating her own laugh. Her mirth is infectious and I find myself falling onto the floor, gasping along with her.

We're still howling when the door opens.

"Rissie, I just talked and Damie—" Matthias and Damien freeze at the threshold and their faces adopt a look of almost cartoonish surprise at the sight of me on the floor, grabbing My-Linh's hand, as she doubles over clutching her stomach.

"'Rissie?' Don't you mean *'hellion?'*" My-Linh shouts, and we fall back into laughter, ears bursting from the sound,

When we look back up, the door is closed and the guys are gone.

"Clarissa, tell us more about your club? Matthias has been raving about it to anyone who'll listen to him for ten seconds. But I'd love to hear it from you!" My-Linh says, settling down next to me on the flower bench when there's only the family left at the rehearsal dinner.

She tugs on Kiara's arm and plops her down on the seat next to us. Kiara hasn't said much to me, but that's not surprising. She's definitely My-Linh's protector, and is playing her role as bridesmaid to a T. It's hard not to brand her as a bitch, but in moments where she thinks no one is watching her and Kylian, she becomes putty in his hands.

I finish my drink and set the glass down next to me. "Well, um, the club has only been open about six weeks, so we're still in very early days. But it's going well. Actually, we're thinking of using the space during the day as a cafe. I'm really excited, because the truth is, I could use help to pay the rent."

"Just ask Matthias for it," Kiara says, eyeing me.

I honestly don't blame her for suggesting it. My monthly rent costs less than what they spend on restaurants monthly. "Well, I'm trying to do it on my own right now. It hasn't been easy, but it's been really fulfilling."

My-Linh smiles at me but nudges her friend with her elbow. "Don't mind her. She's mad because she's away from her business. Kiara stepped away from her family's fortune, too." She covers her face from her friend and mouths the word *'billions'*.

I laugh. "It's hard. The number of things I didn't know about just living." I grimace, remembering. "Why did no one ever tell me how much the phone bill costs?"

Kiara sits up, the bored look on her face fading. "Right? Or milk!"

"Milk costs so much!" I yell.

My-Linh chuckles next to us. "Never thought being former spoiled brats could be something to bond over."

Kiara elbows her friend, returning the one from before. "Says Damien Baxter's soon-to-be wife. Damien bought her parent's apartment building so they wouldn't have to pay the rent rise."

My-Linh's cheeks burn. "Hey, we weren't even together when that happened. Maybe it was the good influence of someone else." She winks at me.

And even though I know there could be nothing further from the truth, for a second I know what it feels like to have someone think good of you.

Forty

MATTHIAS

THE WEATHER GOD CAME out to bless the day for my brother's wedding.

Even our father who moved to Australia from England because he could not stand the grey skies, looks like he could not have asked for a bluer sky. Baxter blue, as Clarissa would say. I can't wait to sit down and talk about to him, it's been months since I had a chance to spend some time with him. It's one of the things I'm jealous most of when it comes to Damien, being so close to our father.

Damien fidgets as he stands at the altar, playing with our grandfather's cuff links on his wrists, tugging at his shirt. "Does my hair look okay?"

"If you ask me that one more time, I'm going to grab a handful and pull it out so you can see for yourself," Kingsley grumbles. He's hardly a people person at the best of times, and there are a lot of people here.

"You look good, man," Kylian pats Damien on the back. Not surprisingly, Kylian is Damien's best man.

Damien had come to Kingsley and I separately and explained to us why he had chosen Kylian. And wanted to know if that would hurt our feelings.

God *fucking* no. I've never wanted to be anyone's best man. Flattering, maybe, but the responsibility? If it was just about throwing a party, then I'd be all for it. But a Baxter getting married? Not a simple task.

And I say "not surprisingly" not because he thinks he's every-one's favorite. But because without Kylian, there probably would not be a wedding. He helped when Damien fell into a drunken depression when our mom come back into the picture, and he helped when My-Linh was in the hospital after they broke up and didn't want to see Damien.

He was the glue in some difficult situations.

And he hasn't let Damien forget it, going so far as to print "Am I the glue?" on a T-shirt that he threatens to wear to the reception every time Damien says something to piss him off.

And now he's standing there, proud as punch that Damien and My-Linh are taking their next steps to a happy life together.

No doubt thinking about when it's going to be his turn.

Both Kylian and Kiara have separately and together threatened to have the longest engagement in history, so who knows if he'll ever have to choose which one of us will be his best man. I vote not me.

I watch as Damien tenses, his jaw twitching as the last of the wedding party makes it down the aisle. I want to reassure him, but I also want him to sweat it a little. They both worked through a lot to get here, why not stretch the moment out a little?

Silence descends as the harp music fades out, and there's a gasp as My-Linh appears at the other end of the aisle. She looks beautiful in a simple white princess gown.

Damien hasn't seen her yet. He's too busy staring down at his hand, running through his vows in his head.

Kylian nudges him. "Hey, man. Look!"

Damien blinks and turns to her.

And tears spring to his eyes.

Keeping You by *Tanya Donelly*, the song My-Linh chose for her entrance, starts to play and everyone rises to their feet.

As My-Linh floats down the aisle, eyes trained on her very soon-to-be husband, her smile grows wider and wider as his cheeks get wetter and wetter.

Kylian leans back towards me "He's going to drown in those tears before she even gets here."

Kingsley lets out a tiny laugh behind me, stifling it immediately. "Shush. He'll die happy, okay?" I say.

After a few more seconds, Kylian leans back again. "It's still flowing. I'm starting to get really worried."

"Shut up, I'm not going to drown," Damien hisses without taking his eyes off his bride.

"Famous last words," Kylian whispers.

Kingsley reaches around me and pushes Kylian back to his position just as My-Linh reaches the front.

Her father lifts her veil and presses a gentle kiss to her head.

"Hi," she says, taking Damien's hand. He just swallows. She gives him a reassuring smile. "You look hot. You going somewhere?"

"Just to the end of forever with you, kitten."

Out of the corner of my eye, I see Clarissa, sitting in the front row, covering her mouth, shoulders shaking.

I remember nothing about the rest of the day until I'm in the middle of the dance floor with My-Linh, Kiara, Clarissa and Kylian, while Damien and Kingsley stand on the side of the floor, arms folded, looking around at the decorations, talking about how weddings are such a big business that maybe Baxter should look into.

"Bride! This is the song we were dancing to the first time I met you!" Kylian shouts at My-Linh.

"I remember, Best Man! Then Damien dragged me off the dance floor and took me—" She blushes. "Never mind."

Kylian takes Clarissa's hand and twirls her before returning to My-Linh. "Naughty Bride! Do you need us to tell you what happens on the wedding night?"

"Why don't you worry about what you're going to do on my wedding night," she shoots back, gesturing to Kiara dancing with one of the other guests.

I love that she never misses a beat. She's our sister now. And I won't let anything hurt her ever again.

Sometime in the middle of the song, Clarissa grabs my hand and drags me off the dance floor. Grabbing a bottle of champagne from the table, I follow her around the corner into a quiet part of the estate.

"I'm exhausted," she pants, taking a swig of the champagne straight from the bottle and rests her back against the wall. I take the bottle from her and pour it into my mouth, the cool fizz cooling my sweating body.

"Having a good time?" I ask, nuzzling my face into her neck, breathing in her sweet and salty skin. We've barely had a moment alone since My-Linh invited her to the wedding. The women have included her in everything and I've been busy with my brothers. "I missed you."

"Today?"

"No. *Always.* I think I've always been missing you in my life. I just didn't know it."

Her eyes sparkle, catching the moonlight as she looks at me. Then she grins. "So, you tried to find me in the beds of every woman who crossed your path?"

I snort. "Guilty."

My arm comes up to bracket her body again the wall over her head as I lean in to kiss her. It's felt like an eternity since we were this close.

For a moment it feels like I've forgotten how to fit my body with hers, but when she moans softly against my lips, everything makes sense again.

Her lips drift to my ear. "I miss you inside me."

My breath catches in my throat, and I clear it with a cough. "Well, darling, I'm happy to fix that for you."

I start to move, but she grabs the front of my shirt, balling it in her hand as she yanks me harder against her. "I can't wait. Here."

Need flares in the pit of my stomach at her urgency. "Anything for you, little hellion."

Tugging at the straps of her dress to untie them, she pulls down the front of her bodice to reveal her bare breasts. Her fingers find her nipples, stroking them as she locks her eyes with mine.

I brush her hands away, the buildup of not touching her for over a week instantly ignites my arousal. My lips find her breast in the dark, devouring it, as my fingers play with her other nipple. They harden like stone under my touch immediately.

"Matthias..." she moans, and her voice tornadoes around me, making me heady.

Fumbling with my pants, we laugh when she doesn't succeed in getting my cock out.

"Hellion, don't tell me you're out of practice," I tease her as I slide my zipper down, giving my aching cock a few strokes.

Her eyes darken and she turns around, bending over, bracing her face against the wall, pulling her dress up to bare her pussy. "Are you going to fuck me or not? Or am I going to have to find someone else to make me come, Matthias?"

Her words send a streak of jealousy in me and I grab her hips, positioning my cock at her entrance. The scent of her arousal mixes with the earthy cool night air. she's been ready for me to fuck her for some time now.

"I'd like to see you try, darling. I'd like to see you try to get far enough from me to let another man anywhere near this pussy." I slam forward, the force of my cock driving into her, knocking the air out of both of us. "This pussy is mine."

She clenches her tight pussy around me and I groan, grinding my hips forward, needing my cock surrounded by her.

"Matthias..." she moans, pressing back against me, meeting my thrusts.

"Yes, darling..."

She doesn't have anything to say. Just a string of moans and intelligible words as I fuck her.

"I love the way you take my cock. God, nothing feels as good as your sweet pussy wrapped around me."

We lose ourselves in the sensations as I slam into her, not a sliver of grace in the way I'm using her pussy for my own pleasure. "Reach under you, darling, feel my cock fucking you," I gasp.

She obeys, her fingers grazing against me every time I pull out and slam back in. The extra stimulation throws me over the edge and my orgasm rips through me. I shudder and empty into her.

When I'm done, I pull out, dropping to my knees and spreading her legs as I reach around and grind her clit hard with my thumb. Clamping my teeth in the flesh of her ass, I bite down hard, as I ram two into her cum soaked little cunt. She screams as she comes, pussy rippling around my fingers, dripping her wetness down my arm.

Still shaking, she collapses onto me as I run my fingertip along her tremoring pussy.

"I missed this," I tell her. "I missed you. It hurt me to be away from you. You're a part of me, Rissie."

The look she gives me sends shivers down my spine. A shared look of understanding. "I'm yours, Matthias. I'm yours."

I cup her face and kiss her tenderly and lovingly, and answer in my own way that I'm hers, too. "Come on, let's get back to the party before someone comes looking for us." As I help her to her feet, there's a giggling from the bushes to our right, and two disheveled figures emerge.

"Oh, hi guys," Kylian grins. "We were, you know, just out for a walk."

I grin at Clarissa. "Yeah, us too."

"Well, of course, that explains why you're out of breath," Kylian teases.

Kiara groans and pulls him away, "Can't you ever just say the right thing in any situation?"

Kylian nuzzles her neck. "I said the right thing to get you to come out here, didn't I?"

Kiara huffs but her face is smiling. "Clarissa, if you're ever looking for a different Baxter brother, I'm happy to step aside!"

Helping Clarissa fix her dress, I drop a kiss on her neck. "Remember what I said. I'd like to see you try to get away from me."

We fall back into our rhythm when we get back to New York City, just like it was before something happened and she pulled away.

But this time it feels different.

We talk.

We talk about almost everything.

I tell her about work and the things I'm working on for Baxter as well as my own ventures.

She tells me about the things she dreamed of doing as a child and having to repress them when her life made her believe she couldn't achieve them.

She tells me about her anxiety, and how it developed. She tells me about her first ever anxiety attack was when she was at prep school and someone told her that her father was having an affair, and that one day she was going to have an evil stepmother.

Worry about the future, about things she thinks she can't control, is another trigger. And confrontation. They all trigger her brain into fight-or-flight response, causing the dumping of too much adrenaline into her blood stream.

We make promises that she'll call me when she's having an anxiety attack, and no matter what I'm doing and where I am, I will make my way to her.

As much as possible, I try to work from home in the mornings, so that I can be there when she wakes up, and I can make sure she gets some food into her before she works all night.

Nights after the club closes are spent eating picnics on the bed as we wind down from the day. Public outings are reserved for occasions where we are to be photographed, keeping up the appearances of our engagement.

For all the things we talk about, there's one thing we don't mention, not even once - what is going on between us and this 'fake' engagement that we're barreling towards.

When it was just a PR ploy, I had no problem signing a marriage license, but now that she's become the most important part of my day, can I let her continue thinking that it's all for pretense?

The research comes back telling me that her stabilizing influence on my public image plays well with the investors and the board has stopped hounding me. A case of no news is good news.

My plans for Patrick continue to fall into place. His last two deals fall through in the space of as many days. I spend too much time and money on my personal vendetta, and I don't have a single regret about it.

He wanted me to finish him off? *Be careful what you wish for, Patrick.*

It's the only part of my life that I keep from Clarissa. Sometimes, in a quiet moment, I see her lift her hand to her temple, and her eyes mirroring fear, remembering the incident. The only time I'll ever bring his name up to her is to tell her that she never has to worry about him again.

Whatever happened to make her pull away before the wedding seems to have been resolved, and even though I'm glad to have her back, a part of me remains on edge, wondering if today is the day I'll wake up... and she is gone again.

I live and breathe Clarissa Masters, and without her, I don't know what would be left of me.

Forty-One

CLARISSA

I CHANGE QUICKLY IN the car, not wanting to show up at the apartment in a skirt stained with a spilled Bloody Mary. Matthias had asked me during the day if I could come home a little earlier so we could spend some time together because he goes out of town in two days. But the club has had a few social media posts go viral over the last few days, and there were more people than ever lining up to get inside. It was past eleven p.m. before I felt comfortable leaving my staff in charge.

I jump out of the car and check my reflection in the elevator's mirrored walls on the way to the penthouse. I clean up good even if it's in the backseat of a car. The thought of seeing Matthias after both of us being busy all day plants butterflies in my stomach.

But it's dark and quiet when I get to the apartment.

"Matthias?" I call out, dropping my things on the table as I make my way to the bedroom. Maybe he's taking a nap before coming to pick me up from the club.

He's not there, nor in the bathroom.

His iPad is still on the nightstand, and he never leaves the house without it, so I know he must be somewhere here.

The eeriness of the silent apartment quickens my breath, and I make my way to his office. There's a soft light emanating from under the door, and when I push it open, I'm not sure what I'm going to find there.

But it's just him, laying with his head back on the couch, snoring softly. His laptop teeters on the arm of the couch, suggesting he was working before he took an impromptu nap.

My heart swells with emotion at the sight of him, his blond hair tousled from a stressful day, shirt sleeves rolled and pushed midway up his forearms. Will I ever get sick of looking at him? I can't imagine I will.

I just hope he feels the same way about me.

Trying not to wake him, I gently pull the laptop off the couch and lay it on his desk. Folding up the papers next to him, I put them on top of the laptop thinking about how I can turn off the lamp without disturbing him.

When I turn around his eyes are open, gazing at me.

"You're home," he says, rubbing his eyes.

"Not as early as I wanted to be, I'm sorry."

"Come here." He holds his hand out to me.

I take it and he roughly wrenches me onto his lap, kissing me deeply, like he's woken up from a hundred-year slumber, hungry, thirsting for me.

Arousal hikes up from my core, and I lean into his kiss, his tongue dipping into my mouth as I open for him.

"You taste so sweet," he murmurs, his hand raking down my back.

"It's the Caramello Koalas," I joke.

A soft exhale whistles out of him. He wraps himself around me as he stands up and lays me back down on the couch, pulling at the straps of my halter top.

"Did I ever tell you I'm a tit man?" he asks, as he flicks his tongue over my nipple.

"Erm, no, but I may have picked up on it," I say, arcing my back.

He chuckles against me before he tugs on my hardened nipple with his teeth, making me hiss. "I'm also a pussy man. Yours."

His hands roughly rip at my dress, tearing it all the way down the middle. It falls, ruined on either side of me, baring me to him. Heat flares in his eyes as he looks over me. "No panties? You were flashing at the club, hellion?"

My blood burns from the proximity of his need. "I got changed for you. I might even have left my panties behind on floor of the car."

He glides a finger from my neck all the way down my body to rest right between my legs. "Dirty girl, I should punish you. How should I punish you, darling?"

He doesn't give me a chance to reply as he pushes my legs apart and dives in. Usually he starts gently, building me up to an orgasm, but tonight it's like he *needs* me, can't breathe without having his tongue inside.

"God... Matthias..." My hands fist in his hair, all my defenses incinerated in the onslaught on my pussy.

My calling his name makes him moan with approval. His moan rumbles through his body, then vibrates against my clit.

Rough hands pull my legs up around his shoulders as he devours me, plunders me with his mouth. Pleasure tingles in the base of my spine, climbing to an orgasm that threatens to break me.

But every time I'm close... oh, so close, he pulls back and runs his tongue along my inner thighs.

The anticipation is agonizing.

Over and over, he leads me to the edge, then yanks it away.

"You're a fucking mess, darling," he growls against my inner thigh, teeth grazing a line along my skin. "Look at you, dripping all over my couch. Your wetness running down my arms."

There's nothing to do but beg. "Please..."

"I can't hear you. Please what, darling?"

"Please... ohhhh..." A moan shatters through me as his lips drop around my clit. But again, as soon as I'm about to fall, he pulls off me, leaning back as he collects my wetness on his face and licks it off his fingers. "Please... let me come. Please..."

He grins. I can feel his mouth curl against me.

Then, without a word, he lowers my legs, then gets up and walks over to the edge of his desk, leaning against it with his arms folded. My hands come down over my midsection, trying to cover up from his intense gaze.

"Don't *fucking* move or I'll make sure you don't come for a month," he threatens.

My hands freeze on the flat of my stomach.

He doesn't say another word, just stares at me, eyes raking up and down over my body.

After a minute of lying there, I wriggle, trying to slide back up on the couch. It elicits another growl from him. "I said, *don't fucking move*. I'm going to have to teach you how to listen, aren't I?"

A shiver scatters through every muscle so strongly, I'm sure he must see my move body move. I want to do everything he wants but something in his eyes tells me... he wants a fight.

"I can *listen* just fine," I say. "Maybe there's something wrong with your delivery."

He rewards me with a smirk. The same smirk that used to piss me off so much, and now I can't get enough of. "Little brat. So then get on fours, ass facing me."

The argument tickles on the end of my tongue, and I'm not sure how far I should push him, but the glint in his eye makes the decisions for me. "Why don't you make me?"

His tongue digs into the side of his cheek, his thumb rubbing unconsciously over the back of his other hand. The same thumb that just tortured me to within two breaths of an orgasm. He fucking owes me. "Get. On. All. Fours."

I slide my body up the couch, pressing my legs together, depriving Matthias of seeing me bared for him. If he wants me, he's doing to have to work for me. "I said, *make me*. Or are you scared you can't?"

Suddenly he's there, spinning me around and practically throwing me onto the floor. I'm just a rag doll in his arms, and the level to which I trust him makes my clit throb. Roughly, he nudges my knees wide apart, the air cool on my dripping pussy.

He steps back, breathing hard, footsteps echoing in the quiet room. "Art, darling, you're a fucking piece of art."

Then, without a word, his palm slaps down on the flesh of ass. I cry out, both out of surprise more than the pain. It stings, but nothing unbearable. But the second one isn't as gentle; my ass is primed for his hand and it comes down harder.

"Are you going to listen to me now? Or do you need to be punished more, hellion?" He doesn't give me a chance to reply before his hand stings my ass again. I'm dying to reach around to touch my skin to see how hot it feels. The heat warms every inch of my body, leaving me hot and tender.

His fingers shove inside me again, pumping in and out as he grabs handfuls of the tender skin of my ass. I scream from the sensations flooding me.

"So fucking drenched. This cunt was made to have my cock in it, wasn't it, darling? You can't wait for my cock to ruin you," he growls, dark and promising into my ear, before he drags a tongue down my neck.

"Please... god, Matthias... please...I need to come."

"Not yet, darling. Not yet."

He pulls his hand out and reaches forward to cram it into my mouth. I lick it up like I'm parched and he's an oasis in the desert.

Suddenly he's gone; when I look over my shoulder, he's back at his desk, pulling his cock out, fist stroking the tip.

"Come here, my little darling."

I start to get off my knees but he stops me. "No. Not on your feet. On your knees. Crawl to my cock, darling. Show me what a cock hungry little slut you are."

I spin, not losing a second as I brace on my hands and shuffle forward, my arousal dripping all the way down my legs.

"Good girl. Look how hard you make me."

He strokes his cock in time with my movements, and every second imprints itself on my brain. I'm nothing but a collection of cells vibrating at the frequency of pure lust, and I could combust at any moment.

The sound of my legs slapping wetly together is vulgar and sensual both at once. When I reach him, I lean back on my knees, locking my hands behind my back to arch my back. "You're a fucking goddess."

Hands reaching down to my head, he feeds his cock into my mouth.

The saltiness of his precum coats my tongue as his cock glides into my mouth.

"Fuck," he hisses, pumping the head of his cock into my lips. "I could come on your face right now, darling. But I want something more."

He pulls me to my feet and bends me against his desk, fingers flicking my clit from behind. I'm so close it doesn't take more than a few seconds before I'm begging to come again.

And this time, if he doesn't... I might just die right here. "Let me come, Matthias... please. Fuck me."

"Louder." His thumb presses into me as his index finger circles my clit, pulling back every few seconds.

"Please. I'm begging you, please... fuck me and let me come."

"I said, *louder*."

I let go. Shouting the words, making my throat hoarse. "Please, I'm begging you. I need your cock inside me, ruining me. Please... please...Fuck me, make me your little slut." I sob with need.

He spins me around, lifts my ass onto the table and shoves his cock inside me.

"Fuck," he roars. "Darling, you're so fucking wet," he growls, leaning over, bracing his hands against the desk as he rams into me.

His cock stretching me, along with the friction of his pubis against me, finally send me over the edge and I grab his head, kissing him as my body shatters into a million pieces.

He doesn't stop, just fucks into me, grunting from the exertion, pulling my legs up over his shoulder.

Another wave of pleasure crashes over me, blinding me with an orgasm that rips through me.

I'm breathless.

I'm his, every part of me is his, as his cock grazes parts I've never felt touched before, I whisper it. "I'm yours. My pussy is yours, Matthias."

"You're going to kill me one day," he growls. "I don't know what you've done to me, but I'm yours."

His words touch me just as he drops his head on my nipples and bites down. His cock drives me to another then another climax, and another.

Until I'm nothing but cum and sweat and dust and tremors.

Only then does he grip my chin, forcing my eyes on his and he roars, erupting inside me, as I wrap my legs around him.

Wrecked, he falls on top of me, gasping for air. His head on my chest, I hold him, hold him with every part of me, until I know, if we're ever separated, I will bleed out and die.

"It's my birthday."

"Hmmm?" I say, lifting my head from the desk to watch him as he gently extricates himself from me.

"It's my birthday today. Well, it was yesterday." He stands by the desk and pulls his shirt off, and gently dabs it between my legs. He's never stopped doing that, and it's the most intimate experience, even after everything we've done together.

Shit.

I'd missed his birthday even though he'd asked me to come home a little early. Talk about selfish. "Why didn't you tell me? Matthias!"

He goes over to sit on the coach, running through his messed-up hair, giving me a sheepish smile. "I didn't want to make a big deal out of it. Everyone has birthdays. But it's the first time I haven't been with even one of my brothers. Damien usually makes a big deal out of it because... he knows I'm the only one who really cares about birthdays, but..."

I sit up. "But he's on his honeymoon."

He shrugs. "Yeah. I mean, lame excuse, right?"

"You should've told me."

He shrugs. "It's fine. No big deal. Just thought I'd mention it. Since you might have wondered why I asked you to come home earlier."

I come over and sit in his lap, wrapping my arms around his neck. "We'll do something. Tomorrow night. I can't take the whole night off, but I'll come home early. And I'll get you a present. A Rock 'Em Sock 'Em Robot toy or something."

He chuckles, kissing me softly. "Firstly, I'll take one of those any day. Secondly, you already gave me my birthday present."

I frown.

His face buries against my neck, breathing in deep. "You crawling on your knees, your cunt dripping, begging me to fuck you. I could never ask for anything more."

I laugh. "Well, I didn't even know it was your birthday... maybe I should give it to you again tomorrow."

He lets out a small chuckle, but there's a sadness in his eyes that breaks my heart. I should've come home earlier. Who knows when this bubble is going to burst.

"Actually," he whispers, his lips tickling my ear, "I have a gift for myself too, but I'm going to wait until tomorrow to show you what it is."

And I'm determined it up to him tomorrow.

***

"Guys, I'm going now. Try not to call me, okay? It's Matthias's late birthday celebration," I call over my shoulder as I push on the back door.

In the dark, someone grabs my arm and slams me against the wall, his hand gripping around my throat.

I try to scream, but I can't.

Fear clouds every pixel of my sight, and I force my eyes open.

Out of the dark, Patrick's face leans into mine, eyes crazy. "You fucking bitch. You ruined everything! I'm going to make you pay for everything's that happened. Take it from your flesh."

He lifts his hand and I brace for impact, praying to a deity I've never been on speaking terms with before. But before his hand lands on me, I see a hand grab his forearm and yank him back.

He spins around and Matthias is standing there, his blue eyes a bottomless pit of clear crystal, red seeping into the whites of his eyes.

"Why won't you just fucking die?" Matthias says, low, dark, scary. Primal. "Fucking waste of space."

Patrick stumbles back a step. "Baxter. Glad you're here. You can watch me fuck up your fiancée, and know that it's all your fault."

"What-what is he talking about?" I ask, confused. Scared.

Both men ignore me. Matthias widens his stance, getting balanced. Patrick sways, obviously drunk.

"You took everything from me," Patrick slurs. "I can't compete with you in business, but I can take back one thing that's mine."

Matthias rears up. "Didn't I tell you if you even so much as laid eyes on her again, I was going to kill you? Well, I don't make promises I don't keep."

With a yell, Matthias launches himself at Patrick.

Patrick, older, shorter, less fit, has no chance. Not that any of that matters. Matthias only has one thing on his mind; finishing Patrick off once and for all.

He flips Patrick onto the ground and kicks his leg into his side. Patrick lets out a blood-curdling scream.

"Matthias!" I yell. But it's in vain.

He straddles over Patrick, who's writhing on the ground, and wails on his face. Blood pools on the ground next to Patrick's head as Matthias pounds into his face. Again and again.

It turns my stomach and I have to look away. "Matthias! Stop! He's not worth it!"

But he doesn't hear me.

It's worse, it's so much worse than the last time.

Finally, he gets up, staggering around as if he's looking for something. "A brick. I need a fucking brick! I'm going to bash his fucking brains in."

A couple walking past the alley, curious about the shouting, peers in, covering their mouths when they see what's happening. "Oh, my god. Someone call the police."

"Matthias!" I run to him, grabbing his hand. "We have to go!"

He looks at me, like he doesn't even recognize me, Patrick's blood dripping down his knuckles.

I touch his face. "Come on, darling. We have to go. Now." I take his hand and pull him into the club, and out through the front door where his car is parked. "Keys!" I shout and he hands them to me in a daze. I can't remember the last time I drove on the right side. The last time I drove was when I lived in Australia.

But it doesn't matter, we have to go.

I turn the car into traffic. Where we're going, I have no idea.

Just out of there, out of where Matthias can be blamed for any of this.

It's dark. Maybe they couldn't see who it was.

The engine revs as I press too hard on the gas. How does he drive this fucking thing? No wonder he's always getting pulled over by the cops.

Think. Think. *Think.*

Shit.

There's one person I know who we both can trust.

Leanne. I turn into onto Perry St. and can only hope that she's home.

Forty-Two

MATTHIAS

"FUCK, YOU'RE IN BAD shape," Leanne says, grabbing my hand and pulling me into her apartment. Behind me Clarissa is panting from the run here. She'd parked the car a block down the road hoping no one would notice it there.

"Nice to see you too, did you redecorate?" I say to her.

"Just shut up and go inside," Clarissa loud whispers and pushes me inside.

Leanne slams the door shut and looks me over. "What the fuck happened?"

Clarissa sinks into a couch, her head falling into her hands. "Patrick."

At the sound of his name, the red cloud descends again. And I have to restrain myself from going back to finish the job. He was still breathing when Clarissa pulled me away.

That wasn't the desired outcome.

Leanne comes over and throws a towel over my head. "Go take a shower. You smell like a slaughter house."

"It's always good to see you, Leanne." But then I turn back. "Thanks."

She shakes her head and joins Clarissa on the couch.

The shower is hot and long; I wait until the water runs clear and cold before I even contemplate leaving, replaying the last hour over and over in my head.

I would've killed him. I would've bashed him brains in and peeled every inch of skin off him, just as a warning to anyone who thinks they can even think of hurting Clarissa.

What happens now, I don't know.

I just know that she's safe for now. What comes tomorrow, we'll deal with tomorrow.

The two women are standing in Leanne's kitchen when I come out, a tea cup in each hand. It must be Clarissa's influence. Leanne only drinks drinks that come in a wine glass.

When they see me, they finish their conversation in whispers. Leanne walks out and taps me on the shoulder.

"Glad to see you're the one left standing," she says, giving me a hug and then leaves.

Exhaustion rams into me like a Mack truck and I stumble out to the couch, sinking into it.

"We need to talk about what we're going to do now," Clarissa says from the kitchen.

But I don't want to talk. The severity of what I've done is dawning, and even though, in the moment, I wouldn't have done anything differently to keep Clarissa safe, I'm not violent by nature. The image of his limp body under me on the ground is already starting to haunt me. And Leanne was right, I had so much of his blood on my body, I can still smell the metallic scent.

"Matthias, we can't just ignore it... someone is going to come looking..."

"Clarissa. I'm really tired. And I... I have to think about things before I decide what I'm going to do, okay? This... is not a small thing. But... if you knew how I felt when I saw him pinning you against the wall, hand raised... I had no choice."

The memory makes my mouth dry, and then fill with saliva. I run for the bathroom, and empty the contents of my stomach into the toilet.

I don't know what's going to happen, but I can't undo it.

I need sleep.

I need to feel Clarissa sleeping next to me reminding me why I did what I did.

But when I fall asleep, it's only me in the bed.

Forty-Three

CLARISSA

REFLECTIONS OF CAR LIGHTS against the window are the only movement in Leanne's apartment. Matthias went into the bedroom after he was sick, but I'm not sure I'm ready to join him.

The images of Patrick lying on the ground in a pool of his own blood haunts me, but more so, I know this isn't going to be good for Matthias.

If he's lucky and Patrick walks away from this, there's no way that he won't press charges, and any prosecutor with eyeballs is going to know they have a case. A young prosecutor looking to make an example out of the rich and privileged is going to go after this with everything have. And Matthias is certainly a good example of both.

He might think that he can talk his way out of this, but even a cat has only nine lives.

The stark reality that he would not even have been in this situation if he weren't trying to protect me is the hardest part of this. And now he's in so much trouble, I don't know if there's anything anyone can do.

There are no answers.

But if this last year has taught me anything, nothing comes from doing nothing.

He helped me, now I have to help him.

I pick up the phone, a grapefruit in my chest, knowing our time has come to an end. The phone is answered on the other side and the sound of his voice makes my stomach churn.

"Can we talk?"

***

Forty-Four

MATTHIAS

IT TAKES ABOUT FIVE minutes before I realize the banging is at the door, and not just in my head. I roll over to see Clarissa rubbing her eyes, just as confused.

"Is that the door?" she asks, her voice adorably sleepy.

"No idea. I'll go have a look."

She grabs my arm. "No! It might not to be safe, you don't know what her neighbors are like."

I give her a gentle kiss as I roll out of Leanne's bed. "Actually, I do. I always make sure I double check my tenants before I let them rent one of my properties."

The banging becomes more insistent just as I reach the door. "It's the police. Open the door, Mr. Baxter," someone calls through the door.

Fuck.

The police?

"Matthias!" Clarissa hisses in a whisper behind me. "Don't open the door!"

"I have to Rissie, it's the police."

"But—"

I give her a reassuring nod. "It's okay, darling. What happens, we're going to work it out, okay?"

I reach for the handle and even before the door is fully open, the police barge into the apartment, pinning me around, slipping a pair of cuffs on my wrists.

"Matthias Baxter, you're under arrest. You have the right to remain silent..."

"No!" Clarissa yells, trying to surge forward, but they hold her back. She cries trying to fight them. Her fear spears me all the way through, and I hate that she has to be here for this.

"It's okay, darling. Go to the office and call Hannah, tell her to call Kylian and Paula. They'll know what to do. And then go back to the apartment or the office. You'll be safe there. I can't worry about you, okay?" Someone swings me around and almost bangs my head against the door frame. "Hey, easy! I'm not fighting this. And I'd prefer it if my fiancée didn't have to watch me get hurt."

"Matthias!" she sobs.

I call over my shoulder trying to calm her. "I'm going to be alright, darling. Do what I told you to! I'll see you soon, hellion."

As I get led down the stairs, the sound of her tears follows me. And the last thing I see when I'm pushed into the cop car at the curb is her tear-stained face on the third-floor window.

And I can only hope it's not the last time I'll see it.

Forty-Five

CLARISSA

MATTHIAS'S THREE BROTHERS, ALONG with Kiara and My-Linh, arrive as fast as their planes can bring them.

But nobody has any answers either.

"Tell me again what happened," Kingsley says when we all congregate in Matthias's office in Baxter Tower.

"She's told you everything, man," Kylian says, with a look of understanding. "You know as much as she does at this point."

My hands come up to run through my hair. I'm exhausted and I haven't had a shower in who the hell knows how long. "I'm sorry. I wish I knew more, but I don't. Matthias is currently being held at the jail, but it's a weekend, and there's been no word except for a short phone call with his lawyer when he was first taken."

I'm going crazy. It's been almost eighteen hours, and we've heard nothing more. Every breath feels like I'm swallowing broken glass, and everything everyone says just grates on me.

My-Linh pats me on the shoulder and I turn around to see she's holding out a cup of tea. It smells familiar; it's the first tea Matthias made me that night. The smell instantly pulls the tears from my eyes.

She looks alarmed. "Oh, um. I can make you a different kind. It's just that this one is good for..."

I take it from her, trying not to seem like an ungrateful bitch. "No, no. Thank you. It's just that Matthias made it for me once when... Erm, once when I wasn't feeling well." Fuck that, there's no reason to hide from them what Patrick did to me, and almost did again. I square my jaw. "He made it for me after Patrick hit me. I had some bad injuries and I fainted once."

Kiara stands up and goes over to the far side of the living room and launched a cushion at the window. They all know the back story, and why Matthias was so violent with Patrick, but I guess giving them the details really hammers it home.

"I hope he dies," Damien says. Kylian shushes him, but it doesn't matter. "I *do*. I hope he fucking dies. Not just because of what he's doing to Matthias, but because of what he's done to Clarissa."

The room descends into complete silence.

Despite being at his wedding, and now here, Damien has never actually looked me in the eye or said a word to me. I don't know what it means that he just said what he said, but when My-Linh goes over and pats him gently on the arm, I wonder if he and I can make some progress after all.

"Is this going to affect the upcoming Kids and Care IPO?" I ask.

"It's doesn't matter, Clarissa," Kylian replies with a shake of his head.

But it does.

Aside from each other and the women they love, these men love their company. It is their flesh and blood, sweat and tears that have been poured into this business, and when something goes wrong, they take it to heart. Blaming themselves.

"I don't want him to blame himself for this. He's worked so hard on it for the last few months. This whole thing with us was because he was trying to do the right thing."

Kiara comes back, her face angry. Kylian hugs her to him, winking at me over the top of her head. "Kiara's pet peeve, what she hates most, is when men take advantage of women."

The two sisters-in-law are like sunshine and shadow. My-Linh's gentleness against Kiara's fiery protectiveness. I don't know if I deserve to be the recipient, but it gives me the first sense of family in a long time.

Matthias's phone on the coffee table rings and we all turn towards it. I nod to Kingsley who answers it. He has a short conversation and then replaces the phone on the table, rubbing his forehead as he thinks.

"Well?" Damien speaks.

"His arraignment is in an hour, they're going to charge him with grievous bodily harm."

"What?" Kylian and Damien shout at once. "Is he going to be okay though? He doesn't have any priors for violence? He only has two for—" They stop glancing at me.

"Let me guess - reckless driving," I finish for them. "But that shouldn't affect this charge, should it?"

Kingsley sighs and shakes his head. "It shouldn't. But who knows?"

I wish, just once, that someone had the answers.

Forty-Six

MATTHIAS

My ENTIRE FAMILY IS waiting outside the courthouse when I'm finally released, something I'm sure both the board and our PR department is absolutely thrilled about. I'm also sure that Damien told them he did not give a flying fuck, and was the first one on the scene.

But the board and the PR department would've been right. Because other than the family, the paparazzi are out in full force to support my stint in jail.

"Matthias! Tell us what happened? Were you trying to murder Patrick Linzer?"

"Is Clarissa Masters engaged to you just for a green card, like she did with Patrick before he dumped her?"

How the fuck do they know that? The fucker must be awake and running his mouth off. I really should've finished him off. They'd hold a freaking parade for me, I would've have gotten a key to the city if I didn't already have one.

"I'm not answering questions, so you can just stop asking." I shout, even though there's no point. If vultures were human, they'd be the paparazzi.

Clarissa pushes through the crowd to me. I grab her and pull her into me for a tight hug. Seeing her just brings me peace. How can one person both stir up so many emotions and yet be my calm in the storm all at once?

"Hey, you okay?" I whisper in her ear. She nods, but it's clear she probably hasn't gotten any sleep since she saw me handcuffed and driven away in a cop car. "Let's go. I could really use a shower."

We take a step down to the footpath and they swarm around us with nothing but a cop or two pushing them back.

I drape my arm around Clarissa and shield her as we make it over to where the rest of the family is standing next to my car.

"Hey. How's the honeymoon?" I say to Damien, who pulls me in for a tight hug.

"Eh, once you've seen one beach, you've seen them all." He pulls away and gives me a wry smile. "You might owe My-Linh a trip to Bora Bora though. That was our next stop." He opens the car door for me; Clarissa climbs in, and I follow.

Before he gets into the driver's seat, he turns toward the paparazzi and yells. "My brother is the single highest donor to the Children Are The Future fund, he runs the New York City marathon every year and raises more money than most of you will see in a lifetime. Maybe that's what you should be writing about instead of this bullshit. Get a life. Before I buy up every single newspaper and the lot of you will be out of a job." The car door slams as he slides behind the wheel.

"Well. Good thing Paula isn't doing anything right now," I tease him.

He ignores me and turns the car into traffic.

Despite how good it is to finally see Clarissa and my family; I've spent the last twenty-four hours stewing over my arrest. Who could've known I was there?

Leanne?

Who was she going to tell? With her job, she deals in confidentiality, having such a high profile client list. If this got out that she released my location to the cops, the only houses she'd be designing would be doll houses.

Someone must've seen us last night.

Maybe even one of the other tenants.

Either way, I'm going to get to the bottom of this. And I'm going to make sure that Patrick wishes he never got up off the ground.

"You want to go home?" Damien asks

"No," I say leaning forward, "to the office. I need to go to work. I've got to figure out what happened and where we go from here. Kids & Care IPO is in a month. We need to spring back from this."

The news had evidently spread through every corner of the office and when I get there, everyone makes a really concerted effort not to look at me, but also not to avoid my eyes. I would love to see that interoffice memo explaining what happened and how to act.

"Matthias!" Hannah jumps up from her desk when she sees me, purple rings circling her eyes, just like the rest of the closest people to me.

"Hey, Hannah, fancy seeing you here. I thought you would've taken advantage of me not being here to do some shopping on the company credit card."

She hugs me, and there's the tiniest little sob. It does nothing to help the lump that's been growing in my throat since I saw how much my family has cared about me.

"Get back to work, okay?" I say softly, and she nods, wiping her eyes, while everyone suddenly finds something in the floor or carpet really interesting.

Her face hardens and she leans and whispers, "Matthias... you have some people here to see you."

"Who?"

She swallows. Whoever it is, she doesn't even want to tell me. That can't be good. Can't be worse than the police, though.

I run into my office and see them, sitting on my couch like they fucking own it.

Terry, Gerry and fucking Patrick.

The three fuckerteers.

This has got to be some sort of sick joke.

Patrick looks better than I expected him to. His left arm is in a sling and his face is basically one giant bruise. Too bad it doesn't cover up how dog shit ugly he is.

"What the fuck are you three doing here?" I fume.

"You two"—I point my fingers at Terry and Gerry—"aren't even supposed to be in New York."

In the background, I hear footsteps as everyone follows me into the office, seeing the shit show in front of me. I hear a woman gasp, or maybe it's all three.

I don't blame them.

Seeing all three of them here is like a sign of the apocalypse.

"Matthias, how are you feeling, son?" Gerry asks, saccharine sweet, and it makes me want to actually throw up.

I take a step towards them. "Just answer the question. Actually, you know what? Just get the fuck out. All three of you."

He stands up, tugging on his shirt cuffs. "I don't think that's going to happen, son."

Anger swarms around me. "Gerry, I swear to God, if you call me 'son' one more time, I'm going to break every fucking bone in your body."

He sighs and shrugs. "It's exactly these violent tendencies that have you gotten into this... pickle, son. We're going to have to do something about this."

"You don't have to do anything about it. *I* will take care of it."

Terry steps forward, and I can't help looking over to see Clarissa covering her mouth with her hand. I wonder if she'd seen him since he disowned her. If I had to decide, I don't know who I want to kill more, Clarissa's uncle or my uncle.

Terry speaks, "I'm sorry, Matthias. But I don't know if you understand how serious this is. Look at what you did to Patrick. You know that you're going away for this."

The thing is, I do know. I know this got way out of hand, and that there are going to be repercussions. I couldn't do anything from the cell. But they're wasting my precious time now.

"Patrick, tell Matthias what the ADA said to you."

Patrick coughs and winces, grabbing his side. It fills me with a sick sense of satisfaction. "Grievous bodily harm, second degree. You're looking at some hard jail time."

"It was worth it if it stopped you from doing the same to Clarissa. Don't pretend that you're some victim. Why don't you tell them what you were going to instead, and see how many are on your side?"

Patrick poses, turning to Clarissa, his voice filled with deception. "I was just there to talk, Clarissa. I swear, I was just there to talk."

Clarissa lets out a little choked gasp and My-Linh and Kiara immediately flank her, taking her hands in theirs.

What a picture my office makes right now, us against them.

Again.

When are we going to have to stop fighting for our lives against this man who is supposed to be our family?

For the first time in a long time, I wish my grandfather was there to come between us. How can Gerry let his memory down day after day?

But there I was, being led away in handcuffs from my hideout. And someone had to have reported my location to the police.

It had to one of them. It had to be. But who?

"You called the police on me, didn't you?" I ask.

I get the answer I'm looking for, though, when Gerald and Terry turn to share a look. I knew. Fucking in cahoots. I'm going to get them for collusion.

"Which. One. Of. You?" I ask, needing to know.

Gerry shrugs. "You committed a crime, Matthias. You should be punished. You're not above the law, *sonny boy*, no matter how much you think you're untouchable. I've told you before, one day your recklessness was going to get you and us in trouble. And look what happened. You almost killed someone."

I step forward to fling myself at him, when I feel Damien hold me back. "You asshole. You are so fucking hungry to be CEO you'd put the company in jeopardy?"

His face breaks into a smug grin. "I hate to tell you this, Matthias, but I am the CEO."

Damien steps forward. "*Interim* CEO. For another six months. Enjoy your time when you can, because when you're out, there's not a single Baxter business that you're going to be allowed to step a slimy foot in."

I can't think about that right now. I need to know more about who is responsible for this. "But how did you know I was there?"

This time, instead of sharing a look, they both turn to look at... Clarissa.

She glances at me nervously, then over at them.

"No," she shakes her head.

The air in the room thins, and nobody breathes or moves for a second

"Clarissa?" my voice comes out small and scared. "What is going on?"

"I think it's time you tell them what's going on, why don't you, sweetheart?" Gerry says. "Might as well tell them now."

"Tell us what?" I'm panicked.

Clarissa moves away from the other women and toward me. "I don't know what he's talking about, Mathias. I didn't tell him you were there!"

"Then how did I know where he was, sweetheart?"

I want to wrap my hands around his neck and squeeze until there's not a single breath of air inside him for the way he keeps calling her "sweetheart." But I also need to know what's going on.

Gerry knows, and he keeps pushing. "I'm giving you one last chance to tell him, sweetheart. Or I'm going to. And I think it's better if they hear it from you."

The suspense is throttling me. "What are you talking about? Just say it!"

"Well..." Gerry starts.

"No! I want to hear it from her. Clarissa, what is he talking about?"

She just shakes her head back and forth, the hair around her face flying back and forth, face tinted green. For a split second, I consider grabbing her hand and taking her away from here. And living in sweet oblivion, but together, for the rest of our days.

Gerry gives up waiting for her. "This was always what was going to happen, Matthias. That's what she's not telling you. She's planned this for the longest time. Haven't you, Clarissa? You were just waiting for the chance."

"No!" she shouts. "Please stop."

But he doesn't. "Tell them. Tell them all how much you have always hated the Baxter name. Tell them how humiliated you were when Damien called your engagement off. Tell them how you came to me for help. Tell them how you swore you would do everything to take them down, you were just waiting for your chance."

"Clarissa..." I gasp.

Her face blanched. "It wasn't like that!"

"Oh my god," My-Linh exhales, echoing my own thoughts.

"It's not what happened!" Clarissa yells, backing up.

Gerry keeps going, the only one whose voice stays even, calm. Cold. "You were angry at Damien... Don't lie about that."

She nods. "I was. But everyone knows that. But that has nothing to do with Matthias. I was mad at Damien, and I was stupid. But that's all over."

Gerry continues, "Is it, really?"

Her eyes fill with tears and she pleads with him. "Please. Please, Gerry, stop! Why are you doing this to me?"

His face doesn't even move when he says, "We had a deal, sweetheart, that's why. The deal we made when you were lying in bed. Or don't you remember?"

"Gerry! Stop!" she wails.

I can't breathe

I don't want to hear any more but I can't stop before knowing the truth.

I face her, the question on my lips. "Did you sleep with him?"

"Matthias. Please." Tears stream down her cheeks.

I want to look away, but I won't know the truth unless she says it to my face. "I asked you a question, Clarissa. Did you sleep with him?"

Gerry interrupts, "I—"

I swing around, feeling murderous. "You shut the fuck up. God, if you value your life, you're going to shut the fuck up." I turn to her again, my head suddenly pounding. "Clarissa. I'm going to give you one last chance to tell me the truth. Did you sleep with my uncle?"

Her face tells me everything I didn't want to know. The pain in her eyes cuts me like a serrated machete, slashing, tearing, maiming me forever. I want to reach out for her. I want to hold her until we forget about this day.

"Say it," I whisper. "I need to hear you say it."

She shakes her head, her entire face crumpled into sobs. "God, Matthias, please don't make me. Please. It's the biggest mistake I ever made."

"Say it!" I roar.

"Matthias," Kingsley says, in a soft, but warning voice. But I don't care. I can't know how I'm going to move on from this moment if I don't hear her say it. Or else I won't let myself believe it.

"Matthias, please. I lo—"

I shake my head, not wanting to hear what she's about to say. "Stop. That's not what I asked you. Say it."

"Yes, I slept with him." Sobs wrack through her chest and tremor the entire room.

The admission knocks the air out of my lungs, and my veins burn with betrayal. My heart breaks, shatters, like someone dunked it into liquid nitrogen and then slammed a sledge hammer right into the left ventricle, breaking it into a million pieces, scattering all over the remnants of whatever existed between her and me.

Realization dawns. "And you told him I was at Leanne's house."

"I didn't call him!" she says, panicked. "I swear I didn't call him!"

"Then how did they know, Clarissa. Tell me how they knew?"

"I don't know!" She looks over at her father, but he just looks away. "Matthias, please." She reaches for me.

I rip my hand away from her, disgusted with myself that I had trusted her, when everything inside me, when everyone around me had told me not to. "I don't believe you, Clarissa. I don't trust you."

My words hover between us, like a billboard broadcasting everything thing that was ever wrong between us.

The life drains from her eyes. "Matthias. I promise..."

I turn away, looking at her hurts too much. "Don't. Don't promise anything. It's not worth anything." I brace against my desk, taking a deep breath, pushing back the devastation in my soul. "You know... you know how I felt about you. You know how much this company means to me. But you did it anyway. They told me not to trust you, and I should've listened."

"Matthias!" she cries, and it tears at me.

"Get out. When I turn around, I don't want to see you here. I don't ever want to see you again."

She doesn't go. Her sobs fill the room, and no one says a word for minutes. And then she runs out of the room, and there's nothing but the pounding of my own heart aching in my ears.

Finally, Gerry, fucking Gerry, says,

"Well, that's too bad. but I guess it's better that you find out now before if you got married."

I spin around, spitting. "You're a piece of work, you worthless piece of shit."

He doesn't even falter. I guess it's not news to him. We always know ourselves best. Instead, he touches me on the shoulder, and I shrug off his slimy hand. "So, now, let's figure out what we're going to do here. Patrick here is willing to talk, see what you're willing to do to make it up for him, and he might ask the ADA to drop the charges."

"Not now," I growl.

"We can't leave it too long. We need to give the reporters something else to focus on. He's generous enough to even sit down with us."

"I said, not now!" I yell.

Gerry snickers, amused by my anger. "Patrick, maybe you should leave. We'll get in touch soon. Don't worry, we will make sure that you're taken care of."

I turn out just in time to see Patrick slither out of my office, cradling his arm. The next time I see him, I'm going to break his other arm as well. What the fuck did he think he was doing coming here? Seeing him in the same room as Clarissa took every last ounce of restraint I had.

Clarissa.

A sob threatens to dislodge itself from my rib cage.

"Gerry. Get out."

"Oh, sonny boy, that was just the minor issue. Now we have to talk about your place here at Baxter Enterprises. Matthias, you violated the morality clause in your contract. It was put in you contract for this exact reason. Do you want to know what they're saying about the IPO? They're saying we should postpone. After all this time, after all this and money, they're saying it's going to tank. All because of you."

I grip the edge of the desk, glaring at my uncle. "It wouldn't have happened if you hadn't made it into a scandal. I bet you called the paparazzi to the courthouse as well, didn't you?"

He doesn't deny it, and I'm stunned by how far he will go to get what he wants. "Blaming me for your mistakes, just like the child you are. But before we go, just know, you should all expect some very big changes soon." He joins Clarissa's father on the other side of room. "Come on, Terry. I'll buy you a drink."

"Get your hands off me," Terry mumbles, shrugging off Gerry's hand just as I had done and follows him out of my office.

"Fuck," Kylian exhales. Speechless for the first time in his life.

Damien comes over and pats me on the back. "Ladies, could you give us the room, please?"

"Of course," My-Linh answers. "Come on, Kiara. Let's go talk to Hannah, she always has the best gossip." She comes over and lays her head against my arm for a moment, and the gentle action breaks the dam in my chest, and the tears cascade, freely flowing down my cheeks.

"Actually guys, could I... I really need to be alone," I choke out when the women are gone. "Please."

They linger for a few seconds, then there's a collective sigh, and then I'm alone.

Utterly, achingly, alone.

I stumble over to my desk, grabbing a bottle off the shelf, foregoing a glass altogether.

The first drink burns.

Deliciously, distractingly, painfully.

By the third sip, I'm numb.

But I keep drinking until the bottle is empty.

The silence in the office is deafening.

But it's still not loud enough to drown out the memory of her words.

"I slept with him."

I replay it over and over and over, until my stomach flips and I grab the wastebasket by my desk.

And try to purge, purge the hurt, purge the memories, purge the feel of her skin under my fingertips, purge her scent first thing in the morning, purge those thoughts that whatever forever I had imagined, was nothing but lies.

Forty-Seven

CLARISSA

"THEY TOLD ME NOT to trust you and I should've listened."
Nothing I do helps.

Nothing I do brings me even a sliver of respite. Nothing helps the sound of his voice in my head. Nothing stops the memories of his face when he heard I had slept with Gerry. Nothing eases the ache of the way he said, *"I don't believe you. I don't trust you."*

Maybe he never did.

Maybe this was all doomed from the start and we had no right letting ourselves fall into a bottomless, hopeless pit of lust.

It was more than lust, Clarissa.

Was it? Maybe that's all it was. Maybe everything else was just blinded by the white heat that ignited when we were in the same room.

Whatever it was, they were the most beautiful moments of my life. Maybe it wasn't supposed to have been forever, but for that short time, I had felt seen, felt understood, felt adored. Even lo—

"No." I say it out loud to make sure I hear it.

It was never *that*.

If it had been that, he would've listened. He would've stopped for one minute and listened. But he didn't. He didn't even give me a chance to explain. He didn't trust me enough to even hear me out.

Understanding knifes into my heart.

Because he never trusted you. Never, ever did.

And I gave him everything.

But did I trust *him?*

I could've gone to him about Gerry, told him everything up front about what was happening, but I was afraid.

I didn't trust him to take my side, to believe me even then.

This was all doomed from the start.

But now it's too late.

And I'm forever stuck in the purgatory of having him once be mine.

***

The phone rings, and I grab it, eagerly glancing at the screen. But it's not him. It's never him.

"Yes?" I ask, not recognizing the number.

"Clarissa."

I suck in a hissing breath. "What do you want, Father?"

"Can we talk?" He sounds like he's a million miles away, his voice quiet, tired.

"There's nothing left to talk about, father. You've proven just what kind of man you are. And I want nothing to do with you ever again."

"You need to underst—"

I cut him off. I don't want to hear it. "From you, I need to understand nothing! I protected you. But I shouldn't have. Because I finally realize it's *your* job to protect *me.* And you never, *ever* have." My hand comes up to rub my chest, trying to ease the ache that hasn't lessened from the day he kicked me out of his life. "You gave me the advice once to pretend that I never knew the Baxter's existed. And I didn't listen. I'm going to give you the same advice now. And you should take it - pretend that you never had a daughter. She's forgotten that she ever had a father."

I hang up.

And for the last time, cry over the loss of a father I never really had.

Forty-Eight

MATTHIAS

"HE SMELLS."

"Like, *really* bad," another voice adds.

"Should we hose him down or something?" That has to Kylian.

"It won't reach." Damien. Always the pragmatist.

"Okay, I have an idea. Everyone, grab your perfumes and colognes! And on three, we'll spray. Ladies, you take the top half, Damien and Kingsley will take the bottom half." Kylian. Again. Whatever the opposite of pragmatist is.

Someone snickers. A woman. Definitely Kiara. "What about you?"

"I'm the foreman," Kylian says. "Sheesh, we all have our jobs. Ready? One. Two. Thre—"

I crack open an eye. "Get away from me."

"It speaks!" Kylian screeches.

I squeeze my eyes shut. "When I get up, I'm going to grab grandfather's letter opener, and I'm going to hold it out, and I want you to run towards it really, really fast."

Kylian scrunches up his face. "That actually sounds like it might hurt quite a bit. No thanks."

A hand grabs my arm and pulls me upright. Kingsley.

I groan. "Kingsley. You, too. You can take turns impaling yourself. Please. It can be my late birthday present."

"I think you're not getting birthday presents for a while," Damien says, nudging me with his foot.

I open my eyes again, taking a moment to figure out where I am. Still in my office, still wearing the same clothes I was wearing when I woke up at Leanne's apartment. How long ago was that? I couldn't tell you if it was a day or a year. I'm on the floor by my desk. How I got there is anyone's guess.

An empty bottle lays at my feet, and it all comes crashing back.

My chest thrums with an aching that's making it hard to breathe. My fingers tingle with the need to see her, to touch her.

But I know I can't.

"Why are you all still here? Don't you have your own jobs? And aren't you guys supposed to go back to your honeymoon?"

"We're here because of you," My-Linh says, kindly. "We can't leave you like this."

"I'm fine." I get to my feet, feeling around for my phone, even though I know I shouldn't hope for a text message or voicemail, I do.

I just want to hear her voice one more time, one more time, to tell me why she did this. Tell me, so I can get over it once and for all.

And move on.

Move on to where?

Somewhere where I don't need to drink my body's volume in scotch to get through the day? That doesn't sound as appealing as you'd think it would.

"She didn't text," Kingsley says, pulling my phone out of his pocket and sliding it onto my desk.

"I didn't say anything. I don't care." It sounds sulky because it is.

"Don't insult me," Kingsley scowls. "Guys, I need to talk to Matthias alone for a bit."

Kingsley talks in two situations: work, and when one of us is in trouble.

I don't like my odds.

The rest file out of my office, Kylian grumbling under his voice and getting a slap to the back of the head from both Kiara and Damien.

"What's up?" I ask, trying to keep my voice light.

Kingsley just stares at me.

Ah, the age-old interrogation technique. Let me talk myself into a hole. Unlike when I was seventeen and crashed a car into Eton on graduation day, I can keep my mouth shut now.

Or not.

"Isn't it funny that there are two more people in our family now?" I say after a while, the silence digging into my skin like a tick. "And girls. Ew."

He doesn't look impressed. Tough room. "What are you going to do about this?"

"Wow, not even going to respond to what I said? Keep going like that and you won't have any friends. Oh... wait."

He just stares back at me. He's really good at this.

So I talk. "Fine. I have to talk to my lawyer about our defense. Maybe self-defense or something. I can talk to Jordan about testifying, he examined Clarissa the night that Patrick attacked her. The first time. Not sure I should take the stand, though; pretty sure I'll just blurt out that I should've killed him.

Kingsley barely blinks. "Not that."

"Oh, well, the IPO? I don't know. We have a month. I'll have to talk to Paula and the PR department. It might be a lost cause though, what with the engagement being over..."

"Not that either."

That annoys me. "Then what the fuck are you talking about?"

"You *know* what."

I shake my head. It's a mistake. My brain feels like it's rattling around in my skull. "I'm not talking about that. There's nothing to say."

He sighs, and then sits down on the floor next to me. "Well, I don't care, because I'm going to talk about it and you can listen, you little shit. And I can call you that because I'm your only big brother." He smooths out the creases in his pants. It's probably the first time he's sat on the floor in twenty years. "You need to think, really think, about what really happened. Don't get blinded by your hatred for Gerry. I get it, we *all* get it."

"What are you talking about? What is there to think about?"

He shifts, obviously uncomfortable. That makes two of us. "Why would she do this? I know we've all been wary about her, but what does Clarissa really get out of this? Doesn't she have more on the line than you do with this ridiculous arrangement?"

I scrunch my face up. "I thought you were here to say *'I told you so.'* I think I would've preferred that."

He rolls his eyes. "Tough shit. Something's not right, man. I don't know what it is, but something's not right. I saw her at Damien's wedding. Literally the worst place for her, considering their past, but she didn't care. She was there for you. She couldn't take her eyes off you. And that's saying something because I still maintain that you're ugly as fuck."

His words pound against my head like a blunt mallet, barely able to get anything through my thick skull. "I think I prefer when you're quiet."

Annoyingly, he doesn't look offended. "I'm just going to say one more thing. No one ever said it was easy to trust someone else. Nothing that's worth anything is easy. Think about that before you convince yourself that everything in the last two months with her didn't happen."

He pats me on the shoulder as he leaves. "Either way, nothing that you're looking for is going to be at the bottom of a bottle."

But I'm just not ready to listen.

Days bleed into night and into days.

Nothing but my telephone screen tells me it's been almost a week since I last saw her. Why does it feel like a fucking century?

One drunken day leads into another until even my brothers give up on me and stop visiting. The only person I see is Hannah, who comes in and throws a bottle of water and a granola bar at me now and then, and makes a plea for me to get showered.

I do, one time, crawl into the bathroom, and sit on the shower floor, fully clothed, the water cascading over me, for hours, until Hannah comes in, turns the tap off, and tries to dry me off as well as she can.

A week after the confrontation in my office I get an alert on my phone that reminds me of the reservation at Blue Hill at Stone Barns I'd made for Clarissa to celebrate three months of Malt being open.

Fuck.

A week. That's too long.

Get the fuck up, Matthias.

It hurts. Everything hurts.

Or maybe it's from the sheer act of standing up after being horizontal for over a week.

And for the first time since I last saw Clarissa, I leave my office.

I take another drink while I wait outside the back door of the club. She usually arrives around eleven p.m. but who knows where she's been staying since I kicked her out of my life.

It's over an hour before I hear her footsteps down the side alley.

"Matthias."

Her voice twists in and around my head and I take in the sight of her, dressed in a strappy summer dress, sunglasses covering her eyes, coffee cup in her hand.

How had I never realized what my name could truly sound like until the right person said it?

The wrong person, Matthias, *the wrong person.*

She walks by and reaches for the door.

"Wait." Her hand freezes on the handle, waiting. But what is there to say?

"You shouldn't be here," she responds when I don't say anything.

Anger streaks through me.

She's right. I shouldn't be here. I shouldn't need to see her, need to hear her voice for even just a minute. I should be able to just walk away from her. I fling the half empty bottle of scotch down the alleyway. It crashes onto the ground in a mess of glass and amber liquid.

"Where am I supposed to go then, Clarissa?" I ask her, desperately. "Where else is there for me?"

"I don't know." The catch in her voice squeezes my heart. "But it's not here."

How can she be so cold?

Because she never felt anything, anyway? It was all a lie?

Her hand pushes down on the door handle, but I grab her wrist, pulling her back

"Tell me. Tell me why did you do this! Tell me why. Please." A week ago she had said the same thing to me. *Please, Matthias.*

"Why, Matthias? You wouldn't believe me, anyway. You were always just waiting for me to break your trust."

I recoil. "That's not true."

"Isn't it? Didn't you believe everything Gerry said without even giving me a chance to explain? Gerry! The person you hate most. Except for me."

Her hands rest on my chest for a nanosecond and for a moment I think she wants to touch me, but then she pushes as hard as she can. I stumble back a few steps out of sheer surprise.

"Don't come back here, Matthias," she pleads. And when she runs inside, I catch the glisten of tears on her cheeks.

That's it, Matthias. No more.

I slump against the wall outside her club, knowing she's just on the other side. Forever just out of reach.

Forty-Nine

CLARISSA

"Boss, the—"

James's voice fades into the abyss as I run past him and into my office.

"Shit!" I yell, swinging the door shut with a loud slam. The sound momentarily provides some release, but then the sound of his voice drowns out everything else again.

After a week, I'd finally found a way to get through the day without needing to hide in my office for hours on end, sobbing.

What was he even doing here? Other than to twist the knife. Doesn't he know how much it hurts to see him?

"I hate you, Matthias Baxter. I hate you so fucking much," I sob.

And I feel myself about to slip into another bout of tears when my phone rings.

Composing myself, I answer. "This is Clarissa."

"Clarissa, it's John."

My immigration lawyer. I hadn't heard from him in over a month, since Matthias and I had seen him to submit my spousal green card application.

"I've been waiting to hear back from you," he says.

That's weird. I hadn't heard anything about him needing to hear from me. "Oh, were you needing something from me?"

"Well, there's a time limit when we can resubmit your application for a business visa."

"I don't understand..."

There's a pause before he explains. "Oh, Mr. Baxter didn't tell you? It was found that someone had tampered with the agent who processed your application. He has been fired and all of his cases are now in review. Mr. Baxter is actually the one who told me about it. So, I asked him which application you wanted to go ahead with and he said he'd ask you and get back to me. But we only have another month to submit the paperwork for your original application."

What I am hearing? Is this what he came here to tell me? Why hadn't he just said so? "Um. I... I'm going to have to get back to you, John."

"Of course, sometime this week would be best."

"I will. John? When did you talk to Matthias about this?"

He thinks about it for a bit, flipping some pages. "Oh, it was almost a month ago now. I'm sorry to nag you, I just wanted to make sure you didn't miss the deadline.

A month.

When we came back from Milan.

A whole month.

And he never brought it up once?

Why?

Had he been so desperate to make sure I went through with this stupid fake marriage that he's kept this from me?

My body stings with betrayal.

Who's the liar now, Matthias? Who's the fucking liar now?

MATTHIAS

OVER THE NEXT WEEK, I make more enemies than I ever had friends.

Everyone and everything annoys me and I get increasingly more irate. By Friday afternoon, I'm downright tyrannical.

"Hannah! Where the fuck is the Henderson report? I said I wanted it on my desk at two p.m. It's three now. God! Can't anyone do the simplest tasks around here?"

I storm back into my office, ignoring the looks of everyone on the floor. When they're the ones with my responsibility, then they can comment on my behavior.

"Hannah!" I yell again. The papers on my desk are a fucking mess. I can't find anything. "Where is my iPad?"

She comes in, slams it on the table and slaps the back of my head. On her way out of my office, she pulls the double doors of my office shut, but not before saying, "Maybe when you stop throwing tantrums, you can keep your door open."

Except for that morning outside of the club, I haven't seen or heard from Clarissa.

And I thought it would start to get easier, but with each ticking second, the missing of Clarissa buries deeper inside me, an ever-present ache in my chest that sometimes overwhelms every other sensation.

I miss every fucking thing about her.

I've only been able to go back to my apartment once, her scent drowning me when I walked into our... *my* bedroom. Her toiletries in the bathroom, her clothes still hanging in the walk-in wardrobe, a lip-stained glass on the kitchen counter that I couldn't bring myself to ask Marika to wash. They all haunt me.

I don't want the traces of her gone.

Saying goodbye is hard when you know it's going to be the last time.

I leave a note asking Marika to pack up her things. But on my way out, I scrunch up the note and throw it away.

Maybe one day, when I can stand being here without her actually there, the ghost of her will be enough.

My office door opens and Hannah steps in, her face about as stormy as mine has been.

"I'm not done throwing a tantrum, you might as well keep the door closed."

"Mr. Masters is here to see you," she says through gritted teeth. She might not say anything, but Hannah knows everything that's been going on.

She steps out as he comes in.

Being based in New York while Terry lives in London, I only see him in person three or four times a year. I guess the last time he was here; I was too busy trying to wrap my head around the three of them in my office to really look at him.

He looks old. His hair is completely white now; his face lined with wrinkles that look an inch deep, eyes devoid of color. I guess not having a heart makes you age badly.

"We need to talk," he says, still standing by the door.

"I don't think that we do. There's a board meeting next week. I can talk to you there. I mean, you called it to talk about my 'bad boy' behavior after all," I say, the bitterness clearly evident.

If I ever forgive him for his part of my possible firing, I'll still never forgive him for what he did to Clarissa. Just because she turned out to be the traitor her father is, doesn't mean I can't hate him for what he did.

"Matthias. You need to listen to me."

I lean back, piercing him with my look. I could just kick him out, but while he's here, I'm going to make it as hard for him as possible. "What makes you think that?"

The wrinkles deepen a little. "It's about Clarissa."

I sit forward in my chair. "Then I definitely don't have to listen to you. You raised her, giving her everything she ever wanted, and then, because of one mistake, you took away everything she had ever known. You're not only a bad father. You're a cruel person. And to tell her it's what Damien would've wanted is the biggest load of bullshit I've ever heard. If Damien had wanted to punish her, he would've done it himself. Good thing he's much more forgiving than I am." The more I talk about it, the more I get agitated. "A chairman of the board is supposed to put the company's best interests at heart. How does getting the Director arrested supposed to be in the company's best interests? When Gerry told you where I was, you should've talked him out of it."

Terry squirms, frowning before he drops a bombshell.

"He didn't call me. *I* called *him*. Clarissa didn't call him. She called *me*."

My mind blanks. I don't know if I actually heard him or my brain conjured it up. "Say that again."

"Clarissa didn't call Gerry to tell him where you were. She called me. For help. She thought I could help find a way to mitigate the effects of what you did. *I'm* the one who called Gerry. And together, we decided to anonymously report you. She didn't call him. She was telling you the truth."

Confusion scatters all over my brain. "I don't believe you. You're lying."

"It's the truth. I can show you." He holds out his phone. I take it because my body feels unable to process anything just yet.

I look down at the phone. Clarissa's number, two weeks ago, at two a.m.

"This doesn't prove anything."

He shrugs, "That's because you're trying not to believe me. But it's the truth."

I stare at him. "Why didn't she say anything?!"

He takes the phone out of my hands and tucks it back into his pocket. "Maybe because she was protecting me, I don't know. But she's not speaking to me. And I don't think she ever will again."

I just stare at him, openmouthed. "Why, Terry? Why the fuck would you do this? I was going to handle it!"

His eyes cement in hate, jaw hardening. "Your family, you Baxter's"—he spits my family name out of his mouth like it's acid—"have ruined my daughter. My beautiful daughter, who could've achieved anything, done anything. But your brother turned her head and then abandoned her. Left her like she was trash by the side of the road."

I shake my head. "That's not what happened."

But he doesn't hear me. "And then you. Pulling her under with your reckless behavior! It was only a matter of time before you hurt her. She was doing so well here. She was taking responsibility for her own life for the first time and then you just screw it all up! I needed her to get her away from you as soon as possible, by any means possible. And if she hates me for the rest of her life, at least I knew what I needed to do for her." He sucks in a rough breath. "I didn't know the history with Gerry. He never told me. But... now. I can't have anything to do with him. With any of you."

Terry is the hero in his own little story, the one where he did the right thing by his daughter, until it was his ass on the line. "You're a piece of work. You've turned everything in your head. She was never the victim, with Damien or me. Only with you. You've hurt her more than anyone else ever has."

"Until now," he says, his eyes glinting. "You say I hurt her, but she risked everything she's worked for, all the work she's done to distance herself from her family.... for you. She called me. For you. She did the one thing she never wanted to do again. For you. And what did you do? You didn't even have the decency to hear her out."

He's right. "So why are you telling me this?"

"Because she doesn't deserve you thinking she did this. I'm done with the lot of you, I'm handing in my resignation, I'll let you all figure out how to fix this bloody mess. But I don't know if you're going to even still be here to see it all. Your days are numbered here; your uncle has seen to that."

The room spins and I have to lean back into my chair, watching him walk out of my office, leaving the debris of the bomb he's just detonated.

Clarissa didn't betray me. She didn't collude with Gerry. Whatever happened before has nothing to do with us, but she didn't betray me.

Elation sparks in my chest, the first feeling of life I've felt in weeks. But it's immediately stomped out by the dread that comes with the memory of her face when I saw her at the club.

"You wouldn't believe me, anyway. You were always waiting for a reason to distrust me."

Was she right? Had I been carrying around the baggage of the past without realizing it?

Guilt blasts as understanding dawns.

She couldn't have felt like she could tell me about Gerry because I would've acted like she was fulfilling every betrayal that I was just waiting to happen. Maybe that's why I had tried to hold on so tightly. So that maybe when it came time for her to run, she'd be bonded to me.

I just hadn't expected that I was going to be the reason we weren't together anymore.

I hadn't given a fuck that she'd slept with Gerry. I didn't like it, but I knew what kind of slimy weasel he could be, and it's not like I was some saint before we'd gotten together.

It's because it was a confirmation of everything he was saying.

It was confirmation that she had turned to him in my worst hour.

I need to see her. I need to talk to her; tell her I know everything. And hope that she can forgive me.

"Hannah, don't call. I'm going out," I call out as I run out of the office.

"Good. About time."

Me: Meet me at the tree in Washington Square Park. I need to talk to you. Please.

It's been two hours since I sent the text for Clarissa to meet me. I chose the spot we've favored for our picnic lunches. The park always gave us ample things to watch and talk about, with one of our favorite times being when we'd watched a father teaching his daughter how to wolf whistle from a YouTube video, but he was about as bad at it as she was. So, I went to meet them, and after a hilarious ten minutes, all three of us were whistling like old pros. I'd learned a lot about myself when it comes to teaching, and the father and daughter left, both having learned a new skill. I'd come back to see Clarissa with a smile on her face, watching intently, although she'd pretended to be focusing on her phone.

It had been hard not to think about her watching me and wondering how I'd be as a father. Not that that was a concept we had even come anywhere close to talking about.

But it had stayed with me.

And sometimes, when I was having a particularly rough day at work, I would imagine the softness in her eyes, the way she'd looked at me when she thought I wasn't looking.

Now here we are, her hating me for not believing her. And me, saturated in guilt over how I'd treated her. Wondering if she would ever forgive me. And knowing I can't blame her if she doesn't.

Two hours and fifteen minutes.

Soon, it's going to be too late for her to leave the club. She has only missed a handful of times to open the club, and most of those involved me.

Her work ethic never ceases to amaze me.

How she has transformed from having every last thing handed to her on a silver platter, to now making sacrifices so that her staff are taken care of.

Fucking Terry.

He talked about loving her, but he never knew her at all. Clarissa didn't need to be forced to learn how to take care of herself.

She is strong, capable, a hard worker and kind in her own subtle way. Creative and resourceful. All the things he thought she never was because he forced her into a life that made her believe she wasn't good enough.

But she was better than all of us all along.

Better than me most of all.

Fuck.

What have I done?

She's not coming.

She's not coming, and it's all my fault.

Brushing the dirt from the back of my pants, the hopelessness sinks my stomach. My fist meets the tree trunk, sending a sharp pain up my arm, making me forget for just a moment.

I need more.

Alcohol isn't doing it anymore.

But I can't keep feeling like this.

It's going to rot my soul away.

As if it matters that I have one without her.

I wave a cab down. "Teterboro Airport. As fast as you can, man!"

Don't be stupid, Matthias. Don't be stupid. It'll pass, I try to tell myself.

The cab turns into traffic just as my phone buzzes. Something at the last moment compels me to check it even though I have no need for contact with anyone but her.

The text, it's from her.

Relief floods my body.

She's coming. Something held her up, that's all.

I open the text.

Clarissa: *"Anxiety attack. At the club. Please."*

No. No, no, no, no. Not an anxiety attack...

Heart thick in my mouth, I jump out of the cab, anyway. It's barely half a mile. *I'll be there soon, darling.* My lungs expand and squeeze, sending oxygen around my body as I run. Shit. I didn't even reply. She doesn't even know I'm on my way.

I can't waste the time. It's going to stop now.

One more block away.

I'll be there in a minute, darling. Just breathe.

The front entrance is locked when I get there. I race around the building until I get to the back entrance.

"Matthias!" James shouts. "She's upstairs. She wouldn't come down."

I sprint up the stairs, legs burning with each step.

She's on her knees in the middle of the room, clutching at her chest as Clementine kneels next to her, rubbing her back.

"Get me a glass of water, now!" I yell, falling onto the ground next to her. "I'm here, Rissie. I'm here."

The looks she gives me is pained, but she doesn't push me away. Instead, her eyes beg me for help.

"I'm here, okay. You're going to be okay. We're going to get through this. On three, we're just going to take a little breath, okay?" I grab her hand and squeeze it, grounding her in that action. "One, two, three. Breathe, darling."

She takes a little breath, and then it shoots out of her almost immediately.

"Good, Clarissa. We're going to take it nice and slow. One more. Ready?" I drag the air into my breath, and she does the same, her face still panicked. "And out." The air is forced out of my body with a *whoosh*. "One more, in. And out."

She copies, with each repetition, it becomes a little easier.

I settle on the floor, rubbing her back. "The park was so crowded today, and I saw a few kids using those skipping ropes they hung up." I talk, talk to distract her, get her brain to focus on something other than the desire to flee. "One more breath. In, hold it, and out. Good."

I talk.

I talk for ten minutes while reminding her to breathe.

I tell her about Damien and My-Linh traveling around the U.S., instead of their original honeymoon plans. And how My-Linh volunteered Damien as an audience member for the show when they went to Disney, and there's a picture of Damien wearing some sort of cloak, apparently at the was the moment when he was going to commit. And then there's another picture of him smiling into the camera, because My-Linh is standing next to him.

I tell her about how Hannah went on a date the other day, and came to work in the same clothes that she was wearing the day before.

I tell her about getting some pictures from the owners of the ranch, and how they are willing to discuss selling. But I don't tell her, that I can't bear to buy it, if she's not going to go there with me. That she's the reason I went there the first time. And I won't go back unless she's by my side.

She listens.

Zoning in and out as she fights with her brain. But soon, she focuses for ten, fifteen seconds at a time. She even nods at once point. Her eyes losing the erratic way they flick back and forth, her hands no longer white-knuckled.

When she breathes on her own, I scan her body, making sure that there are no other injuries. Sometimes when the attack comes on unexpectedly, she inadvertently hurts herself.

"And Leanne finally told me who it was she's seeing. You're not going to believe it. It's with the older guy who lives on the second floor! Little wench. How's she going to bring home other guys now?"

A little smile tickles on the corners of her mouth. "Funny."

My heart soars at her first word since I arrive. "Yeah." I give her hand another squeeze before laying it gently on her leg. "Alright?"

"I think so." She takes a deep breath and inspects her hands, like she just realized they were attached to her.

It's horrifying what she goes through each time. But I see her working so hard to prevent them, I can't help wondering if she's had one in the time I haven't seen her.

She frowns, and looks at a point just a few inches from my head, avoiding my eyes. "Thank you."

I nod. "I told you, wherever I am in the world, whatever I'm doing. If you need me, I'm going to be here, Clarissa."

She stands, brushing the dust off her bottom. It reminds me of the same action I did just a half an hour ago. And I know I shouldn't but I can't stop myself asking, "Why didn't you come?"

Confusion leaches into her eyes. "Come?"

"I sent you a message. I was waiting at the park. I wanted to talk."

She shakes her head. The way her curls fall around her face makes my insides ache. I have to take a step back to stop myself from reaching out and tangling my fingers in her hair.

"I didn't get the message. I've been busy. We've been busy," she explains.

And my heart sinks all over again.

I reach for the glass of water Clementine left on the table. "Have a drink."

She takes it, and as brief as it is, when our fingers touch, I'm instantly breathless.

"Sorry," she mumbles into the glass as she drinks.

"Your father came to see me today." Emotions light the kindle of distance and she takes a step back. Two steps between us, but it feels like a lifetime of misunderstandings and baggage. I wish I could incinerate it all with a wave of my hand. "He told me what actually happened. He told me you didn't call Gerry, that you called him. And that you made him promise not to tell anyone. But he didn't keep the promise, did he?"

"No."

The confirmation doesn't bring the relief that I had hoped. "Why didn't you tell me? Why didn't you tell me when I asked you? Why did you let me believe that you'd called Gerry?"

She flinches with every word. "I *didn't* let you believe that. I tried to tell you I didn't call him. But you didn't listen."

She did. She did. This wasn't her fault. It was all mine. "Clarissa."

But she's not done. "You put two and two together and came up with some ridiculous number. When you should never, ever have believed Gerry over me!"

Guilt stabs at my chest. "God, I know that, I know that now. I'm so sorry. I should've known better."

She nods, eye glistening. "Yes, you should've. I didn't tell you because we both promised that night that we weren't going to tell anyone we'd talked. And I kept my promise even if he didn't." She takes such a deep breath, I worry that she's having another anxiety attack, but she continues, "I lived my whole being poisoned by him about how to treat people. It took getting to see the world on my own to see how bad my behavior was. You called me a bitch. I was one. I am one. But I'm trying. I'm not going to let my father ruin all of that."

I want to pull her to me, I want to tell her that she's achieved so much. "Incredible. He said that I was the reason you'd give up all the progress you made. He said I was the reason that all that you'd learn was going to waste. "

She doesn't answer for a few seconds, then she says, "Maybe neither of us should've trusted the other."

I frown. "What do you mean?"

"I mean my green card."

Oh, my god. I had completely forgotten about that. I had meant to tell her about it that night. But then the whole debacle happened with Ravel and then we went to Milan and it completely slipped my mind. I had meant to talk to her about what she wanted to do.

"You kept it from me," she accuses me.

I shake my head. "I didn't mean to. I forgot. I really did forget."

Her eyes narrow. "I don't believe you. You should've told me the second you got the phone call." She's right. I hadn't wanted to tell her until I'd figured out what I wanted her to do. "You're no different. You didn't hit me, you didn't kick me out of my house, but you didn't let me make my own decision either, Matthias! How am I supposed to trust you, if I can't even trust you to tell me about things that affect me like this? You had no right!"

We stand there, two broken people, scarred by our good intentions on our ways to a separate hell.

Tears splash onto her pale cheeks, and I ache to brush them away. To absorb her pain with mine. But there are still things she wants to say, and she deserves for me to hear them.

"I'm so tired, Matthias. I'm tired of my anxiety. I'm tired of crying over you. I'm tired of having to explain and apologize for things I did when I was a different person. I'm tired of having to show everyone I've changed only for them not to see it. Because each time I do, instead of reminding myself how far I've come, it pulls me back to the past. And that's a very unhealthy place for me to be."

"So, don't. Don't look back to the past." My hopelessness deepens. Burying so deeply inside me, it feels like there's no way it can ever be dug out.

Her chin lifts, and she smiles sadly through the tears. "You don't get it do you? You're the one pulling me into the past."

There's no holding back the hurt that causes me. "I'm so sorry."

She gives me a tear drenched smile. "I know. Wouldn't it be great if we didn't have to keep apologizing to each other? I'm not good for you, either. Look at your life. It's just as much of a mess as mine is. Don't you want to find someone who makes everything easier instead of harder?"

I reach over, taking her hands in mine. Her touch feels as new as the first time. "Do you honestly think that I will ever be with another woman?"

She doesn't answer my question. "Doesn't it hurt just being together? Wouldn't your life be better without me?"

My hand cups her face, and she leans into it, just a little, molding her cheek to my palm. Fitting perfectly. "Oh, my darling, show me a loss that will hurt like losing you." I swallow the sob stuck in my throat. "Do you need time? And space? Tell me what I can do?"

Her hand cups mine. "You need to let me go. You need to release me from this pain. I can't take much more, Matthias. I'm not strong enough to push you away. You need to do it for me. It's what's best for me."

Fresh pain slashes at me, and I know I have to go. Without knowing when I'll see her again. "I don't know what made you think that I was a good guy. Don't wait for me to do the best for you. Maybe if I loved you a little bit less, I could put you first. But you're not *the first* in my life. You're the only. Don't you ever forget that." Her shoulders shake with an eruption of wracking sobs.

I wrap my arms around her, holding her until the gasps stop, and my shirt is drenched with the evidence of her agony, and hers holds the only tears I ever shed over a woman.

Finally, when there's nothing left, I pull away, my thumb brushing away a tear teetering on her eyelash. I drop one last kiss on her forehead.

Fifty-One

MATTHIAS

"WE HAVE EVERYTHING," DMITRIK says, opening the folder and spreading the contents over my desk.

My eyes scan the scattered papers and pictures on the table. It makes me sick just looking at it. But that's exactly how I should feel. Only a heartless fucker could do these things and walk around like he doesn't give a shit.

"You ready to go tonight?" I ask. I want this done as soon as possible.

"You know I am." Dmitrik's face is a picture of disgust. He wants to take this asshole down as much as I do.

I nod. It's now or never. "Okay. Pick me up at ten. That should give us enough time."

**

We sit in the dark of Patrick's living room for almost an hour before we hear muffled chatter outside the apartment door.

Keys drop and someone giggles. Probably not Patrick. There's some fumbling, and then the door flies open. He had a harder time getting into his own apartment than we did.

Being cocky, and probably cheap as fuck, he has the barest of security systems. Getting past the lobby was even easier. When you have a recognizable face, you can convince anyone that you're meant to be there.

And now we wait.

I let him stumble around for a little after the lights don't turn on as they should when they reach the living room.

"Stupid fucking light," he grumbles. "Oh well, who needs light?"

"Works for me," the female voice says. Not half as drunk as he sounds. She's either being paid to be here, or she's going to be leaving with some things that he didn't know he was giving away.

I wait until they fall onto the couch, and fumble around for a minute before I flick the light on.

"What the fuck?" he shouts, covering his eyes instead of bothering with his unzipped pants.

"Hello Patrick."

He scrambles to his feet when he realizes it's me, snuffling like a warthog, his eyes already filling with fear. "What the fuck are you doing in my apartment?"

I smile, cold and thin. "You know what, I get asked that a lot. I must keep showing up where I'm not wanted. You must know what that's like, not being wanted."

The woman gets to her feet, watching the scene play out with a look of amusement on her face.

"Right, miss?" I say to her.

And she just shrugs. "I don't know him that well."

I pick a photograph off the pile sitting in front of me on the coffee table and slide it across to her. It's a picture of Clarissa's bruised temple. I can't look at it for too long if I don't want to end this whole thing too fast by pushing him off his balcony. "If you don't want to end up with one of those, I suggest you get out of here while you can."

She pales, probably wondering what might have happened to her tonight. And that's just it. He looks harmless. Those are always the worst ones.

"I... I'm just working," she admits.

"I know. It's okay. You're not doing anything wrong." I cock my head and Dmitrik steps out of the shadows. "Can you help the lady and make sure she didn't waste her time here? And get Kevin to take her where she needs to go."

He grunts and leads her out of the room, his hand on her elbow.

Patrick stands, legs awkwardly spread, trying to stop his pants from dropping to his knees, shirt half unbuttoned, eyes glazed. With a wipe of his hand, he smears the lipstick on his mouth. Marks of the punches I'd gifted him have almost fully faded.

A picture of a mess of a loser.

"You're a fucking piece of work," I hiss and then spit on the ground by my feet, trying to get the disgust out of my mouth.

"Get out of my house," he says. But there's not conviction. Every time it's been just him and me, he's always come out the loser. Maybe he should've thought of that before he not only hurt Clarissa but countless other women as well.

"I will. I wouldn't be caught dead in this dump," I say, looking around with a sneer. "Too bad we won't be able to say the same thing about you."

I place a hand on the top picture on the pile of pictures and fan them all out over the length of his table.

I start listing off names. "Lindsay McIntyre. Janet Seabra. Melanie Anson. Michelle Powers..."

With each name, he pales a little more.

I stop, lifting my foot up onto the coffee table between us so he can see my steel capped boots. "Would you like me to continue?" I don't even need to glance at the list, I'd made a point to remember every woman on that list.

The Adam's apple in his throat bobs. "How do you know those names?"

"You know something, Patrick?" I stand up, grabbing the gaudy paperweight on the table, and weighing it in my hand. "Do you know the difference between having a fifteen-million-dollar inheritance, which I'm sure you've pissed away on hookers and alcohol that you don't even know how to enjoy, and having fifteen *billion*?"

He swallows and takes a step back, eyes locked on the paperweight.

I tap the paperweight on the table, showing him how solid it is. "Do you know what 'fuck you' money is?"

A head shake. "No."

"Well, it could mean all sorts of things, it could mean you can buy and sell people, it can mean you can put a price on someone's head and if you pay it, everyone will look the other way, and you can do whatever you want with that person."

I round him, stepping in so close I'm sure he can smell my cologne, and I can smell the days-old undershirt he's wearing. "You don't have 'fuck you money,' do you, Patrick? You have what you think is 'fuck you money.' There's a difference. Like the amount you paid all these women is laughable. You hurt them, and then you took advantage of them again. Do you know what that creates? People who hate you with a passion and want to see you dead." I stand behind him, nudging his foot with mine. "But that's what you do, isn't it? Prey on the weak, the needy. It's what you thought Clarissa was, didn't you? She was beautiful, came from a good family, a family you thought you were going to be able to associate with. She needed a green card, and you made sure she needed you for that."

The irony isn't lost on me. But I'll deal with my guilt later. For now, I'm focused on him. Sniveling. Little. Fucktard.

"*I* have fuck you money. Specifically"—I kick my foot out, swiping it under his shin and he goes toppling the floor, his head grazing the corner of the coffee table and screams out in pain—"I have fuck with Patrick Linzer money. And when I pay someone off, they stay quiet. Or even better, I pay them to talk about you."

I lean in, whispering against his ear. "And guess who I paid to talk, Patrick?"

"Ginnifer Pope, Brenda Notting. Wow, Brenda was actually happy to talk for free. But I couldn't have that. So, I paid her what you should have. Should I go on, Patrick?" I stomp on his legs, it gives way under my foot, not breaking, but he still screams.

He screams like a little bitch. "Please. No."

"No?" I grab his shoulder and shove him onto his back. "But I'm just getting started." I step on his arm so he can't move it and dangle the paperweight over his face. "You know what, Patrick? You're actually not that bad looking. Could use a spray tan, maybe, and a haircut. But I hate to think what will happen to your prospects of finding a wife if you have a giant scar on your face. Now I don't give a shit about a scar, but you can't really rely on your personality, can you?"

I pretend to drop the paperweight, catching it a few inches from his face, so close my knuckles brush against his nose.

"God! No!" he whimpers. "What do you want?"

"Me? Aw, I don't want anything. I have 'fuck you money,' remember?" I pull my keychain out of my pocket. "I'm just havin' a little fun with you. I mean, that's what you tell them, don't you? Just a little fun." I bend at the knee and drive the stem of a car key right into his shoulder socket. Until it breaks skin and his scream fades into a whimper. "Don't worry, I'm not going to break any bones or anything. Just seeing how much you can take until you break. Shouldn't take too much."

"Please," he pants, "what do you want?"

Oh, the thing I want, I can't have. I want him cremated alive. But I'm not the person he hurt. They're the one who should get to decide what happens to him.

So I play with him instead. "Well, I don't know. What do you have, Patrick?" I look around the room. "I mean, I was going to send a file with all of your transgressions to the media, but I'm willing to listen to see what you might want to trade me for it. We don't really have the same taste in art. I mean that Degas"—I point to a painting on the wall—"I own the original. So, what else have you got?"

I stand, one leg on either of his head, and he sweats, looking up at me. "I... I can drop my charges."

I pull him up so he's kneeling again, blood staining his left shoulder.

"Well, that's not really how it works. I mean, you can tell them you're not going to pursue them, but I could still get prosecuted. And for what? Making sure you didn't do to Clarissa what I did to you? I mean, I don't really think it's going to trial. And why is that?"

I grip a handful of his hair and yank his head back with a crack of his neck. "B-B-Because you h-have f-f-fuck you money."

"Very good! Look at you learning. So... tell me again, what are you going to give me if I take it easy on you?"

"I... I'm not going to press charges and... and... whatever you want. Please."

I whisper into his head. "And you're not to hurt another woman again. Because I'm telling you now. I'll find them. I'll find every single one of them. And I will have what you did to them done to you, but so much worse. So, so much worse, Pat. Do we have a deal?"

He nods like a bobble head. "Yes. Okay."

"Good. And you're going to release a statement that you're going to donate $500,000 to a women's shelter."

He tries to shake his head, but I'm still holding it. His pupils narrow instead. "That's... too much. Please. I don't have much left..."

I smile a smile that doesn't reach further than the corner of my lips. "Make it $600,000. Keep talking. I can count all the way to fifteen million."

"Okay! Okay...."

I let go of his hair. "See how easy this was? We're almost done, Patrick. We have had a lot of fun here, haven't we?"

I sink into the sofa while he kneels there, drooling, dripping down one side of his face as his lip swells, a look of both fear and loathing in his eyes.

"Just one more thing." I put my phone on the table before sitting back, arms folded. "I want to know everything that Gerry said to you. Every single fucking word."

When I leave an hour later, Patrick is no worse for wear. Maybe his thighs are a little tired and his finger a little sore. That can happen if someone drops a paperweight on it. I liked that thing. I took it with me.

My head aches from all the things he told me about Gerry, his plans, his renewed motivation to make sure that Kingsley never takes his rightful place as CEO of Baxter Enterprises. He tells me things that turn my stomach. And those are just the things that Gerry would tell a slug like Patrick. What else he has planned, is going to come out of nowhere...

I hand Dmitrik the envelope with the pictures and testimonies of the women who agreed that it was okay to release their stories.

"Wait until he releases the statement and then send those out."

He nods.

I change my mind. "Actually, you know what? Send those out now. Fuck him if he still wants to come after me after that."

Dmitrik nods and tucks the envelope into his jacket. "You okay? It got serious in there."

We stop under a street light, waiting for Kevin to return. "Has someone ever hurt someone you loved?"

His eyes darken.

"Then you know. There's not such a thing as too serious."

Fifty-Two

CLARISSA

ALL IN ALL, I couldn't be prouder of my risk.

But what's the point of joy in your achievements when you don't have someone to share it with?

Although Matthias and I haven't formally announced a break up, it's been weeks since the last of our public sightings and the tabloids are rife with theories about what has happened.

It's a sunny summer day when James comes back after a weekend away. He's excited because he came first place in a national bar-tender competition and is going on to compete in the international heats in a few months.

I could not be happier for him. He's a drawcard for the bar, and it's only fair that he's recognized for his contribution.

"James, can you come here for a moment?" I call out to him one day.

"What's up, boss?"

Over the months we've settled in a professional closeness, and when I need to take a few hours off, he's always the one who steps up, somehow keeping an eye on the club even from the behind the bar. He's training two others to take over so he can take a night off a week, and go off for his competitions without feeling guilty about leaving me in the lurch.

He comes to stand next to me outside the front of the club. I point to a newly painted addition to the club's front window.

"James Spritely – Winner of The Barley and Mint Bartender Competition."

He yells in surprise and pulls me in for a side hug, and I don't fight him off. It's been a long time since I've hugged someone. It feels nice. It reminds me that my brain isn't encased in a robotic body. I'm human. And sometimes it's okay that I need another human too.

Just not *that* human.

It's not okay that I need *that one*.

"You're okay here for a few hours?" I say, once he releases me. "I'm meeting someone at the coffee shop on Cornelia Street."

He shoos me. "Get out of here. You're blocking my sign."

I laugh and walk away, turning only to wave him a goodbye over my shoulder.

Breath empties from my lungs.

Matthias.

I freeze, dragging in a breath, and then turn back to where James is still standing.

No Matthias. I must've imagined it.

Thinking about him for every moment of the day has me seeing him everywhere. On the other side of the bed when I open my eyes, sitting in my office at the end of the night if he needed to get some work done, standing at the Vietnamese cafe counter, laughing at me because I always order without peppers.

Everywhere.

His voice in my head, talking to me when I'm alone, encouraging me, talking problems out with me, reminding me to breathe when the anxiety hits.

And sometimes, just sometimes, I let myself remember how he told me that I was his only.

I wonder if his presence will ever fade from my brain. And I don't know if I should wish that it will or won't.

Halifax is waiting inside when I get to the café.

We're about a month away from opening the club as a morning coffee spot. For now, we'll only open from eight a.m. until twelve p.m. to see if there's a demand, and then we will figure it out from there.

Halifax talks about coffee like James talks about ice and glasses. And it's a privilege to listen to him.

"Sorry, I'm late," I mumble as I hang my bag on the back of the chair and settle into my seat.

"All good. Try this one." He pushes an espresso cup towards me. I lift it to my mouth, almost drunk from the fragrance. Thick, with hints of tobacco and caramel. I take a sip as he looks at me expectantly.

Wow," I say, the coffee hitting me in the back of the throat in an explosion of flavor. "This one, definitely."

"Great!" he grins. "That's my favorite from the Australia trip."

"I see why."

He scribbles something down on the notepad on the table and I lean forward, reading as he writes. "You smell like coffee." I giggle.

"Thanks," he says with a warm smile. "You smell nice too, but not as nice because you don't smell of coffee."

"I smell better, brat!" I yell, reaching out to slap his hand. He grabs my hand and squeezes it, his laugh fading.

"Hey. I wanted to talk to you about something."

Oh no. I was afraid of this. Over the last month, every time I've seen him, Halifax has acted more and more like he was interested in pursuing something a little more than friendship.

But I had hoped he'd see that I was in no mind to be wanting to be in any sort of romantic relationship. And probably wouldn't be for a long time. He'd been there when I'd cried all over his shoulder about Matthias, telling him all about the fake engagement.

I'd been a little better in the last few days, and I guess he took that to mean that he should admit his feelings.

"Halifax. I don't think you should say what you're wanting to say."

He sighs. "I need to."

I sigh and lay my hand on top of his. "Okay, but I'm going to warn you I'm not ready for anything."

His eyes take on a sad air, exactly the thing I was hoping to avoid. He blinks it back and decides against his better judgment to keep going. "Clarissa, I think you are so amazing. From that first day, I knew you were unlike any other women I've ever met in my life before. I was wondering if you would like to go on a date with me?"

I take a beat, trying to think of the kindest way to let him down when someone speaks for me.

"No, no, she wouldn't."

I jump about a foot in the air and land back in my chair from Matthias's voice. Halifax looks about as confused I am.

We both crank our neck upward to see Matthais standing there at the table, his face a perfect storm, Baxter Blue eyes swirling with so much simmering fury I'm afraid Halifax might be smitten right here and leave nothing but a coffee smelling burn mark.

"Matthias!" Halifax and I both say at the same time. Halifax in surprise, me in anger. What is he even doing here?

"Tell him, Clarissa, tell him you would not like to go on a date with him." His voice is low, almost inaudible, but the message is clear. He's jealous.

Emotion kicks up like a dust storm around the two of us, air cracking with electricity. When's the last time I was this close to him?

"Tell him," he repeats, eyes boring down on me. "Now."

My hackles rise at the command. "You can't tell me what to do, Matthias."

"I'm not. I'm telling my fiancée she shouldn't go on a date with another man. I shouldn't even have to tell her. She should know."

"I'm not y—" I don't even get to finish the sentence; he grabs my arm and drags me to my feet. "Matthias!

It never took much effort for him to move my body into any position he wanted, but I'd never fought against him in bed before.

I struggle to pull my arm from his hold, he swings me around so that we're face to face. Shoulders and chests heave from the effort of our struggle, and then his mouth is on mine.

The rest of the world burns away, leaving nothing but the two us, intertwined. He kisses me like he hasn't seen me in a century, and in many ways, it feels that way. I wish we could stay like this, but the ever present hurt in my stomach intensifies with each second that we're kissing. Because nothing has changed.

We are still Matthias and Clarissa, two people cleaving towards each other on opposite ends of the universe with no way to reach the middle without tearing ourselves apart.

Every part of my soul wants nothing except to fall into his orbit again, but the gravitational pull of my hurt keeps him just out of reach.

I can't do this.

I push him away, my lips being the past of my body to pull away from him.

"You are my fiancée. You will be my wife. It's fated. Don't you understand that?" His voice howls with a pain I know is mirrored in my own heart.

"Matthias."

His fingers press against my lips. "You are. If being married means being forever bonded to you, then I'm already your husband. Always and forever." An arm snakes around behind me, and he molds his body to mine, brushing another kiss against my lips. "These lips are yours. My body is yours. My heart is yours. My life is yours. And I'm going to spend the rest of it showing you that no one will ever make you as happy as I'll make you. And that no one will come close to making me as happy as you do."

One more kiss, and he lets me go, trailing a finger down my cheek.

On the way to the door, he walks back to our table and lays a hand on Halifax's shoulder. "Halifax. you're a good guy. So, I'd appreciate it if you kept your hands off my fiancée. No matter what she says, she's mine. "

"Hi, Clarissa, it's John here. Just letting you know that I've submitted your application for a business green card as Mr. Baxter has withdrawn the spousal green card application. I think we should have no problem; I've already gotten verbal confirmation that it will be processed today. They really don't want too much scrutiny over that immigration agent taking bribes. I'll call you with good news soon."

"Mr. Baxter is here to see you," Clementine says later that day, a glazed look in her eyes.

Which one?" I ask. Because it really could be any of them, and I'm done being ambushed in my own place of business. Unfortunately the glazed look in her eyes doesn't help narrow it down They all have that effect on women on some level. Except Gerry. It's definitely not him.

"Um," she says, her cheeks blazing. "I don't know this one."

Okay, good, so it's not Matthias either.

Kingsley is a force of nature, like a Greek god. A really good-looking, *grumpy* Greek God, so while women can't take their eyes off him, he also scared him. If it was Kylian, Clementine would be laughing. It's got to be Damien.

And I'm right.

"Damien. I'm surprised to see you here," I say, walking into the club room.

He has his back to me, head tilting toward the ceiling. Turning slowly on his heel, he looks like he's taking everything in.

"Clarissa, this place is remarkable," he says, genuine surprise in his voice. I'm not offended. I'm surprised every day by this place. But I also know, I was only a very small part of what made it what it is. But getting a compliment from Damien Baxter is not really what I'm expecting today.

"What can I do for you?"

He looks at me unblinking. "I came to see you."

"Well, you've seen me. What else?" I know I'm being rude, but I don't really feel like standing there waiting to be accosted by my ex-fiancé.

"Have you talked to Matthias?" he asks, throwing me off guard. "He said you're not really returning his calls."

I shake my head, not quite trusting my voice. "I ran into him a few days ago. He showed up at a meeting I was having. Again."

"He's a mess."

Me too. "What are you doing here, Damien?" Apparently, that's a question I'll be asking the Baxter men until the end of time. "I'm very busy."

"Can we sit somewhere and talk? Like, really talk?"

I know I shouldn't. Nothing good can come of it. I know I should just tell him to fuck off and enjoy his married life. But I know it must've taken a lot for him to come here. And I like to think that teenage Clarissa, who followed him and his brothers around like a puppy dog, would never forgive me if I didn't let her have this moment.

I gesture to the bar, and James discreetly makes himself scarce.

Before he even has a chance to say anything, I confess what I've been feeling. "I guess karma did a good job on me. Everything I did to you, happened to me. I actually...I feel relieved. Like I've paid back my debt. I know I have a long way to go to make myself a better person, Damien. But I'm working on it."

He doesn't say anything right away, just rubs his forehead the way he does whenever he's trying to find the right words. Then finally speaks. "In Barossa Valley, the day before the wedding, when Matthias came to see me, I told him that even though he was my flesh and blood, My-Linh is my heart and soul. And that if I had to choose, it wouldn't be him. I don't know if he knew what I meant when I said that, or if he just thought I was making some grand statement to make a point. But... now, I think he knows. He's experiencing it for himself." He takes a breath. It's the longest speech I've ever heard Damien give outside of a board room.

He continues, "He loves you. He loved you that day. I saw it on his face, he just didn't know it yet. Sometimes... it takes something to happen for you to realize. Especially if you're a Baxter. Eight months ago, you gave me that push. I've spent so much time resenting you, it blinded me to what you did for me. You're the reason My-Linh and I made it. Sometimes it takes an outside source. So... that's why I'm here. I'm that outside source."

"Matthias didn't trust you because of me. I'd done nothing but talk about all the ways you weren't to be trusted that when it came time to make a choice, all he heard was my voice. And for that, I'm sorry. I see you've changed, Clarissa. And I trust you now. I'm so sorry it took so long."

I'm scared to breathe in case I wake up from this dream. "What are you trying to say, Damien?"

"I'm saying that Matthias loves you so much, he doesn't know what to do with himself. I'm saying that he's hurting, not from anything you've done, but because he hurt you. I'm saying that for the part I played in that, I'm sorry. And so much has happened between us that I don't know if we can ever be friends again. But that I hope we can. Because if my brother had to choose between you and me. I know who he'd choose. He loves you. He's always going to love you. And he fucked up, but haven't we all?"

He gives me a look that takes me back eight months. Sitting there with him at a Sydney rooftop restaurant, about to make the biggest mistake of my life.

It's been a long time getting here, but even Damien doesn't see me as the same person anymore. And I don't know if I could've gotten here without Matthias. In the time we were together, he did nothing but make me feel like I could do anything. I miss that.

"I have anxiety attacks," I blurt out. "I've always had them, but they get worse when... when I left Sydney. And I had a really bad one before Matthias was supposed to come to Australia. That's the only reason he took me. I didn't want to ambush your wedding."

He sighs, tugging at a napkin. "Did you have them when we were together?"

I nod. "But nobody knew."

"I'm sorry you couldn't tell me. I was a bad friend." Damien slides off the bar stool and tucks his hands into his pockets. "He didn't tell me why he wanted you to come to Australia. He just told me that he couldn't leave you. And that's when I knew that what you two have... it's real. Don't waste it, Clarissa."

And for a moment, we stand there, old friends, wanting the best for each other.

"Thank you, Damien. And... I need to say something. I should've said a long time ago."

He smiles and stops me to say, "I'm sorry too." He takes one last look around the club. "And I'm proud of you, Clarissa. You're going to do amazing things."

And when he leaves, for the first time in a long time, I wonder if there's a chance for Matthias and me after all.

Fifty-Three

MATTHIAS

PATRICK LINZER FACES CHARGES of *multiple counts of sexual assault. Investigators say they have been combing through an anonymous report containing evidence of years of Linzer's treatment of sex workers and women he met on dating apps. He's currently in custody and bail has been denied. This follows weeks of reports that Linzer's firm is leaking funds after a mass exodus of his highest ticket clients. Stay tuned for updates.*

I press the button on the remote and the TV fades to black.

"Well, I guess that's that," I say to Dmitrik over the phone. "Job well done."

"What's next?"

"The same thing we've been working on for years. Clock's ticking. We have six months left."

"I'm on it," Dmitrik answers, hanging up the phone.

Hannah comes in, her face worried. Which is a rare sight.

"Your uncle just called. He's called an emergency board meeting. They're meeting in an hour; your brothers have all been informed."

I'd expected this. After Terry Masters's resignation two days ago, I've been waiting for Gerry to make his next move. The board is split, half in our camp, half firmly in Gerry's camp.

It's going to be a dog fight. And Gerry fights dirty.

"Call Paula. I need to see her five minutes ago," I say, sitting up in my chair.

The corners of Hannah's mouth twitch. She knows, *she knows*, I don't give up without a fight either.

Half an hour later, Paula is standing at a podium in the lobby of the Baxter Tower, reporters surrounding her. "Guys, we're going to start in just one minute, okay?"

She turns to me. "You sure you don't want me to look over your statements?"

"Paula, they would require that I have written some down." I grin. The look on her face is priceless, and I only hope that the bonus she gets when this is over will help her pay for the Botox from all the wrinkles I've given her this year. "I'm ready."

She nods, and speaks into the microphone. "In light of the recent allegations about Mr. Matthias Baxter's personal life, it is only fair that he gets a chance to respond. Please hold for questions until he is finished." She steps off and gives my arm a tight squeeze.

As soon as I step in front of the microphones, the flashbulbs go off at double speed. It takes me a moment to adjust to the flashing lights in my face, but I can't stand here forever. The longer I take to get to my point, the hungrier they're going to be.

I take a deep breath and speak from the heart.

"I lied." Well, that's a good start. And I thought the flashbulbs were going off before. "I'm thirty-seven years old and up until a few months ago, I told myself I didn't believe in love, I didn't look for it, and I never expected that I'd find it. And I realize now that I lied. I lied to myself. I was just scared because I thought that I would never find the right person for me. It turns out she was right in front of my face the whole time."

"I know you've heard so many stories about me being a playboy, about me breaking hearts everywhere I go. Well, that is only half true. I enjoyed the company of many amazing women, but no heart was ever broken. And if you hear that, then it's not the truth."

"But the media coverage was getting out of control, and with the Kids & Care IPO coming up, the focus was on me when it should've been about the company. Kids & Care has been consistently ranked as the best child's care and pre-kindergarten service country-wide. We provide parents with peace of mind when they leave their children with us. And they know that at the end of the day, their children will be safe, well fed, have their emotional needs taken care of, as well as giving them ample opportunity to learn more about the world in a fun environment. There are so many things that we want to achieve with the company, take it into rural areas and lower socio-economic communities who deserve to have access to childcare they can trust as well so they can go to work without worrying."

"And my coverage in the media was hindering that. So, I took action. I not only lied to myself, but I lied to you as well. My engagement to Clarissa, while real, was not based on love. Not initially. We were engaged to give you all something else to talk about other than my scandals. And I am so sorry for misleading you. It was absolutely the wrong thing to do. And I see that now. A relationship has to be based on trust. And I understand if your relationship with me has been irrevocably damaged."

"I want you to know I am sorry. But that while we may have started out as entering into the engagement on misleading terms, I can tell you that now, I want nothing more than to marry her. For all the right reasons. But even more so, I want to get to know her, and for her to get to know me, from the start. To see me for all that I am, without all the lies. And for me to see her without being clouded by the past."

I swallow. I wish I knew if she was out there watching. "So, Clarissa, if you're watching, I would like to ask you a question. Would you please go on a date with me? Because even though I will always love you, I think you need to learn how to love me again."

I stop. Done with the words. I wish I could just know if she is watching.

Something occurs to me.

"I... have somewhere to be," I say and jump down from the podium as someone yells out, "Matthias, where are you going?"

I feel a smile spread across my face, and I yell back, "I'm going to ask a girl out on a date!"

Chaos ensues and without turning around, I know the entire gaggle of reporters is following me out of the building and out onto Wall Street.

"Mr. Baxter," Paula pants, catching up with me. "Where are we going?"

"You didn't hear me?"

"You're going to Malt?" she asks, trying to keep up with me.

"I am. Wanna come with?" I walk, no, I *run*. I expect the group of reporters to fall away, but they don't, yelling questions out to me on our impromptu jog around Manhattan. "Come on, guys. Keep up. You don't want Anna from Heard It Here to have an exclusive, do you?"

There's something freeing about running up Hudson Street in the middle of a Tuesday afternoon. I wave to a group of tourists watching me running to the Village with ten reporters and their cameramen chasing behind me. All in an Armani suit.

"Run!" one of them shouts.

"I'm trying!" I shout back, with a laugh, my body filling with excitement.

Half a mile from the club, I realize she might not be there. I pull my phone out of my pocket and dial her number.

For the first time in weeks, she answers. "Hello?"

The sound of her voice energizes me, and my legs kick faster under me. "Rissie, where are you?"

"I'm at the club," she says. Not friendly, but not angry.

"Great. Stay right there."

There's a pause, and then she says, "Why are you out of breath?"

"I'm running. I feel like I've been running for a long time. Too long."

She doesn't say anything, but she doesn't hang up either. I cross the road, almost getting run over by a passing cab. The car horn echoes down the street and into the phone.

"Was that a car horn?"

"Yes, Rissie, it was." I feel like laughing out loud. This is so ridiculous. In the reflection of the nearby shop, I see the crowd running behind me. But instead of growing smaller, more people have joined. They must have caught onto something happening and didn't want to be left out.

The more the merrier.

"Clarissa, do you remember the first day we ran into each other at Leanne's place?"

"Yes." She sounds hesitant, she doesn't know where I'm going with this. I don't blame her.

"Remember when I told you that I wasn't a simp?" I ask, through breaths.

She pauses. I don't know if she doesn't remember or if she doesn't want to. "Yes."

"I was wrong."

"Matthias. I don't have time for this."

"Wait! Don't hang up," I shout, panicked. It feels like if she hangs up now, I'll never have another chance. "Listen to me. I was wrong. I've been so wrong about so many things. I was wrong when I didn't see that you were right under my nose for twenty years. I was wrong when I didn't steal you from Damien. I was wrong when I let you walk out of my office that day. I was wrong so many times. Every day that we've been apart, I was wrong. I should've been there every day, and every night. Because, darling, if there's a thing I am... it's a simp. For you, Clarissa."

She sighs. "Matthias... I never wanted that from you. I just wanted you to give me a chance."

We're only a hundred yard away. Once we turn the corner, the club will be in sight.

"I know. And you wanted me to fight for you. Darling, I'm fighting. I'm fighting for you right now."

I'm almost at the corner, in my life I've never been scared to do anything. But I'm scared to do this. And that tells me just how much I want it. How much I want her.

Then, as if she's connected to my brain, as well as my heart, her voice is small as she says, "I'm scared."

I stop running. Just for a moment. Because once again, she's proven she's the woman for me. "I am too, Rissie. I am, too. So, we'll start slow. But I want to start again."

Silence. Then, "When?"

I turn the corner, expecting to see the painted window of the club.

But I don't.

All I see is her. Standing there. Waiting for me.

I sprint, dropping the phone on the ground, getting rid of anything that's going to slow me down.

The crowd catches up, a chorus of panting behind me.

I stop in front of her.

Phone still in her hand.

"Ask me the question," I pant.

"What question?"

"Ask me when we're going to start again."

Hope and fear fill her big brown eyes. "When are we going to start again, Matthias?"

"Now, darling. Right now." I take her hand and pull her into me, crushing her lips with mine.

She presses into my body, mouth giving way for me.

And everything else fades away.

"I missed you so much, darling. I missed you so fucking much," I say, only once we're both gasping for breath.

Her hand comes up to touch my face, like she's wanting to make sure I'm there. "I missed you so much, Matthias."

"What were you doing standing out here?" I ask, remembering the way my heart jumped when I saw her there.

"I was waiting for you," she admits with a smile. "My-Linh texted to tell me to turn the TV on. You were all over the channels."

I slide my arms around her back, hugging her. Tight. Possessive. Protective. "Did you hear what I said?"

She nods. "Did you mean what you said?"

"Every single word. You need to know I'll never walk away from you, or push you away ever again. But I'm ready to take things slow. I'll wait for you, forever."

She leans back, giving me a look that fills me with a calmness that only she can give me. "I love you. And what if I want forever to start today?" She grabs my shirt and yanks me against her, and I pin her against the windowpane, kissing her until I'm dizzy from happiness.

Finally, she looks over my shoulder and shakes her head.

"Quite the romantic gesture."

I grin and give them a wave. "Any for you, darling."

"Me and everyone in the tri-state area!" she teases.

I nuzzle my face against her neck, taking deep breath after deep breath. Never wanting to be far from her scent ever again.

The flash bulbs go crazy again and I chuckle against her temple.

She shakes her head and laughs. "You can't do anything without causing a scene, can you?"

I give her a grin like no other. "Guilty."

Fifty-Four

MATTHIAS

AFTER THE REPORTERS AND the crowd disperse, I follow Clarissa inside to be alone so we can be alone for a moment.

We kiss for what seems like forever, trying to make up for lost time. Her lips taste like... her. I've spent months trying to place what the flavor is, but there's nothing like it in our existence. They just taste like *her*.

"I have to go," I say, resting my forehead on hers. "I have to go to the board meeting. And possibly get fired."

She grimaces. "I hope not."

"Me, too. But with your father gone, it's anyone's guess about what's about to happen. And I need to be there. It's my company."

She brushes her cheek against mine with a little purr. "I know. And I'm coming with you."

I think about telling her no, and then I realize I don't want to. I want her there. And if I want her to share every aspect of her life with me, then I need to do the same for her.

"Let's go."

My brothers, My-Linh and Kiara, are standing outside the conference room when I get to Baxter Tower. The women's eyes light up when they see Clarissa, but she steps in behind me, hiding.

I reach for her hand and whisper, "It's okay. They want you to be here."

Only then does she give them a little wave hello.

"What's going on?" I ask my brothers. The response I get is three very serious faces staring back at me. "That good, huh?"

"We said that we weren't going to start the meeting until you were here. If they want to talk about you, then it's only fair that you're here," Kingsley explains.

Keeping one hand still gripping Clarissa's, I reach for Kylian, and give him a one-armed hug. He looks more worried than the other two put together. Sometimes he still really is our baby brother.

"Well, I'm here now. So, let's go do this."

I step into the conference room first, with my brothers following close behind. We take our seats while everyone watches us with what can only be described as morbid curiosity.

When we sit, the vice-chair, Leonard Applebaum waves his hand for silence. He was the second longest serving board members, before Terry resigned. Now he's the one who's been here the longest. An ally to my grandfather when he was alive, he neither likes nor dislikes us.

"Gentlemen. To expedite proceedings, while we were waiting for you, the board voted for me as interim chairman. Until we can put the chairperson position to a proper vote, I will be in charge of running today's meeting."

The four of us glance at each other. This is probably the best outcome, for now. Kingsley gives Leonard a nod, signaling that we will not oppose it.

Leonard, seated at the end of the conference table, stands. "This meeting has been called due to extraordinary circumstances. One is the recent resignation of Terry Masters. And the other, being the conduct of our director of the America region of Baxter En-

terprises. Some of our members have argued that recent events
have clearly violated the morality clause of Matthias's contract.
It has been raised that Matthias be suspended from his position
until a general shareholders' meeting is held. I'd now like to invite
statements from members of the board."

For the next hour, I sit and listen as people I've sat with on
this board for over ten years, debate my character, my work, my
intentions, my failings.

I hear things that aren't real, that are merely perceived, that are
plain lies. I listen while others speak with tears in their eyes about
my contributions to the company and the city of New York.

Through it all, I look each person in the eyes as they're speaking.
I don't interrupt them to argue, and I don't take notes. I'll remember every last word that is said in this meeting and how I'll conduct
my relationship with each person when it's all done.

When it's my brothers' turn to speak, they talk about the person
I am.

They talk about what was always most important to my grandfather when he left this company in our hands. They talk about
why I was born to do this. And they talk about the detriment to
the company and its standing in the region if I'm removed.

And when Damien seems like he's almost done, he pauses, taking a second to look around the table.

"My brother, Matthias, does something that most of you sitting
at this table have not. He puts the company first, over and over and
over again." Without taking his eyes off our uncle, he continues,
"Putting the company first doesn't always look like what you think
it is. Sometimes it's being quiet when you want to speak up and
vice versa. Sometimes it's about knowing the long-term gain is
more important that short-term satisfaction. Sometimes, it's about
doing something you would never do, but to appease you, the
board, and the public, it gets done. And that's what Matthias has

done time and again. If you're prepared to have the most popular member of the Baxter family stand down from representing Baxter Enterprises, then I hope you're ready to accept responsibility for the consequences." He sits down, breathing hard, and stares down at his hands.

Gerry pushes to his feet. "It's my turn."

My three brothers look at me, offering their support.

When we all turn to look at our uncle, it's with nothing but contempt for him in our heart.

"You say that Matthias has always done what is best for the company, so is having one personal scandal after scandal after scandal doing what's best for the company? Is having his name splashed all over the tabloids about his womanizing doing what's best for the company? Is organizing a press conference just so he can chase after his little girlfriend, the same woman he just admitted to using for his own agenda to deceive the public, doing what's best for the company? He's an embarrassment to the company and the sooner we remove his name from our company's the better!"

"That's enough!" Kylian jumps to his feet, eyes wild. "You don't know what you're talking about!"

I stand up next to him, pulling on his arm urging him to sit in the chair. "It's okay, man. I've got this," I whisper to him. When he sits, I compose myself and face Leonard. "If Gerry is done, Mr. Chairman, I'd like to speak now."

Leonard glances at Gerry, nods and who sits down, still glaring at me.

"Ladies and gentlemen of the board. Thank you for everything you've said today. For the most part, everything that I've heard was spoken with the express intention of wanting the best for Baxter Enterprises. And what I've realized is nothing that's been said today is convincing anyone of thinking differently. So, to not waste any more of the board's time, I think we should move to the vote. But before I step out of the room, I would like to use my time to share something with you."

I pull my phone out and press a button on a recording.

Patrick's voice fills the room.

Explaining all the plans that Gerry had confided to him about ways he intended on sabotaging my brothers and me, about replacing members of the board who he deemed against him, about schemes he was working on to manipulate the directors.

For ten minutes, everyone listens in complete horror. Even Gerry sits glued to his seat, unable to move.

Once the recording goes quiet, I pick up my phone, and silently step out of the room and close the door shut behind me.

Heart pounding in my chest, I reach for Clarissa, who runs to me, and wraps her arms around me.

"How did it go?" she whispers against my neck.

"I guess we'll find out soon."

I debate going up to my office while I wait, but my feet refuse to move. Kiara and My-Linh make room for Clarissa and me in the office next to the boardroom, saying that they'll be back with coffee. Kiara shares a look with me and mouths "good luck."

Emotions swirl in my stomach as I think over everything that's happened today. First, reuniting with Clarissa, now, sitting outside my own boardroom wondering if ten minutes from now, I'm still going to have my job.

Clarissa rubs my back in circles. "Just breathe. We'll do it together, okay? After three."

The gesture, mirroring all the actions I'd done the same for her, unravels the knot of tension in my chest. I rest my head on her shoulder with a sigh. "Can I come work with you? If I get fired?"

She chuckles softly. "Sure, I need someone to stand outside and do crowd control."

I laugh and kiss her neck. "I think I'd actually like that. I can use my brainpower to think up ways to spoil you."

Her fingertips brush through my hair as she whispers comforting words. It makes the waiting slightly more bearable.

Almost an hour after I've left the boardroom, the door finally opens, and the board files out, none of them meeting my eyes.

Finally, Damien steps out first, followed by Kylian and then Kingsley.

I can't tell from the looks on their face what's happened. Which is surprising in Kylian's case. Kiara must've been teaching him to work on his poker face. Either that, or they're just really trying to hold back showing the bad news on their face.

They walk over to me, my heart in my throat.

"The vote was nine to ten," Kingsley says, without elaborating.

Clarissa touches my back.

"You're safe," Damien finally adds.

Relief blankets me like a warm cocoon and a single sob bubbles out of me. "Oh, my god."

They give me a moment to celebrate before the serious look is back.

Kylian leans in an says, "There's more."

"Gerry?"

Kingsley nods.

Before he can tell me what else was discussed in the meeting, Gerry storms out of the boardroom and makes a beeline for me, his face contorted with hate.

"You. You are going down for this. We're not done, you little fucker. You think you're so smart, but I'm smarter."

He looks behind me, sees Clarissa, and lunges for her. In the background, I hear My-Linh shout, "Clarissa, watch out!"

I push Clarissa out of the way. Reaching for Gerry's shirt, I shove him to the ground. "When are you going to learn? I keep my promises. Stay away from her."

He scrambles to his feet and leers towards her. "You made a grave mistake, sweetheart. You'll realize that soon enough." When he turns to my brothers and me, his eyes are wild and red. "You all are about to realize you've messed with the wrong person."

"We're ready," I say. "Let's settle this once and for all."

His nostrils flare and then he hurls himself towards the elevator.

"What the hell was that about? What happened in there?" I ask once he's gone.

Damien fills in the holes, his face grim. "The board voted nine to ten to suspend him over that tape. They said that it was hearsay. But I know a lot of them are looking at him differently and definitely are going to do some digging. He's going to take things up a notch now. It's coming close to the CEO vote. He's going to think like he's got nothing to lose."

Kylian comes around and hugs me from behind. "Then let's give him a fight."

My-Linh steps in next to Damien and lays her head on his arm since she's so short she can't reach his shoulder. He wraps his arms around her and drops a kiss on top of her head.

It makes me smile, and I do the same with Clarissa just as Kiara moves next to Kylian and he follows suit.

Kingsley looks at all of us like we're crazy. "Look at you three, all whipped." He's joking, but it's true.

Kylian shrugs, "Not me. I've always been husband material. Not my fault it took Kiara so long to come around. Why My-Linh loves Damien is anyone's guess"—he grins when she pokes her tongue out at him—"and Clarissa, well, we all know why she's with Matthias." His eyes flick down to my groin.

Clarissa looks him dead in the eyes and says, "Guilty."

And then all seven of us laugh, laugh until we forget that Gerry just threw down the gauntlet, and work is about to get just that much harder.

But we know that if we do it together, we're going to be okay.

Fifty-Five

CLARISSA

MATTHIAS AND I DECIDE to walk back to the club, while the others grab a bite to eat before joining us there later. I see-saw between utter exhaustion after everything that's happened today, and feeling more energized that I have in a long time.

Matthias is here with me, his hand in mine as we walk in silence.

After Damien's visit the other day, I couldn't get his voice out of my head. He'd said something that I needed to hear – that we all make mistakes. Matthias had forgiven mine, maybe I needed to do the same with him.

"What are you thinking about?" he asks when we're about a block from the club.

"That your brother is very wise."

"I wouldn't call Kylian wise, so much as just talkative," he jokes.

I roll my eyes. "I meant Damien. He came to see me the other day."

"Does My-Linh know?"

I shrug. "I have no idea. But I don't think she'd care. I think that in that relationship Damien is the jealous one, not My-Linh." He laughs, nodding. "No, he said something that made me realize that we deserved a second chance."

We reach the club, and I lead us around the back.

For the longest time, I couldn't come back here without replaying the night with Patrick in my head. But it turns out that it took having Matthias with me to vanquish those demons.

***

"To Clarissa and Matthias!" Kylian shouts, lifting a glass in the air.

Music plays around us, but it feels like it's just us sitting at the bar. Matthias's family had been nice enough to free my table when a big group showed up and now we're crowded around the end of the bar, no doubt annoying James by messing up his carefully organized system.

"And to Malt, a happy three-month anniversary to Clarissa and her team," Matthias adds.

I'll drink to that. I gesture to James and once he's done serving his order, he comes over with another bottle of Japanese whiskey in his hand.

He holds it out to Kylian, who empties his glass and holds it out to my bartender. "I heard you're the Hibiki expert around here," James says. "If you're around later, I'll get out a bottle I have hidden in case the boss and her boy toy decide to drink themselves stupid again."

"Ooooh," Kiara says, and gives me a wink.

"Wait, " I glance at Matthias who just shrugs. "How did you know about that?" I ask James.

"How did I notice when eight thousand dollars of liqueur goes missing?" he laughs. "That's what you pay me for. But I did get a delivery today." He goes to the other end of the bar and comes back with an ice press. The same one Matthias had told him about. "I guess I can forgive you guys if you keep these gifts coming."

Matthias grins. "It's not a gift, it's a bribe. If you ever want to get out of here, our bar, Bottle, in London could use your influence."

I punch Matthias in the arm. "Hey! Stop trying to steal my bartender."

His hand comes around to cover my mouth as he leans in closer to James. "Don't listen to her. She's actually thinking of getting rid of you. Says you cost too much. And—ow!" he yelps, pulling his bitten hand away from my mouth.

James laughs and returns to his conversation with Kylian while Matthias rubs his hand, giving me a hurt look.

"I would never steal from you," he sulks.

"No?" I pretend to hug him, and reach into his pants pocket, pulling out two Caramello Koalas. "Then what's this?"

"That... is not... what you think it is. I took them so that you would...er, have something to eat...um, if you needed it."

I scrunch up one of the empty wrappers. "And this one? Where's the koala?"

This time there's no scramble for an explanation. "I ate it, and I enjoyed. Trust me, I'm going to need my energy for later." His lips graze against mine when he whispers, "I have a lot of time to make up for."

A sparkler lights inside my stomach as I take a sip of my drink to hide my blush.

"Mr. Baxter, are you in lust with me?"

The depth of feeling in his eyes makes me shiver as he holds me close, and it's just the two of us in a crowd of bodies. "No, darling, I'm desperately and unequivocally in love with you."

And when I say the same to him, I know that it's forever.

EPILOGUE

FROM BUSINESSTODAY.COM:

Kids & Care Smashing Projected Share Sales in Scandalized IPO

Baxter Enterprises subsidiary Kids & Care raised 478 million in their initial public offering yesterday, with a share price of $17.37. 22% higher than expected after months of reported in-fighting over the future of the IPO and Baxter's public image.

After a shock public confession a week before the IPO, Baxter's reunion with former Baxter board chairman Terry Masters's daughter, garnered universal support leading to the IPO opening at a record high.

Early numbers from today project a close of $19.43.

Baxter Enterprises owns 78% of the shares Kids & Care's shares and will retain control of the company.

***

This comes to the end of Matthias's and Clarissa's story but they will definitely show up in Luna, the last book in the The Baxter Billionaires series. You can preorder it here (https://www.amazon.com/dp/B0BQNDRJPV) . And read Kingsley's story.

CONTENT WARNINGS

This book depicts scenes of violence and anxiety attacks. Sexual assault is briefly mentioned with no descriptions.

ACKNOWLEDGEMENTS

You never write a book alone, even though it can feel that way sometimes when you're awake at 3:48am looking up the difference between toward vs. towards and having to make a decision.

So I just want to thank every person who put up with me being grumpy, asking random questions in the middle of the night, and who always supports me no matter what crazy thing I'm doing.

But most of all, thank you to those of you who took a chance and read this book. You don't know what it means to me.

Other Book Type Thingos Daisy Allen Wrote

Don't forget to subscribe to Daisy Allen's email newsletter to receive information on upcoming new releases and bonus offers just for subscribers!

Click here to subscribe or go to: https://bit.ly/daisyallento sign up
You can also follow Daisy on Facebook for ramblings and extras:
facebook.com/daisyallenauthor
or TikTok at @authordaisyallen

All Books by Daisy Allen

Available on Amazon and Kindle Unlimited
The Baxter Billionaires

Luxe

Luck

Lust

Luna (out late 2023)
Rock Chamber Boys

ABOUT THE AUTHOR

First thing you should know about the author, is that she really, really hates writing these About The Author things. Who came up with these things? Cursed marketing people, that's who! Damn you marketing people!

The second thing you should know about the Author is that she has an MBA...specialising in marketing.

The irony is not lost on her, even when many other things are...like going to bed at a reasonable hour or how the economy works.

The Author, other than laughing right now at referring to herself in the third person, currently lives in Maine, USA, although she identifies as Vietnamese, who lived most of her life in Australia, and was born in France. I'm...I mean, she is a veritable one woman international food court.

She likes wining and dining, and whining when she's not being wined and dined.

Is a dog person, and professed not cat person, even though there is a cat currently sitting on her lap right now.

She wants to thank you for reading this book.

Writing is all she's ever wanted to do in life.

Happy Reading.

Printed in Great Britain
by Amazon

26837598R00256

BAXTER ENTERPRISES

EST 1923

LUST

THE BAXTER BILLIONAIRES

by

Daisy Allen